PART ONE

ONE

When their mother called them to leave their games in the garden and come back into the house, it was the beginning of something so unbelievably meaningful, so big and yet so problematical, so influential, so determining, so full of traumatic consequences and so absolutely shattering in their lives. At least that was what bothered his mind and sometimes his conscience through the later years of his more mature life.

"Boys! Where are you? Come back in, I want you here in the kitchen at once!"

This call wouldn't have been such an unusual event – their mother often called them in from the garden, usually when lunch was ready – had it not been for the time of the day and for her tone. Manfred understood at once that there had to be some important matter, much more important than an announcement of potato soup and sausages. He did not know about Thomas, who was older but somehow less sensitive, but Manfred thought he could detect not only the importance of the matter at hand, but equally a slight concern or even worry in his mother's voice. It was her wording as well as her forced tone.

When the boys arrived in the frame of the kitchen door, their mother was wiping her hands on her apron. She was such a beautiful woman, always pale and sometimes a little frail. But she maintained the authority required of all German mothers of her generation. A role, Manfred sensed, which did not always come easy to her. She seemed nervous. "I want you in the house because I just had a message from your father. He'll be home earlier tonight because he has some great news. He asked us to prepare for a celebration."

"What are we celebrating?" Thomas asked.

"Shall we get presents?" Manfred wanted to know.

"I don't think so. But you will see. I don't want to spoil your father's joy in telling you himself. He'll expect us to be ready for him when he comes home. So, quick, quick! We haven't got a lot of time. Thomas, you take this brown purse and run to Frau Helmbrecht's shop round the corner. Here's a list of things I need."

"But Mama, Father can bring all these things from his shop."

"Don't argue, Thomas. He's not coming from his shop, he's coming straight back from a meeting in town. And you, Manfred, you get the fine tablecloth from the bottom drawer in the sideboard and the fine silverware and lay the table for dinner in the dining-room. Don't forget the Bohemian crystal glasses; they're at the back of the middle shelf. Off you go, boys. I want your father to be proud of you."

What could it be that was so important? Manfred was puzzled and a little apprehensive. He knew he couldn't always rely on his parents' word. Especially Father liked to announce things in a theatrical manner, usually standing in the middle of their living-room, so that you expected some really great things to follow. But more often than not, things turned out to be some silly news that only concerned the grown-ups. For the boys it was often a disappointment. He remembered the flamboyant announcement only just over a year ago, when it turned out Father had merely decided to refurbish his shop. Why should that have been of any concern to the boys? Sometimes he asked himself why parents did what they were doing. This puzzle, or rather the extended version of this question, was to become one of the repeated enigmas to occupy his adult mind: Why do people do what they do? He puzzled over the logical concept that there had to be reasons, ideas, objectives, motivations behind people's actions.

***

Of his early childhood he would remember very little in later life. It was a peaceful period of unspoilt happiness, and he would remember it as a time of permanent summer with clear blue skies and comforting temperatures. He particularly liked to listen to the blackbirds in spring and to the rasping sound of the crickets in July. Despite the blissful nature of those early years, one of the earliest memories concerned his brother's attempt at superiority. His brother Thomas, who was two years older and whom he admired in every possible way, was convinced that he was responsible for their games, their choice of trees to climb and the formation of all their friendships.

"Now, look here, Freddy," he admonished him from time to time when his reign appeared to be questioned, "I'm a lot older than you. So, it's only natural you should have to obey my orders. It's the way of the world."

Though he hated to be called Freddy, Manfred usually went along with this order of things. After all, this arrangement also had its advantages. Thomas's spirit of adventure and courage was far greater than his own, which meant that the older boy initiated most of their more daring games and led his younger brother into many an adventure that Manfred wouldn't have missed for anything in the world once he managed to look back after all had gone well. It certainly was the case with the huge oak that Thomas climbed first and that proved to become their look-out over several neighbours' gardens. Under his leadership, the boys built what they considered their tree-house, which in time became Manfred's favourite retreat, even long after his brother had lost interest in watching other people's private activities in their back gardens. It was hardly a tree-house but rather a higgledy-piggledy accumulation of wooden pieces, boards, planks, rafters and the like which they could get hold of. The largest pieces came from a near-by building-site on the Galgenberg, appropriated on Thomas's initiative and under his guidance.

Thomas was tall for his age, with dark brown hair that hung down in wisps over his eyes when he moved his head too quickly. He didn't seem to mind that, and his younger brother often wondered how anyone could live with his hair in his face most of the time. Their mother, who seemed to be quite relaxed about their appearances as long as they didn't get into real trouble with any of the neighbours, also tolerated it and only very occasionally remarked that he might need another haircut. He was her first born, clearly her favourite, and she considered him very handsome even from childhood. It was true, he had a winning smile on his broad face with prominent cheekbones, his brown eyes were beautiful, although he would often keep them narrowed to two slits, which, together with his relatively broad nose, gave him a slightly Mongolian look. One of his classmates would later call him Genghis Khan when he wanted to annoy him. Thomas didn't mind what he looked like, certainly not during his childhood. Puberty and adolescence were still far away.

Manfred was different. In fact, he looked so different that people were often surprised to learn that they were brothers. He was a small boy, even small for his age, with very fair and curly hair, and with clear blue eyes. Also, he was rather shy and generally preferred to remain silent while all the other children fought over vocal supremacy. He just couldn't see the point of raising his voice to convince others. He believed that truth and the right way of things would always win in the end anyway. He knew he wasn't his parents' favourite child, and he accepted the fact that whenever there was a treat for only one of them it was always his brother who would get it.

However, as he approached kindergarten age, he sometimes thought he would show them all one day. One day they would all see what he could achieve. He sensed that you didn't need to shout when you wanted people to listen to you. There appeared to be enormous charisma and a capacity to exercise power over others in a quiet and even voice if you put enough energy and conviction into what you were going to say.

Life in Thuringia in the 1920s was a strange experience, although the boys did not know this, being quite unaware of the social and political upheavals of the time when they attended the overcrowded kindergarten in Untermhaus, an older and more established quarter of their hometown of Gera. Their father explained to them why the area was called Untermhaus. It was because those streets were first developed and built up in the time after the Thirty Years' War, in the 17th century, just below the castle – hence *Unterm Haus* – which dominated the valley. The Reussen Schloss obtained its name from the dynasty that had first built or at least first occupied it – in those days one never knew how legitimate such occupations were – and the name of course first means "Russians". Later in life, Manfred would read that fascinating picaresque novel by the seventeenth-century writer Hans Jakob Christoffel von Grimmelshausen, enjoying those long Baroque names, that early novel set in the Thirty Years' War, where the Russians were still called "Reussen". When he discovered that so many years later, he remembered his father's explanation. But already during his childhood, Manfred had heard many interesting facts and stories about the castle and the Reuss dynasty. Father often told them stories about the development of the town, the various achievements of its inhabitants and particularly of Heinrich Posthumus, the Reussen prince who was born after his own father's death – a fact that Manfred found hard to believe – and who founded the first high school or "gymnasium" for the boys of the town, back in 1608. When he died in 1635 his sons tried to govern the town together, but they couldn't prevent the Swedes from burning it down in 1639, which was why the town had to be rebuilt in the following decades. Manfred found himself reminded of that part of local history again and again throughout his life. Somehow, the period of the Thirty Years' War and the atrocities committed in those days never left his consciousness completely.

The town's kindergarten in Untermhaus was a happy institution that allowed children of different ages to mix freely, so boys and girls from three to six played together very happily, and the young teacher managed to keep them in order very easily. After all, most children came from middle-class families that still kept up the old German virtues of strict obedience and military-like discipline. Thomas and Manfred were among the few children from more liberal-minded families. For them, kindergarten was great fun. At the time, it was the only such institution in Gera, and neither Thomas nor Manfred minded the fact that they had to walk the distance from their home on the Galgenberg all the way down and across the Elster to Untermhaus every morning and back again every afternoon. It took them about thirty-five minutes down and about forty-five minutes back up again. This was not only due to the geographical conditions but equally to the demands of their social life. Their house on the Galgenberg had only just been constructed, it was one of the first houses to be built in Ypernstrasse, sometime after the Great War, and it took well into the late 1930s for the remaining plots to be developed and built up. This meant that their home was cut off from most of their friends, up there on the Galgenberg, overlooking the town centre, almost like the Reussen Schloss, only on the other side of the valley. The area was to become a prime site of Gera in the 1930s, with National Socialist Party members having some of the finest villas built for themselves as long as their standing could afford it, and with Russian officers and administrators taking over after the Second World War. But at the time of Manfred's childhood, the beautiful hill of the Galgenberg still consisted mainly of pastures and orchards, with the town's cemetery further to the southeast on the slope of the hill.

When their house was built, their father considered this the peak of his financial success. He was a jolly man with a bald head and a round belly who liked to laugh a lot. His name was Thomas, like his first-born son's. His delicatessen business in the Sorge, Gera's main shopping street, was thriving indeed. His shop was the first delicatessen in Thuringia to import spicy Italian sausages, caviar from Persia, *graved lax* from Norway and real Emmental cheese from Switzerland. He sold a range of first-class cold meats and cheeses from France and Italy, as well as a large selection of sausages from every corner of Germany. His Hungarian paprika sausages, his Polish quail's eggs and his stuffed vine leaves from Greece created quite a stir among the wealthy merchants' families in the area. Though he did not see himself as a political man, he found it hard to go along with most of the other citizens of the town, who seemed to have given up all national pride after the Versailles Treaty and displayed a lazy *laissez-faire* attitude when it came to political opinions. Thomas Weidmann was different. He strongly believed that Germany got such a bad deal after the War that it had become a national duty to hold one's head up again. So, when the still reasonably respectable NSDAP approached him with their reformist views he was really taken with the visions of a once again proud and self-confident Germany.

***

When Manfred entered the dining-room dressed up for dinner, he felt uneasy because it was really too early for dinner. Why all this fuss over some news their father had to tell them? His parents often exaggerated things. They liked to make a big deal about things that seemed uninteresting or irrelevant to Manfred. So, their big announcements often fell flat in an awkward anti-climax. It wouldn't be any different this time, he was quite sure. But then there was that undertone of apprehension and worry that he had detected in his mother's voice. What was it going to be?

Thomas joined him in the dining-room. Manfred, though in admiration of his elder brother, knew how much more gullible Thomas was, so he wouldn't have any misgivings.

"Here's your father," came Mother's voice from the hall.

Thomas Weidmann planted his portly figure in the middle of the hall carpet, placed his hat on the hat-rack, took off his raincoat and beamed at the prospect of his home and his family. The boys stepped into the hall and stood in front of their father, who didn't give them his usual stern look, but produced a hardly perceptible smile. At least that was what it seemed to Manfred. Nevertheless, they did as was expected of them, standing still and upright in a row of two, like soldiers standing to attention in front of their officer. As usual, their father patted their heads, first Thomas's then Manfred's.

"I am so proud of you boys, and today you can be proud of your father," he announced in a booming voice. Then he placed a quick peck on his wife's cheek, mumbling, "You look absolutely ravishing today, Elfriede."

"Well, let's go to the dining-room first," she suggested. "And listen, Manfred, you stop jerking your shoulder. It looks disrespectful." She was right, of course. Manfred felt embarrassed about his bad habit of jerking his left shoulder whenever he was excited. He didn't mean to be disrespectful. He just couldn't help it.

They marched off, and in the dining-room they took their positions for important announcements made by their stern father, fully confident that behind that stern façade there was a liberal mind with a capacity for irony and a healthy sense of humour. Father placed himself in front of the fireplace, one hand on the mantelpiece, the other hand behind his back, his jacket open, displaying his fine silk waistcoat and the gold chain of his pocket-watch dangling across his round belly; his family facing him in a row of three at a distance of more or less exactly one metre fifty. This theatricality, Manfred had perceived long ago, was meant to lend more weight to whatever their father had to communicate. Whereas his mother and his brother seemed to be happy to go along with such a charade, Manfred couldn't help feeling a little ridiculous. But he lacked the courage to do anything about it.

"Well then, my dears. Today you can be proud of your father. And listen, boys, in decades to come you will remember this as a historic moment, a moment which marked the beginning of your family's participation in the noble rescue and rehabilitation of your Fatherland."

He paused for a few seconds to let this sink in. Then he uttered a small puff through his rounded lips and continued.

"Today your father has joined the Party. It is the party that will save us all from the humiliations of our enemies in the Great War. It is a party that will give us all back our self-respect and our national pride. Yes, boys, I have joined the NSDAP. Now, what do you say to that?"

Manfred knew that no answer was called for. It was the usual rhetorical question at the conclusion of his father's announcements in front of the fireplace.

So, the Weidmanns celebrated their father's historic decision and accepted it as the right step to be taken in such a volatile political climate. Manfred had no idea how his brother saw it, but he felt that such a step could mean many things he couldn't explain yet. Mother's nervous reaction seemed enough to sense some degree of danger, while Father's attitude opened the door to endless possibilities.

Over the following few years, everyone accepted the developments as inevitable. There was nothing one could do to influence the situation in the small town. To Manfred, it seemed that the authorities weren't doing anything about the crowds of people loitering in the streets, the growing unrest over more and more unemployed men hanging around the town centre, smoking, talking in low voices, some of them shouting political slogans, others just staring down at the pavement in sad silence. But Manfred was just too young to understand. And while he could discuss practically everything else with Thomas, the political situation of the day was a topic which was always avoided between them.

While politics were still only a haze on the horizon of Manfred's consciousness, albeit a haze that was charged with possibilities and future developments that might very well encroach on his own life one day, the here and now of his life at kindergarten and then at primary school absorbed the greater part of his energies, his happiness and his fears. The most powerful force that occupied his mind in the years following his father's entry into the Party was the increasing unease about girls. Whereas girls had merely existed incognito alongside boys in earlier days, they now suddenly stepped out from obscurity and monopolised his awareness of the world, of himself, of everyone's social behaviour.

In particular, there was a girl called Anna. She was slim and had long blonde hair with a touch of ginger, eyes as blue as Manfred's, and she moved around the playground with a refreshing lightness. He sometimes stole a glance at her while she was jumping like a rubber ball round the big elm with Thomas and some other children, and it seemed to him that she could fly through the air. He also liked her bubbly laugh which sounded like a small silver bell from the distance. Manfred had always taken it for granted that Thomas was naturally entitled to the better treats in life. He got the larger pieces of cake on Sunday afternoons, he got the more valuable Christmas presents and he was the recipient of more attention when they had visitors. Manfred had never questioned that. So, it was also quite natural that his brother should get more attention from Anna when they walked home from school, first together as a crowd, then, as they passed their various friends' homes, gradually reduced to the three of them. Anna was walking in the middle, Thomas to her right, Manfred to her left. Manfred wanted her to listen to him and to look at him, but she seemed to give more attention to Thomas. She seemed to laugh louder at Thomas's jokes and she seemed to take a keener interest in his plans and visions. Feeling excluded, Manfred wanted her to turn her lovely face to him more often.

One day, when the brothers were on their way home, just the two of them, Thomas asked him, "What do you think of Anna?"

"I think she's very nice," answered Manfred carefully.

"You know what?" his brother asked. "I think she wouldn't mind if I told you that she agreed to be my *Schätzchen* – my sweetheart."

Manfred didn't quite know what to do with this information. Nor did he know why his brother was telling him, but he was clearly puzzled. He had heard from other children that you ought to get yourself a *Schätzchen* sooner or later.

"So, what are you going to do with her?"

"Well, you know," Thomas hesitated, "I don't really know that I'm supposed to DO anything in particular. It's more, like, you know, how we feel about each other. But now that you've asked, well, we might go for walks together."

Manfred thought you could go for a walk with a girl without having to call her your *Schätzchen*. He himself liked Anna very much. Should he call her his *Schätzchen*, too? He wondered.

"Can she be my *Schätzchen*, too?" he asked.

"Of course not, you daft boy!"

"Why not? If you can, why can't I?"

"Because, because, because… It's very simple. A girl can have only one boy who calls her *Schätzchen*, and a boy can have only one *Schätzchen*. That's how it is."

"All right then," Manfred stammered, "in that case I don't want one. It's too complicated for me."

Thomas laughed. But despite his loud laugh he felt a sense of relief. How awful if his little brother had become his rival!

Manfred, on the other hand, was too young to know jealousy. If Anna could only be his brother's *Schätzchen*, that would be all right. He could still enjoy looking at her, and she might also walk with him. What difference did it make?

Things changed when Thomas left kindergarten for school. All of a sudden, Manfred found himself in a new role, the role that his older brother had occupied before. Only about three weeks into the new school year, one morning in the playground of the kindergarten compound, Anna came up to him and asked him, "Will you walk with me after school?"

The children all referred to kindergarten as "school", a habit that Thomas resented once he had joined proper school. He asked his younger brother to be more precise in this matter. So, Manfred found himself on the brink of correcting Anna, but when she gave him a playful wink, he discarded the impulse and just answered, "Of course, that would be fine." He hoped she wouldn't notice the slight jerking twitch in his left shoulder.

When, after school, they walked around the streets of Untermhaus, Manfred found it a very pleasant experience to have Anna to himself. Up until that day he had always been with her in the company of other children, mostly his elder brother. Now, alone with her, he was just a little excited. He didn't know why, but it was a very good thing. They talked about the games they had played during the day and about their families.

"I'm an only child," Anna explained. "So, I haven't got anybody to play with when I'm at home. My parents say I can always bring home other girls to play with."

Over the following months, the two became a fixed item. The other children accepted the fact that Manfred and Anna were together most of the time when it was possible. It was also clear to everyone that the two of them shared everything. If you told Manfred a secret, you could count on Anna to be informed, and vice versa. One evening, walking up the Galgenberg after saying good-bye to her at her garden gate, Manfred remembered his discussion with his brother about a *Schätzchen*. He smiled to himself, confident that by now Anna was his. He had no need to call her *Schätzchen*, because they had a tacit understanding that they belonged together, at least for the foreseeable future.

One of the places that they felt particularly pleasant was the huge sandpit at the back of the kindergarten compound, a happy place where many other children liked to play too, but Manfred's new roads through the sandy mountains were only embellished by castles and turrets along the way by Anna. No other child cared about the artistry of his even roads and daring tunnels. One afternoon in September, Manfred was digging a tunnel through the sand, his right hand already into the tunnel nearly up to his elbows, when all of a sudden, his hand was met by Anna's hand, digging from the other side. Both of them worked quickly to shovel out the remaining sand at both ends, which finally allowed their hands to clasp each other in the middle of the tunnel. They held on to each other for several minutes, while neither of them spoke a word. They just smiled over the top of the sandy mountain and enjoyed the feeling of secrecy. What an adventure! Holding on to each other's hands when nobody could see or know about it!

Suddenly Wolfgang, the pompous bully, stomped over the top of the sandy mountain and crushed the tunnel underneath. It was the end of a magic moment for Manfred and Anna. They never repeated that special digging adventure, but they would never forget that magic moment.

The children were still blissfully unaware of what was going on in the big world around them. The adult population, on the other hand, felt themselves gathered into a maelstrom of social and political developments that allowed no sentimentality. One had to make hard decisions. Thomas Weidmann also found himself in an uncomfortable dilemma over his allegiance to the Party.

While he was proud and satisfied over some of the measures backed by the Party because they promised to fight the terrible evils of mass unemployment and galloping inflation even before the Crash of 1929, he was made increasingly uneasy by some of the slogans emerging from some hardliners in the Party. He was particularly disgusted by the stupid and short-sighted opinions about foreigners, Jews and Gypsies, propagated by certain Party members. He found it unfair, because he knew that many of the industrialists of the town who managed to attract all those commissions from Russia during the two years following the great Crash – commissions that secured thousands of jobs for the people of Gera – were in fact Jews. Without the so-called *Russenaufträge*, the working population of the town would have been a lot worse off. Also, many of his friends and customers were Jews, and he tried to maintain a balanced view on the causes and effects of the War. The *Siegermächte* may very well have treated Germany very badly at Versailles, but then he had to admit that his beloved Fatherland was certainly not without blame either, if one wanted to be fair. Also, if the German government wanted its old enemies to relent and allow Germany to become great again, if one was hoping for a remission of debts and for permission of rearmament, then wouldn't it be a lot wiser to be proactive in diplomacy, rather than to antagonise all the other nations?

Early one Saturday evening in the summer of 1932, he attended a political gathering in the market square. There were men in brown shirts and black boots, with black leather belts and red armbands displaying black swastikas in white circles, standing in rows around the square as if they had to guard the entire gathering. He suddenly felt cold and terribly uneasy. Fear crept up in him. Was this going to be the new healing force for Germany? He began to doubt his own role in the midst of all those over-confident faces. To him, they had a threatening aspect. Flags were waved, a military band played several brisk marches, and then there were speeches. Thomas listened to all three speakers very carefully and was horrified. What these men advocated amounted to sheer stupid blindness. To him, the Jewish population, together with all the other minorities attacked by those hardliners, formed part of German culture, they were all part of German heritage. He wondered why nobody in that crowd seemed to realise that what was being put forward was against the principles of mutual human respect, principles that Thomas considered of prime importance. He also found it absolutely unacceptable that all three speakers referred to British and American politicians as well as international banking and business leaders as "the Jewish Conspiracy", blaming them for all the evils and all the social problems in Germany.

On that day, Thomas went home a disillusioned man.

Only a few weeks later, on the 13th of September, the National Socialist government of Thuringia dismissed the mayor of Gera, Dr Arnold, along with his assistants, and the *Staatsbeauftragte* Dr Jahn established his direct dictatorial rule over the town. When Thomas Weidmann was told this bad news in the afternoon, he was truly shocked. The old mayor had been elected, whereas this new *Staatsbeauftragte* had no democratic legitimacy. This was the end of democracy for Gera and probably for the whole of his Fatherland. In the evening, he went home to his house on the Galgenberg, assembled his family in the living-room and told his wife and his children that he was leaving the Party. Their ideals no longer had anything to do with his world and his convictions. They were an uneducated and uncultured *Lumpenpack* – a pack of scruffy scoundrels. Criminals.

His wife Elfriede seemed relieved when he told her, for she had already felt rather uneasy about everything that she heard from the National Socialists, but she hadn't wanted to contradict her husband. She was a weak and frail woman, very thin and very pale. Her skin had an almost bluish hue, and her grey eyes looked quite sad. She never spoke against her husband's wishes. In fact, several of the Weidmanns' friends thought she behaved like a slave. But the truth was that her husband was a very gentle and considerate man. He was always kind to his wife and never even raised his voice in her presence. Quarrels were extremely rare, and differences in opinion were usually resolved by her leniency. To those of her friends who made critical remarks about her weakness, she justified herself that she was just very happy in her role of voluntary submission. For her, it was the proper role of a good German housewife. Everything in their marriage appeared to contribute to their common bliss. If only it hadn't been for her poor health.

A few days before Christmas, one of his customers chatting with him in the delicatessen shop mentioned the greatness of Adolf Hitler. Thomas Weidmann hesitated before he carefully answered, "I'm not so sure about him. He seems a bit too radical for my taste." He did not dare to go any further in his mild criticism. This might be a secret agent, one could never know.

"Come on now, Herr Weidmann, a businessman like you must be in full support of Hitler. Men like you have the potential to become the true backbone of our great nation. You should read the new book that's only come out. It's about the Party, about its history."

"How can anyone write a book about the history of a political party that's only been tottering about for a decade or so?"

"Oh, you see, Herr Weidmann, this is a very clever book. Konrad Heiden, the man who wrote it, indeed calls it *History of National Socialism*, but what he gives us is a view into the glorious future of the Party and our glorious Fatherland. So, it's a case of future history, very clever, can't you see?"

Thomas Weidmann mumbled, "That looks like a contradiction."

The man looked at him with big eyes. He was clearly fascinated by this new book. Such gullibility could hardly come from a secret agent, Thomas thought.

Walking home in the evening, Thomas Weidmann thought about what that customer had told him. If indeed such a book had been published, he had to get hold of it. Two days later he got it, and between Christmas and New Year he sat down in his study every evening after Elfriede had gone to bed and devoted his attention to Konrad Heiden's new book. As he read page after page, a gradual feeling of unease rose in him. What this book showed him was not really Adolf Hitler's greatness, but rather his despotic methods and his hypocritical and dangerous rhetoric. It pretended to show the way towards the country's future greatness, but if you could read between the lines, as it were, you could see a clear warning. Such a leader might easily lead the country into total disaster.

Finishing the book, Thomas felt a cold shiver down his spine. He had been right to leave that *Lumpenpack*, and it was only to be hoped that the intelligent people in the country would eventually succeed in getting the people away from such a Rat-catcher of Hamelin.

***

Life for Manfred became more serious when he moved up through school. He was placed in the same class as Anna, but they were not allowed to sit together. The girls were seated in one row, the boys in another, and school life gradually took on a more military-like atmosphere. Their teacher sometimes yelled at them like a drill-sergeant, and he wanted them to stand up straight, put their heels together, keep their arms stiff down their sides and always address him as "Herr Lehrer". When their country had elected a new *Reichskanzler* in January 1933, the teacher explained the importance of this event to the children.

"This new *Führer* of our Fatherland is going to save us all from those who only want to destroy our nation, our culture and our German heritage."

Manfred wondered who that might be, who wanted to destroy the country. He was too young to understand politics. After school, he asked Anna.

"Do you understand our teacher? What does he mean when he speaks of those who want to destroy us? Who are they?"

"I don't really know," Anna answered, "but my father says it is the Jewish Conspiracy."

Neither of the children knew what the "Jewish Conspiracy" was supposed to be. They both knew several Jewish families in Gera, but they couldn't connect them with any conspiracies. They discussed the word "conspiracy" and came to the conclusion that it had to mean something like getting together to plan evil things. But neither of them could imagine any of their Jewish friends being involved in evil plans. Manfred thought of Isaac, a very nice boy, about the same age, the son of his father's business acquaintance Mr Rosenbaum. The Rosenbaums sometimes came to lunch on Sundays. Mrs Rosenbaum was a very sturdy woman, always very charming and cheerful, and she always brought some sweets for the boys when they visited. Isaac was a very gentle boy, and Manfred really admired him a little because he was so clever and so knowledgeable.

Anna said she also liked their Jewish neighbours, the Mendelssons, but her father had already warned her not to become too intimate with them. They couldn't really be trusted. "So perhaps we'd better be careful," she mused.

"I don't care what they say," Manfred stated categorically, "I won't believe that Isaac has anything to do with any conspiracy. He's a really nice chap, and I like him a lot."

They left it at that.

A new development in Manfred's life was his relationship with Wolfgang. The big boy with his rasping voice and his bullying manner used to be someone to be avoided. Manfred even used to be a little afraid of him. And now, gradually, Wolfgang became more agreeable, and before long Manfred began to like him. When Anna asked him about Wolfgang, it came as a revelation to him that one could actually change one's feelings towards another person in such a way that he found it hard to explain his new attitude to her.

All he managed to say by way of an explanation was, "I was wrong about him. He's actually quite nice."

Anna accepted this. She admitted to herself that if there was one thing about Manfred that she particularly admired it was his easy way of finding other boys "nice". To her, this was a sign of a gentle nature, a positive view of humanity.

Only just over three weeks later, the country was shocked because some Communist – a Dutchman, a foreigner, of course – had set fire to the *Reichstagsgebäude*, the National Parliament Building in Berlin. In Gera, two days earlier, Dr Jahn had dismissed many of the local councillors and appointed new ones from his own party, the NSDAP. The official explanation was that it was done in order to strengthen the local government against the threats of the Communists. Again, Manfred and Anna discussed these events. They had heard about the evil nature of Communists before, but this was really too much. And when the media reported the national duty to eliminate all Communists and supported the stricter measures taken by the government, the children thought they understood the logics of it, but Manfred couldn't help feeling uneasy when he watched the faces of the men marching through the streets in their brown uniforms and their polished boots.

However, as the months went by, the political indoctrination, which had crept in on them so surreptitiously at first, gradually became more recognizable. Big new swastika flags were set up in every corner of their school building, and at the front of their classroom, on the wall just above the blackboard, there was a large portrait of the new *Reichskanzler*, Herrn Adolf Hitler. Every morning, their school day would begin with the singing of the national anthem, all children standing straight behind their desks and raising their right arms stretched out in a stiff salute. When the singing was over, the teacher would ask with a firm and strict voice, "Who is going to save our Fatherland?"

"It is our *Führer*, Herr Lehrer!" the children had to shout at the top of their voices. After which ceremony they could sit down, and regular teaching would begin. This routine persisted over the next six years, and before they realised what was going on, the children found themselves at an age where they began to ask some new questions and gradually understood that they had to make some important decisions for life. While they were learning to add and subtract, to multiply and divide, to spell correctly and to understand the intricate rules of German grammar, to know the secrets about plants and the anatomy of the most common domestic animals, things were easy, though some of the ideas about human races that entered the curriculum in biology seemed to Manfred to be the teachers' particular hobby-horses. When they were learning about geography, naturally it was quite straightforward, where towns, rivers and mountains were on the map, the names of the world's capital cities and the oceans around the globe, but their teachers began to add political aspects wherever they could. For example, it took Manfred by surprise to learn that certain countries were geologically so deprived and had such a poor climate that it affected their inhabitants over generations so that they became underdeveloped, some even became *Untermenschen*, inferior human beings. America was particularly affected, and that was why they had so many Jews. When it came to history and *Reichskunde*, things really amounted to pure political propaganda. The children learned about the rightful claims of the German race, indeed the Aryan race, over vast portions of Europe and beyond.

In the early years, Manfred and Anna would sometimes discuss these elements of their curriculum, and they both felt sorry that some of their old songs were frowned upon, some music was declared un-German and more and more books were banned by the teachers. As time went by, however, they tended to steer around such discussions, and they gradually learned to avoid any critical remarks about some of the more debatable things that they had to study for school. Besides, their curriculum was so demanding that it left them very little time to speculate over the relative importance or the future relevance of their subjects. They admired Wolfgang's ease with which he seemed to sail through the subjects. After every test, Wolfgang came off with flying colours.

For Manfred, the best side of those years was his friendship with Anna. Thomas had long lost interest in her, and Manfred observed that his brother liked to walk home with another girl from his class. Her name was Charlotte. She was taller than Anna and had nice brown hair. Manfred did not really get a chance to get to know her; Thomas seemed to hide her from his younger brother. As the months went by, the two brothers, though still very close in their home and in matters of boys' activities and interests, drifted apart when it came to girls. They no longer exchanged their impressions about particular girls, and they no longer talked about what they would like to do with a girl once they found themselves alone with one. Such discussions had never had any connection with what Manfred really felt for Anna and what they did when they were alone together. What the brothers had been imagining was childish and sprang from boys' fantasies anyway. Sometimes Manfred regretted the loss of their former intimacy, and he wondered if it might have something to do with the way things had gone with Anna.

More and more of the children's energy became absorbed by sports. Both Weidmann boys loved the challenge of athletics, and while more and more of their school life became regulated by Party rules and political propaganda, their sports activities left them a space of relative freedom. They enjoyed the camaraderie and the spirit of a common interest which they experienced in the sports club. Thomas was fifteen and Manfred was thirteen when they became fully immersed in their sports activities. While Thomas excelled in such disciplines as middle distance running and high jump, Manfred found the 100 meters and long jump more to his liking. And since both boys were growing fast they soon joined the basketball teams of their sports club, too. It was a happy time, and they did not mind the fact that they were only allowed to run or jump in their sports outfit with the swastika on their chests. Such emblems had meanwhile become normal elements of their lives so that hardly anybody took note of them these days.

When Manfred wasn't busy for school, engaged in activities of the *Hitlerjugend* or occupied by his sports activities, he liked to go for walks along the Elster with Anna, although a great deal of her time was also taken up by her activities in the BDM – the so-called *Bund deutscher Mädel*, the League of German Girls – and her role in the girls' volleyball team. While her activities as a *Jungmädel* in the BDM took place in sports halls and in parks where Manfred couldn't see her, he had the opportunity to admire her from time to time during her volleyball training. Often, he would meet her after her volleyball. Early one Friday evening, he entered the sports complex a bit earlier than usual. The girls were still playing their game of volleyball. Manfred spotted Anna at once. Though he had seen her regularly over the past years and never questioned the fact that he knew what she looked like, she suddenly seemed to look different. At first, he thought it had to be her seriousness and her commitment to the game, but then he realised it was her figure. When she jumped in the air to slap the ball the front of her sports shirt jumped, too. He couldn't keep his eyes off her newly discovered femininity, the beautiful round shapes of her breasts. Up until now, she had just been his best friend, but this discovery gave him a stab in his stomach, and he realised he had to see her in a new light. She was becoming a woman, a real woman with a woman's breasts and more rounded buttocks. After his initial shock, he had to admit to himself that this new discovery made him very happy in a way he had never experienced happiness before. He decided to treat her with even more respect than before. She deserved it. She was so beautiful. He would never forget this moment, his first glimpse of Anna as a woman.

One afternoon that summer, Manfred wanted to meet his old friend Isaac. They had arranged to do some of their maths homework together. When he arrived at Isaac's house he found the door closed and no one seemed to be at home. One of the neighbours, a stout woman with a ruddy face and an ugly headscarf tied at the back of her head, looked over the fence, broom in hand, and brusquely asked Manfred what he wanted there.

"Can you help me, please? I'm looking for Isaac. I arranged to meet him. Do you know where he might be?"

"That whole Jewish lot ran away last night. The cowards sneaked off in the middle of the night. Well, good riddance, if you ask me." She snorted through her pressed lips and threw him a significant glance charged with self-righteousness.

Manfred didn't know what to say. On one hand, he was shocked. Why did they leave so unexpectedly and without saying good-bye? On the other hand, he began to think that perhaps there was some truth in what people were saying about Jews. They just couldn't be trusted. Everybody was saying it, especially his leaders in the *Hitlerjugend*, a movement that Manfred had been forced by peer-pressure to join like all his classmates. And then there was Anna, who had told him that Wolfgang had explained to her how the banning of Jews was an international thing, it was the way of the modern world. The English also banned Jews from becoming boy scouts or girl guides. And from his history lessons he knew that the Russians had already persecuted the Jews in the 19th century because they were mean swindlers and criminals and the non-Jewish population had to be protected from them. So, the Jews must be a very treacherous race, after all. He must have been deceived by his former friend Isaac. Manfred knew that he was not in agreement with his father's views in this matter. In fact, both boys thought their father was a blind romantic. Whenever it was reported that yet another Jewish family had disappeared from Gera, he said he was very sorry. One day, shortly after their mother had been sent to a health spa in Czechoslovakia, they had a fierce argument. It began with their father's report about the disappearance of a Jewish family that he used to know very well.

"What a pity the Levis from Weimarer Strasse have left. They were such nice people and good customers. You know, boys, I used to play cards with Chaim Levi, and he – "

" – Filthy people!" Thomas interrupted his father, "We're better off without them."

"How can you speak about the Levis like that?"

"They were thieves and swindlers. Everybody knows that. We were just taken in by them. They were never really part of our town. They never really belonged. They can't have made their money in any rightful way. You can't believe that."

"And Wolfgang told me," Manfred joined in, "that they were lucky they weren't arrested for worse crimes. Very cowardly of course, to sneak off like that in the middle of the night."

"Yes," Thomas added, "they say they were really American spies."

"Nonsense!" their father shouted. "I knew them very well, and I can tell you they were perfectly honest."

"And I can tell you," Thomas snarled back, "you'd better not say such things when other people can hear."

"What next!" His rage mounted, as he could sense his authority melting away in front of his sons. "I can say what I like in my own house."

While their father grew angrier and angrier by the minute, his sons remained relatively calm. They knew they were on the winning side. The whole country was behind them. Their father's romantic views belonged to the past. And as the sons knew very well, these days, such blindness was even becoming dangerous.

Thomas said to his brother, "Come, let's go. We don't want to be associated with such seditious babble." Of course, he wanted Father to hear this. The provocation was fully intentional.

The boys didn't know that their disrespectful behaviour towards their own father was the result of two strong factors, puberty and political indoctrination. These two forces united in their minds and set them more apart from their father as the months and years went by. While their father could cope with the rebelliousness of his sons' puberty, he found it an almost impossible task to save them from what he considered the dangerous and inhuman influence of their teachers, their sports coaches, their peer groups and the general hysterics in public life. He hadn't even been able to make them see the terrible danger of the new legislation on racial segregation that the *Führer* had announced at Nuremberg recently.

They left their father sitting at the dinner table. Only three years earlier, such rebellious behaviour would have amounted to an act of high treason within their family, deserving the harshest punishment. But these days, Father's pompous ways were getting him nowhere, and with Mother's absence, the mitigating factor had also disappeared. Manfred could see that his father's face was swollen with anger and disappointment. But this wasn't the time for sentimentality. If they, as members of the *Hitlerjugend*, were going to be the builders of the new Germany, they had to place public well-being above petty little family disputes. They didn't want to be left out of things on the dawn of the new Germany. They wanted to be part of it. Surely, this was a truly noble aim. As the *Führer* had said in his recent radio broadcast, this was the beginning of a new era, the future would be a future without *Untermenschen*, and the German Empire would last for a thousand years once it had got rid of all the undesirable elements.

TWO

It was a grey Thursday afternoon when Manfred came home from school earlier than on other Thursdays because their history teacher was absent, attending some further training course on new research findings about the origins of the German people. The headmaster said the school was understaffed since they had lost two of their teachers recently, the maths teacher Dr Feigenbaum and the physics teacher Herrn Kahn, who had both disappeared unexpectedly, which had caused the headmaster not only to drop a number of maths and physics lessons but also to refuse to ask other teachers to replace any of their absent colleagues. This was his personal protest aimed at the education department of Thuringia, who should have sent more teachers to replace those who had left. After all, the headmaster had lost seven teachers in the course of the past eighteen months, and all without pre-warning. His protest led to an increase in free lessons for the pupils.

Manfred closed the garden gate and stepped up to the front entrance. He had hardly closed the front door and reached the hall when the telephone rang. This was still an unusual occurrence since it had been only about three months ago when they'd got their telephone. There weren't many of his classmates whose parents had a telephone, but several houses on the Galgenberg had them. At that time, the telephone was primarily considered to be a communication tool for business purposes. Who needed such a contraption for private conversation? That was considered an absurd luxury by the general public. Naturally, Father had one in his delicatessen shop in the Sorge, so whoever wanted to reach him could call him there. And it was only two years ago when the telephone network in Gera was upgraded to a self-dialling system. Before that time, you had to call the operator to get a connection. Father told the boys that Germany was at the head of technical development in Europe. Three decades later in England, Manfred would remember this when you still had to get through the operator in Britain. But now, in the mid-thirties, he still felt very nervous when he had to answer the telephone. After all, it was a pretty strange thing to be talking to someone you couldn't see face to face. So, it was with mixed feelings that he picked up the receiver from the hook on the new contraption hanging on the wall, opposite the clothes-rack in the hall.

"Hello, this is Manfred Weidmann speaking."

"Oh, good afternoon. This is Dr Wolfsohn calling from the St Wenzel Sanatorium in Karlsbad. Can I speak to your father, please?"

"I'm sorry. My father is not here. But I think you can reach him in his shop." Manfred read the telephone number of his father's shop from a notepad by the telephone and wondered why the doctor from the sanatorium wanted to talk to Father. It must have something to do with Mother; perhaps they wanted to change her treatment. He was worried. Could it be a more serious situation? He was never told what Mother's illness was, and neither was Thomas, or he would have told him. Two months ago, they had driven to Karlsbad in their new car to visit their mother at the sanatorium. Their new car, yet another emblem of middle-class affluence becoming quite common on the Galgenberg, was a dark blue Adler saloon-car with a sliding sunroof. Father had insisted it was a German car of the highest quality. Manfred liked the musty smell of its leather seats and the comforting purr of its engine.

After he'd rung off, he sat down at the kitchen table to do his homework. He opened his English book and began to memorise the list of three dozen irregular verbs that they had to learn for the test on Friday. Some were dead easy, others were quite tricky. Easy ones were verbs like "put, put, put", "hit, hit, hit" or "cut, cut, cut" where all three forms were identical. Difficult were verbs like "come, came, come", "hold, held, held" and others where you were never quite sure which of the three forms was different from the others, the present, the past tense or the past participle. And the really tricky ones were verbs like "lie, lay, lain" and "lay, laid, laid", even the regular verb "lie, lied, lied" because it was so like an irregular one, those were verbs you could mix up so easily. Manfred was sure the teacher would try to trick them on these on Friday. Herr Frank was an unpredictable teacher, some of Manfred's friends said that was because he had been abroad for too long. Everybody knew he had spent at least a whole year in Great Britain, and of course it was general knowledge that he must have got under the influence of lots of Jews and Gypsies over there. So, he could probably not be trusted one hundred percent. All the boys expected some foul-play from Herrn Frank, even though they had no concrete reasons for that. There were moments when Manfred found himself liking Herrn Frank – who, one had to admit, sometimes gave them proof of a very pleasant sense of humour – but it was only a fleeting whim that he immediately dismissed from his mind because he felt he had to go along with the other boys, who had to be right. Herr Frank was bound to have been infected by Jewish tricks during his time in such an untrustworthy society. Their history teacher had given them some examples of how the Jews dominated public life in Britain, particularly the British banking system, which in turn dominated the world of business all over the world. That was one of the things that the new Germany saw as its duty to rectify.

His thoughts drifted off, away from English grammar and irregular verbs. He remembered their last visit to Karlsbad in the Adler. Mother had been sitting in a wicker-chair under a group of very old trees in the large park at the back of the main building of the Sanatorium. There was a Scottish tartan rug in red and green spread across her legs, even though the weather seemed quite warm to Manfred.

"I'm so happy to see my dear boys," she said, when Manfred stepped up to her. She gave both boys an extremely long and tight embrace. And Manfred could detect a tear running down her left cheek. He wondered what could have made her so sentimental. It wasn't her usual way.

Manfred liked his mother's aura, her smell, the touch of her cheek when she kissed him, and he felt safe in her embrace. He was sad that her embraces had become a lot rarer over the past year or so. Also, they had become physically altered, somehow, he wasn't quite sure why. Could it be that she looked thinner and her bones stuck out more clearly? Did her tears have anything to do with her emaciated appearance and her pale blue complexion? While she was talking to Father, Manfred observed her body language and her general appearance, and it struck him that he didn't really know his own mother. Was this pale, thin, fragile wisp of a woman really his mother? Was this the jolly, well-proportioned and well-balanced woman he had known in his early childhood? Where was her charming smile and her full face? Where had her air of self-confidence gone? Looking at her now, Manfred felt sorry for her and mysteriously estranged from her. He had to fight off a cold shiver down his spine, and all of a sudden, the day had lost some of its generally agreeable and comforting atmosphere. Thinking back to this moment in years to come, he became convinced that that afternoon in the park at Karlsbad had really marked the end of his childhood. It was the moment when he realised that he wouldn't have his mother forever. It was his first taste of human mortality, although he couldn't have expressed it as such at the time.

Their parents talked about the good air of Karlsbad, the healing power of its waters, the efficiency of the doctor and the nurses, and eventually the boys were sent on an errand to fetch the German paper from the Sanatorium's reception area, an errand they knew was just a pretext to get them out of the way while their parents were discussing things the boys weren't meant to hear.

When the boys returned with the paper, Manfred had the impression that their father looked more earnest. They handed him the paper, and while Mother was chatting to Thomas about his progress at school, Manfred was observing their father. As he was turning the pages of the paper, the frown on his face was getting deeper by the minute.

"The *Führer* really seems to have lost his mind," he said, shaking his head.

"Father! How can you say such a thing?" Thomas countered.

"Well, just read the papers. His new legislation – "

"Oh, please, stop it!" Mother begged, "I don't want any arguments between you, and I don't want to hear about politics. Everyone seems to go on and on about things the *Führer* is going to do, especially the Czech nurses."

Although they respected their mother's wishes, Manfred could hear his brother mumbling under his breath, "And they've certainly got their reasons."

It was difficult to open another topic, so their visit drew towards its end. The boys said their good-byes and their parents embraced in a controlled manner.

So, what could be the matter with Mother now? Manfred, sitting over his English grammar, alone in their big house, found it hard to concentrate on his homework. He hoped his father would return from work soon, so he could tell them what the doctor had told him about Mother's health. It could very well be good news. Mother might be released and come home, a healthy woman again.

The front door opened, and Father stepped in. His manner was brisk and business-like. He didn't lose a lot of words, but merely informed Manfred that he'd come home earlier because he had to drive to Karlsbad.

"It's about Mother. I'll leave the shop in Herrn Wachtveitl's hands while I'm away." Herr Wachtveitl was his Bavarian office clerk, an able man with a funny accent and a ruddy face. "He can look after things in my absence. Now, be a good boy and tell Thomas when he gets home. Frau Müller can cook for you, I arranged it with her." Frau Müller was their neighbour in the dark green house behind the tall fir-tree. This wasn't the first time she was helping the Weidmanns in an emergency.

After a very quick good-bye, Father was out of the door again, and Manfred could hear the engine of the Adler being revved up. Looking out of the kitchen window, he could see the car reversing into the street and then shooting forward in the direction of the broader street leading down to Berliner Strasse.

The house was very quiet. Manfred could hear the ticking of the hall clock.

It was in the evening three days later when Frau Müller came over with a saucepan full of carrot soup, two pairs of Viennese sausages and a chunk of dark bread for the Weidmann boys. She placed the food on the table, where the boys had already laid out their water glasses, their plates and cutlery. She heaved a deep sigh which told Manfred that she had something to say to them.

"Well, well, my boys, it's a sad business," she began. "I don't know how to tell you."

Thomas looked up from his soup and demanded, "What is it, Frau Müller?" But Manfred didn't need to ask, he already knew.

"It's your dear mother. I'm so sorry to be the one to tell you. You see, she passed away peacefully this afternoon. I had a phone call from your poor father. He begged me to tell you immediately, tonight." She slowly walked round the table while she told them, and when she had delivered the bad news she stood behind the boys and placed her heavy hands on their shoulders for comfort.

Thomas looked down, staring at his bowl of soup as if he could see their mother in the food. Manfred couldn't help himself; the tears ran down his cheeks and he couldn't keep his jerking left shoulder under control. He tried to be brave. After all, bravery was one of the virtues that education had been trying to breed in boys of his generation. But he just couldn't help himself. He felt embarrassed in front of Thomas, who managed to take it so bravely. Not a sound emerged from him, not a single sign of emotion. He just stared down. Manfred stood up and climbed up the stairs, reached his room and closed the door behind him.

Through the rest of the evening and through the whole night, he had the impression that the house was particularly quiet. He listened carefully from time to time. There was nothing but complete silence. For Manfred, this was the silence of the angel of death, a notion he had picked up from one of their old aunts the year before, when there was a distant death among her acquaintances. He had no idea what or who the angel of death was. Now he imagined it to be some kind of ghost that visited every living being who had known the deceased person. So naturally, it was also visiting them now.

He couldn't go to sleep because his head was full of memories and conflicting emotions. He remembered the comforting warmth of his mother's embraces, her blue eyes, her smiling face, her gentle voice and her serving attitude, especially towards her husband. Manfred didn't know if he should blame his father for his mother's sad life. But then he wasn't so sure if her life had really been so sad, after all. Didn't she love her husband? He had never seen his parents exchanging caresses or other tokens of love. The kisses that they exchanged were more perfunctory than tender, and he thought he couldn't remember them ever looking at each other with any degree of true affection.

It was early morning when he finally dropped off into a troubled sleep.

***

Elfriede's death marked the end of the Weidmann family as it had existed in their grey house on the Galgenberg. It affected her widower as well as her two sons, each in different ways.

The widower, Thomas Weidmann, delicatessen merchant and shop-owner, liberal-minded free-spirit and romantic, admirer and sponsor of the arts and head of the respected Weidmann family on the Galgenberg, a true man of substance in many respects, was so shattered by his beloved wife's untimely death that he seemed to lose his hold on things. He no longer uttered any of his former romantic notions, he no longer opposed his sons' ideas of a proud and new Germany about to rise from former humility, and he no longer avoided any dealings with the *Staatsbeauftragte* and with the Nazi mayor of Gera. When a large order came from the town offices, an order of exquisite delicacies for one of the official functions of the NSDAP to celebrate the *Führer*'s birthday, he accepted it without comment and even went so far as to come along with Mr Wachtveitl to deliver the goods to the town hall and help him set up the sumptuous buffet in the great hall with the old oak parquet floor, the dark paintings of German battles on two of the four walls and the long red wall-hangings with their swastikas all around. It was as if he had suddenly surrendered his former misgivings about the *Lumpenpack* and decided to go along with them, at least to profit from them if they wanted to become his most lucrative customers.

To cope with his new widowhood, he felt it was good for him to travel to Berlin every three weeks or so. It took his mind off the many places in Gera that reminded him of his happy times with Elfriede. They had only been to Berlin a few times, and now that the capital of the new Germany was undergoing so many changes under the guidance of the *Führer*'s architect, Albert Speer, the *Reichshauptstadt* had nothing to remind him of happier days. He would drive up in his blue Adler, park it near Unter den Linden and then walk through the Brandenburger Tor and into the parkland to the west of it. He liked to watch mothers with their children and stared with an empty mind at groups of young men in uniforms. In the evening, he liked to go to the theatre. The new developments that the *Staatstheater* had undergone recently seemed to justify his newly-found *laissez-faire* attitude towards the Nazi régime. After all, the Nazis had not only reopened the theatre under its old name, Schiller-Theater, but also appointed Heinrich George, one of the most popular actors, as its new director. Thomas Weidmann remembered how the stocky George with his Berlin accent had originally been a Communist and opposed the budding NSDAP only a few years ago when he worked with people like Brecht and Piscator. But within a very short period George – Georg August Friedrich Schulz with his real name – had accepted the leadership of the Nazis and even played in one of their propaganda films, *Hitler Youth Quex*, which Thomas had seen in Gera. At the time, he had found himself quite surprised that the great George should lend his talent to the Nazi cause, but now it served as an excuse for his own change of attitude. Also, the great name that George replaced as the director of the Schiller-Theater served as a similar model. Gustaf Gründgens, who only ten years earlier had been connected with Max Reinhardt and with the family of the celebrated novelist Thomas Mann – working with his son Klaus Mann and marrying his sister Erika Mann – had also been taken in by the Nazis and joined some powerful arts councils set up by Hermann Goering, Hitler's right hand. So, if such important figures in the arts – among them Wilhelm Furtwängler, the gifted conductor of the outstanding Berlin Philharmonic Orchestra – accepted and even served the leadership of Hitler and his Party, Thomas argued for himself, he could very well acknowledge that at least the Nazis supported the arts and gave new impulses to the literary and musical life of Germany. And this was enough to give up one's opposition to them. Wasn't it possible that some of the awful things about the Nazis that were being rumoured would prove to be just that: rumours? Perhaps some Jews really deserved the bad treatment that they were given these days?

Like that, Thomas Weidmann's regular visits to the *Reichshauptstadt* helped him not only to cope with his bereavement but equally strengthened his decision to go along with the Nazis and to deal with them in his professional capacity. His change of mind came just in time, because the Nazis had found out that he wasn't a Party member and demanded that he should prove his allegiance to the great cause of the new Germany. They sent for him, and he had to appear for an interview at the town hall.

"Now, Herr Weidmann," the young official behind the desk asked him, smiling benevolently, "how do you justify the fact that you refuse to become a Party member and at the same time you profit from your business connections with the Party?"

Thomas Weidmann managed to hide his nervousness and hesitated for a short moment. "Well," he answered, "in fact, I was a member only a few years ago. But when my dear wife's health declined I fell behind in my membership fees and decided it was more honest to quit."

"Aha!"

"Yes. I felt it was a matter of honour. How could I profit from something without paying for it?"

"I see. German honour."

"Yes. I have always believed in the importance of German honour."

"All right," the young man smiled. Thomas was relieved. The magic word "honour" had saved him. He hoped this was the end of the interview, but the official cleared his throat and looked at him in a questioning way.

"How do you intend to prove your allegiance to the Party now and in future?"

"What options do I have?"

"Naturally, your most obvious move is to join the Party again."

"Or else?"

"Well, you could serve the Party in other ways. If you choose this option," the man winked at him, "I will make a note on this form, which you will sign, and I will refer your business to Standartenführer Obermayer, who will in turn contact you. There are many ways in which you can be useful to us. And if you want to keep your business, you will be wise to cooperate. There's just one condition, though. Do you employ, or have you ever employed, any Jews in your business?"

Thomas hesitated. Young Salomon Feigenbaum had run some errands for the shop, but that had been more than two years ago, and he'd never been properly employed, just a boy doing small jobs for pocket money. Besides, the Feigenbaums had left a while ago.

"No."

"Fine, Herr Weidmann. A true German man of honour, as you say. You will hear from us in due course."

When, a few days later, he was contacted by Standartenführer Obermayer's office, he had to agree to spy on his customers. It was understood that housewives would exchange gossip while doing their shopping, and if they ever mentioned anything suspicious – like feeding more mouths than could reasonably be wanting food in their homes or listening to foreign radio stations – Thomas Weidmann was expected to make a note and report such instances to the same office, which he came to understand was an office working in liaison with the Gestapo, the *Geheime Staats-Polizei*, the secret police. He was to report regularly every fortnight.

As for his older son Thomas, the loss of his mother made him harder. He turned his back on his family. Often, he would not come home after school, but spend the rest of the day at the local headquarters of the *Hitlerjugend*, where he took over a range of new duties. One day he declared over breakfast that he wouldn't be home in the evening, and from that day on he became a rare presence in the house on the Galgenberg.

Manfred was affected in a different way. Instead of shutting himself off and presenting a hardened face to the world like his brother, he suffered terribly and was nearly crushed by his need for comfort and emotional warmth. He was under enormous pressure during the funeral. Instead of giving him comfort, the ceremony merely served the purpose of showing off to the people of Gera. The message was clear: Weidmann's Delicatessen was a thriving business employing and serving only Aryans, its wealth and its success were reflected in the sumptuous decoration in church and around the grave. The mourners were valued customers, business connections and a few distant relatives that Manfred didn't even know existed. It was obvious they weren't here for mourning, commiseration or comfort, but for the display of their latest fashions in black clothing and for the marking of their social territory, the affirmation of their social standing as citizens who could afford to shop at Weidmann's Delicatessen in the Sorge. Not everyone could boast to be a customer of the town's finest retail business. One had to let the world see who was who.

Manfred felt lost.

Two weeks after the funeral, a Tuesday, Anna approached him after school. She had such a look of compassion that Manfred's heart went out to her, and tears began to roll down his cheeks.

"Oh dear! Can I walk home with you?" she asked in a gentle voice. "Will you let me be with you? We don't have to talk. Just walk together. Will this be any good for you?"

Manfred was too overwhelmed to utter a word. He just nodded. Her voice was so good for him, so clear and honest, so free of pretence and melodrama, quite the opposite of those hypocritical mourners at the funeral.

"It's a sad business. You must be lost." This statement was such a comfort. It was just a statement, but it was the truth.

"It will take time," she added.

They walked along the banks of the Elster. When they were alone they stopped, and Anna hugged him tenderly. She laid her head on his shoulder, which for once did not twitch. There was no need for words, the rippling sound of the Elster was enough. They remained like this for several minutes. Manfred didn't even hear the loud croaking of the crows as they were flying past, he just wanted to be like this, to be held by Anna for the rest of his life. His tears dried off while he felt her heartbeat against his own chest. The softness of her body against his, the sweet smell of her hair near his nostrils, her warmth, her proximity, the mere fact of her being here: all this was so good. He didn't want it to end. Ever.

After a while, Anna loosened her hold and gently drew back. For a split second, he was disappointed, but then he spotted some people approaching them on the footpath. It was an elderly couple.

"Good afternoon," Anna said in a clear voice. Manfred merely muttered some undefined greeting. He didn't want these people to see his tears. But the elderly couple just mumbled their greetings and walked past them. When they were about five metres away the woman looked back and gave them a strange nod.

"Let's walk on," Anna suggested. "That is, if you are ready."

They looked at each other for a few seconds, and their eye contact gave him courage. So, they began to walk on along the river bank.

Soon, their mood changed, and Manfred spoke his first words. "She was such a good mother. But she was never a happy woman."

This was the beginning of an unhurried and unrestrained conversation between them as they were walking along the bank and then up towards the Galgenberg. Anna didn't press him, she just responded to his statements, went along with his opinions and musings, and like this she gave him the very support that he needed most in this hour. When they reached the grey house in Ypernstrasse it was the most natural thing in the world for Anna to come into the house with him. In the hallway, she hesitated and looked around. It was her first time in this house.

"Would you like a cup of tea?" he managed to ask.

"That would be perfect," Anna smiled back. He felt that this was a special occasion. To him, it seemed that even though she smiled at him it was a very serious situation. There was a strong earnestness behind her smile, and he felt he could connect to her through this earnestness. A genuine connection he had never experienced with anyone before.

When she left him half an hour later, he knew she would come to him again. And so she did. From that day onward, Anna came to his home every two or three days, but only through the week, never on weekends, because it was clear to both of them that the presence of other persons – Father or Thomas – would disturb the wonderful thing that they had now been building up between them. They didn't know what this thing was, but it was good.

He saw her as his best friend. Whenever she arrived at his home and before she left, they embraced and re-lived that first embrace on the banks of the Elster. Sometimes they went for a walk, but they preferred to stay indoors in the grey house, where they were undisturbed, with his father being at the shop and his brother mostly away. Their embraces were a haven of tranquillity and well-being for both of them. They didn't dare to exchange such intimacies on their walks, being wary of other people's reactions, also feeling uncomfortable when others saw them, not only because they saw it as a violation of their intimacy but also because they wouldn't have wanted anyone to tell their parents. Gera was a small town; many people knew their parents. Another reason for their preference of the indoors was the autumnal weather, which rendered their walks less comfortable.

This state of things continued for two months. They would usually meet at his home on two or three days of the week. They would embrace, they would look at each other, and they would talk. They talked about his mother, what she had meant to him, the meals she used to cook, the things she used to say, her sad moods, her failing health and about what a lovely person she was. They also talked about Anna's family, about their sports activities, their plans for the future and their immediate duties in their respective youth organisations, Manfred in the *Hitlerjugend* and Anna in the *Bund deutscher Mädel*. Sometimes they discussed common friends, especially Wolfgang Löffel, and sometimes Thomas was briefly mentioned. Only very rarely would they discuss what was happening in public life, and both of them really hated politics, for which, however, they had to feign an interest at school and in their youth organisations. During this time, Manfred had mixed feelings about international politics. He had his particular problems understanding Germany's relationship with England. During the past few months he had begun to like the English language, and he was fond of several British heroes, such as Isaac Newton, Charles Darwin or Lord Baden-Powell, different figures though they were. From his teachers, his mentors and his leaders, however, he had learnt a great deal about British treachery, about the atrocities committed in the English colonies, especially in the Caribbean and in India, and about the poor standard of living in Britain due to the Jews, who exploited the country and corrupted its people. When the news came about the *Führer*'s meeting with Neville Chamberlain, the British Prime Minister, in late September, Manfred and Anna discussed this development and agreed that now things would go well, there wouldn't be a war – as some of their friends were saying – but Germany and England would agree on most things in international affairs, especially about the Fatherland's rightful claims to the annexation of the Sudetenland, which they understood were the Czech border areas. So, after all, Manfred would be allowed to admire his British heroes and wouldn't have to hate a country and its people that he really liked. That was a comforting thing.

One afternoon in October, as Anna was taking off her brown corduroy jacket, Manfred became aware of her fine womanly figure. And as they embraced he felt a new sensation creeping up within his whole being, a sensation he could hardly identify or control. Without realising what he was doing he began to move his hands up and down, along her figure, down her back to her buttocks and up again to the nape of her neck, all very gently. This caused her to move her body in a way that electrified him. She pressed herself to his body more than ever before, and because they were wearing their uniforms he could feel the soft but firm mounds of her breasts against his chest. A strong force was pulling his mouth towards hers. She turned her face to his and put up her lips in such a way as to invite him to kiss them. The moment his lips touched hers was absolutely magic. He realised he could feel her breath coming from her nostrils and caressing his cheeks while the touch of their lips remained unbelievably exquisite. Slowly she opened her lips, which made him open his, too, and so he carefully and very tenderly entered her mouth with his tongue. The softness and the wetness inside her mouth surprised and overwhelmed him. First slowly, then more eagerly, their tongues moved around and explored each other's mouths, both treading on new territory for the first time in their young lives.

He pulled her down onto the sofa in the living-room, and she let herself be pulled down ever so gladly.

Sitting comfortably on the sofa, they could really lose themselves in their kissing, which lasted for centuries, they felt, but was still not enough when they gently pulled away from each other after a while. Manfred had the impression that his lips were feeling a bit numb after the long contact with hers, but he also felt a strange and hitherto unknown intoxication. They relaxed for a few minutes, their faces only millimetres from each other, each feeling the other's warm breath very close. They couldn't explain what was happening to them, but they wanted more of it.

When they took up their kissing again, he found it was even better than the first time. He felt more confident, and he could feel that she, too, was obviously more willing to continue for as long as he liked. After several minutes of kissing and imaginative exploration with their tongues, Manfred cradling Anna's body in his right arm against the soft back of the sofa, he had a sudden urge to move his left hand down her front, and when his hand reached her right breast and felt its softness through the thin fabric of her blouse he thought he was the happiest man in the world. He cupped her breast and moved his hand around it, and all the while they kept up their kissing. Quite unexpectedly, he felt something harden at the tip of her breast, even though there had to be at least two layers of material between his hand and her skin, and at the same time a deep moan escaped her throat and she slightly widened the opening of her mouth without giving up their kissing.

He moved his hand up the front of her white blouse and slowly loosened her black neckerchief – he knew the girls called it their *Fahrtentuch* – and pulled it out of its brown leather knot, which wasn't so easy with only one hand. Once the neckerchief was open, he could begin to unbutton her blouse, which he did with relish. For him this was an utterly new experience, which had an air of forbidden adventure and a very joyful element of revelation. He had never seen a girl or a woman take off her clothes, and up to this very moment he had never really wondered what girls looked like underneath their clothes – except in their silly fantasies as young boys, which had no connection with reality. But now, right now, he suddenly wanted to know, to see, to experience. He was too young to know the difference between sexual desire and mere curiosity, and he would probably never be fully capable of such a distinction. While he was so completely occupied with his own urge he was still slightly surprised that she allowed him to do all this. She even appeared to want it, too.

Once her blouse was open, a new world presented itself to him, and his hand stroked over the cotton fabric of her singlet or undershirt, he didn't care what it was called, he only knew that now he could feel the softness of her breasts more directly. What absolute joy! With a bold move, he shifted his hand beneath this last layer and at last touched the velvet skin of her naked breasts, where he felt he could keep his hand forever and ever. He cupped the full roundness and could hardly believe that Anna had such unimaginable treasures hidden beneath her clothes. Now he also realised what the hardness at the tip meant, he had a very strange feeling when he felt the hardness of her nipples, at the same time aware of the heaving movement of her entire upper body, the movement of her breathing, as well as her heartbeat.

They continued like this for a long time, until suddenly the mood changed. He felt that Anna wanted to put an end to their caresses even before she made the first move. Slowly they disentangled themselves from each other. She pulled down her singlet and began to button up her blouse, while he tried to recover from the overwhelming experience he had just gone through.

"I think we should stop here," she breathed.

He wondered if he'd done anything wrong, but she smiled at him in such a blissful way that he was relieved. While she was busy buttoning up her blouse, she felt she had to give him some form of explanation to make things right. Not to leave him disappointed.

"You know, we should give it more time. It is really lovely with you, but I just feel we shouldn't go any further."

He nodded. However, at this point, probably neither of them knew what "further" there was for them, because it was all new territory, and neither of them had been told the facts of life by their parents. These things were never mentioned in those days in German society of the 1930s. All they could feel was that there had to be a "further" because they could feel it so strongly and almost overpoweringly in their bodies.

After another long kiss, fully dressed and ready for the outside world, they parted, and Anna left for her home. He offered to walk her home, but she declined.

"You should be at home when your father comes home, and I think I need to be alone after what we just had. I need to think." After a pause she added: "And I want to live through it again in my mind. It was so beautiful."

He closed the door behind her. The house was very quiet. He put his left hand to his face and tried to catch Anna's scent on his palm. Nothing could be better.

THREE

During the two days following his earth-rocking experience with Anna, Manfred walked on clouds. His whole being was so immersed in his memory of her, her being, her presence, the intimacy with her and the common experience of their bodies. He thought he could still feel her warm breath on his face and his hands could still be in close contact with the soft skin of her lovely body. In his mouth, he could still feel the touch of her tongue and his whole person shivered with the memory of everything that was her.

The nights were almost unbearable. The intensity of her presence in his mind was so overwhelming.

Why couldn't they be together all the time? What was she doing or thinking at this very moment? Was she thinking of him, too? Were her feelings the same?

He came to admit to himself that this was probably what was generally understood when people talked about falling in love. If this assumption was right, Manfred could totally agree with the notion of "falling", because he knew now that it was no use resisting what was happening, one was just drawn into it and it was indeed like falling into a new world. He couldn't quite decide whether this new world was paradise or hell, because he was constantly drawn between the two extremes of either rejoicing in complete bliss over this newly-discovered love or sinking into utter despair over his dependence on her when she was not with him to give him the assurance of her love. He found he could hardly concentrate on his school work because his mind was not free. She occupied it completely and exclusively. Struggling with the enormity of his emotions, he suddenly remembered a poem that promised to give him some confidence now. It was a poem by Catullus, which he remembered from his Latin classes mainly for its brevity, but whose beauty and real meaning he was only now beginning to comprehend:

Odi et amo.

Quare id faciam fortasse requiris?

Nescio. Sed fieri sentio et excrucior.

At this moment, he couldn't care less for the poem's chiastic structure or any other theoretical facts that they had to study at school, but it was its meaning that caught him and made him remember it at all. How perfectly accurate this observation was! For Manfred, it caught the very essence of his present state. In the middle of the second night he got up from a troubled half-sleep and sat down at his small desk. He took a large sheet of paper and wrote the poem on it in beautiful large letters. It took him nearly an hour because he wanted it to look really good. Then he stood up and nailed the sheet on the wall above his bed. Back in bed, he looked up at it and wondered if it might not be even better if he had a good photograph of Anna that he could put up next to the Catullus poem. But then, Father and Thomas would discover his secret. They certainly had no idea of how far advanced he was in the love department. He decided to postpone this question and tried to go back to sleep.

It was hard to sit at his school desk and listen to what the teachers were telling them. He had to steal a glance over to where she was sitting. To his amazement and disappointment, she never looked back at him. This made him very uneasy after two days. So, on the third day he decided to seek her out after school and ask her about her feelings. But there was no need to seek her out, since she was already waiting for him just outside the schoolyard, behind the holly where they couldn't be seen by everyone.

"Hello, Manfred," she said, looking him in the eyes, "have you stopped liking me? Did I do anything wrong?"

"How can you say such a thing?"

"But you never called me after... you know what."

"Oh, Anna! I've been thinking of you all the time, of you and of us. It was so wonderful with you. I was hoping to be with you again every day."

"Were you?" She began to smile in a teasing way. She looked absolutely ravishing.

"Yes, of course. What were you thinking?"

"So, you really like me?"

"Oh, much more than like you." He was looking for words. The magic word "love" would still require more courage than he could muster at this stage. It was on his tongue, but he decided to keep it for later. If and when they could be together again like they were the other day, then he might bring it up. He felt he had to hold her in his arms when he told her.

"Would you like me to come to your home again?" she slowly asked.

This was good news indeed. "Yes, of course, let's go right now."

As they were walking up the Galgenberg, she took his hand. The renewed touch of their skin was phenomenal, it gave him all the happiness and reassurance that he needed at this moment. Soon they were in the house again. This time he didn't offer her a cup of tea, he couldn't wait. Hardly had they taken off their jackets when he took her in his arms. Obviously, she was equally anxious to renew their intimacies, because he could feel how hard she pressed her whole body against his, and this time it was her tongue that eagerly entered his mouth first. His mouth received her gladly, and from this moment on it was clear to them that they were both willing and their love was mutual.

Their embraces, their kisses and their caresses became more passionate.

"Can't we go to your room this time?" she whispered in his ear.

He was surprised and extremely excited over her initiative. But because he remembered her restraint of last time he asked her, "Are you sure?"

"Yes, I want to be in a place where nobody can detect or disturb us. Here, in the living-room, you never know... Your father or your brother might walk in any time. I would feel a lot safer in your room."

He looked at her beautiful face for a few moments before he took her by her hand and led her up the creaking stairs to his room. They closed the door behind them, which immediately gave them a sense of never-before experienced intimacy. They sat down on his bed. She looked up at the wall.

"Oh, what made you put that up there?"

"Don't you remember this poem? We had it in Latin, I think it was in February."

"I was ill with my bronchitis for most of February."

"Oh yes, of course. Well, you couldn't be expected to catch up with everything that you'd missed. This is the short love poem that the Latin poet Gaius Valerius Catullus wrote for his mistress Lesbia."

She read it out carefully, first stumbling over the elision in the second line, but she managed to get its meaning. Then they both remained silent for a few moments.

"It's beautiful. And so full of a deep truth. Can't we light a candle?" she suggested. "It would be so romantic, wouldn't it?"

He stood up and found a thick red candle at the bottom of his desk drawer. It was already burned halfway down, but it still had many hours in it. When he'd lit it, the flame stood up to a nice size and gave the lovers the atmosphere that they required to make things perfect. When he sat down at her side again, she took his head between her hands, leant back and pulled him down with her until she was lying on his bedcover and he was halfway on top of her. Like this, they could kiss in a relaxed position for a very long time.

Naturally, his left hand began to explore her again. This time, she didn't wear her BDM uniform but a dark red jumper with a thick grey skirt. It was easy to shift his hand underneath her jumper, then under her shirt. Her skin was soft and warm. While he was enjoying what his hand found, her kisses became more and more passionate. And when his hand finally reached her naked breasts and felt her hard nipples again she emitted a deep and long sigh.

"Oh, Manfred! I do love you so."

So, she'd had the courage to utter the magic word first. He was so happy he could hardly believe this was really happening. But after her declaration, it was easy for him to respond in kind and tell her he loved her too.

Their mutual declaration had given him encouragement, so he began to lift up her jumper and her shirt and eventually he pulled them over her head, which she readily allowed. She even helped him by lifting her head slightly. Then she took the discarded articles from him and threw them away on the carpet.

In the dimming afternoon light, with the flame of the candle tinting the room in an orange hue, Manfred now admired her upper part in its natural state. He had never seen a woman's breasts naked, and what he saw now made him gasp with pleasure. He began to kiss her belly, then slowly moved his lips upward until they reached her breasts, kissing first one nipple then the other. What absolute bliss! Anna enjoyed this. He could feel her shivering with pleasure. When she shivered her breasts wobbled slightly, which he considered particularly captivating. He spent a very long time just kissing her in a relaxed way and stroking the soft white velvet which her breasts represented for him. He was convinced that he could spend the rest of his life just caressing her lovely breasts.

It was natural for her to take off his upper clothes, so they continued their kisses and caresses with the pleasure of having this exciting and reassuringly beautiful skin contact. Like this, they lost themselves in their loving activities for the following three hours, forgetting everything else in the world during this time. It was what they had both been wanting for quite some time. Now, at last, they were together.

***

On a Tuesday morning, about four weeks later, Anna came up to him before their first lesson at school. She took him aside and whispered in his ear.

"Have you heard the news?"

He didn't know what to answer. Ever since they had begun their intimate phase he had hardly ever listened to the news on the radio. He knew their teachers and the *Hitlerjugend* leaders would tell them everything anyway, so he could shut himself off in order to concentrate on his more academic schoolwork and dream of Anna and their kisses.

"What happened?"

"There has been a Jewish attack. In Paris. Against Germany."

"How can there have been an attack on Germany in Paris? That's in France."

"I don't remember the details," Anna shrugged her shoulders, "but I'm sure the teachers will tell us everything. I just wanted to tell you. I hope there won't be a war now. It would be terrible if we couldn't be together, wouldn't it?"

She looked him in the eyes with such an expression of worry that his heart went out to her. Looking round to make sure nobody could see them, he quickly hugged her to comfort her. Then they entered the school-building together without touching. But they both knew that they belonged together.

"Yesterday, our country was attacked by a treacherous Jewish conspiracy," Herr Mollenhauer, their young Latin teacher, announced at the beginning of their first lesson of the morning. "They sent one of their agents, a seventeen-year-old Jew called Herschel Grynszpan to kill one of our diplomats in Paris. The Jew was as filthy as his name suggests: *Grünspan*, verdigris. May he rust and rot away in hell!"

"Herr Lehrer! What's going to happen now?" one of the boys in the first row asked.

"Well, naturally, our government is in uproar. And justifiably so. Some act of retribution is now called for, I am sure."

Manfred felt a twitch in his left shoulder. He was extremely uneasy. But there was nothing he could say or do to feel any better.

After school, he sought out Anna, and they went for a walk along the Elster to discuss the political situation, something they had hardly ever done. Normally they discussed things that concerned their personal lives, their families, their common interests, or they talked about things that helped them to get to know each other better. But today, the tense atmosphere that seemed to lie on the town like a dark blanket affected them like most other people. When he held her close, he could feel her nervousness.

"What do you think is going to happen now?" she asked.

"I don't know," he sighed, and they realized their own smallness within the order of things. Within this world, they were so tiny and probably so insignificant. But for each other, they mattered enormously. Again, Manfred was reminded of his old question: Why were people doing what they were doing? Why were the Jews trying to destroy their Fatherland?

He reached home alone, because Anna had to go to her own home to do some schoolwork and to help her mother with some household chores. They didn't have a charwoman like the Weidmanns, so Anna had to help sometimes.

He was surprised to find his elder brother at home.

"Oh, it's only you, Freddy," Thomas mumbled as he looked up from the kitchen table where he had his leather things spread out for cleaning and polishing. He held up his waist-belt to check its shine in the light of the lamp over the table. Then he spat on it and started polishing it again.

"Are you here for longer?" Manfred asked.

"Don't know. Just getting ready for things tomorrow."

"What about tomorrow?"

"Don't ask stupid questions. It's nothing for little boys. But if you have to know, well, you must be aware of the necessity to act against the filthy Jews now."

"Oh," Manfred was surprised. "Are there any concrete plans already? Is there going to be a war?"

"Of course there won't be a war, silly. But we were ordered to be ready for a big action tomorrow night."

"What big action?"

"As I said, nothing for little boys." And with this curt comment he stood up and put on his belt. He put his feet in his polished boots and arranged his uniform. The swastika on his sleeves looked brilliant. Manfred did not know whether to be afraid or proud of his brother in his resplendent brown uniform. He looked so fierce, but then he was only doing his duty for their beloved Fatherland, wasn't he?

Hardly had Thomas left the house when Manfred turned on the radio. There was music. Wagner, he recognised that at once. When the music finished there was a programme to commemorate Ernst vom Rath, the diplomat who had been shot in Paris. His life and career were highlighted in a detailed report. It was clear that the death of this brilliant man, who would have achieved great things, had he lived, was a very sad loss for his family and for Germany. Manfred listened to the whole programme, before he switched off and began to prepare something to eat. His father would probably be home later, so he heated up a pork stew and some potatoes from the day before, sat down at the kitchen table to enjoy it and made sure he left enough for his father.

On the following day, a Wednesday, everything appeared to be normal, at school, in the streets, all around, but Manfred's sensitivity registered a strange atmosphere of impending doom. He couldn't put his finger to it, but he was convinced something was going to happen soon, something that would concern them all. It was a sort of end-of-the-world mood which lay in the air.

After school, Anna came home with him. From her general attitude as well as from her relative silence during their walk home, he registered that she shared his assessment of the general mood.

When they were in his room, lying together, the upper parts of their bodies bared, their caresses began very tenderly and slowly, both of them savouring every moment, but after a while they both became more excited, more passionate, more desperate. It was as if the general mood had affected them in such a way that they felt they might as well give up all their restraints because the world was coming to an end anyway.

Manfred lay on top of Anna, grasping her breasts with both hands and nuzzling his face between her now flat mounds, fully enjoying their softness on both his cheeks, when he realised he wanted to know more of her. Slowly he shifted to her side, slid his right arm under her back and with his left hand began to stroke her legs, first over her thick skirt, then down below her knees, from where he moved upwards along the inside of her thighs. He gently unfastened her suspenders and rolled down her woollen stockings, discovering areas of her naked skin he'd never believed would be so soft. She helped his movements by lifting her bottom, and when her stockings were completely removed she began to pull down her skirt. He took it from her and threw it on the floor beside the bed, where the other clothes already lay in a heap. As he saw she was now only wearing her knickers he realised it was unfair that he was still wearing his trousers. So he took them off, too, and they caressed each other for a while like this. Eventually, his hand moved down from her bellybutton and slid under her knickers, where he was surprised to find such a thick bush of hair. When his hand moved further into this most intimate region of her body and he discovered her wetness he felt himself go crazy with desire, and his own underpants could hardly hold his stiffness. He withdrew his hand and moved it up to her breasts again, kissing her deeply, both of them beginning to moan softly. He pulled his mouth from hers very gently and whispered into her ear.

"Are you all right?"

"Yes, it's so wonderful. Don't stop. I'm so happy!"

She sat up and took off her knickers. Then she grabbed his underpants and pulled them down, too. He could tell she was surprised, perhaps a little shocked, but also very happy to see his enormous erection. They took a moment to enjoy looking at each other's beauty completely naked, an experience they would never forget for their whole lives. Then they lay down and embraced, kissed and caressed each other.

She emitted a light squeak, with pain and pleasure combined, when he at last entered her slowly and carefully. Then the world enveloped them both in a whirlwind of passion.

Outside, daylight was fading away, and the November evening began to sink into ever deeper darkness. The lovers were utterly unaware of what was going on in the outside world. It was only when the noises of breaking glass, the shouts and the cries became louder and more desperate by the minute that the outside world entered their awareness again.

At first, Manfred thought he was dreaming. He rubbed his eyes while he was reluctantly loosening his body from Anna's. His mind was still a bit dizzy, even though he was fully aware of what they had just done. He didn't regret anything, and when he saw the blissful smile on her face in the dim candlelight he knew that she didn't have any regrets either.

"Listen! What's that? What's going on?" he demanded.

"It sounds like some drunks smashing windows in the street."

"Yes, but it's not in our street, it must be down near Berliner Strasse. There must be lots of drunks if they can cause such clamour."

"Let's get up and see," she suggested. "I have a bad feeling something terrible is about to take place."

While they were getting dressed, all the lovely feelings of a short while ago gone, he remembered what Thomas had insinuated. Was this the beginning of a war? No, it couldn't be, but it sounded pretty awful. Especially the loud cries, which indicated that people were in terrible agony.

As they reached Berliner Strasse, they realized that the main noise was coming from the town centre, so they turned left and walked along the tramlines towards the centre, marching quickly and holding hands.

What awaited them was mayhem. The streets were full of running people. There were lots of uniformed men with sticks, clubs and guns. They smashed shop-windows, they yelled commands and they caught hold of some of the terrified men and women running from their houses and shops. Lorries drew up, and many of the civilians were manhandled brutally and thrown onto those lorries. Only very few of them fought back, but to no avail. The uniformed men were stronger. It looked as if all these people were being arrested. What for? Manfred wondered. Anna turned white and nearly fainted. She held onto her lover, and they withdrew into an empty doorway. On the left, down a narrow alley, they could detect a fire.

"What's that?" he asked, well aware that she wouldn't be able to answer him.

They spent more than two hours in dark corners and doorways, looking with open mouths, Anna no longer able to hold back her tears, Manfred so shocked he couldn't make any comments on what they were witnessing. They saw shops being ravaged and looted, windows broken, houses set on fire, and they saw the local synagogue going up in flames. All the time they heard the barking voices of the brown uniforms and the terrible cries and desperate wails of the people trying to escape this hell.

Later, they couldn't remember how they ever got home, but it was late at night.

***

When Manfred woke up, it was still dark outside. He looked at his alarm clock on the bedside table and saw that it was half-past five in the morning. As his mind was crossing the bridge between sleep and wakefulness, the events of the previous day and the night slowly began to sink in. He began to realize that within the past twenty-four hours – even less, the past fifteen hours or so – he had experienced the greatest happiness in his young life and witnessed the most shocking scenes in public life. What a terrible contrast! How could he cope with such extremes? Again, he returned to his repetitive question: What made people do what they were doing? This enigma could be applied to both extremes, the intimacy of their love-making as well as the horror of the brutal scenes they had seen in the streets of their home town.

What made Anna give herself so completely to him, what made her offer her body and mind to him in such a wonderful way? Yes, it was love. But still, it was such a complete surrender in a way. Was that what women always did when they really and truly loved a man? If this was the climax of pleasure that his life as a man had to offer him, indeed, he could face anything in the future. The mere knowledge of such bliss and the satisfaction of such an experience would always give him strength and confidence. He could do anything, achieve any high goals he could ever aim for, put his stamp on the world, render his life meaningful.

And what made men destroy other people's houses, their shops, their livelihoods, even their lives? There had to be very powerful forces behind such naked hatred. Manfred felt divided between pity for the families whose lives were destroyed so brutally and critical empathy for the perpetrators. If men could be driven to such extremes they must have very good reasons. Their fury might appear blind, but it could have sprung from frustration and then been channelled by their leaders into such action as he had witnessed. If the Jews hadn't pushed so many good citizens to the brink of poverty, and if Jewish arrogance hadn't robbed so many hard-working men of their self-respect, surely such outrages could never have taken place. It had to be a case of the underprivileged people reaching their breaking-point.

Through his ruminations and evaluations of the recent events, Manfred's subconscious ego told him that he could personally gain insight from what was going on. Really, what he had experienced – at both extremes of the scale of human experience – was educational. This was how one learned about the world. What had happened must have some larger meaning. He never thought of himself as a religious person, but he suspected that the recent events – his private erotic experience as well as the public escalation of civil conflict – had an element of holiness about them. Some higher force had directed them. It wasn't a divine creature or such humbug, but it was some higher force.

The important question that presented itself to him now was how to cope with this. How to behave in the near future? How to ensure that the wonderful state of things he had reached with Anna could be maintained into eternity? On the other hand, how to react to what was happening to his home town, his country, his beloved Fatherland? In both spheres, he became convinced, it would be best to be patient, to wait and see. In Anna's case, he would first get to the bottom of her feelings. He wouldn't take such liberties with her again until he was totally and completely convinced of her own free willingness, her ardent desire to repeat what they had done and to continue doing it into the foreseeable future. In the case of the current state of things in his country, he would wait and do nothing, say nothing, make no comments to any of the other boys, give no sign of his own position. Only when things became clearer, would he decide on his own course of action. Lie low and keep one's mouth shut, that was the watchword of the day, he was now convinced. When he reached this conclusion at last, he felt he was ready to get out of bed and face the world.

As he was getting up, stretching his body in its upright position, he wondered at the twitching of his left shoulder.

***

Of course, when Manfred walked to school he could still see a lot of evidence of last night's destructions. Some of the buildings had broken windows, some had black marks on their façades. He could see a few people standing around in small groups, probably discussing last night's events. He wondered on whose side they were. But he couldn't understand what they were saying, and he didn't dare to approach them. He had to find his own place within the general chaos of emotions and attitudes. Every individual was now thrown back on his or her own resources.

At school, naturally, everyone had something to say about the situation. Some boys were very loud and voiced their satisfaction over what had at last been set right, while others discussed things more quietly and with serious faces. Manfred realized that not a single word or a single argument that was uttered by his peers could influence his own opinion. He had come to his conclusion in the early morning. He wouldn't let anyone else shake him out of his own solution.

The teachers dealt with the events in their different ways, but the general tenor was one of satisfaction. What had happened had at last put the Jews in their proper place. It was the right of good citizens to take things in their own hands and teach a long-overdue lesson to those *Untermenschen* who still lived in the town.

The media were full of praise, too. After a while, Manfred caught the name that was given to the events by the authorities. They called it *Reichskristallnacht*, the Imperial Night of Broken Crystal Glass. For a brief moment, he thought that it was quite a beautiful name, too beautiful for such horrible things that had been done, but he dismissed the thought immediately. After all, important events had to be remembered in the history books by the vehicle of memorable names, while the sordid details were buried. Otherwise, no historian would be able to study the events of the past without being blinded by those details – which could be a lot more horrible than the recent events if one came to think of all those wars of the past, the Greeks fighting the Persians, the Romans fighting the Goths, and many other big historical conflicts –

and the historians would be led astray from the true interpretation of those events. That was surely what it was.

The great disappointment of the day for him, however, was Anna's absence from school. He wondered if she might have changed her mind, she might be angry at him. He had gone too far with her last night. How could he know?

After school, he walked to her house and rang the bell. It was the first time that he had the courage to do that, the first time he mustered the courage to face her mother, who might open the door. He had prepared a suitable pretext for his visit. Since Anna appeared to be ill, he was bringing her their homework from school. But when the door was opened, it was by Anna herself. Her face looked pale and her hair was in disorder. She looked sleepy. But when she saw him, her face lit up with a very happy smile. Her eyes lost their dullness and began to shine, and her whole body stood more upright. She cleared her throat.

"Oh, Manfred!" she croaked in a hoarse voice.

"Hey, are you all right? I've been so worried. When you weren't at school, you know, after last night..."

"I've been feeling ill. My head spins, and I feel weak in my knees," she said, touching her forehead as if to prove her condition with this gesture. "But now you're here I feel a lot better. Do come in." She opened the door wider.

He stepped in and asked, "Are you on your own?"

"Yes, but not for much longer. Mother should be home within the next half-hour or so. You'll have to leave soon."

Once the door was closed behind them they fell into each other's arms and kissed with all their passion. But after a minute or two, she disengaged herself from him. It was an effort for both of them.

She assured him that she had no regrets, that everything was good between them and that she would be back at school after another day or two. He gave her the homework from school, they had a quick peep in their English book and he explained which exercises they had to do in writing for the next English lesson. Then, after another very tender embrace, he left her house and walked home along the banks of the Elster and then up to the Galgenberg. As he was walking up the hill, it suddenly dawned upon him that the name Galgenberg was the opposite of what he had found out about the naming of historical events. It reminded you of the most terrible punishment that humans could inflict on others. Then he dismissed the thought and accelerated his steps up the hill. It was a cold day.

FOUR

In the hot summer of the following year – Manfred had only just turned seventeen – he was walking along one of the faceless streets in Untermhaus when he came across Wolfgang Löffel, who was wearing a very stylish new grey pin-striped, double-breasted suit, which gave him a much more adult look.

"Wow, you do look something!" Manfred smiled. "You look like a really grown-up man in this suit."

"I am a grown-up man," Wolfgang answered.

Manfred remembered that Wolfgang was a year older because he had been ill for a long time when he was a small boy, and that was why his education was delayed by one year. Since they had spent most of their school years in the same class, Manfred had forgotten their age difference.

Wolfgang straightened his back and adopted a proud attitude. *"Da staunst du, was?"* he chuckled and snorted.

Manfred had to admit he was impressed. "Indeed, I *am* surprised. You even look taller. But what are you wearing such a gorgeous outfit for? Are you leaving school? That would be unwise, only a year before our *Abitur* exam."

"Of course not. But I have to plan my career." Wolfgang hesitated, then after a pause continued, "Can you keep a secret?"

"It depends."

"Oh, you are a deep one. Always evasive, the true *Zauderer*, like Hamlet."

"Don't say that. It's only... I mean, how can I promise to keep a secret before I know what the secret is? That's a childish attitude, asking people to make promises they don't know they can keep."

"Keep your hair on, man! I only meant to find out if you can be told things in confidence – "

" – and you wanted to make yourself more important. You've always been fond of putting on a great show about yourself."

"Well, my friend, you seem to know me better than I know myself. But let that be and listen to what I've got to tell you."

"Ok, but let's go to that café over there. If we have to discuss such important secrets I feel more comfortable sitting down and having a cup of coffee to help me digest it all."

The two young men sauntered over to the small café on the street corner. It was a place they both knew well. When they entered, the young waitress greeted them as regulars. She was quite good-looking, with a slender figure and fine legs, as most boys were quick to detect. She wore the usual black dress with a frilly white apron.

They sat down by the window and ordered their coffees. As the waitress walked away from their table they both followed her with their eager eyes.

"A real head-turner, that one! I wouldn't mind getting my hands on that bottom of hers. I wonder if she'd let me get a taste of her," Wolfgang remarked.

Although Manfred had also looked at the backside of the young woman for a brief moment, he felt uneasy about his friend's vulgar comments. Ever since he'd got together with Anna and enjoyed the real pleasures of a truly fulfilling love-life, he felt a little disgusted about the way some of the other boys spoke about girls. He decided to let it pass this time, but he made a mental note of Wolfgang's low opinion of women.

"Well, what's that secret of yours?" he asked.

"Nothing's certain, as yet. But I'm seeing good old Finkenschmidt later this afternoon."

"You mean, the Finkenschmidt who used to be our physical education teacher until last year? Herbert von Finkenschmidt?"

"That's the man. Good old Herbert has built up his connections since he left teaching, and he's going to help me."

Manfred noted the familiar use of the first name but didn't comment on it. "How is he going to help you?"

"You see, Herbert has joined the *Wehrmacht*, the Army, and he indicated he might put in a good word with his superior officer. The thing is, I am so desperate to join up. I can't stand this hanging around, waiting, waiting, for what? For a war that's never going to happen? I'm so sick of waiting. I want to do something for our country."

"Can't you wait until after our *Abitur* exam?"

"That's too far off. I have to act now."

"Well, as for myself, I can't say I'm so desperate. The longer we can keep peace the better, if you ask me."

"And let the English and the bloody Russians taunt us and exploit us into eternity? The German people have to stand up now!" Wolfgang's voice had reached a high pitch, which made an elderly couple stare at them from another table.

Silence followed. Manfred didn't know how to react to this outburst. The waitress appeared with their coffees. When she walked away, Wolfgang's eager eyes followed her again. Manfred didn't look at her.

"To come back to more immediate desires," Wolfgang smirked, "I really think I ought to do something about that fine piece of female attraction."

"Haven't you got a girlfriend?" Manfred asked, hoping to get his friend onto a more civilised level.

"Pah! You don't have to go in for a girlfriend, you know all that mumbo-jumbo about holding hands, saying you love each other and swearing everlasting faithfulness. Bullshit, that is! All a man needs is good sex. And believe me, women are the same. All they're after is a man who can give it to them."

"I find that vulgar and disgusting."

"Oho! You've become a softie, a sissy. You're not saying you go in for all that soft talk, are you?"

"I admit I am. But in that department, we probably have to agree to disagree. Let's just leave it at that."

"Ok, man. But I can tell you, there're a number of girls at our school that are only waiting for it. They're hot."

"Oh, come off it!" Manfred tried to steer their conversation in a different direction. "Let's talk about something else."

"No, wait. Let me just finish this. There are at least two hot girls that spring to my mind when I think of our school."

"Now, who would that be?" Manfred asked just to humour him.

"Charlotte Landmeyer and Anna Kleinschmidt."

Manfred felt a stab in his chest. Not Anna! How could Wolfgang see her in such a light? And how could he speak of her in such vulgar terms? He knew that Thomas was still with Charlotte, although he'd never seen them together recently, but he felt he had to defend his wonderful Anna, his love. It was expected of him by common decency. But he was so shocked he couldn't utter a word.

"Hey, man! Do you agree? Aren't they hot? I might try to grab one of them for myself one of these days."

"I don't want to hear anymore," Manfred said and emptied his cup in one gulp. Then he stood up, placed the money for his coffee on the table and turned to leave.

"You can't just go like that!" Wolfgang protested.

Manfred didn't care for Wolfgang's awful designs on girls. He left the café and walked to the riverbank, where he sat down on a wooden bench. The backside of the bench carried a brass plaque, "Sponsored by the NSDAP Section of

Untermhaus". Manfred registered the plaque and saw his own impression confirmed that the Party had now really infiltrated and drenched every aspect of their lives. How could it be wrong then? He remembered that only a year or two ago he had had his doubts, but now he'd come to the conclusion that the Party – despite some of its negative slogans and its flaws in some other aspects – was in truth the instrument his country needed to set things right again. The Party had the willingness and the means. He knew from his brother that the most effective sub-organisations of the Party, especially the *Schutz Staffel* and the Gestapo, by now had control over who was getting into high positions in the armed forces and in the administration. So, it was probably only a matter of time until they would start something that would rock the whole country and put their enemies in their places. A war? They were probably only waiting for a provocation from either of their political opponents or their neighbours. Would it be initiated by the English, the Russians or even the Poles? Somehow, Germany's eastern neighbours seemed more likely to start a war.

Then his thoughts turned to Wolfgang. He was really someone who could get what he wanted, but Manfred was sure he wouldn't get his dirty hands on his beloved Anna. In a way, Wolfgang's attitude reflected the whole nation's present state. Manfred suddenly stumbled over this parallel. The vulgarity, the frustration, the ambitions. Probably, individuals as well as nations sometimes needed such attitudes: the vulgar elements to do the dirty work, the frustrated minds to see the stark reality of their own position, and the ambitions to act and do something to change this.

Over the next few weeks, the weather turned even hotter, and in August it was extremely hot, hotter than Manfred could remember. On some days, the thermometer would climb up to 37 or even 38 degrees in the afternoon. He wiped the sweat from his face when he entered Frau Helmbrecht's shop on his way back from school one Monday afternoon. He had to get some groceries for his father and himself, not a great deal these days since his brother was away.

"Oh, these are bad times," Frau Helmbrecht sighed as she was handing him the small bag of groceries. "Everything still all right at home?"

"Well, Thomas has been away in the *Wehrmacht* for nearly two months now."

"Has he? I was wondering, I haven't seen him for a while. Do you know how he is? Is he stationed far away?"

"We don't know. In his letters he tells us it's a good life in the Army, but he isn't allowed to let us know where he's stationed. It's all secret."

"Of course. It's the same with our Christian. In April, we knew he was stationed in Danzig, but after that we weren't allowed to know. Well, let's hope it's all for the best."

On leaving the shop, Manfred came across Frau Müller, who still helped the Weidmann men sometimes. She never appeared without a sad phrase about their poor mother and always managed to be of use in the household. Sometimes she brought a cake, sometimes she did a few chores in the kitchen or in the garden. She was a good angel for the Weidmanns.

"Oh, Manfred dear, how are you?" she beamed. Despite her sadness over the loss of poor Elfriede Weidmann, even after all these years, she was generally a cheerful and optimistic person.

"Thank you, Frau Müller, we're fine. And how are you?"

"I know I shouldn't complain, I mean I didn't have to suffer such a loss as you poor boys, losing your dear mother and having to cope on your own now. But it is a sad thing to have both my boys in the *Wehrmacht*. I only hope they're getting enough to eat where they are."

"I'm sure the *Wehrmacht* is feeding them well, Frau Müller."

"Are you? Well then, I won't complain. But it is so sad to come home to an empty house. It was bad enough when my Reinhold had to join in January, but now my Horst, my baby, my little Hottie, had to go, too. And I don't even know where they are."

Manfred couldn't help smiling in his mind when Frau Müller called her youngest son Hottie. He was called Horst, a good old German name, but whenever her emotions overwhelmed her she would call him Hottie.

"Haven't you heard from him, then?"

"Oh yes, I had a letter from him. He's all right. In fact, he has fallen in love with a girl, he writes. He doesn't write much about her, but I think she's got a Polish name. Now, what good German boy would fall in love with a dirty little Polish girl? That really gets me worried."

"Many German families give their children exotic names. I wouldn't worry too much. The good thing is that he has fallen in love, isn't it?"

"You think so?" She didn't sound convinced.

They said good-bye. Manfred walked up the garden path to the front door and let himself into the house. He put away his meagre shopping and sat down to his homework for school. But he found it hard to concentrate. So many of his friends and acquaintances were in the *Wehrmacht*! When would his *Stellungsbefehl* come? When would they call him up? Suddenly, he came to a conclusion. He would take the initiative himself, like Wolfgang. But he wouldn't just join the *Wehrmacht* and let them make him crawl around in the mud in awful infantry training. He would aim for some higher task, something where he could do his service in a comfortable office.

He remembered that Father had told him about one of his customers who had been in high places for over three years. What was his name?

When Father came home in the evening Manfred asked him. "Who was that customer of yours, you know, the one who made his career in the Party and works for some important government office?"

"You mean Adolf Keppler?"

"That's him. Yes. Do you think he could do something for me if I approached him?"

"What have you got in mind?" Father asked, looking him straight in the eyes. "You know, you can't get a decent position unless you join the Party, and I wouldn't allow that."

"Don't worry about me," Manfred lied. "I can look after myself. But will you give me his address and phone number, please?"

"If you promise to stay away from that *Lumpenpack*, the Party. And mind you, you'll get your *Abitur* exam before you join the Army or any other organisation involved in politics or government. It's bad enough to have one son in the *Wehrmacht*. I want you to stay at home for at least another year. Is that understood?"

"That's all right, Father. Don't worry."

"Will you promise?"

"Yes, Father," he lied again.

When Manfred lay in bed later that night, he thought about the discussion with his father. It was fine. Father had given him Adolf Keppler's address and phone number. This was good. He could contact him now. Nevertheless, he had a strange feeling about the promise he'd given his father. He knew he wouldn't keep it. Of course, he would join the Party, there was no other way. He realised this was the first time ever that he had lied to his father. These were hard times, he told himself. One had to take hard decisions. And after all, these were only white lies. Small lies that were necessary for some greater cause.

He still couldn't go to sleep. After about two hours, he had to get up to go to the toilet. As he was sitting on the toilet, listening to the silence in the house, he felt a twitch in his left shoulder.

After that, it took him a long time to go to sleep. And when he finally dropped off it was into a very troubled sleep.

***

Adolf Keppler received him personally in an office in the town centre. On the telephone, they had only briefly discussed possible opportunities for Manfred if he wanted to be of use to the cause of his Fatherland, to the Party and to the *Führer*, without having to join the dirty low business of infantry training in the Army. Keppler had told him to come to his office on the following day. Now, Keppler's secretary, a strikingly beautiful woman in her thirties, led him to Keppler's inner office.

"So, what do you have in mind?" Keppler asked after their initial greetings and customary polite phrases. He was a very tall man with an impressive figure, very short-cut hair, a long scar on his left cheek – probably from a cut by rapier in some initiation-ritual in his old students' brotherhood, his *Burschenschaft*, Manfred speculated – and a ruddy complexion. His eyes were a steely blue, and his clean-shaven face ended in a square jaw. He smiled.

Manfred explained his dislike of dirty Army work and his aim of some higher task, preferably in a dry office, and possibly with some important decisions to take. He was ready for a challenge.

"Well, young man, I must say I like your attitude. Are you a member?"

"I want to apply today," Manfred answered, the memory of his promise to his father stowed away in the deepest recesses of his conscience.

"Good. That's a beginning. But I'm afraid it won't be so easy. Can you come for a more detailed interview on Friday?"

"Of course, Herr Keppler."

"I'm warning you. The interview won't be so easy. The interviewers will want to know a lot of things about you. But if you pass the interview, I will investigate what we can find for you. It's for your father's sake. Mind you! Do not disappoint us." With these words he stood up, came round his big desk and led him to the door.

Back in the street, Manfred felt proud. He had taken the first step in his own career. Even though his father had given him his first entry ticket, he would now take his life and his career in his own hands. He thought it was strange to find Keppler such a hardliner of the Party even though he was friendly with Father, who was opposed to the Party. It was probably because Father kept his opinion well-hidden. Most of his customers knew he wasn't a member but they tolerated it because of his good business and his excellent service.

At school two days later, Herr Mollenhauer winked at him in the corridor. "Well done, young Weidmann!"

Manfred was going to ask him what he meant, but the young teacher had already turned round the corner to the staffroom. Could it be that the Party officials were making enquiries about him at school? Did they already collect information about him to have some reliable background knowledge about him for the interview on Friday? Well, he wouldn't have to worry on that score. His school work was brilliant. He was nearly at the top of his class, especially in English and Maths.

When, after school, he told Anna about it she was full of enthusiasm. "It could be the making of you. Of course, the

Party leaders have to make sure of a candidate's loyalty before they entrust him with any task of importance. You're lucky your father has this connection. It's obvious you need connections to get anywhere these days."

"But won't you mind if I have to leave Gera? I've heard most of the opportunities in a Party career are not to be found here in the province. I may have to go to Leipzig or even Berlin."

"Of course, I want to have you here with me, that's obvious," she said and kissed him. "But if the greater cause for our country takes you to another place, you have to go, and I'll wait for you. You know I'd always wait for you."

He thought he was a lucky man to have such an understanding girlfriend. It was comforting to know she wouldn't oppose his plans. The only problem would be his father. It was better not to tell him too much. When, in the evening after the visit to Keppler's office, Father had asked him about it, he had been unspecific and only gave him some general answers. Keppler had been friendly and sent him his best regards, Keppler had said he might help him into a career when the time came – he didn't say it could be soon, long before his *Abitur* exam – and Keppler hadn't made any promises. Manfred didn't know how much of this his father believed him. He suspected him to understand more than he let on. It was quite possible his father knew exactly what his younger son had in mind, and it was equally possible that he fled into his own romantic notions ignoring the hard realities of the times and believing his son would first follow his education before any other plans. Whatever his father's insight, Manfred would have to be careful not to let him know too much. He wasn't going to let anyone thwart his noble plans.

At the interview on Friday, which took place at the same address as his first meeting with Keppler, only in a different room, Manfred was surprised to learn how much the three interviewers already knew about him. They asked him lots of tricky questions about his political views, about his past, about his family, and about his ambitions for the future. They even knew about Anna. One of the interviewers smirked when they mentioned her, just as if a relationship with a girl was a special asset, but of a nature that Manfred didn't like. He was reminded of Wolfgang's vulgar behaviour and realised he hadn't had a private word with him since that day at the café. He wondered if Wolfgang had reached his desired posting in the *Wehrmacht* by now. He was just speculating on running across him again one of these days when the first interviewer pulled him out of his thoughts with another unexpected question.

"And how do you think you could make your amorous relationship with Fräulein Kleinschmidt useful for the Party?"

He was shocked. Why and how was he to make use of his love? It wasn't something *to make use of*. He abhorred the expression. But he had to give these men something. He had to throw a bone to these dogs.

"I believe she could become very useful when I need to procure sensitive information for the Party." It was a phrase he remembered from a cheap spy novel he had read on his last holidays on the beach of the Baltic Sea, a book his father had brought along, and he only picked up because he'd run out of his own reading material.

There was a pause. The three interviewers exchanged meaningful glances, then continued with less sensitive questions about his school work. The dogs had obviously accepted his cheap bone.

They were highly impressed by his excellent school work. One of the interviewers tried to show off his own knowledge, asked him a tricky calculus question and went on to elaborate on a lecture about a graph of which he only had superficial knowledge. It wasn't really a question but rather a discourse to display his love of his own importance. The other interviewers didn't seem to be very happy about it, but when Manfred explained the mathematical problems associated with the graph that was under discussion, they smiled. He knew he had impressed them, and he hoped this would get him the desired success.

At the end of the interview, they told him he would hear from them in due course. They dismissed him in a friendly manner and shook hands with him.

A week later the results came. Manfred took the letter from the letter-box with a twitch in his left shoulder. His father was not at home, so he could devote himself to his career at his leisure. He opened the letter and read it through several times. It explained that he fulfilled the requirements for recruitment as an elite *Jungmann*, which meant he wasn't admitted into the *Wehrmacht* or any other combat organisation yet, but he was ordered to complete his secondary education first, and this had to take place at Pirna, an elite educational institution at Sonnenstein Castle near Dresden in Saxony. It said he was to report at Pirna immediately upon receipt of this letter.

Manfred sat down. His feelings were divided between disappointment and excitement. He was disappointed that they didn't accept him immediately into one of their organisations and thus ensure that he wouldn't have to join the *Wehrmacht*. But he was excited over the new prospect. Of course, he had heard about so-called Napola Schools. They were really called *Nationalpolitische Erziehungsanstalten*, National Political Institutes of Education, officially abbreviated NPEA, but everybody called them Napola, short for *Nationalpolitische Lehranstalt*, National Political Institute of Teaching. The location, Sonnenstein Castle in Pirna, promised to be a very pleasant place, so there was something to look forward to.

When he came to think of it, he realised that he was probably very lucky. Naturally they wanted him to get his *Abitur* first, he was still only seventeen, but from Pirna his brilliant career would be waiting for him. He was a truly privileged young man.

He rang Anna at once. She took the news without emotion, it seemed to him. He thought she might have shown more disappointment over their impending separation.

When Father came home in the evening, Manfred had his suitcase packed and ready to leave for Pirna. Father accepted the news with a stony face. Manfred saw he wasn't pleased. Nevertheless, he said, "I'm proud of you, my boy. But be careful and critical about what you're letting yourself in for." That was all.

Manfred spent his last evening with Anna. She came to his home, and because Father had to go out again, they were alone, which was wonderful. But it was a sad evening. Even though they made love, the atmosphere between them remained strained. Neither of them could throw off their nervousness. After all, their separation for several months was imminent.

The next morning, Manfred got up early. His train would leave around lunchtime. To pass the time, he switched on the radio. The news at ten o'clock announced a speech by the *Führer*. He barked into the microphone:

"Seit 5 Uhr 45 wird zurückgeschossen..."

The Poles had attacked Germany, and this was a Declaration of War!

FIVE

It was the barking of the dogs that made the place so daunting. They were huge and black. Two of them were Labradors, one appeared to be a Rottweiler. At the slightest noise or movement, they went berserk. The smallest disturbance would set them off on a barking rampage. They certainly guarded the place like no other animal, and any intruder would have to cope with them. There was no way around them.

When he climbed over the fence near the edge of the forest in the dim twilight of the early-morning dawn, he believed the place might give him some shelter for the day. But hardly had he stepped away from the fence towards the barn when the barking began.

The barn loomed dark but inviting against the grey sky. It wasn't raining, but it was a bit cold, even though this was July. He wished the summer would come at last. He rubbed his hands.

The barking didn't stop. On the contrary, it seemed to grow in volume. He decided to wait a few moments without movement, hoping the barking might stop eventually. He froze into a statue and kept his breathing low.

It wasn't the first time he'd been surprised by fierce dogs, but he usually managed to get them used to his presence. It was only a matter of patience. His experience had taught him that you could just outstay the dogs' patience, and they would normally give up after a while. Some took two or three minutes, others kept barking for nearly ten minutes, but in the end, they would all get used to his presence and accept the situation.

But not these dogs.

He waited for what seemed like an eternity, but the barking wouldn't abate. The dogs just refused to calm down. What tenacity! He couldn't help admiring these animals, even though they were making life a lot more difficult for him.

He began to think of alternatives. How far could he make it under cover of the dark? How far was it to the nearest farm on the other side of the forest?

He decided to give them another five minutes. His wrist-watch was still in working order, which was important for him in his present predicament. The minutes crawled along while the dogs kept up their frenzy. He knew that the way we experience the passage of time was relative. The same five minutes would appear like a quick flash if he was in a different situation. For example, if he was active doing something exciting, or if he was in the middle of a joyful intimacy with a lovely woman. He nearly grew angry with himself for having such thoughts, for even imagining or remembering beautiful moments in his life. To be honest, he had to admit that he hadn't really experienced unaffected, pure happiness for more than five years. He considered the possibility that he might never have any beautiful moments again. Who could tell?

It was no use ruminating on philosophical questions like the passage of time or the likelihood of renewed happiness in his life. The here and now needed his full attention.

When, after those five minutes, the dogs were still barking, he turned round and walked back to the fence. Reluctantly, he climbed back over the fence, leaving the alluring barn behind his back and making his way into the darkness of the forest.

Fortunately, it was a dry day. After walking through the dense undergrowth for another half hour he found a suitable spot, secluded and protected by thick bushes all round and with a soft, mossy ground. He sank to the ground, folded up the small bundle he was carrying and covered himself with his worn army-greatcoat. He was so tired that he soon drifted off into a troubled sleep. His uncomfortable physical position couldn't keep him awake. It wasn't the first time that he had to spend the day in similar circumstances. He had been lucky most of the time, finding a dry spot in some barn or hayloft, but when such luxuries were inaccessible he had to make do with a snug corner in the woods, which wasn't really so bad when the weather wasn't wet.

His sleep was troubled because he couldn't shake off some of the recurring images and dreams. Were these mere fantasies or genuine memories? He didn't know for certain. No longer. The past few months had been so earth-rocking and traumatic that he had begun to doubt his own memory. He couldn't dismiss all the images of dying men from his mind. He saw them again and again. There was one man in particular, not very old, with a narrow face and dark curly hair. It was shocking and utterly unbelievable how a man could face his own death with such equanimity. He knew they were going to shoot him. When they'd pulled out his fingernails, he'd confessed he'd been working as a spy. After such a confession he must have known his fate. His life was worth absolutely nothing. They let him watch some of the other executions to give him a foretaste of what he had coming to him. One never knew, he might even tell them more. But the man remained completely calm. How could he eventually walk up to the trench full of dead bodies, knowing he would be one of them in just a few moments, and keep up his calm dignity? He'd looked him in the eyes. Not a flicker, not a tear, no sign of panic! This image came to him almost every night. The man's calm dignity. His eyes. His firm step up to the trench. His silent acceptance of his imminent death. No begging for mercy, no crying, and worst of all, no accusations.

Then there was that woman. A Jewish whore. She had been caught in the cellar of a grocery store during a raid in Wolgast. They'd taken her to the brothel they'd set up for their own entertainment in Greifswald, and they'd drawn lots over who could enjoy her first. She was so beautiful, they all wanted her. His turn came third. But when he walked into her room at the brothel – a bare room with a bed and a chair – he found her dead on the bed, her throat cut, blood everywhere. He couldn't remember the results of their short enquiry into her suicide, whether they could find out how she'd got hold of the knife, all he could remember was the sight of her on the bed and his mixed feelings. Disappointment over a missed opportunity to enjoy her merged into something like respect for the woman. He knew she was nothing but a worthless Jewish whore. But he just couldn't forget her, her fine features, her bold eyes and her personal dignity in spite of her humiliating situation.

Today was no exception. His bad dreams and visions came to him like almost every day in his sleep. There were other images, besides the spy about to be executed and besides the beautiful Jewess who committed suicide. There were those groups of Russian prisoners of war that they'd picked up somewhere north of Minsk. As they were being paraded in the dirty snow on the edge of that forest, to be shot presently, they began to sing. He remembered the silencing of their fine bass voices by the rattling of the machine-gun that mowed them to the ground. He had the impression that the sound of their singing voices was buried in the snow and would re-emerge in the spring when the snow melted.

Faces, eyes, voices, shaking bodies, calm postures, terrible fears, unexpected surprises of human behaviour; men, women and children *in extremis*: They all haunted him in his sleep.

His back ached with stiffness when he woke up. It was late afternoon. He stood up and stretched his worn back. He would walk to the other end of the forest hoping to find another farm where he might be able to steal some food. If the farmer or his wife looked trustworthy he might beg for food, but he had to be careful. He hoped it would be easier to find a farm, now that he'd reached the other side of the hills in Thuringia Forest. The area ahead would be slightly more densely populated, which was a danger and an opportunity. There was a higher danger of being betrayed and caught, but there was a higher probability of finding food and shelter. He still had to be careful. He still didn't dare to show his face during the day. There were too many military patrols. Russians, Americans? He wasn't sure. He walked all night. He had crossed the main road between Suhl and Schleusingen yesterday. He hoped to reach the border to what promised to remain of the American zone in another two or three nights. It was over a month ago when they'd announced on the radio that the Americans were going to hand over Thuringia to the Russians. So this part of Germany was becoming too dangerous for him. However, things had gone well so far. Apart from that farmer near Königsee who had tricked him into a shed with a promise of a piece of bread and a bowl of hot soup while he had sent his wife to telephone the military administration in Ilmenau. That had been a close shave. He'd only just got away when he saw an army jeep approaching round the bend on the narrow road from Dörnfeld. It was a tricky business. You never knew who you could trust.

Meanwhile, he had developed a certain radar awareness of a farmer's political allegiance. Those who were still proud Germans and couldn't accept the foreign occupation usually had softer features. They seemed somehow familiar. Whereas those who welcomed the occupation had sly faces. They were dreamers who were hoping for a better future. They were wrong, of course. The future wouldn't be better, but a lot worse.

This morning he was lucky. As he was approaching the farm, he heard the farmer grumbling and complaining to his wife, as it seemed. He was complaining about the shortage of seeds and about the arrogance of the new Russian regional administrator who had sent him home with empty hands.

"How am I supposed to grow crops if the bloody Russians won't let me get any seeds?" he shouted at the fat woman who stood near him, her furrowed face under a colourful headscarf and her large front behind a dirty apron, her arms akimbo. She just shrugged her shoulders. His face was livid with rage. He dropped down his pitchfork and threw his hands in the air.

"Wasn't it a lot better when we had good German law and order? *Deutsche Zucht und Ordnung*! I don't believe the *Führer* is dead. He'll come back one day and show those barbarians. We'll have him back!"

This was a farmer one could safely approach. So he walked up to the fence and begged for something to eat. The farmer calmed down when he saw his dirty appearance, his emaciated figure and his military greatcoat. He looked the poor visitor up and down.

"Escaping from the bloody Russians, heh?" he asked.

"Yes, and I fear I might be in danger because I am a good German. I fought at Stalingrad, and I really did my bit for our Fatherland."

"Well," the farmer stroked his stubbly chin, "you're a lucky bugger."

His wife remained silent.

"I'm honoured," the farmer added, "to meet a man like you, a true German. Do come in, you must be hungry."

So this was a lucky day indeed. They invited him in and gave him a hearty breakfast of dark bread, butter, eggs, cheese and cold sausage. They didn't have any coffee, but they gave him a hot drink of some sorts and fresh milk.

"You see," he explained to them while he was chewing the bread, "I have to be careful. So, I only travel during the night. Otherwise, the Russian patrols might find me. Because I was a German soldier, they would imprison me or kill me or send me to a camp in Siberia, those awful barbarians."

"But you're not a deserter?" the farmer asked with a sly face.

"No, my unit was mostly slaughtered by the Russians, and only very few of us remained, so we had no alternative than this. We decided to split up and walk west, hoping to reach the American zone. The Americans might help us build up a new Germany again, a solid and proud Germany, as we used to have." He added the last sentence hoping to avoid any further questions from the farmer, who looked as if he could bring up the illusion of a duty to fight any forms of *Wehrkraftzersetzung.*

They were interrupted by the appearance of a young woman dressed very much like the farmer's wife.

"Good morning, Liesel," the farmer beamed. "Come and meet a good German soldier!"

After exchanging their polite greetings, the young woman, who was the only daughter of the house, was instructed to take him to the bathroom at the back of the farmhouse. He was offered a bathtub, a towel, a brick of hard soap and some fresh civilian clothes. His old and worn clothes were half-military, half civilian. Now he would be safer with only civilian clothes. As he was stepping out of the bath and beginning to rub himself down with the green towel, the young woman opened the door and peeped in. She smiled. He realized what she was after, and he quickly dressed to avoid any misunderstanding.

"Won't you stay with us for a while?" she asked in a cooing voice, with a heavy local accent.

He knew what that would mean, and he explained to her that he was in great danger if he was found out by the Russians. He made his situation very dramatic to impress her. She was disappointed and tried to convince him of his safety as long as he stayed in the farmhouse, with her. She stepped up to him.

"Won't you give me a kiss?"

"All right, Liesel," he smiled. "I'll kiss you, but I'm leaving you. I can't stay. Please, understand this." And with these words he kissed her on the lips. Then he disengaged himself from her attempted embrace and left the bathroom.

Liesel's mother showed him his room. He suspected she knew what her daughter was after, but neither of them said anything. Once in the bedroom, he locked the door with the big black key. He wanted to be safe from any intrusion, and he didn't trust Liesel's acceptance of his refusal.

It was late afternoon when he woke up. He dressed in his new outfit, brown baggy trousers which were a bit too short, a blue farmer's shirt, an old black waistcoat and a grey jacket with holes in the elbows and a greasy stain on one of the lapels. There was even an olive-green pullover, which he decided to take along as an alternative to the waistcoat or the jacket. These were rather shabby clothes, but it was a good and warm civilian outfit. He saw it as an advantage to look poor and shabby. Like this, he would melt into the civilian crowds more easily. He didn't want to look too conspicuous. He walked to the kitchen, where there was some food on the table, but not a person in sight. They were out in the fields, so he could fill his stomach plus a small bag for provisions and an old rucksack that they had left on a chair for him. There was a dirty slip of paper attached to one of the straps of the rucksack: "For you, good German."

As he was walking away from the farm in the descending dusk, he looked back and wondered what would have become of him if he had accepted Liesel's invitation. Quite apart from the danger threatening his life from the Russian occupation forces, he couldn't imagine a life with a girl like Liesel. He had lost the ability to love and respect a woman. He could never again be natural with a woman, and he could never trust a woman again because no woman could ever trust him again.

He walked through the whole night. Towards the early dawn showing on the eastern horizon he crossed the main road between Themar and Henfstädt. The country was a lot more open here, with undulating green fields and great distances between the farmhouses. He would have to be extra careful in this new environment. After a while he came to a farm near a village whose name he couldn't find out. They had removed a lot of village signs when they had to withdraw from their positions in view of the advancing invasion of the Allied Forces. He remembered the same procedure from the eastern front. You didn't want the enemy to find out where things were, you hoped to confuse them, thereby gaining some valuable time for your own retreat. To the south of the village, which had a narrow road running through its middle, he discovered a small lake or pond whose shore was overgrown with reeds and small hazel bushes. This gave him excellent cover from which he could observe the shed on the pond's southern shore. It looked unoccupied.

He sat down among the bushes and ordered his thoughts. The experience of his last encounter with a farmer and his family had taught him the necessity of a new biography. Naturally, he had to give people a name and a story. To Liesel and her parents, he'd been Hans Meyer, a name he'd just invented. But he would have to be more careful. He would have to invent a more convincing name, not too common and not too special. And he would have to invent a better story than the one he'd told that farmer. Fought at Stalingrad, and now his unit disbanded, that was rubbish, altogether too general. He decided to take a rest once he was in the American zone and take time to think of a convincing new biography. It would have to be a lot more detailed, and he would have to season it with a sprinkling of exciting anecdotes that would catch any listener's attention and steer things away from suspicion.

Carefully, he walked up to the small shed. The door was open, and it was empty. No wonder it wasn't occupied, he realized, when he saw the few gaping holes in the roof. There was no threat of rain, so he decided to spend the day in this shed.

After eating the last piece of bread he had and drinking some water he'd scooped from the pond, he was tired from his long walk through the night and lay down on his bed of grass and straw and covering himself with his greatcoat. It was the only piece of military clothing he had allowed himself to keep, because as he had seen in many places, people wore such greatcoats even though they had no connection with the army. Coats were rare, and the nights could still be cool.

As he was slowly falling asleep his thoughts returned to Liesel. She was the only young woman he had been close to for several months. She was not beautiful, but she was young and radiated a healthy constitution. He remembered her well-developed breasts which he couldn't miss when she stood in front of him in the bathroom. However, in spite of Liesel's possible female attractions, his own sexuality was not aroused. It was rather the naive trust which she seemed to offer him that touched his heart in a strange way. He knew he would have disappointed this innocent farmer's daughter. It had been the right decision to say no.

He jumped up when he felt a hand on his shoulders. Someone had awoken him. It was about noon. The sun shone through one of the holes in the roof and it was a lot warmer. He looked up. A man's face with a stubbly beard stared at him.

He wanted to stand up and either defend himself or run out of the shed, but the other man held up his hands and smiled.

"No fear, my friend. I'm not going to harm you or betray you."

"Who are you?"

His question reminded him of his own need. The situation in which he needed a name had come right now, earlier than he had expected. He cleared his throat and decided to go first, and before the other man had time to answer his question he uttered the first name that came to mind. "I'm Dieter Wolff."

"My name's Karl Huber," the other man replied.

After this introduction there was silence. Karl Huber sat down, and they remained seated on the floor of the shed, facing each other.

"So, Dieter, we seem to be in similar circumstances." There was no need either to deny or confirm this. It was so obvious.

"Got any food about you?" Karl asked, inclining his head in the direction of his new companion's bag.

"Not much left. You hungry?"

"I wouldn't refuse a good dinner now," Karl smiled.

Dieter – as he now decided to call himself until he could think of a better name – took an apple out of his bag. "I've got two of these. You can have one if you're desperate."

It was a small gesture, but in these hard times it was a very generous offer, and it immediately sealed a sort of companionship between the two men. They both relaxed and began to chat of things in general, first about food and drink, then about life in the Army, and about the War, which they both agreed was now definitely over. After a while, their talk turned to their families. They didn't tell each other any details, numbers of their units, military ranks or where they came from, they just talked about their parents and siblings. Karl also had a lot to tell about an uncle of his who had disappeared during the War. Dieter mentioned his father and his brother. Then it was girls, women. Both men had lost touch with the female half of the world, as Karl was putting it, and they both gained some degree of consolation from the stories they told each other about their intimate experiences with women, some true, some not so true. Dieter thought he might as well invent some good stories about women. These were small lies that made Karl happy. White lies.

They never touched upon any awful aspects of the War. Dieter was sure Karl must have seen some horrible things, too, but it was better to let those things be. They would have to forget a lot of terrible experiences during the rest of their lives anyway. They might as well begin to forget them here and now.

It was afternoon, but they were both still tired. So their stories gradually petered out, and they fell asleep again.

***

It was pitch-dark when he woke up. He heard Karl, who was still snoring. He got up and opened the door. There were stars in the sky. Without disturbing the other man, he managed to get away from the shed and from the small lake. He headed west. He made slow progress and lost a lot of time when he had to wait for a group of middle-aged men walking home from a drinking spree to disappear towards the village to the north of the pond. He didn't want to take any risks with them. From what they were shouting into the night he gathered they were Germans, but their celebrating mood indicated a certain sympathy with the occupying forces. In the dim moonlight, he could see that his way lay through a valley between two small hills. After another hour, he found that the village to his left was called Bibra because a broken sign with this name lay in the grass beside the country lane.

The first signs of dawn appeared in the east when he reached another village. He thought he had to be quite close to the border. Better be extra careful.

On the edge of the village he observed a farmer entering his cowshed. The cows mooed with the prospect of being milked. Dieter peeped through the stall door and tried to assess the farmer. Could he be approached safely?

It was getting light, there weren't many alternatives, he had to take the risk. If the farmer was opposed to giving him shelter or if he was in league with people who could be dangerous for him, he would just have to run. Run back to the nearest woods. He looked back to where he'd come from and took a mental note of a wooded area which might give him enough shelter if the need arose.

He knocked on the upper half of the door, which was left open. At first, the farmer didn't hear him because he was too busy with a cow's udder, but when the knock was repeated he looked up.

"Who's there?" he shouted.

"My name's Dieter Wolff. I'm on my way west. I'd be very grateful if you could give me some food and if you allowed me to take a rest in your hayloft."

"Can you milk a cow?"

"I've never tried."

"A city-boy, then, heh?" the farmer chuckled.

"But I can help you in other ways, perhaps."

The farmer was silent. He continued with his milking. Dieter saw pail after pail being filled with fresh warm milk that made his mouth water. After a while the farmer reached for a small metal container. "Go on then, help yourself, city-boy."

Dieter helped himself to fresh milk. When the sweet warm frothy liquid touched the tongue in his mouth he nearly choked with shock. It was so unexpected and so absolutely wonderful to taste this fresh milk. He gulped down a fair amount before he handed the container back.

"Thank you very much. This is very kind of you."

The farmer completed his milking task and loaded the milk cans onto a bicycle trailer.

"Wait here. I'm taking the milk to the village dairy. I'll be back in ten minutes. Don't go and frighten my wife. She's very frail. Wait for me." Then he disappeared round the corner of the cowshed, riding his bicycle and pulling the trailer with two cans of milk.

Dieter waited at the back of the cowshed. Soon, the farmer was back. He took him to the farmhouse which they entered through the back door. They stepped through a sort of utility room before they reached the kitchen.

"Why must you invite every tramp to our kitchen?" the farmer's wife pleaded when they entered.

"Don't mind her," the farmer said to Dieter, ignoring his wife's protest. "She's afraid the Russians might come and rape her. You can't blame her. I mean, from what you hear about the Russians. But I always say: No need to worry. If you treat them with decency they'll be decent with you." While he was offering this piece of advice he began to fry himself an egg on the old stove. His guest sat down at the kitchen table. The woman remained standing at the back of the kitchen, observing the two men and keeping a watchful but frightened eye on the newcomer's appearance.

"So they're here for good now?" Dieter wanted to make sure.

"Yes, so they are," the farmer explained. "They've now taken over the whole of Thuringia. The Americans have left."

"How far is it to the American zone from here?"

The farmer handed him a cup of hot milk, a cold pork sausage and a chunk of fresh brown bread, and he sat down to his own breakfast, which consisted of the same items as Dieter's, with the additional delicacy of the freshly fried egg. For a few moments, not a word was spoken, and only the chewing and slurping noises of the men filled the kitchen. Dieter wondered if the farmer hadn't heard his question or if he didn't want to answer.

"It's just over there," he replied at last. He underlined his vague statement with a gesture in the direction of the kitchen window and a loud burp. His plate was empty. "You see, Olga dear," he remarked, turning to his wife, "this city-boy wants to go west. He doesn't like the Russians, just like you. Why don't you go with him?"

She did not reply but lowered her face in shame.

"Ha, I was only joking," the farmer chuckled. He was the only one who laughed. "But listen, city-boy," he continued, "you can just walk over there. That's Henneberg, that village over there. That's where you can join the main road from Eisenach to Würzburg, and that's where you'll be certain to walk into Ivan's arms."

"Do you know a better way, then?"

"If you can get round Henneberg alive, you can find a forest area to the west of Hermannsfeld. That's where it's quite easy to get across without running into a military patrol. But the problem, as I say, is getting past Henneberg. The village is full of Russian soldiers, and the border is heavily guarded. You better walk south. Just before you get to Schwickershausen, you turn right. That'll get you to an easier crossing. Mind you, it's guarded, too, but you can wade across in the dark. Just don't go too near the bridge. And there's another problem. The country round there won't give you a lot of cover. It's mostly open fields. But if you ask me, I'd go for it rather than meeting up with Ivan in Henneberg."

"Thank you. You're very well-informed."

"Do you think you're the first fellow who's looking for a way to get across?"

"No, probably not. You must have seen a few people like me, living in this place. Haven't you thought of crossing over yourself?"

"Why should I leave my farm? The Russians will need bread and potatoes, too. They'll have to treat the farmers with respect. Otherwise they're going to starve to death."

The two men continued to talk about general gossip for a while. Eventually, the farmer told him where to hide in the barn and told his wife to get an extra blanket as a mattress. "You won't need it to cover up, it's going to be a warm day, but the floor is quite hard, so use it to sleep on."

The farmer was right. The day turned out to mark the end of the cool weather, and it became quite hot in the afternoon, which made it difficult for Dieter to sleep.

He began to think of his situation. It was a good thing the farmer had warned him about the village to the northwest. He would try his luck where the farmer had suggested, further south. This farmer must have met quite a lot of people who were on their way west, people like himself who were hoping to find better conditions in the American zone now that the Russians had taken over Thuringia, probably not only ex-soldiers, but also refugees, some even from the east, from East Prussia and Poland.

He realised that once he was across and safe he would still have to go a long way. If he wanted to start a new life in the west, he would have to walk as far as Frankfurt or Wiesbaden, where he was hoping to find a new start if his old great-aunt and his distant cousin were ready to take him in.

The Frankfurt area was full of Americans, he knew. He might try to get a job doing some translation work for them. His English was quite good. They might be happy to employ him. At least it would be a beginning. At least he could try.

When dusk had fallen, the farmer's wife appeared with a bottle of beer and a small pack of cold food for him to take on his journey west. He thanked her, but there was no reply from her. He felt uneasy with her. He wondered if she could see through him. She had such a witch-like manner. Could she guess what he had been? Could she sense what he had seen, what he had done?

He set off in the dark. It was so dark he found it difficult to follow the narrow road. After a long bend to the left he suddenly saw a military patrol vehicle, hardly more than fifty metres ahead. Without hesitation, he jumped into the undergrowth on the slope to his right and tried to suppress his breathing. If they found him, it would be the end of him.

The vehicle stopped. Some of the men got out to continue their patrol on foot. One remained in the car. He revved up the engine, made some awful crunching noises with the gearbox and turned the vehicle round. Those on foot began to walk in the direction of the undergrowth.

They approached slowly. There were four men. They were carrying rifles, chatting in Russian and smoking. He could see the red glow when they drew smoke from their cigarettes.

What would they do if they caught him? Would they shoot him point-blank? Would they take him prisoner and send him to one of their death camps in Siberia? What if they found his tattoo?

Dieter Wolff thought of positive things to fight his mounting fear, of his first kiss, of beautiful Latin poetry, of his mother's warmth... but he didn't manage to avoid a violent twitching in his left shoulder.

They were only a few metres from him when they burst out laughing.

PART TWO

SIX

Nora was searching through her narrow cupboard. There were lots of old toys, dolls with and without clothes, cheap plastic jewellery, fragments of an old doll's house, board games with rubbed-off edges, a dirty hairbrush and elements of toy kitchen equipment with tin plates, tin teacups and an array of twisted aluminium-like teaspoons. At the bottom, she found several girls' books, some Enid Blyton titles, two by Louisa May Alcott, one by Jacob Abbot, one by Samuel Griswold Goodrich, also L. M. Montgomery's *Anne of Green Gables*, a poor copy of Eleanor Porter's *Pollyanna* and several Mark Twain books. There was a musty smell.

She didn't even remember she had those old things in her cupboard. She hadn't looked at them for years. They had always been covered by clothes she had just thrown in there when they wouldn't fit in her larger wardrobe, which stood on the opposite side of her room, next to the window overlooking the backyard of their home in this leafy suburb.

"Nora dear! Will you be much longer with your things?" her mother's voice came up from the hallway.

"Nearly done, Mummy," she shouted back.

"When you're ready I'll need your help down here."

"Okay, Mummy, I'll be down shortly."

She was always polite towards her parents. Even though she found it a bit troublesome to help her mother with her packing, she wouldn't give vent to her moderate anger. Father could do his own packing. So could Margaret. Then why couldn't her mother?

The family was busy packing for their big move to England. Nora had never been outside the States. She'd been to California, to New York to see the Empire State Building, to Mount Rushmore, to the Grand Canyon, and she'd seen the battlefield at Gettysburg, which was important because they had studied Lincoln's Address at school, so it was quite eerie to see the place where it had actually been delivered. So she had seen something of the world. But overseas? This was going to be a great new adventure.

She didn't know if she should be happy or sad about it. Her parents had told her they were going to live in England from now on. She didn't mind losing her friends so much. Most of them weren't really *friends*, but just people she happened to know. Still, it was strange to imagine she might never see Chicago again: the lake, the lakeshore, the el-train and all those familiar buildings. She might also miss her sports club. And then there was the question of language. She had heard British people speak on TV and sometimes in films. She remembered the British Prime Minister, Edward Heath, speaking to President Nixon at some international conference, and the contrast was mind-boggling. Heath sounded as if he had his mouth full of horse-chestnuts. And how could the British speak with such a clipped accent and in such staccato voices? She truly wondered if she would understand her new friends or even people in general in England, and if they would understand her. Or would they just laugh at her?

At thirteen, Nora was too young to be interested in politics, although she loved history, but from her father she had heard what his boss, Paddy Malone, had said about the English and how they were murdering lots of Irish in Northern Ireland. That may or may not be true, she thought. What had been troubling her more over the past few months – apart from her worries about the strange accent – was what they had learnt in their maths lessons about British money: twelve pence in one shilling and twenty shillings in one pound. The teacher had shown them English coins, and they could see that these coins didn't even give the real value but only some fancy names like "Half Crown" or "Florin". And to top it all, the teacher had explained that there were shops that didn't accept payment in pounds, but in Guineas, just to make things as complicated as possible, probably to confuse American tourists. But how would she ever be able to calculate simple sums of money?

Two weeks ago, however, it had come on TV that the British had now changed and simplified their money. At last, they could no longer ignore the logics of a decimal system. What a relief! But then her father had told her that they were still driving on the wrong side of the road. How would she be safe when she was going to cross the street?

She also remembered some of the things their civics education teacher had told them about the British deficit in democratic rights, but she had forgotten the details. She wondered what she would learn about that aspect of British culture once she was going to her new school in England. The English people might not even be aware of their inferior political system and their lack of civil rights.

Her mother's voice pulled her out of her thoughts. "Are you coming down?"

"Yes, coming!"

She decided to leave things as they were. She had packed everything she would need in England, and those old books and toys could very well stay behind. She would get new things over there.

She went down the stairs and joined her mother.

"Ah, here you are," her mother sighed. "You can help me pack those tablecloths." Mother was very nervous. Nora felt that she was worried about the whole adventure of moving from one continent to another.

"Mummy, am I going to have my own room in England?" Nora wondered.

"Well, Daddy said they were keeping an apartment in readiness for our arrival. But once we're settled we can find our own house. Then you'll certainly have your own room. Promise!" Nora didn't believe what Mummy said when she added, "Promise," because it was usually a sign of insecurity. Her mother merely wanted her to stop asking anymore questions.

Mother and daughter spent the next three hours packing all manner of household stuff. While they were folding things, closing boxes and labelling them, they kept up a conversation about what awaited them in England. Father had been given the directorship of his company's UK Headquarters in Newcastle-upon-Tyne. It was a company producing a range of chemical substances, mostly detergents, but also chemical products for industrial purposes. He was going to be paid very big money, and he was going to have a lot of responsibility in England. Mummy and Nora were to fly out on the next day, whereas Daddy was to follow one day later with Margaret, Nora's older sister. They were going to meet up at a big hotel in London before travelling north to Newcastle two or three days later. It was early spring, so it would still be quite cold up there, more or less as cold as it was in Chicago, only a lot more humid, raining almost every day.

Margaret was staying with one of Mummy's aunts in Connecticut. She had already done all her packing before her short holiday on the East Coast. Nora envied her because she didn't have to help Mummy with the packing of household stuff. She decided to remind her parents of this inequality once they were in England and it came to the task of unpacking everything in their new home. Margaret would have to do more then.

Daddy had already left for the East Coast. He said he had things to do in Boston before he was going to fetch his older daughter for their journey across the Atlantic Ocean. So Nora and Mummy were left to their own devices until their family reunion in London.

In the evening, when everything was packed and ready for the removal men, mother and daughter went to have their last American meal in a small restaurant about two miles from what was still their home. There was no more food in the house, and the kitchen was empty. The restaurant was what people called a diner. The outside looked like a railway carriage in shiny metal stripes, while inside the tables were all fixed in a row along the window front. There were ketchup bottles on all the tables, and the menu looked a lot more elegant than the atmosphere of the whole place suggested. The diner offered a large selection of healthy dishes with salads and vegetables, apart from the regulation hamburgers and hot dogs. Mummy said this was because the owner was Italian. When they arrived by taxi – their family car having been sold already – they found the diner half empty. They were directed to one of the tables, took off their anoraks and sat down.

"What's my new school in England going to be like?" Nora asked, when they had given their orders and the waitress was waddling back to the kitchen.

"We don't know yet. Daddy said he was going to look into it once we're there. As it appears, there'll be a choice of several schools. He's negotiating with the head office over here. He thinks they should pay for private schools for you and your sister. The English call them public schools, but they're not public but private. That's the English for you!"

"Yes, I know. They do everything upside down or the wrong way round."

"We'll all have a lot to get accustomed, Nora dear."

"What if I don't want to go to one of their public schools?"

"Daddy says they're a lot better than the ordinary state schools. You see, it's all a question of social class over there. So naturally we only want the very best for our girls."

"But I don't want to become an arrogant bitch. I've seen some pretty awful girls in private schools in films. That's what you become when you mix with people who think they're better than everybody else."

"Well, don't worry. There's plenty of time to make up our minds. Daddy will know what to do when we're there. And I'll make sure you'll have your say, too."

Back at their home for the last time, Nora said good night to her mother and immediately retired to her room. Standing in front of her bed, she slowly looked around and examined every detail. So, this was the end of her childhood, she felt. She knew she was really too young to actually believe that, but she was overwhelmed by such a feeling when she told herself that she would never be back in this room. She looked in the long mirror on the wall where she could inspect her own person. Was she still a child? Or was she already a young woman? She had her period; so technically, biologically she was a grown woman who could bear children. And yet, looking at herself in the mirror tonight, she tried to see herself in this new role. She saw her size, hardly more than five foot four, her shiny brown hair falling down to her shoulders, her slim face with that small mole near her left eye, a birthmark she had often felt embarrassed about – an embarrassment she had left behind long ago – and with those thin eyebrows which her school-friends said gave her a very adult look. Her green eyes seemed rather large. Her glance travelled lower and took in her undetermined figure, a straight girl's figure with small breasts and only a hint of a woman's hips. She still couldn't believe that a boy could ever find her attractive, but her intellect told her that this might very probably be the case one day in the distant future. Only, she couldn't imagine it at this stage in her life. What must it be like to be really close to a boy? What would a boy say to her? What would he do? What would she do? Yes, it was a fact she knew from her mother's explanations and from biology books that a man and a woman would eventually lie naked in bed together and he would put his thing inside her, an act she simply couldn't imagine.

She touched her cheeks, then she shifted her palms down to her neck, and eventually she ran them down the length of her jumper down to her jeans. What if she had no clothes on? How would she feel if these were a boy's hands? She shivered. Unimaginable! Impossible! How could a girl ever allow such a thing? And yet, there was a strange feeling running through her entire being, a feeling she had never known before. Was it awful or was it somehow pleasurable? How irritating!

For the first time in her young life, Nora realized a discrepancy between herself as the person she'd always believed she was and her biological role as a childbearing woman, which the future held in store for her. How would she cope with this discrepancy in future? Would she undergo more changes than hitherto? She was quite satisfied with who she was, but she admitted to herself that she wouldn't mind if her figure became a little womanlier. She wasn't like her friend Karen, who had confided to her that she never ever wanted to grow up physically. Karen stepped on the scales several times a day to check she hadn't put on a single ounce, and she was extremely worried about every single new layer of fat on her body. Nora could still hear Karen's protestations, "I hate women's breasts, and I hate big hips. They make a woman look so ugly. I'd get rid of such protuberances if they ever grew on my body, I tell you!" They had argued over this, but eventually Nora kept her own thoughts to herself. Now, in front of her mirror, she didn't have a problem with her figure, rather with the present moment in her life.

For a moment, she was going to undress in front of the mirror, to see herself better, to discover her numerous imperfections in more detail and to be able to assess her figure more accurately. But she changed her mind. The next time she would see herself like that, with her clothes off, it would be in her new life, no longer a child, in England.

***

When their taxi was taking them from Heathrow to their hotel in London, Nora looked at the strange new world that presented itself to her. On the motorway it wasn't so much the fact that they were driving on the wrong side of the road, it was more obviously the smallness of the cars and the dirty but quaint aspect of the houses that took her by surprise. It was a rainy day, and everything looked awfully grotty. When she looked out of the side window, she could observe the people in the other cars. The drivers had very grim faces, they didn't look relaxed like American motorists. Even though most men wore collars and ties they still looked unkempt and greasy. Many of them had longish hair that was in need of a haircut. Nora wondered if they didn't have good hairdressers in England. The cars were as dirty and rusty as they were in Chicago, but they were driven at higher speeds. Some of the manoeuvres she observed were quite dangerous.

In London itself, the streets were very narrow, and traffic was quite chaotic. Nora was glad when they could at last get out of their taxi in front of a big hotel with an extremely posh entrance. Brass handrails, red carpets and a lot of bevelled glass all round.

Once they had checked in and made it to their room, Nora felt better than outside in the taxi. Being in a hotel room abroad, alone with her mother, gave her a sense of adventure. She had never been alone with her mother like this. There had been intimate moments between them before, but never like this. They were two Americans in a strange country, while everyone else around them was foreign. Nora felt that her mother was more like a friend than a parent. Somehow, she had the impression that her mother was in a similar mood. The father was absent, the sister was absent, it was a new atmosphere of togetherness, like a secret pact, a new bond between mother and daughter.

"Shall we go down for lunch?" Nora asked, sitting in the deep armchair near the window and looking out onto the wet roofs of the surrounding buildings.

"That's a nice idea," her mother replied. "Let me just put away these last few items." She was still busy folding their clothes and placing them in the large chest of drawers. "We could have left everything in our suitcases, but I'm not sure how long Daddy wants to stay here before heading north to Newcastle, so it's better to settle in properly and keep our things nice and tidy."

When, a few minutes later, they were walking down the broad staircase that led to the reception area, Nora was searching the faces of the people she could see standing or sitting around the lobby. They all looked quite still and lifeless.

Mother and daughter had ordered their food and were holding their glasses of water, looking round the large restaurant, when the feeling of their hotel room came back.

Nora felt she could ask her mother anything she liked at this moment.

"Why did you agree with Daddy to come and live in this country?"

"Because it's a wonderful step in his career. And it's a new experience for us."

"I know. But what about you? Don't you mind?"

"I'm your mother, your daddy's wife. So naturally I go where he goes."

"Have you always done what he wanted?"

"Well, it's what we do when we're married. And your daddy is such a good husband and a wonderful father."

Nora had heard this general explanation many times before. They were silent for a few moments. The waiter arrived with a glass of wine for the mother and a coke for the daughter. They both took a sip from their drinks before Nora asked her next question.

"I know he's a good daddy, but what makes him such a good husband for you?"

"He's so reliable, and he has such high standards. You know, he went through a terrible time in his young days. That's taught him his high principles."

"You mean that's why he's often so strict with us?"

"He's only what you call strict when he feels he has to defend important moral principles. He has seen such awful things in his life, but he believes in the good roots in us."

"What's it got to do with good roots and high moral principles when he forbids us to wear fashionable clothes, I'd like to know?" Nora remembered the conflict she'd had with her father only two weeks ago. It had been one of those rare occasions when she forgot her good manners and shouted at her parents. She still believed they didn't want her to look too good in fashionable outfits. They probably feared she might look too grown-up, and they wanted to keep her in eternal childhood.

"Oh, that was only the material you wanted. It was what they call camouflage."

"And what was wrong with that?"

"You know your father doesn't want his daughters to walk around in military outfits."

"It's not military, it's a fashion!"

"You know your father's standards. Because he's been in the war and he's seen such awful things, he's against military equipment, and he thinks it's immoral to wear such stuff just for fashion's sake. A soldier's uniform is worn for the purpose of killing people. Camouflage is a killer's outfit."

"You know that's ridiculous."

"I respect your father's moral standards, and I want you to do the same. Please, don't go against your father in such things. We can call ourselves very fortunate to have such a model of a man at the head of our family."

Their food arrived. The steaks were hard and dry, something they had been warned about before leaving the States. All their friends and neighbours who had visited England before had told them about the awful food they would get there. Nora wondered what the food would be like in her new school. The business of cutting up their steaks and loading their forks with chips – which Nora still called French fries – and tasteless watery vegetables kept them silent for a while.

"You see, Nora dear," the mother began, looking into the middle distance with wet eyes, "when I met your father he was still suffering very much under his awful experiences. He must have experienced terrible things and seen lots of suffering in the war. He must have been very fortunate to have survived such horrors. It was in Chicago, back in 1954, only nine years after the war. We were both looking out over the lake on a cool but sunny day. I was with my Aunt Sally, and he was on his own, munching a sandwich for his lunch, when we happened to look at each other. I was immediately taken with him, such a handsome man. He was the first to say something. I was far too shy. I'd come to the big city from my small town, Davenport, Iowa. I can't remember what he said, but despite Aunt Sally, we managed to arrange to meet again."

"You never told me that bit. What was it like for you to come to Chicago from Davenport?"

"Oh, it was just fantastic. Davenport was so provincial, and Chicago was the world. As a young woman, I was simply overwhelmed. The big shops, the traffic, the fashions, the concerts and theatres, the people..."

"So Dad was part of this new experience?"

"In a way, yes. We fell in love at once. Looking back now, I think what made him so attractive for me, besides his dashing good looks and the ironic twinkle in his eyes, was his sadness. The sadness he was carrying inside himself after what he'd seen in the war. It gave him a slightly mysterious look, which I found very romantic. And then there was his funny accent."

"Yes, it's German, isn't it?"

"It's Swiss German, he insists on this detail. You know that."

"Yes," Nora admitted, "but we've never talked about it, have we?"

"What more is there to be said?"

"Well, for one thing, I often wondered why Daddy could have been in the war if he grew up in Switzerland. The Swiss weren't in the war. We had that in our history lesson."

"He didn't grow up there. He had to escape from the Nazis in Germany, so he came to Switzerland as a refugee."

"Why doesn't he like to talk about it? Whenever we ask him about his past in Europe he says it's all too awful. He must have seen things that we have to learn about in our history lessons today. Why can't he tell us more?"

"It's because some of the things are just too bad. He doesn't want to talk about them."

"But when you first got together in 1954, you must have asked him things about his past. I wouldn't marry a man whose past I knew nothing about."

"Why do you keep on? Why do you insist on those distant things?"

"It's just that we've never been told as children. I'd like to know more. Do you know the details of his escape from the Nazis? Was he really in a concentration camp? How long did he live in Switzerland before he came to the States?"

"Come on, finish your vegetables." This was the end of the little *tête-à-tête* discussion between mother and daughter. Nora knew it was no use trying to get her mother back to the topic once it had been closed like this.

The next morning, they went for a stroll around the neighbourhood of their hotel. They saw Hyde Park and Marble Arch, Oxford Street and Regent Street. There were lots of shops and lots of people. It was a cool but pleasant March morning. When they got back to the hotel, the receptionist handed them a telegram.

"Oh, Dad's not coming for another two days," the mother said when she had read the telegram. "He's being kept in Boston a bit longer than expected." She folded up the telegram and slid it in her handbag.

The new situation gave them two more days of togetherness as mother and daughter. They decided to take a sight-seeing tour around London to make the most of their first day. When they got tired of following their guide – a young woman with a bright red umbrella as a beacon – they sat down on a bench and told her they'd make their own way back to the hotel. This was in the park at Hampton Court Palace. They looked at the early daffodils that surrounded them.

"We saw this place in a film back in the States," Nora began. It was about Henry VIII and his wives. I think I remember that the king took the palace from the archbishop and gave it to his young wife, you know, the one he had beheaded only a few years later. Did you know that?"

"No, I don't know a great deal about British history. In fact, I don't know too much about history at all. Back in Iowa, all we learnt about in our history classes was the Boston Tea Party and the Declaration of Independence and all that. There wasn't a lot about European history. Of course, we knew a few English kings and queens, and we knew about Henry VIII and his wives, but no details, and that was about it. I was never any good at history."

"But meeting Dad you must have learnt a lot about recent history, the war, the Nazis, Hitler, Stalin and all that?"

"Not much. Only what he told me about his own experiences, and as you know that wasn't very much."

"I know," Nora agreed. "And I know, as you told me yesterday, he doesn't like to talk about it. But can you tell me what you know? I think I'm old enough to know."

"Well, my child," her mother hesitated, "as I told you last night, I met your father in 1954. He told me he'd grown up somewhere in Germany, I don't remember the name of the place. When Hitler and the Nazis came to power he was in danger because he was a Socialist. So one day, after he'd fought for them in the war for more than three years, they suddenly arrested him. They were going to deport him to a concentration camp, when he managed to escape. He told me how he walked all the way to freedom. He had to walk at night and sleep in barns and haystacks during the day, to avoid being caught by the Nazis. Anyway, eventually he got to Switzerland, where he got political asylum. Then, a few years later, he came to the States."

"Did they give him his tattoo in prison, you know the one on his left arm?"

"Yes. All the people they sent to their concentration camps were tattooed like that. But how do you know? Have you seen his tattoo? It's not very clear. In fact, it's hardly visible, just those two letters inside his arm. I think he tried to get it off, but tattoos can't be removed so easily. To me it's obvious he hates it."

"Of course, I've seen it. When I asked him one day he said it wasn't for little girls, but it reminded him of our duty to respect all humans. So, it must remind him of his bad days in the Nazi prison."

"Oh, come on, Nora. Let's walk over there. I'd like to look at those flowers." Mother steered them away from their bench and from their topic.

On their second day in London, they went to have a look at pictures in the National Gallery, which Nora found rather boring. In the afternoon, they took a boat down the river and visited the Maritime Museum at Greenwich. It was an exhausting day. So they went to bed early. The topic of Dad's past in Europe was never mentioned again.

***

Nora was sitting on her bed, her mother was at the small writing table in their bright hotel room, when the telephone on the bedside-table rang. It was a call from the lobby to inform them of the arrival of Dad and Margaret. Shortly afterwards, they were all together, hugging and kissing, happy about their reunion. Nora moved to the next room, together with her sister, while Dad moved in with Mum.

After lunch downstairs, the parents retired to their room, but the two sisters decided to go for a walk in Hyde Park. The weather wasn't as bright as in the morning, but it was dry, and the grey atmosphere suited the girls' melancholy. They were both a little insecure about what to make of their new lives in this strange country.

They had a lot to tell each other. Margaret told Nora about her time in Connecticut and about Boston. Then they fell silent.

Sitting on a park bench near the Serpentine, Nora began to open the new topic she had discovered in conversation with her mother the other day. "Did you talk a lot to Dad?"

"Well, yes. We had a lot of time to talk. He told me lots of interesting things about his new job in Newcastle."

"Did you talk about his past?"

"Why about his past?"

"Did you never wonder why we hardly know anything about our own father? What he was before he met Mum?"

"Wasn't he a German refugee originally? Then he was in business in Switzerland before he came to the States. I think he became an American citizen a few years before he met Mum. Why do you want to know?"

"Don't you want to know more?"

"Why should I? He's our dad and we love him. Isn't that enough?"

"Well, yes, but... I don't know, it's just that...," Nora faltered.

"What do you mean? Is there anything wrong? Did you have a row with him or what? What's wrong if he doesn't like talking about his time in a Nazi prison?"

"You're right. You know I love him, too. And I admire him as much as you do, for his high moral principles, for what he does for us, for Mum, for other people and so on. But, ... well, I may be wrong, but there are these moments. Sometimes, when I'm not with Dad, when I'm separated from him and just thinking of him, I have the impression he's not really my father, he's some stranger, some person that I don't really know."

"Oh, my little sister! These are just the shifting moods of puberty. I was like that, too, when I was your age. Don't worry, it'll pass."

"Oh, please, don't talk down from the high horse. You're not all that older, Margaret."

"Three years make a big difference at our age, believe me. I know. I've been through it all." With these soothing words, Margaret took her sister in her arms.

After their embrace, the sisters forgot their discussion about their father, and turned their attention to what they could do in London. They expected to have another two or three days in this grey city. Margaret suggested Madame Tussaud's for an outing the next day, and Nora agreed with pleasure. She had read that there were not only wax figures of famous politicians as well as English kings and queens, but also of Elvis and the Beatles. That might be good fun.

They walked some more through the park, and when they reached the gate that led them out onto the pavement of Bayswater Road, the sky opened up and the sun peeped out from between the clouds. With the wind easing off a little, it became quite pleasant. It was a pity about the noise, Nora thought. In the park, they had heard the twitter of birdsong, but here the traffic noise drowned it all. And to add to the noise, a big aeroplane on its approach to Heathrow came roaring quite low over the park.

Artists were exhibiting their works along the iron park fence. The sisters looked at some of the pictures. Even though they didn't think much of them in terms of artistic standards, they were touched by some of them. It was an agreeable afternoon, they had to admit. The better ones among the paintings certainly worked wonders and lifted Nora's spirits considerably. Especially one picture of a northern landscape appealed to her. The artist had managed to compose the setting and match the sombre colours in such a way as to render the bleak landscape in a light which wasn't altogether void of a certain hidden cheerfulness. Or was it rather confidence and assurance?

It took the girls nearly an hour to get back to their hotel.

Next day, they visited Madame Tussaud's, and on the following days they mainly went shopping with their mother. Three days later, they boarded the train from King's Cross to Newcastle.

Looking out of the window of the train speeding through the flat landscape, Nora lost herself in her thoughts about what had happened between her and her mother in London. The more she thought about what Mum had told her about Dad's past, the more blank spaces appeared in her image of her father.

At her former school in Chicago, history had mainly consisted of an enumeration of the glorious aspects of American history, such as the War of Independence, the early years of the independent states, the victorious conquest of the West up to Little Big Horn, the victory of the North over the South which sealed the abolition of slavery, the rise of the country to the leading industrial nation in the world and finally America's great roles in the two World Wars. They had to learn by heart some of the most important sections of the Constitution and even some of its Amendments. And, of course, they had to memorize the names and dates of office of all the American Presidents. European history, on the other hand, remained mostly blank, except for some of the horrors committed by the Germans in the two wars, and Hitler's perverted mind and aggressions were treated at length. Nora found herself hoping that she would learn a lot more about Europe, now that they were going to settle here, and history was one of her favourite subjects. Once she knew more about the whole Nazi era, she would explore a lot more about her father's life.

The flat country that she was staring at was very bleak.

SEVEN

The language was the worst shock. Nora was worried she might never understand these people. They all appeared extremely friendly and warm-hearted, but their language was utterly incomprehensible. It wasn't really English, Nora and Margaret thought.

"I was wond'ring if your hinny could mind the bairns on Saturdeeah," Mrs Henderson asked. She was their next-door neighbour. Mother had to ask back twice before she understood the smiling woman.

"Of course, Nora will be happy to do some baby-sitting for you, Mrs Henderson," she replied.

"Why-ay, that's canny," was Mrs Henderson's comment.

When the door had been closed behind Mrs Henderson, who was walking down their garden path, Nora asked her mother what the friendly woman had wanted.

"She wants you to do some baby-sitting for her. Look after her two children on Saturday. They want to go out, and she'd be so happy if you could do that. She'll give you a whole pound. That's very generous. So, I said you'd be happy to oblige. Was I right?"

"Yes, Mummy, that's ok. But I wish you'd ask me first."

"Oh, I'm sorry. I was so overwhelmed by her language. It was such an effort to understand her, so I completely forgot to ask you first."

"So, you find it hard to understand these people, too?"

"Of course, I do. It's a real nightmare."

"Then I'm glad we're not the only ones. Margaret and I find it extremely hard," Nora complained.

"Never mind, we'll all get used to it. I tell you, in a few weeks we won't even notice the difference."

Nora did not believe her mother. But she was right. After only a few days even, both sisters felt as if a switch had been turned in their ears and they could understand the Geordies – as the people called themselves – as well as any other English-speaking people. But they still liked to make fun of them when they were alone together. They tried to imitate the typical sing-song of expressions like "why-ay" and to get the long "aw"-sound right in simple words like "no" or "low". With other people, their school-mates and their neighbours, however, they wouldn't dare to imitate this charming dialect. They continued to move on the safe ground of their American English and only gradually replaced certain American expressions with British ones. The first of these replacements was "pavement" for "sidewalk", and soon others followed.

At school, only very few children made fun of their American accents, most of them admired what they called "the Hollywood accent" and thought the two American girls sounded rather posh, but in a pleasant way.

After the first few weeks, both sisters began to like their school. Especially Nora was glad their parents had let them choose between the two school systems. They had both opted for the state school system, or – as the English called it – the maintained system. To have chosen the private school – called public school – would have gone against their American sense of equality and democracy. Their school, which was called a grammar school, was within walking-distance of their new house in a suburb called Gosforth.

Dad had insisted on a school which offered Latin as a major subject. He had always been fond of that dead language, and he liked to quote phrases whenever an opportunity presented itself. The girls had already grown up with phrases like *cum grano salis* or *mutatis mutandis* from early childhood. And when, at the end of a minor quarrel about some disagreement, he gave in to one of his daughters he usually chuckled, "*in dubio pro filia*", but as little girls they never found out what was supposed to be so funny about the expression.

In their first Latin lesson at their new school they were surprised to hear yet another way of pronouncing this language. Dad didn't pronounce it as the American teachers had done, and this English teacher now pronounced it differently again. It was all very puzzling. Margaret did not really mind. Nora wondered if it was only the Geordie way, but the teacher, a friendly elderly man with a bald head, called Mr Carr, assured her he had grown up down south, somewhere in Bedfordshire.

Gallia omnia divisa est in partes tres. This was the first sentence in their new Latin book, *De Bello Gallico*, written by Gaius Julius Caesar. Nora was so proud. At last their lessons didn't only consist of Grammar exercises and translations from English into Latin, at last they were actually reading their first book in that language. She brought it home, and when Dad came home in the evening she ran up to him and showed it to him.

"How wonderful!" he exclaimed. "Now you are a big girl."

"Will you help me if I run into any problems understanding certain sentences?" she wanted to know.

"I'll be delighted. You know, I always loved the language. I believe that it has a positive influence on our minds and actions. It's character-building. When I was going through the darkest moments of my life, back there in Germany, it was my memory of Latin poetry which virtually kept me alive."

Nora found this hard to believe. But she was glad to see her father happy. So, through the following months she often sought his advice when it came to the task of finding the meaning of words and expressions that mostly had to do with weaponry and warfare. It was amazing how many words Caesar must have known for swords, spears and other weapons. Sometimes she wondered why her father didn't protest against such a text. He always took the pacifist view wherever possible, and he still forbade them to wear camouflage clothes. So how was it possible for him to like Caesar's text? She asked Margaret's opinion.

"It's because Caesar's wars happened long ago," Margaret explained. "It's ancient history. It's not like the recent World Wars, which are so close. For Dad, the Second World War isn't just history, for him it's reality, personal experience."

Such discussions about their father made Nora see him in a new light. The change of scenery, away from their homely Chicago to this quaint new British environment, and also their new life in this still unfamiliar house: these triggered a new sense of awareness in her. In this context, she began to look at her parents with new eyes, and she thought she saw her father – whilst he remained a parental authority – more clearly as just a middle-aged man. Some evenings, sitting over their supper and listening to the parents discussing the day's events, Nora studied her father's face. She saw his thick greying hair, his deep eyes with those wrinkles at their edges, his narrow face and his firm jaw. It was the face of a very determined man, a man who knew what he wanted. She felt proud of her father.

After the summer holidays, Nora's class welcomed three new fellow-pupils. One of them was Ned Robson, a shy boy with dark hair. Nora immediately liked him. Soon they walked home together after school. He lived just round the corner. Margaret was the first person to notice the new development in her sister's life.

"You like him a lot, don't you?" she asked Nora one evening. They were lying on Nora's bed, a situation which always gave their talks a very intimate atmosphere. Like this, they could discuss everything, there were no taboos.

"How did you guess?" replied Nora, blushing.

"It's obvious. I can tell from your new behaviour. You have changed."

"No. It can't be. I'm still my old self," Nora protested.

"But I can tell," Margaret insisted. Then there was silence for a short while. The silence was fraught with meaning.

Nora remembered a sentence she had read in one of her father's books: "She took refuge on the firm ground of fiction, through which indeed there curled the blue river of truth." She wasn't sure, but she believed it was from Henry James. It made her wonder indeed whether she should tell her sister the full truth about her feelings for Ned or whether she should take refuge on the firm ground of fiction. She chose the blue river of truth.

"Yes, you're right. I think I might fall in love," she admitted.

"You think you might? Ha ha, you've already fallen in up to your ears," Margaret laughed. "It's wonderful. I'm so happy for you."

"It's not so easy," Nora moaned. "It hurts so much."

"I know. It hurts at first, because you don't know if he loves you back, and you don't know what to do about it."

"Yes, that's it, exactly. And it hurts so much when I can't be with him, which is most of the time. Those few moments when we're together are so precious, but they're so short. It's only when we walk home from school."

As it turned out over the following weeks, Nora felt more and more that her mother no longer understood her. She imagined her mother loving her father with the same painful intensity as she loved Ned, and the sheer idea nearly made her sick. She tried to imagine her parents in an intimate activity, as she had seen in films, but even though she was normally quite gifted when it came to a colourful imagination, she failed completely when she tried to imagine them in the act of love. True, Dad often called Mum "my darling", sometimes "darling Emily", and she usually kissed him on the cheek, but never on his mouth. When they embraced, it was usually a fleeting affair. There just didn't seem to be any real passion lost between her parents.

As for her own development in this department, she found herself in the wonderfully exciting but equally daunting phase of exploration. She knew she loved Ned with all her heart, and her body felt strangely drawn to him, but she didn't quite know where this was leading her. She wanted to do more, to experience more, to find out what lovers did, but at the same time she was afraid of the unknown. She had heard and read so much about possible disappointments, about the dangers of sexual activities among teenagers, and her mother had warned them of what men and boys wanted. She had never been particularly specific, but it was precisely the hazy nimbus surrounding the topic as it was treated by Mum which suggested unfathomable dangers and disappointments.

Ned was a pale boy with long thin arms and gangly legs. He never walked fast, he rather slouched along. Nora found this endearing. His long thin face was quite feminine, with smooth white skin that had yet to experience the novelty of facial hair. Nora began to imagine what it might feel like to kiss those thin pink lips. His voice was very manly and stood in harsh contrast to his soft looks. Nora wondered why his voice had already broken while he still looked rather boyish and didn't need a shave. A highly interesting boy, by all means!

In late September, walking home from school, Ned and Nora found themselves turning suddenly into a back alley. They both wanted it, neither of them had to pull the other or even say anything. They just turned away from the pavement, round some dark green bushes and found themselves alone, just the two of them, in one of those ugly, unkempt back alleys, overgrown with weeds and deserted by human beings. The alley stretched along the back yards of a long row of houses. It was about two hundred yards long, and halfway along the alley a black and white cat was sitting, cleaning its paws with its pink tongue. The cat was the only living creature in this world besides Ned and Nora. The sun, which rendered this autumnal afternoon in a golden light, only reached the back yards, the alley itself was in the shade, and the contrast between the sunny parts and the grey shade seemed extreme.

They slowed down and eventually stopped, facing each other. Ned put his hands on Nora's shoulders and gently pulled her towards him. She looked up into his pale face, trying to detect what he was feeling at this moment. His face appeared strange at this close range. She could make out two small pimples on his chin, about one inch from his lower lip. His eyes looked insecure, searching for hers. His expression betrayed even more insecurity, presenting to her something between a sour half-smile and a fatalistic mood, as if he was about to say, "I'm sorry, what do you expect me to do?"

Nora knew this was a very special and very important moment in her life. When she felt a new and utterly unknown force in her abdomen, as if someone was pushing her body against his, she felt her former shyness disappear. She wanted him to take her in his arms, and she desperately wanted to feel his lips on hers.

When he enveloped her with his arms and their lips touched at last, Nora closed her eyes and let herself be carried away into an unmapped territory that made her believe she was entering a new form of existence, leaving her old and meaningless life behind her and embarking on a significant future. After these first impressions, she just dismissed all intellectual assessments and let herself sink into this sea of warm and velvety water. She was ready to follow him wherever he was going to lead her.

After an eternity of earth-rocking kissing, which had begun with simple lip-contact and gradually grew into a fascinating exploration of their mouths with their active and extremely sensitive tongues, they both began to regain parts of their consciousness. They drew slightly apart and drew some deep breaths. Ned looked at her, their eyes were locked together, as their mouths had been for the last few centuries.

"I love you," he managed to whisper at last.

"I love you, too," she answered.

That was all. Then they continued with their kisses until, after another century, she began to feel uncomfortable. Her back was a bit stiff from their long standing in the alley. This physical unease gradually pulled her out of her dream. She returned to the world and reluctantly faced the facts. She realized that time must have flown. She pulled away from Ned and patted her hair to smooth it down.

"I've got to be going. I don't want Mum to find out about us."

They checked each other's appearance. When they felt they were presentable enough they walked back to the street they had left when they were children, and they continued their way home feeling very grown-up.

Back at home, Nora went straight up to her room. She threw herself on her bed and began to re-live in her mind what she had experienced in that back alley only a short while ago. With her eyes closed, she lay there, forgetting about homework, savouring her memory, until her mother called her downstairs. It was tea-time.

In the morning, Nora made sure she found Ned on her way to school. Together, they walked hand in hand, happy to be together again. No words were needed. Everything was perfect.

During lesson-time, Nora's attention was drawn to the subjects at hand, but whenever the subject got too boring she drifted off and bathed in her memory of that kiss, that long kiss, that first real kiss in her life.

When their history lesson began, she was pulled out of her dreams with a violent realization. The new topic was the Second World War. With a sudden stab in her heart she remembered that Dad had been in the war, in the very same war that they were going to discuss in their history lessons. As long as they had been treating topics like the Great War, the General Strike and the Great Depression, even the Abdication Crisis, things had been as distant for her like the Tudor kings or Napoleon and Waterloo. But now, this was the recent past, nearly the present world, considering that Dad had been part of it. He had suffered so much, Mum had explained, so that the daughters never asked any questions. Dad himself had always been as silent as the grave about his experiences; he only reminded them of the awful terror of a war and forbade them camouflage clothes. One day, he had remarked that he was glad they were girls, for if they'd been sons they might have developed an unhealthy interest in weapons, in guns and pistols, as boys often did, so he was relieved they were daughters. Apart from his aversion to weapons and his refusal to accept the existence of any military equipment in the world, they knew nothing of his ultimate reasons behind this attitude or his role during the War. Nora decided to find out more.

She had to wait for the right moment to approach her father with such a sensitive subject. But she knew he was very fond of her, especially since she'd shown such a keen interest in Latin and ancient history. This might serve as a possible opening.

"Didn't Emperor Augustus and his successors aim for supremacy over the entire Mediterranean as well as most of Europe?" she asked her father, when she found herself sitting alone with him in the lounge on a wet Sunday afternoon.

"Yes, and they managed to build one of the largest empires in history. Roman influence reached from Northern England – you've seen pictures of Hadrian's Wall, haven't you? – to the Sahara Desert and to what would be the Arab World today. I wish I could show you some of their monuments as they are still in existence today. We must make a start with Hadrian's Wall, which is just down the road. In fact, do you remember when we went on that visit to one of our new friends' week-end house near Hexham. That's where Hadrian's Wall is. Shall we go there next week-end? Would you like that?"

"Of course, Dad. It would be fascinating. It's only a pity we can't see all the other monuments. At school, we learnt about Pompeii, about Baalbek and about Palmyra."

"Now, those are too far away for us. Let's make a beginning with Hadrian's Wall. Later we might see other sites in this country, such as Bath, for example."

"That would be wonderful. Thanks, Dad!"

"And what did you learn from ancient history?"

"That empires may be great for a time, but they never last. It's probably because it's always a small minority that profits from such empires. The majority of the people always suffer. Mr Jackson told us that's the case in all empires."

"Did he include the British Empire, I'd like to know?"

"He didn't say."

"I'm asking because the British are notoriously uncritical about their own history. They usually blame all the other nations with whom they've fought a war. For a long time, it was the French they hated, then the Germans. They never question their own role in all those wars, the only mode they know is their own hero-worship."

"But they saved us from the Nazis, as Mr Jackson explained."

"Indeed, in a way they did," Dad smiled.

"Then why shouldn't they be proud of it?"

"Because national pride is the source of dangerous nationalism, which is the breeding ground for new wars. Once people start to believe that they are better than other nations, things become racist and may eventually lead to another war. We should all be humble when it comes to judgments of other nations."

"Are you humble about your own past in Germany?" Nora dared to ask.

Her father was silent for a while. Then he cleared his throat.

"It's all such a long time ago," he said at last, and his shoulder began to twitch slightly.

When she saw a tear running down his cheek, she was sorry. She was going to save him by changing the subject when he spoke again. This time, his voice was soft, and his entire attitude had lost its customary authority.

"You see, my girl, I have made some awful mistakes in my life. But there's no going back. You can't change your own past, you just can't."

"Did you suffer a lot?"

"Yes. But not in a way you could imagine."

"Did you hate the Jews, like everybody else?"

"Not everybody hated them."

"But Mr Jackson said while the population of Germany at the time was seventy million people, they found out after the War that only 455 individuals were recognized as Jew savers, I think they called them *Judenretter*, people who hid Jews in their attics or cellars or otherwise helped them survive, like the people hiding the family of Anne Frank in Amsterdam. Imagine, only 455 out of seventy million!"

"Yes, it was a case of national hysterics."

With this statement, the conversation was closed. Nora would have liked to ask more questions, particularly about Dad's personal experiences, but to approach such a delicate subject proved to be more difficult than she had imagined. She was determined to try again at a later opportunity.

Christmas and New Year came, and Nora's first winter in Britain turned out to be quite cold with lots of snow and ice on the roads, although never as much as they used to get back in Chicago. But everybody said how unusual it was for England.

The public discussions, as well as the conversations in the family, turned more and more often to the present situation in England, especially the dispute in the coal mining industry, which threatened to culminate in a national strike action of the coal miners. In the Newcastle area, indeed in the entire Midlands and the North East, this was felt very acutely. The impending strike action threatened to shorten their supply of electrical power.

"There are going to be regular power-cuts soon, unless the dispute can be solved," Dad announced one evening in January.

"How are we going to cope?" Mum asked.

"I'm sure we'll cope. They say there's going to be power for three hours, like twelve to three, then no power for three hours, like three to six, then back to power from six to nine, and so on," he explained.

Nora listened to this without emotions. She was confident that the strike would still be stayed off. Such a thing could never happen in this country, she was quite sure. But then she remembered all those other strikes in British industry that the news had been full of, ever since they had been in the country. There had been the railways, then the motor industry, there didn't seem to be an end to strikes. So this new threat was perhaps more than likely.

Indeed, the big strike became reality, the power-cuts were implemented, and Edward Heath declared a national state of emergency from the 9th of February. At first, Nora and her school-friends found it quite funny. It was an adventure to cope with these power-cuts. The teenagers began to gather at one of their homes and sit round an electric fire for three hours, warming up as best they could, keeping up their lively discussions with tea and Digestive biscuits, until the power went off and candles were lit. Then things turned out really romantic for about an hour and a half, the talks became more personal, sometimes even quite intimate, and all sorts of daring things were uttered under the cover of the dim candle-light. But then everyone began to feel cold. The outside temperatures on such nights often dropped below freezing point, so even in their rooms things became quite uncomfortable during the last of the three hours without power, and even their talks often died out when everyone had to concentrate on keeping warm in their layers of jackets and coats. So when the power came back on, Nora and her friends cheered with great pleasure, and they all felt like little heroes.

On some of these nights, Ned was among the group of friends. Naturally he was sitting next to her in their circle round the candles on the floor. Both of them found their hearts beating a little more quickly when the power went off and the candlelight rendered the atmosphere more romantic. However, even though they felt they might do more than just sit next to each other they had to restrain themselves. Nobody was to find out that they were having a special thing between them, so they couldn't even kiss. Still, it was an exciting experience.

The "thing" between them remained in its delicate budding stage for several months. They both felt they would like to follow their inclination and explore each other's bodies, but they were just too shy. Nora felt she would like to feel Ned's skin and really wanted him to feel hers, but she didn't know how to let him know and was too shy to start doing anything herself. Where could it lead? She was only going to be fourteen in a few weeks' time, and her mind was full of her mother's warnings. As a girl you never knew what tricks boys could be up to. Thus, her faster heart-beats during those candlelight sessions stemmed mainly from her inner conflict between wanting and dreading.

When the strike ended and regular power supply returned in late February, Nora wasn't sure about how to feel. Her only hope for a more intimate development in her relationship with Ned was gone, but on the other hand she felt more relaxed because they could just continue with their kisses behind bushes and in back alleys as they had enjoyed them before the strike. She only really regretted the intimate atmosphere of the candlelight evenings, not only with Ned but equally with their other school-friends. Nora felt she had now acquired quite a respectable circle of friends after only a few months in the new country. There were several quite nice girls that she liked, and she was glad to have spent all those evenings with them getting to know one another a lot better.

There was Debbie, who lived only two streets away. She had a round face that always had a friendly smile, her hair was something between fair and red, she had an older sister like Nora, she also liked Latin, she could play the piano and her father worked for Barclays Bank. Nora found herself naturally drawn to Debbie, and now, after those intimate evenings during the power-cuts, they realized that they had become best friends.

Another very good friend was Janet. Nora liked her, although she didn't live in Gosforth like Debbie and most of Nora's other friends, but in Jesmond, which was something of a hippie suburb of Newcastle, full of students living in digs, bedsits or small flats in one of those identical terraced houses off Osborne Road. Janet's parents had gone to a great effort to be allowed to send her to Nora's school in Gosforth. The family lived in one of the few mock-Tudor houses with black beams towards the upper end of Osborne Road, which placed them nearly on the same social level as the rest of Nora's circle. All these insinuations about social class really annoyed Nora, but living where she did, in one of Newcastle's posh suburbs, she simply couldn't escape them. After living there for a few months, she realized that she was stuck in this box, there was no way of escaping her family's social label, which was upper-middle-class. At times, she would look back and remember their lives in Chicago in a wistful mood. There had been no question of social class. Or had she simply not seen it?

Janet didn't play a musical instrument, but she was more into modern pop music, of which she had a huge record collection. Also, she was different from Nora in her attitude to school. Perhaps in protest against her parents, who had fought so hard to get her into this school, she disliked most of the subjects, she only made a minimal effort to cope and she considered their teachers stupid people. On the other hand, there was a very special charm about her, a charm that didn't escape Nora. This charm consisted of very good looks, a winning smile, a general sense of easy-going carelessness and an extremely catching sense of humour. Nora felt that Janet was her other half, her contrasting shadow, or some other person who belonged to her despite all the differences between them. Sometimes she thought she needed her to balance her own views of things, like some sort of regulator. Of course, she never spoke to her about this aspect of their relationship. When they were alone together, without any of their other friends, Nora wondered if Janet had similar ideas of their differences and their relationship. But like her, Janet never mentioned anything in that direction. It was as if their unequal relationship was either just taken for granted or was really only a figment of Nora's imagination. After all, Nora's experience of the world was still rather modest. The important thing for the time being was that the two girls were happy about each other and spent a lot of good times together.

There were a few other friends, but none as intimate as Debbie and Janet. When the whole group of friends went to town to do some window-shopping, perhaps daring to buy a small item of clothing – a T-shirt, a pair of tights or cheap jeans – from Fenwick's, the only department store worth looking at in town, Nora, Debbie and Janet were usually accompanied by other girls like Amy, Christine and Sophie, who all went to the same school and lived in Gosforth. The group liked to travel to the City on top of a double-decker bus, and they usually got off the bus near the Civic Centre, laughing and happy about their common experience in the big city, which made them feel quite grown-up.

***

Nora turned fourteen in March, and this spring marked the first anniversary of their residence in England. Although the parents didn't mention it, Nora and Margaret celebrated this anniversary in private. They sat down on the soft cushions in Margaret's room, lit some candles and allowed themselves a few small bottles of Coke.

"Isn't it odd?" Margaret asked, "We've been here for a whole year now, but it feels like ten years?"

"Yes. Sometimes I can hardly remember everything from our old home. And what about you?"

"Well, I can remember enough for my taste. But then I have to focus on our life here, with things as they are at school."

"You're going to take your A-Levels next year, aren't you?" Nora wanted to know. "Are you going on to university then?"

"Yeah, I guess I will."

Nora still admired Margaret and her clear ideas about her own future. She had always known what to aim for, and she seemed to have very succinct ideas about her working life as an adult. This made Nora realize how much she herself was still a baby. She had no definite plans for her future, she didn't even know if she was going to continue with school after her O-Levels. And whereas Margaret had a gift for science and apparently wasn't interested in boys – she probably never even had a boyfriend – Nora's interests lay in languages, history and boys. Sometimes Nora feared her interest in boys made her inferior to her elder sister's abstinence. How could Margaret not be drawn to the other sex? Nora knew she would always "run after boys", as their mother labelled a girl's pronounced interest in boys. She couldn't help it. She was a weak girl, a weak person. Her sister was a firm rock in the wild sea of life.

"Do you think Mum and Dad are happy here?" Nora asked.

"I think they are. Dad likes his work. He seems to be quite a big cheese in his company, which gives him a sense of importance, much more so than back in the States. And Mum is thrilled about her new part-time job. She told me so only last week. So yes, I believe they're very happy here. Why are you asking?"

"Well, I don't really know. Sometimes it just seems to me there's something, ... I don't know, ... Dad seems so withdrawn sometimes. As if I couldn't get near him, as if he was trying to hide something."

"Oh, that's just your changing world, little sis. You're growing up. You're reshuffling your views, particularly your views on our parents, on boys and men, and so on. So you begin to see Dad in a new light, from a more grown-up vantage-point."

In bed that night, Nora couldn't go to sleep immediately. She spent a long time thinking of what Margaret had said and wondered if it was just that.

EIGHT

Mr Woolf – or Didi Woolf, as his business friends liked to call him – was always very busy. His work was very important to him, but he also spent as much time as possible with his family in their comfortable house in Gosforth. He loved his daughters Margaret and Nora, and he was still very fond of his wife, Emily, even after nearly twenty years of married life. He still found her an extremely attractive woman, and she suited him in every possible way. She may be a little boring sometimes, perhaps too "normal", without any sense of adventure or excitement, and their marriage had been bubbling along quite nicely for all this time, but this had its advantages, too. As long as their sex life was still intact. Which it was. At least Didi thought so. They had sex about once a month, usually in the middle of the night. Always on his initiative, never on hers. Sometimes she wouldn't even be fully awake, and if she did wake up, it was usually when he'd already reached his climax and felt like going back to sleep. But they never talked about their sex life. So, he was convinced it was good.

Didi cut a very good figure. He was just under six-foot tall, slim, with a handsome, clean-shaven face and thick, dark brown hair made more daring by a few grey streaks, and he had this successful aura about him that a certain type of American businessmen had. He looked best in his grey suit. When he had his hair freshly washed and wore his narrow blue tie, some friends' wives said he looked almost like JFK or sometimes like some oil tycoon from that American soap on TV. People who met him for the first time were bound to admire him for his charisma. Unfortunately, that brilliant first impression was sometimes a little shaken by his strange clipped accent.

People knew he was American, so they just noted that his accent was a bit different but couldn't define it. However, there was that specific halting rhythm and that slightly monotonous intonation, an idiosyncrasy that only a few people with a fine ear for languages detected, and of those there were few enough in Newcastle in the 1970s.

His wife and daughters knew about this, of course. They knew he had a Swiss-German accent, probably with a little proper German thrown in.

Something that his family found hard to understand was his ongoing interest in German politics. They accepted it as a weird hobby of his, but when he began to talk about it more often in the spring of 1972, his interest seemed to take on a new dimension. His family became fully aware of this when he came home for dinner on the 18th of May. He threw a bunch of newspapers on the sideboard and announced his interest in watching the news on TV in the evening. He said it was very important to follow the news about Germany. Neither his wife nor his daughters knew what he meant, but they went along with this general bit of information. Like all their friends in England, as well as their old acquaintances back in the States, they never cared about what was going on in the world outside their countries. Why Germany? Who was interested in Germany?

Because she had developed quite an interest in history, and not only British and American history, but European history in general, Nora was the first to break out of this family pattern and realized that there had to be important news indeed if their father announced it like that. She knew that the greatest hotspot in the world, where the two superpowers were standing in confrontation, was the Berlin Wall, and that was in Germany.

So they watched the news on TV, and after that only Nora remained in the room with her father to discuss what they had just heard and seen. It was an important speech made by the German Chancellor, Willy Brandt, about the new phase in German politics in relation to its Communist neighbours in Eastern Europe. Only the day before, Brandt had explained the new *Ostpolitik* and the new *Ostverträge* in the German parliament, after which the parliament – called the *Bundestag* – was going to ratify the Warsaw and Moscow Treaties. This meant that, 27 years after the end of the War, Germany could at last begin a new phase in international politics, and the Russians were officially no longer threatening to attack West Germany.

"But what's that to us, really?" Nora wanted to know.

"Oh child, can't you see how dramatically this new development is going to change Europe? It could even be the beginning of the end of the Cold War. After agreeing to these treaties, the Russians will no longer be brazen enough to attack a Western European country, not even enforce their supremacy over Eastern European countries with military force, as they did in Hungary in '56 and in Czechoslovakia in '68. Can you see that?" His voice rose higher with passion.

"Sorry, Dad, you may be right, but I still can't understand."

"Let me explain," the father began, "it's really quite simple ..." but Nora interrupted him, claiming to be too tired to concentrate on politics. So the father gave up, but she could see how excited he was.

Next morning, she asked her history teacher at school.

"I don't really know," Mr Jackson said, "but I think it means that the Germans will no longer have to be afraid of Soviet aggression."

"But why should my father be so excited about it?" Nora wondered.

"Well, didn't you tell us your father had some personal connection to Germany? Perhaps someone in his family resisted the Russians during the War, they may have been afraid of a Russian invasion ever since, and now they may feel safer. I don't really know. Time will tell."

But Nora wasn't satisfied. She only wondered why her father obviously took such a strong emotional interest. She didn't know of any relatives in Germany who could have done anything against the Russians. She decided to discuss this with Margaret.

When she asked Margaret a few evenings later, her elder sister was surprised at Nora's interest in the matter. "What does it concern you?" she asked nervously.

"Aren't you interested?" Nora asked back.

"Why should I be? That's old hat! We live here and now, and all that stuff about Germany, the War, the Russians and the Communists, that's got nothing to do with us. And what if Dad did have some relations for whom things might change now? He never told us anything about his German connections anyway, so just forget it."

After this, they never touched the subject again. But Nora decided to keep her mind alert and find out more. After all, this was real world history within her own family.

Meanwhile, she had more pressing things on her mind. There were some problems with Ned, and also her friends Debbie and Janet had some issues with Christine and Sophie. Through most of the summer, Nora felt that life was getting a bit too complicated for her.

Her relationship with Ned had been going quite nicely through the winter, through the power-cuts, and well into spring. They had gone for long walks, and they'd often sought out secluded spots where they felt safe enough to engage in some pleasant cuddling and kissing. She believed she was in love with him. But as the weather turned warmer in spring,

Ned seemed to lose interest while wanting more from her. He no longer told her he loved her, while he began to place his hands under her clothes and stroke her naked skin in ever more passionate ways. When, at last, he reached her naked breasts with his warm hands, she was puzzled as to how to react. While she found it exciting and very pleasant, she couldn't help feeling the wrongness of the situation. She felt she was mutating into a split personality, one side of her enjoying the titillating physical sensation, while another self was looking down at both of them from a critical elevated position.

Ned seemed to notice her hesitation. He took it for shyness and withdrew his hands, only to try again a little later. This time she let him enjoy himself but decided to draw a line here. She wanted to clear up her doubts about their relationship before she would let things go any further. Eventually, he stopped his caresses, they both straightened their clothes and sighed.

"Let's go for a cup of tea somewhere," she suggested.

They went to a small café in Grey Street, not far down from the Theatre Royal. Nora got herself a cup of tea, while Ned chose a milky coffee. They sat down at a table near the door and spent a while stirring their cups and just looking into the middle distance. She tried to catch his eyes, but he avoided hers, sensing that something was amiss.

"Do you still love me?" she asked.

"Well, I mean, we've been together for quite a while now. We wouldn't have stayed together if we hadn't been in love, now would we?"

"That's not enough," she managed to breathe.

"Yes, me too, I'd like to have more. Why can't we try to find a place where we can do more? You know, enjoy more of each other..."

"I don't mean it like that."

"Oh yes, I have been feeling that you don't really seem to love me anymore. Whenever I want to touch you, you hold back, you just don't seem to enjoy being with me anymore."

"I don't want more in that way. I'd like to have more commitment from you."

"I don't understand you," he moaned, looking at her with dog's eyes.

"That's exactly the problem. We have moved apart. We're no longer the eager lovers we were a few months ago. Things have just cooled down between us. You must have felt it, too, if you're honest."

He was going to contradict her, but he hesitated. "I don't know what to say."

"Let's just give us some time. Let's be good friends and find out where we stand over the next few weeks. We are still so young."

"If you think that's a good idea..."

They were silent for a while, before Nora decided to clear up the gloomy atmosphere which had descended on them. So she changed the subject. "Have you put your name down for the school trip in June?"

"I haven't, but I'm going to," he answered, relieved.

They continued talking about school work, about their common friends and – to please him – about the latest game of Newcastle United, a topic she hated, but she wanted to show him she didn't bear him any grudge.

After this, they didn't meet just between the two of them for several weeks. They only got together in groups of friends and in class. To Nora's relief, they managed to remain good friends without rekindling the former fire. In a way, she was quite happy about this state of things, but as time went by she began to miss being with a boyfriend. She realized she had tasted from the sweet tree of love. Not only her heart but also her body craved for a new chapter in this department.

The issues with her girlfriends were of a different nature. They had some silly dispute over one of the boys at their school, Jeff Benson, who was a tall sixth-form pupil with long dark hair. Christine and Sophie considered him the most beautiful boy they'd ever seen. While Christine thought he looked like Alain Delon, Sophie said he looked more like Alan Bates in *Far from the Madding Crowd*, only taller. Debbie and Janet didn't agree with this assessment of Jeff's looks at all. They agreed that he looked much more like Richard Chamberlain but wasn't really worth looking at because he preferred the Rolling Stones to the Beatles, which proved he must have lost his mind completely. The disagreement escalated, and the girls began to shout and scream at each other. When the yelling got too loud, Nora just walked away from her friends because she thought it childish to get excited over such a trifle. Also, she didn't think Jeff was all that good-looking, and she couldn't care less about the looks of film-stars or the superior quality of some rock-band over another. She never listened to such music anyway. She only heard it, but without liking it, when she couldn't escape it; for example, in certain shops or at certain events, where both the bands under discussion couldn't be shut out. So she made it clear to her friends that she wasn't going to take sides.

"Oh, how typical of you!" they shouted. "You with your nose up in the air. You're too posh to have an opinion on such primitive matters that interest lower-class girls like us."

"I'm not posh. How can you say that I've got something like social arrogance?"

"Just listen to her," they shouted to the world at large, "our teachers' darling with her airs and graces, her Latin and her clever questions in the history classes..."

Then there was only yelling and screaming, and the arguments got lost in the general frustrated atmosphere. It got too much for Nora. So she just walked away, giving her friends the finger and accelerating her steps in the direction of the school's main entrance, her eyes streaming with tears.

How could her friends be like that? How could they think of her like that? And how could they get so worked up over such stupid issues? She knew you could never argue about matters of opinion or taste, because every individual had different opinions and different tastes on most things. Even your best friends didn't have to agree with you on everything under the sun. *De gustibus non est disputandum*, she remembered her father's dictum. But the worst thing was the seriousness and energy behind their weak arguments.

In bed at night, she spent a long time thinking about what had happened. She tried to understand the psychological workings behind the quarrel. But she got lost in the maze of her own thoughts and eventually fell asleep.

In the middle of the night she awoke from her troubled dreams, and a possible explanation suddenly flashed through her mind. Could it be that people lost their intellectual reasoning in a debate when the position they were defending was based merely on emotions and not on facts, but they weren't aware of this and felt frustrated over their own inability to find a better reason – in fact no intellectual argument at all – to give more weight to their position? If the position you argue from is really untenable but you're not aware of this, you are bound to get frustrated and your emotions will play havoc with you.

That had to be the case with her friends. Nora was relieved to have found some sort of explanation. Nevertheless, she blamed herself for failing to see that from the outset and for getting involved where she shouldn't have got involved.

Both problem areas – the boyfriend question and the appropriate proximity or distance between herself and her girlfriends – remained with Nora throughout the following months. However, as the days became shorter and the wet

November days of Newcastle turned the atmosphere into a depressing bleakness, she thought she had found a well-balanced attitude in both departments.

Even though she still admired good-looking boys – without comparing them with film-stars, of course – she had come to the conclusion that she didn't have to press things, she didn't have to get herself a new boyfriend as soon as possible. Things would eventually fall into place. As long as she remained herself and looked at the whole question from her higher vantage point with a relaxed attitude, there would be another boyfriend in good time. Thinking of herself with the best critical distance she could muster, she admitted to herself that she wasn't ready for more daring sexual activities as yet. She first wanted to become a more mature person, whatever that involved. But at the same time, she enjoyed observing boys and sometimes, when she couldn't sleep at night, imagining some sort of satisfying love-making. She still couldn't conceive how to bridge the emotional distance between enjoying a cuddly kiss and going the whole hog. What she knew from her reading and from some films she'd seen on TV, couples just started going to bed with each other and having real adult sex at a certain point, but the emotional side of that great step was never convincingly explained. People just did it. As for her, she needed the confidence that her physical activities would be in full agreement with her emotional needs. So there was no hurry. Her days would come.

With her girlfriends she felt more and more relaxed, too. They all resumed their easy-going relationship and often went to town as a group. They were six young girls who were exploring the world together. On the bus between Gosforth and Newcastle's Civic Centre, they sometimes had such a good time that they kept laughing so loud as a closed circle that other bus passengers tut-tutted and shook their heads.

"Well well, today's young girls! They don't know any shame!" was sometimes uttered by elderly ladies with bitter faces, but only heard by other passengers, never by the girls concerned. When other passengers nodded, the elderly ladies felt confirmed in their view, while the girls continued in their exuberant mood and kept up their noisy chatter.

The group gave Nora more self-confidence, as time went on. Despite the unfriendly cold weather, she felt warm enough when she was with her friends. But of all the girls in the group, it was Debbie who was her very best friend. Perhaps it was because they had so many interests in common, perhaps it was because she lived so close-by. Debbie was often at Nora's house and vice versa. As the year drew towards its end, their mothers knew them as an inseparable pair. Nora's mother would normally ask on a Friday evening, "Will you be at Debbie's tomorrow, or is she coming here?" and then, later, "What about Sunday? Is Debbie going to be with us for our Sunday roast?"

It occurred to Nora that Margaret might be jealous of her good friend Debbie. Margaret not only stayed away from boys, she also never came home with a girl. One evening, Nora thought she just had to know, so she asked her sister if she had a girlfriend.

"Why do you want to know?" was Margaret's reply.

"I just wondered why you never bring any of your friends home. You know how often Debbie comes here."

"So you thought because I don't bring anyone here I can't have a friend? Well, if you must know the truth, I do have a very good friend. Her name's Helen, and she's very nice."

"Oh, I'm glad for you," Nora said, relieved. "Why don't you introduce her to your family?"

"Because I don't believe in such things. My family, I mean Mum and Dad and you, well, you are one part of my life. And Helen is another part. I don't want to mix these two parts."

"But that's very odd. I enjoy the way Debbie is received in our family, as I am in hers. Like this, it's all in the open. Mum never worries when I'm out because she knows I'm with Debbie, or with Debbie and other friends."

"That's different. You're too young to understand my situation. You see, Helen isn't just a friend, she's a lot more. We're very close."

"I still don't understand," Nora begged.

"Well, that's what I just said: you don't understand. But you will one day."

After this final dismissal, the topic was no longer mentioned between the two sisters for a long time.

***

After New Year, the weather turned milder. It was certainly a lot milder than a year earlier. When Nora and Debbie were sitting in Janet's room in her big house in Osborne Road one late afternoon in February; the three girls remembered how they had been freezing at that time.

"Do you remember how we were waiting for the power to come back, freezing in our winter coats, sitting in front of our cold electric fires?" Janet asked.

"Of course. It was an exciting time," Nora answered.

"But my parents were furious," Janet said. "They said the miners ought to be punished. It's all those strikes that are ruining the country. My daddy said if it wasn't for all those strikes, our economy would be in a better state than it is. For example, he said our car industry is suffering so terribly because of the strikes. They affect the quality of our cars, so nobody is going to buy British cars in a few years."

“That’s exaggerated,” Debbie replied. “Our industry is still one of the best in the world, my parents say.”

Nora wondered if she should step into this topic, too, but hesitated because she knew she didn’t know half enough about it. She only remembered her father making similar comments as Janet’s. So she decided to contribute some general remark to the conversation. “I think it all depends on the type of industry. My dad works for the chemical industry, and he says we can easily compete with Continental companies, even with the Germans. Actually, he mentioned a possible business trip to Germany later this year.”

The other girls were impressed with her comment. Then their discussions turned to different topics. Naturally, they soon landed in the question of boys, boys and girls, boyfriends and new discoveries among their friends.

Janet fetched some more bottles of Coke and a few packets of potato crisps from the kitchen. When she returned to her room, Debbie teased her with an unexpected statement: “Christine says she’s seen you together with Jeff Benson. You were holding hands.”

Both Nora and Debbie looked at Janet, who was still standing in the middle of the room with three bottles of Coke in her hands. The packets of crisps lay on the carpet. For a moment she froze, obviously racing through her brain for what to say. But she quickly regained her composure.

“She can’t have seen us.”

“Well, she must have. Come on, tell us more about it. Are you two together?”

“It’s still early days. I can’t tell you more. But please, don’t tell anyone.”

Debbie and Nora knew Janet well enough to know there wouldn’t be any more information forthcoming. So they swallowed their disappointment and promised not to tell anyone.

“But you also promise to tell us more when things move on, won’t you?”

Janet promised her part of the deal. Then Nora mentioned their homework for the next day, which changed the atmosphere and took them away from their more private interests. They discussed the essay they had to write and exchanged some good ideas. And soon it was time to go home. Walking through the park on their way back to Gosforth, Debbie and Nora returned to the topic of Jeff Benson.

“What a sly one she is,” Debbie began. “Who would have thought she could get him. He’s the one. All the girls want him.”

“I, for one, don’t want him,” Nora said casually.

“You must be the only one, then.”

Back at home, Nora went up to her room, sat down at her small desk and began to work on her essay. When she reached a point where she wasn’t quite sure about how to continue with her argumentation, her mind drifted off. She wondered how it could be that so many girls seemed to admire one and the same boy. Jeff certainly wasn’t good-looking. He seemed boring to her. After a while, she dismissed the topic and returned to the matter at hand in her essay.

In the evening, she found herself alone with her father in his study while her mother was busy with household chores elsewhere in their big house. It wasn’t the first time. Such meetings between father and daughter seemed to happen just like that, and they gradually established a new sense of trust and intimacy between them. So it became quite natural for them to approach certain topics that they would never mention with other members of the family present.

“Isn’t it strange how so many of my friends seem to be after the same boy?” Nora asked.

"It often happens. Probably the boy just represents the type of young male that conforms to the current taste and fashion," was her father's explanation.

"I would never run after a boy that all my friends go on about all the time."

"Well, when it happens to you, you just can't help it, can you?"

"Perhaps if I was the first girl to get him, before anyone else became aware of his charms," she laughed.

"Don't laugh. That's exactly what happened to me when I was your age. Well, maybe a bit older than you are now, but that's beside the point."

"Oh, do tell me about it, Dad," Nora begged.

"Let me fetch my glass of wine first," her father said and rose to go to the kitchen. She was afraid the spell of the moment might be broken, so she returned to her question immediately when he sat down again with the glass in his hands.

"Was she beautiful?"

"She was the most beautiful girl I'd ever known," he sighed, taking a sip from his wine and looking into the middle distance.

"What was she like?"

"She was very slim, with long blonde hair with a touch of ginger. Her hair took on a magic colour in the late afternoon sunlight, and her blue eyes were such a deep blue it felt like drowning when you looked into them."

"Well, Dad, – " she was going to say something but realized it wouldn't be such a good idea. He might change his mind and stop.

"Her name was Anna," he continued. "She had a very charming smile, and her laugh was ever so bubbly, so heart-refreshing. She was my first and only girlfriend before I met your mother. I never heard from her again after – "

"Why did you break up?"

"Oh, Nora, my girl, you don't know. Those were such troubled times," he sighed heavily, bent over and buried his face in his hands.

"But there must have been a reason?"

"We were so young, and we were so much in love... then the War came, things became difficult."

Nora saw tears in her father's eyes, something she had never experienced before.

"You must have loved her very much," she suggested.

"Yes, you can say that. You can most certainly say that," he said and blew his nose. "I never saw her again."

"And you never heard from her or about her?"

"Oh, once, only once. Someone told me he'd seen her with someone else, and he told me some awful things about her. I didn't believe him. He was such a bad guy himself. He just told me to hurt me. He knew I'd loved her once, so he knew he could hurt me by telling me such awful lies about her. You see, Nora dear, you couldn't trust anybody in those days. It was a terrible time." He shook his head.

Nora saw he had come to the end of his revelations about his young love. She knew it was no use pressing him for more, but she was confident that she would eventually find out more.

The subject was not mentioned again for several months, but Nora knew that her father was suffering. Their confident talk about his young love had opened a gate between them, and he must have re-opened another gate in his own memories. When nobody was watching him, Nora observed, he would often fall into a sad mood, even shaking his head to himself sometimes. She knew it was all about Anna, his memories of her and what he'd heard about her later. She didn't know why she knew. She just knew.

Meanwhile, her life happily went on with Debbie and her other friends. The spring showers became rarer and the weather turned warmer every day.

It was in early June when the blow fell. The shocking news about her friend Janet struck like lightning, and it changed her group of friends forever.

NINE

Nora had only just reached the classroom when she sensed the strange atmosphere. Everyone was quiet, there were only some whisperings and a few silent coughs. One girl sniffed into her handkerchief.

Debbie looked at her with a questioning face and shrugged her shoulders. She obviously didn't know anything either.

When the class was ready for the school day, Miss Wallace, their form teacher, entered and sat down at her desk to go about her task of registration. Nora looked around and noticed that Janet was absent. When Miss Wallace came to Janet's name she didn't read it out aloud waiting for the girl's response but only quickly murmured something and immediately proceeded to the next name on her list. After registration, Nora expected Miss Wallace to make some sort of announcement because it was obvious that there was something going on concerning Janet.

Miss Wallace looked at her pupils with a stern face, her eyes travelling just slightly above their heads from one end of the classroom to the other. Then she left without another word.

Everyone looked around for explanations. Nora suspected that some of her classmates must have more information because the strange atmosphere had been there before registration, before Miss Wallace's obvious neglect or omission of Janet's name.

If Janet was ill the school must have known, but it still wasn't the usual procedure when one of the pupils was ill. There had to be another reason behind Janet's absence. Suddenly, Nora felt very uneasy.

"I hope nothing serious happened to her," Debbie breathed into Nora's ear. But before she could answer, Mr Brathwaite, their English teacher, stepped in and immediately began to ask them about their reading for the day. Still no word about Janet. So they had no choice but to go along with whatever was required of them in the various lessons of the day. When the lunch-break came, all the pupils stood together in groups, wildly chatting and wondering what could have happened.

It was in the early afternoon between Latin and maths that a rumour emerged. "Janet got herself knocked up by a boy," was the way it was communicated. When, towards the end of the school day, the rumour hardened into certainty because Sophie had overheard two teachers discussing what had meanwhile grown into a big scandal in the corridor when she was on her way to the toilet, Nora and her friends were shocked. It felt like the outbreak of some terrible natural catastrophe, like an earthquake. It was clear to every pupil of the school, and especially to those in Nora's class, that their world would never be the same again.

After school, Nora and Debbie sat down on a park-bench and stared ahead, at a loss for words, before they approached the delicate subject.

"Did you have any idea?" Debbie began.

"No. Did you?"

"Of course not. And she never even gave a hint."

"Well, how could she? This is going to ruin her life forever."

"How do you mean?" Nora asked, surprised. "I know this is a big scandal, and things are certainly going to be difficult for her, but I don't think it'll necessarily ruin her life. Once there is another scandal it'll all be forgotten, and she can go on with her life."

"You have no idea. Everybody is going to pounce on her from their moral high ground. The school's going to dismiss her, and no one is going to give her a job. Besides, she won't have time for either school or work. She'll have to look after her baby."

Nora went home, lost in thought, wondering what was going to happen to Janet. When she entered the kitchen, her mother looked at her with a stern face. "You've heard?" she asked. So the scandal had spread like a wildfire in the African bush.

"It's so unfair," Nora said. "Why do people treat her like that? She hasn't done anything wrong. She's just allowed a boy to do things with her. She probably didn't know what it could lead to. I know her, she's very naive. Most probably her parents haven't even told her the facts of life yet."

"That's a cheap excuse. A girl knows perfectly well how far to go."

"Obviously, Janet didn't know. Or do you think she wanted this?"

"Nora dear, I know she's one of your friends. But how can you be so certain? She gave me the impression that she was asking for it, you know, the way she dressed and all that. She's just not our sort."

"How unfair of you, Mum! Just because her parents don't make the same money as you! She's my friend, and her outfits are just cheaper than mine, but they're always decent."

"I seem to remember she was practically naked when you sat together in your group in the park last summer. That's just to make the boys look at her, if you ask me."

"Mum! That was on a hot summer's day! I had my bathing suit on, too, and so we all had. Hers was a very nice bikini, and that was perfectly decent. I thought she looked great in it, with her figure."

"Well, did she have to taunt the boys with her breasts nearly jumping out of her top?"

"She didn't do anything of the sort. And it's certainly not her fault if her boobs are bigger than most other girls' in our group, now is it? Are you going to give me an operation to cut me down to size when I grow bigger?"

"Don't be silly, my girl! I can see what I can see. She just doesn't belong here. She belongs to the Jesmond lot."

This was too much for Nora. She had really tried to discuss the matter reasonably, but her mother's attitude disappointed her. She felt abandoned with her view of the world. She stood in the kitchen for a few more moments, utterly speechless, before she rushed out, slamming the door behind her.

It was later, when she lay on her bed, thinking of the events of the day, that she turned her mind to Janet and her predicament. She was convinced it was Jeff Benson. Then she tried to imagine Janet and Jeff making love. Where could they have done that: in her house in Osborne Road or at his home? Did they really know what they were doing? Or were they just carried away by their wonderful feelings? She remembered her fragmentary attempts with Ned, their kisses, Ned's eager hands on her breasts, their passionate embraces, but she simply couldn't imagine how she could ever lose herself so far as to allow a boy to go the whole hog. Janet must have this experience now. Did this make her more grown-up?

Over the next few days, the scandal of the lower-class girl who got herself pregnant by a good-for-nothing boy was all over the community. People were shaking their heads over such low morals, parents were warning their daughters of any sexual activities with boys, and the teachers in Nora's school only spoke in whispers about the delicate subject, whispers that could be overheard by most pupils anyway. They were probably intended to be heard, Nora thought. They followed a strategy of keeping up an atmosphere of a horrible natural catastrophe that was just too awful to be discussed in the open, but too juicy to be avoided altogether. Besides, Nora suspected the teachers of welcoming such a scandal which served to cement their power, to strengthen their position of a more elevated moral authority. They worked in close collaboration with the church people. The canon of the local church came and spoke to the whole school in three successive morning assemblies. Of course, he didn't take such filthy words as "sex" or "pregnant" in his mouth, his hypocritical rhetoric meandered around all sorts of phrases from the Bible, and the only half-way intelligible message to the pupils consisted of a thundering warning. He warned them of parties that lasted into the night, he warned them of the consumption of alcohol, he warned them of mixed camping holidays and he warned them of what he called indecent clothing. The rest of his babblings were lost. Nora asked Debbie if any of it had made sense to her.

"Well, not really, except the bits about booze and parties. But don't worry. He had his great field day."

"The worst thing about it all," Nora concluded, "is the fact that nobody seems to care for poor Janet. They're just pouncing on her like a pack of hungry wolves."

The issue of Janet's pregnancy had a series of consequences for Nora and her view of her mother's world and indeed of the entire society in which she lived. She considered the reactions of those in authority callous and hypocritical. From this day onward, she decided to ignore any advice or warnings issued by either the teachers or the churchmen. As for her parents, she overheard a conversation between them which showed her that while her mother was as hysterical as her teachers, her father took a much more enlightened view. She heard him even plead for Janet. "The poor girl needs help," she heard him say.

His wife answered, “A good hiding, that’s what she needs, if you ask me!”

Thus, Nora lost all respect for those in power. Also, she made it her special task to take Janet’s side, to remain a good friend to her, to be there when she needed someone to talk to. And she decided to stand up for her in discussions. No girl deserved to be talked about the way Janet was talked about.

Unfortunately, it became more difficult to keep in touch with Janet because her good friend was not only dismissed from their school. She was also banned from Nora’s home by Mother’s decree. “I won’t have such low riff-raff from Jesmond in my house. No working-class slut is going to corrupt my daughters.” However, what the mother didn’t realize was the fact that such strong language had the opposite effect on Nora. It confirmed her resolution to stay in touch with Janet at all costs, even if Janet had been a working-class girl, which she wasn’t.

Over the next few weeks, while the scandal was artificially kept hot by the righteous people of Gosforth, Nora managed to escape the common witch-hunt and sneaked over to Jesmond to visit her friend Janet, who was rather shy and downcast at first, clearly feeling guilty, but who gradually regained more self-confidence in their meetings. She found a place in a different school, a comparatively new type called a secondary modern school, where the headmaster was informed about her “condition” from the outset and promised to protect her from accusations by teachers or pupils. He even promised to defend her in front of other parents in their meetings. While Nora was glad to be at her own school because of the academic excellence offered there, she couldn’t help feeling a little envious of Janet at her new school, which was obviously more tolerant and more humane.

When Nora told Debbie that she was still seeing Janet, Debbie congratulated her. On one of her next walks across the park in the direction of Osborne Road, Debbie accompanied her. When both of them arrived, Janet was overjoyed. And from now on the three girls maintained their friendship, a friendship based on mutual confidence and on common moral experience. It was to last for many years.

***

In Nora's family, the question of Dad's proposed business trip to Germany became the most important issue debated over the dinner table. He had mentioned such a possibility on various occasions before, and Nora had always wondered why this should be such a big deal. Business people often went on business trips. Dad had been on trips back to the States several times since their move to Britain, and he had been to other countries like France, Belgium and Norway, but never to Germany.

"Why are you discussing this with us?" she asked one evening over their cold supper. "Is there any special challenge for you? Do you have any problems with your German business partners?"

"Oh no," her father answered, "it's not that. I'm just a bit worried about travelling by air, you know, with all those terrorist attacks these days."

"What terrorist attacks?"

"Well, you remember last year's IRA attacks, the Aldershot bombing and the black September, don't you?"

"Of course. But when you travelled to all those other places you weren't worried. Why now?"

"Listen," her mother interrupted. "Don't use such an arrogant tone to your father."

When the father had left the dining room for his study, Nora took up the matter again with her mother. "I just want to know what's so special about a simple business trip to Germany. That's all."

Mother hesitated before she answered. "You know your father originally came from Germany. So he's a bit worried about the language. He doesn't like to admit it, but he's not too confident about his German, which is not only antiquated but also mixed with Swiss German, a thing the Germans will laugh at."

"Okay, I see," Nora mumbled, but she sensed that there was more behind the issue and decided to let the matter rest for the time being.

A few days later, the topic came up again. Dad announced he would definitely fly to Germany in a few weeks' time. He simply had to go to the Leipzig Trade Fair, the world's oldest trade fair, going back to the twelfth century, the most important venue for business contacts between East and West during the Cold War. In his position it was of the highest importance that he should meet some important men who worked for East Germany's state-controlled industry. A whole new market was opening up for many Western companies now that the treaties between West Germany and the Soviet Union had been signed and ratified.

"So, you're no longer worried that people will laugh at your accent?" Nora teased him.

"I have it from the East German Embassy in London that they will treat me as an official guest, which will give me VIP status. So I should be met with the necessary respect."

"Was it really only that?" Nora persisted.

"Well, my girl, if you want to know the truth, I was – and I still am – a bit worried about my past experience. You know I was in a concentration camp towards the end of the War, so my name might still appear on some old lists."

"From my understanding of history, they should rather treat you as a hero if they find out about your time in a concentration camp."

There was a slight twitch in his shoulder. "You don't understand. Things got so muddled up at the end of the War. They might want to put me in prison by mistake, and once you're in you can't get out so easily in East Germany."

Nora accepted this. Even though she had learnt quite a lot of facts about the War, about Nazi Germany and about the concentration camps, she had to admit to herself that the reality in people's minds was often bound to be more complicated or even chaotic. She began to feel more sympathetic towards her father and his latent fears.

A month later, Didi Woolf left Newcastle on a five-day business trip to Leipzig. When Margaret and Nora sat down for a sisterly chat after the evening meal, Margaret asked, "Don't you think Dad was a bit nervous about his trip when we said good-bye?"

Nora hesitated before answering. "Yes, and he told me why. It's because people in Germany might misinterpret his role during the War. You know he was in a concentration camp?"

"Oh, I see. But why do you keep pestering him about all that? Don't you know he doesn't like to talk about those years and all the horrible things he must have experienced? Can't you leave him alone?"

"I never pestered him. I'm just interested in history. And he was a witness to important events in modern history. So why can't he tell us more?"

"Simply because it hurts him too much. You have no idea of what a bad trauma can do to people." Margaret got quite worked up over this.

"Okay okay, hold your horses. You are not interested in history, but I am. Let's just agree to disagree over this."

The sisters didn't like to quarrel. Nora accepted the fact that Margaret just wasn't interested in recent history as much as she was. She also came to the conclusion that, perhaps, she was being a little unfair towards her father. After all, if he had really suffered at the hands of the Nazis, one could understand that he didn't particularly enjoy talking about his ordeal.

So when their father returned from his business trip, the daughters welcomed him with the usual warm feelings, and Nora didn't press him for any tales from Germany.

A few days after his return, however, Dad opened up the topic himself. They were sitting around their living-room, the mother doing some knitting – an activity she had only recently taken up again after having neglected it since her childhood – and the girls lounging on the sofa with their books, while their father had just finished reading the papers. He usually read *The Times* and *The Guardian* – sometimes also *The Financial Times* – in the evening, often taking quite a long time to get through his papers, probably reading every bit of news. Tonight, he was through with them after only half an hour. Outside, it was raining and there was a heavy wind.

"I say, it's truly amazing what the Germans have achieved, how far they have developed their country since the War."

"Even in the East, the GDR?" Nora wanted to know.

"Well, not so much in the GDR, but things are a lot better in the West. I can tell you, there's a big difference."

"But weren't you in Leipzig, which is in the GDR?"

"Yes, that's where the trade fair was, and that's where I spent most of my time. But I had the opportunity to visit the West, too. I realized I could see an old acquaintance in Stuttgart. Someone I thought might become useful if things got unpleasant for me in Germany."

"Oh, that's interesting," his wife interjected. "You never told me you'd still got people you knew in Germany. Who is he?"

"You wouldn't know him, although he's quite high in German politics. His name is Hans. He's high up in one of their federal states called *Bundesländer*."

"You're right there. I don't even know their president or prime minister or any other big shot. But did you actually see him? And did he remember you?"

"Yes, he was surprised to see me. He was surprised that I had survived."

"How did you know him back in the War?" Nora wanted to know.

"Well, I could do him a few favours back then, I think it was in 1944. He was a judge, and I was assigned to do a few jobs for him. Nothing to write home about, though. I don't really remember any details. It's too long ago."

"But you remembered the man, and he remembered you?"

"Yes. We had a chat in his office in Stuttgart. He explained a lot of things to me, you know, about Germany in general, about the way modern Germany, I mean the Federal Republic, the *Bundesrepublik*, has dealt with its recent history. They've even coined a new word for it, long and typically German. It's called *Vergangenheitsbewältigung*. Now, that's a mouthful for you, isn't it?"

"It means getting to terms with your past," Nora explained. "We had it in our history lessons. Mr Jackson explained it to us."

"How clever you are, my girl," Mum said. "The things you know..."

"Hans explained how, ever since the student riots of '68, the political left have gone over the top in blaming almost everyone who happened to be alive during the War. It's all organized by the Communists, of course. His motto, 'What was lawful then cannot be unlawful now,' has become quite a catchphrase, and the Socialists have interpreted it all too seriously, accusing him and many others of our generation of being dishonest. Naturally, many people in Germany who had been there during the War had to re-shape their own past a little, you know, nobody was safe when the Allies took over. Hans explained how he was accused by his political opponents for mendacity and perjury. Of course, everyone had to invent a few small lies. In English we would call them white lies, wouldn't we?"

"Well, that obviously depends on the gravity of their wrong-doings," Nora commented. But before she could ask more detailed questions he went on.

"Hans took me to a fine restaurant in Stuttgart, where everyone knew him. We had some very wholesome German food. It was so delicious, I can tell you. If we had restaurants like that in Newcastle, your Mum and I would go out for a meal more often."

Nora tried to steer the conversation back to the topic of Dad's old friend in Stuttgart, she wanted to know more about their roles in the War, but he had moved away from politics and went on with his praises for German cuisine. He couldn't be stopped in his descriptions of the various dishes that were unknown to people in Newcastle.

After this revelation, Dad didn't return to the topic of the War and the Nazis, and the right moment to ask him more questions had gone.

In the following weeks, Nora didn't often have time for her interest in history because maths was becoming more and more demanding. She had to do a lot of extra work in order to understand their new topic of equations. While she thought she understood what was being demanded, she just couldn't transform the practical problem at hand into a mathematical equation. And when she did manage, she had problems to solve the equation. She often forgot that you had to do exactly the same transformation on both sides of the equation. So, she often struggled. She knew she had to concentrate on her maths if she wanted to succeed in her O-Levels, which were approaching pretty fast. This new focus on maths downgraded her history to a lower priority.

Nevertheless, she sometimes remembered what her father had told her about his meeting with his old acquaintance in Stuttgart. She just didn't have the time and energy to explore more. After all, her father appeared to be quite relieved that his German trip had gone so well. There had been no more talk about his Swiss accent in German or his German accent in English. Nora knew how German accents were caricatured in English cartoons and even in some modern English novels, usually written by authors who didn't know much about languages but just catered for the general cliché, where every German character mixed up the sounds for "v" and "w" and couldn't pronounce the "th" sound, something she had experienced more with Americans back in Chicago than with real live German visitors. In fact, to her ears the German accent was better audible in the staccato rhythm and the different intonation, sometimes in inaccurate vowels – for example, many Germans would say "bed" for "bad" – but otherwise it sounded more like an Irish accent. Besides, she wondered why the English always had such a thing about people's accents, as if it was some serious flaw in one's character if one had some sort of an accent.

Soon, there was another matter that demanded her attention more fully: Janet's baby. It was expected to be born any day now. Nora went to Janet's house more often, sometimes with Debbie, sometimes on her own. Janet told them that everything was as it should be, and the three girls were all looking forward to the arrival of the new human being.

Over the past few months, Janet's parents had given her every possible support. Things had been negotiated with Jeff's parents resulting in Jeff's recognition of his part in the situation. Neither Jeff nor Janet were contemplating a permanent relationship with a view to a future marriage but admitted that the baby was the result of "just a short fling". Thus, it was agreed that the baby should grow up in Janet's home and Jeff's parents were willing to contribute a small sum towards its upbringing. Jeff insisted that the child, once in a position to understand these things, should know him as its father. He was hoping for a girl, while Janet said she would love her child no matter if it was going to be a boy or a girl. Janet's mother said a boy would be easier, girls were known to be more difficult with their changing moods and their hot tempers.

Janet's headmaster gave her ample time off and promised to take her back when she was ready after the birth of the baby. He explained to her parents why he was taking this firm stand towards the board of governors and towards all the parents who objected to such "immoral" practice. The reason was that his own sister had been in a similar predicament back in the fifties, and her school had only made things worse instead of helping her. She had been evicted and sent to a home for "fallen women", a measure which had caused nothing but misery and trauma. It was then that he had vowed that he would act differently if he should ever be in a position to make such relevant decisions.

All in all probably the best of all possible solutions for Janet and her baby, Nora thought. She found that she was looking forward to the baby very much, and of course the situation strengthened the bond of friendship between them.

Soon the time was upon them. It was a cool October evening, and the three girls were sitting in Janet's bedroom, sipping tea and telling each other what they had read in the papers and seen on TV about Sheik Yamani, their new star in international politics. For quite a while they had all heard about the so-called oil crisis due to an Arab oil embargo, and Nora had read about petrol shortages in several countries. Debbie had read that people were banned from using their cars on certain Sundays in many countries, all because of the petrol shortages. And the man behind all that was believed to be Sheik Yamani, the new president of the OPEC, the Organization of the Petroleum Exporting Countries, already founded in 1960, but hardly taken notice of up to now. Sheik Yamani had only recently begun to use oil as a political tool by exercising pressure on the economies of the Western World. The girls admired this courage, as they believed, and they considered the Sheik an extremely good-looking man. Almost every day he could be seen in the news on TV, strutting through a thick throng of journalists, swinging his prayer beads in his right hand, a confident smile on his face, fully aware of how completely he was holding half the world hostage.

"My mother thinks Yamani is a criminal," Debbie said.

"My parents don't care," Nora added. "Dad says things will blow over after a few months and the oil price will drop again. Mum says she's not interested in politics, and after all we can afford the higher price for a gallon of petrol."

"My Dad is furious," Janet said, but stopped immediately. She moaned and placed both her hands on her swollen belly. "I think this is it..."

She stood up to go to the toilet, and they all saw the wetness where she'd been sitting. Nora ran down to tell Janet's mother to call an ambulance. The waters had broken.

Everything went very quickly. Janet was rushed to hospital by ambulance, Nora and Debbie followed soon after by bus, and four hours later the baby was born. The two friends were allowed, together with Janet's mother, to see Janet in the Maternity Ward for a quick visit. Janet was utterly exhausted but very happy, with sweat all over her face. After being hugged by her mother, she gave her two best friends a weak smile and wiped away a tear from her cheek.

"It's a boy," she breathed.

TEN

It was the year 1986. The month of January started off quite mild, but from about the 18th the mercury dropped and soon the snow arrived. By the 23rd, most of Europe was covered in a thick layer of snow, and England was no exception.

Nora wrapped herself in her thickest winter coat and a stylish woollen scarf she had got from Laura Ashley's only the week before. She absolutely hated the cold, and she always felt it more acutely than most of her friends, probably because she didn't have a lot of fat on her bones to keep her warm, not at all like Debbie, who had developed quite a plump figure over the past few years. No, Nora had accepted the fact that most people considered her to be one of those silly young women who nearly starved themselves to death because they wanted to conform to the measurements of the latest fashion model. In her case, it was just her natural shape.

As she was walking through the High Street, heading for the coffee shop where she was to meet a Mrs Thornton, she noted that there were relatively few people around, fewer than normal for this time of day. This was probably because of the cold weather plus the fact that people's purses were often at a low level in January, with little to spare, so the usual shoppers must prefer to stay at home and warm themselves in their houses.

She entered the coffee shop just as the machine behind the counter was issuing a loud hissing sound as it was being operated by a young man with black hair and a thick black beard. He was dressed in the standard black t-shirt, jeans and a green gardener's apron with the coffee company's logo in front.

As she was looking round, she detected a middle-aged woman waving at her from the back of the room. Nora walked up to her. "Mrs Thornton, I presume?"

"Yes, not quite Dr Livingstone," the woman smiled, indicating a seat opposite her.

"Pleased to meet you in person," Nora said, the women shook hands, and Nora took off her thick coat, placing it over the back of the chair. "I'll be with you straightaway, I'll just get myself a cup of coffee."

When Nora had her cappuccino and was sitting comfortably opposite Mrs Thornton, the two women prepared the atmosphere with some small-talk before they eventually came to the topic at hand.

"So, you want to do some part-time work for us?" Mrs Thornton enquired.

"Yes, if that is at all possible," Nora answered cheerfully. She wondered at herself, at her calm absence of nervousness.

"We're always looking for good translators. Since many of our publications are translated from other languages we need a lot of good ones. Unfortunately, many young language students just don't come up to our expectations, so we're looking for experienced professionals like yourself. We've had a good look at the material you sent us, and of course at your qualifications and your CV. It's very impressive. Dr Armstrong, our chief editor, was particularly impressed by the quality of your early translations, you know the bits from Lampedusa's *Gattopardo* that you did while still at university."

"Really? I thought they were youthful exaggerations of what I took for *Italianità* at the time."

"Well, Dr Armstrong considered them very subtle and introspective, especially for a young person that you must have been then. Plus, of course, he was glad to see such able work coming from a graduate of his own university."

"He was at York, too, then?" Nora smiled.

"Yes, indeed. And he often reminds us of the fact that people up north are so much friendlier than down here."

They discussed more aspects of the work that Nora would be expected to do for this publishing house. She was to work as a translator, a part-time job she was hoping to be able to do from her home. She really needed a proper professional challenge to fill her time and fulfil her intellectual ambitions, especially with George away from home so much and with young Andrew needing her at home. She wasn't going to be one of those incompetent mothers who neglected their young children by just plonking them down in front of the goggle-box while gallivanting around town all the time. She wanted to combine her role of a good mother with her professional ambitions.

"So it is agreed, then," Mrs Thornton stated. "You're ready to start at once, and you're willing to take on translations from French, German and Italian?"

"Yes, quite so."

"And the pay is ok for you, at least for the first six months?"

"Yes, that's okay."

Mrs Thornton was beginning to gather her things from the chair beside her.

"We'll send you your contract tomorrow, and once we get it back, countersigned by you, we'll send you the first text immediately. It's going to be one of Kleist's short stories, or novellas, as the experts call them."

"Is this the Kohlhaas novella?"

"Yes, I think it is. Oh, and by the way, is it okay if I call you Nora?"

"That's fine by me, I still haven't got used to being Mrs White," Nora confessed.

"Oh yes," Mrs Thornton quickly added, "before I forget it. We're planning to phase out typewriters. Can you work with a computer? The Kleist text is probably going to be our last text in the old typewritten version. The company is going to give you a Commodore computer for you to use at home, since you work from home, and the texts will come on floppy disks. Is this going to be a problem for you?"

"It shouldn't be," Nora replied. "My husband already works with computers at Gatwick Airport. So he has some experience and he'll be able to help me initially."

"I'm glad to hear it. Well then, I must be off."

The women shook hands again, and Mrs Thornton left the coffee shop in a hurry. Then she disappeared from view among the people in the High Street. The town centre of Horsham had become a bit busier during the time Nora spent in the coffee shop.

Nora walked to the car park, squeezed herself behind the wheel – an unusual but necessary effort because she was wearing her thickest coat and it was too cold to sit in her little car without her coat – and started the engine. She was glad she had this new car, which started even in these cold conditions. When she was younger, especially as a student in York, she'd had a series of what people would call "old bangers", rusty old wrecks which were cheap but often caused problems. When they moved down south and bought their new house in the outskirts of this charming market town, George got her this new VW Golf. She considered herself fortunate. Not only because George was making good money but because they had such a good marriage and such a lovely home.

Sometimes she would miss Newcastle, York, the North East, the Geordie accent, the sooty smell in the air, the black houses and what she considered a different light up north, but generally she was very happy down here, even though she hadn't seen very much of the countryside around Sussex. It was such an ideal location, within easy reach of London, near Gatwick Airport – where George worked – and even not too far away from the sea, Brighton, Worthing, Beachy Head and such lovely spots. There was still a lot to explore for her. Once little Andrew was a bit older she would be able to take him for strolls along the coast. That would be wonderful. She smiled to herself.

As she was driving through Horsham she suddenly remembered that she had meant to call her mother about a recipe for apple pie. Her mother had always made the best apple pie, so now Nora was hoping to emulate her mother's baking skills for her little boy. Andrew was going to be two in March, and he loved his cakes, so an apple pie would be the right thing for his dinner on his birthday.

Back in her new home, Nora took off her thick coat and her boots before she sat down and dialled her mother's number.

"Hello, my darling," Mum was delighted. "How are you, and how's little Andy?"

"He's called Andrew, Mum. I don't like you to call him Andy. I hate it when people use stupid short forms of names, it's an American thing."

"Well, I *am* American, and besides it's done in this country, too."

"Okay, okay, Mum. To answer your question, yes we're all right."

"Have you settled in by now? I always said it was a mistake to move away from your family. You could have built up a life for yourself in York, or even back here."

"But George couldn't. As you know, his expertise lies in airport management, the logistics of airports. Can't you see that Gatwick is much more interesting than the provincial little airport of Newcastle?"

"I only mean it would be nice to have you nearer."

"Thanks, Mum. Now, what I was going to ask you is your recipe for your delicious apple pie. Can you write it down and let me have it? I'd like to attempt one for Andrew's birthday."

"I'll see what I can do for you. I'll have to think about it so I can write it down. You know, it's all just automatic. When I make one it just comes natural..."

"I see. But I'd really be very glad."

"All right then, my darling."

"Is everything okay? Dad okay?"

"Well, I don't know."

"What do you mean, you don't know?"

"He seems to have some sort of problem with one of his German acquaintances. He doesn't like to talk about it."

"Has it got to do with his old friend in Stuttgart? You know, the one he said was high up in German politics?"

"Oh no. Don't you know? You must have been at university when it happened, so you didn't get the story at the time."

"What story? Tell me."

"Well, what happened to his friend. He was denounced, I think it was about eight years ago. He lost his position, and he was accused of being an old Nazi. It was even in the English papers, quite a big scandal."

"I'm sorry, I must have missed it. But how did it affect Dad?"

"I don't know all of it, and your father doesn't like to talk about it. But I think he felt he was losing his support in Germany."

Nora realized that her mother didn't know much, so she decided to abandon the subject. She added a few general remarks and soon rang off.

She made herself a cup of tea. She allowed herself another half hour of peace and quiet before she was going to pick up Andrew from Lucy, her next-door neighbour who often helped to look after the little boy when Nora had to go out.

Over her tea, she tried to concentrate on what she remembered about her father and his involvement with Germany. Before she left school, back in Newcastle, she'd often had a chat with him and he'd told her more than he would her mother. But once she'd left for university she no longer had the opportunity. Meanwhile, her father visited Germany several times, always on business, and Nora herself spent four months in Hamburg to improve her German – just as she spent a few months in Montpellier for her French – before she took her degree in modern languages at York University. Her father's connection with Germany had somehow drifted into the background of her mind. Now she remembered her eager interest in her father's past in Germany which she'd kept when she was a young teenager, but which she'd lost years ago.

So, he had some problems now, if she could believe her mother. What problems could those be? If his old friend, the Stuttgart politician, could no longer be of any help for him, then what? What did Dad need any support for? Didn't he just do his business in Germany? Nora decided to ask him when she saw him next time. He said he would come down to London in February. They would be able to meet up either in London or at Gatwick. Yes, she would ask him then.

The rest of her day was filled with household chores and playing sessions with little Andrew. At half-past five, George came home.

"Hello, my darling," he shouted from the hall. "Have you heard the news? A terrible catastrophe! The Space Shuttle exploded."

They turned on the television and watched the six o'clock news. They were speechless when they saw the pictures of the explosion in the blue American morning sky. They felt pity for the families of the astronauts who were watching it all from the ground and who first believed it was some spectacular special effect, like fireworks on the 4th of July.

"Wasn't there a teacher on board? A teacher who was going to report to the American school children from space?"

"This is like the *Titanic*," George said.

"Not really," Nora remarked. "There were many more innocent passengers on the *Titanic* who perished in the cold ocean, and these are only eight astronauts who knew the risks."

"I don't mean in terms of numbers, but in its symbolic significance," he insisted. "Look at the names. The Titans were mythological creatures who challenged the ancient gods, and this space shuttle was also called Challenger. So, as far as I can see, in both cases it was Humanity who was challenging Nature, and Nature checked Humanity in its attempt. It was a warning for Humanity who was in danger of overreaching itself, its potential."

"I can see what you mean. But the religious innuendo goes too far for my taste."

They watched more programmes that dealt with the Challenger explosion. The various TV stations brought discussions with experts, historical overviews of space travel, repeated pictures of the explosion and even, for the sentimental touch, replays of interviews they had made with the astronauts before the fateful day, especially interviews with that teacher. Nora and George watched the entire evening, having a cold supper on their laps in front of the TV. In between programmes Nora rushed upstairs to give little Andrew his supper and put him to bed. Fortunately, the child was so tired that he fell asleep immediately and his mother could return to the screen without having missed very much.

From that day onward, Nora kept the Challenger accident in her mind in a strange nexus with her position in life. Even years afterwards, she would remember the date not only as the day of the Challenger explosion but also of the start to her new life, even the beginning of her responsible adult existence. It was strange but true that such a watershed feeling hadn't overcome her at the moment of little Andrew's birth, but only now, so relatively late in her life. What had gone before now appeared as a mere extension of her childhood, whereas her days after that date belonged to her real life. She was an adult human being, a wife, a mother and a professional translator of literature. It didn't bother her personal categorising mind that she had to reach almost her 28th birthday to attain this level.

Once the weather thawed, Nora felt more elated about her newly found role. She often went for walks with Andrew in his buggy. Sometimes, she left him with Lucy and went for a longer walk by herself. Like this, she could think more clearly.

Her walks took her out of Horsham, along narrow bridle-paths towards the expansive fields of Christ's Hospital. The relative tranquillity of the green fields with their red brick buildings in the distance and the consciousness of the proximity of such an ancient institution of education and learning both had a soothing effect on her. Here, at last, she could review her situation in life. Every day she walked across the green fields, sometimes closer to the anachronistic brick-buildings, sometimes more through the open countryside, sometimes near the railway-line close-by.

On one occasion she happened to come very close to one end of the main row of brick-buildings. She saw a group of pupils in their terribly uncomfortable and old-fashioned black

– she believed she'd read somewhere that they called it blue – uniform with their yellow knee-socks. A middle-aged man with NHS glasses, black hair with a few grey streaks and a flushed face wearing a gown of sorts – probably a house-master – was calling out to the pupils, who turned back to where they'd come from. The seemingly blind obedience of the pupils and the distant incomprehensibility of the house-master's orders somehow reminded her of Jacques Tati and the tourists at the French railway station in *Les Vacances de Monsieur Hulot*, and this helped her to see everything with a touch of humour. It was like watching a ballet performance without music, a well-planned and carefully-rehearsed dumb-show.

Time and her walks eventually helped her to regain some degree of balance. Up till now, she realized, she had always kept the image of her father as a moral authority. Whatever she did she measured against his principles, or what she believed to be his principles. But now, at last, she found that she could cope quite well without that self-alleged anchor in her childhood. Now, at last, she had emancipated herself from her parents, especially from her father. As for her mother, Nora had long given up taking her seriously.

On another occasion, she came across a pair of pupils who had obviously escaped from their prescribed territory and the stern house-master's watchful eye. They were a boy and a girl, probably about fifteen or sixteen years old. They appeared so absorbed in their secretive togetherness that they were completely unaware of Nora's proximity. She stopped in her walk and stepped behind the concealing branches of a bush because she did not want to disturb them. As she stood behind the bush she felt she had to hold her breath, fully aware of the importance of this moment for these young people. They were behind one of the regular brick-buildings, on the back side where nobody could see them – except Nora.

As if by mutual consent they began to embrace, and their shy kisses began tentatively, but gradually gained in confidence and energy. The boy pushed the girl against the brick wall and ran his hands up and down her sides, while the girl stroked the back of the boy's head, and their heads moved from side to side in the growing passion of their kisses. They looked ridiculous since their outdated school-uniforms clashed with their actions. They looked like a pair of medieval dignitaries engaged in a forbidden ritual. Nora found herself wondering what could possibly be the fun of caressing each other through those extremely uncomfortable thick coats. And when the boy pushed his right knee between the girl's legs and she lifted her left leg slightly to make room for his urgent desire the yellowness of their socks nearly produced a snort of suppressed laughter from Nora.

The young couple continued kissing in much the same way as they had begun, and Nora accustomed herself to the fact that they would probably be going on like this for quite a while, perhaps for hours or until they might be found out by the house-master. So she decided to withdraw quietly. She trod very carefully as she walked away in the opposite direction, so as not to disturb the youthful lovers. As she glanced back from a distance of some fifty yards or so, she thought the girl might be looking at her without really seeing her, looking through her, as it were, or looking right into her soul. The young girl's eyes, in a dream-like trance induced by the passion of kissing, entered Nora's soul and hit her right at the centre of a sensitive spot.

It occurred to her that she had been about the same age as that girl when she'd kissed a boy for the first time in her life. While she felt a lot older and wiser now, at the same time she found herself envying the younger girl's experience, the passionate kissing. Nora had seen kissing scenes and even the occasional sex scene in French films – though never explicitly

– but she had never felt as she felt now. Somehow, that girl's passion touched her and made her yearn for her lost childhood.

Thus, Nora entered her adult life and began to regret the loss of her childhood all within a few weeks, the heavily significant weeks following the Challenger catastrophe.

***

The meeting with her father took place at Gatwick Airport at the end of February. They had arranged to have lunch at Garfunkel's in the South Terminal.

"And how's my little grandson?" Dad began, once they sat down at the table and got the business of ordering their food behind them.

"He's great. He's learning new words every day. It's fantastic to see his amazing development."

They talked about various insignificant things before Nora zoomed in on the topic that was so important for her. "Do you still go to Germany regularly?" she wanted to know.

"Not as much as I used to," her father answered.

"You know, I used to take a very keen interest in modern history, so I often wanted to ask you more about your time in Nazi Germany. But I've lost that interest over the past few years."

"There wasn't such a lot to tell anyway."

"Well, I often wondered. And now Mum tells me that you had some problems when you were in Germany the last time. What happened?"

The father busied himself with the food, which had just arrived on the table between them, before he answered.

"You see, I was wrong to rely on my old acquaintance Hans. Once he fell from grace in seventy-eight, I realized I hadn't played my cards very well."

"Why did you need your friend anyway?"

The father couldn't help a slight twitch in his shoulder. "I believed he could protect me from bad rumours. But as it turned out, he couldn't."

"Why did you think you needed such protection?"

"Oh, my dear girl! Back in the old days, under the Nazi régime, we all did certain things that we weren't really proud of after the War."

"Yes. On a small scale, I can understand that. It must have been difficult or even dangerous to oppose the system openly. The only option was probably emigration."

"That wasn't an option for me and my family."

They were silent for a while, enjoying their hamburgers and chips, brooding over what had been said. At last Nora took it up again.

"So what difficulties are you having now?"

"I don't know if there'll be any difficulties, but there's that awful fellow who's pursuing me. He seems to have tracked me down, and now he's trying to blame me for things I'd never done."

"Do you know the man personally?"

"Well, yes. He used to be a sort of friend when we were children, his name is Wolfgang."

"How did he track you down? Did you visit your home town?"

"Oh no, he must have gone to great lengths. You see, I'd changed my name after the War. It used to be Wolff, with one o and two fs, one of the German forms of the name, and when I was in Switzerland I found that the people hated the Germans, so I changed it to the English form, Woolf. But that didn't prevent him from finding me. One day, in Leipzig, as I was checking into my hotel, he suddenly stood in front of me. I was so shocked."

"What did he say?"

"First, he just stood there, smiling in an arrogant and cheeky way, as if he was some great criminal who'd just found his victim. I recognized him immediately. He'd always been an unpleasant bully, and the War hadn't changed him, obviously."

"What did he want from you? What did he have against you?"

The father hesitated before he answered, "That is a complicated affair. Let's not talk about it."

Nora could feel that the topic was unpleasant for him, so she decided to let it be for the time. She didn't ask any more questions. They remained silent for a short while, eating up their plates of chips and looking down. Nora wondered if she should let sleeping dogs lie and just forget the subject. What did it concern her? Why should she have a right to know what terrible things her father experienced during the War?

Soon they took up their conversations again, but now they talked about Andrew and about her new job.

"I'm very proud of you, my girl," he smiled. "It was a good thing to learn all those languages. And do you remember how glad I was when you took up Latin at school? Latin is the basis for your linguistic skills."

"Of course, I remember, Dad. And yes, I admit Latin helped me a great deal, especially in grammar, but also in the vocabulary of the various languages, you know the etymology..."

"Oh, the big words my girl uses..."

They both laughed. All the former tension about the past and the bully Wolfgang was forgotten.

Nora didn't think of the touchy subject of her father's role in the past again for several weeks. She was too busy with her child, her work and her general situation in life. She still didn't feel at home in Horsham, and she still had to catch up a great deal with her sister and her old friends Debbie and Janet.

Margaret had married an American academic called Doug while Nora was still at university. He was a very bright sociologist from some American small town. They had met at university in London, got married in Newcastle and immediately moved back to the States. These days, they lived in Boston and had two children. Nora and Margaret often wrote letters to each other, sometimes they even telephoned, but that was quite expensive.

Debbie had studied history of art in London. Now she had a job with the Tate Gallery, and she lived on her own in a small flat in Hampstead. But recently, it appeared, she had started on a new relationship with a young artist called Vladimir. Nora was very curious about him. She had still not met him personally. She sincerely hoped this would be a steady thing for her good friend. Debbie had gone through a series of relationships, none of which lasted for more than a few months. Debbie herself believed that was because of her figure. She often complained to Nora that men didn't find her attractive, with her plump body, her fat bottom, her wide hips, her huge breasts, her thick arms and legs and her ugly face. Nora had to contradict her then. She felt she had to rebuild her friend's self-confidence. For Nora, Debbie looked, well, perhaps a little on the full side, but really very attractive. She was sure there had to be hundreds of men who would find her extremely good-looking, especially when she was wearing one of her artier outfits.

And then there was Janet. As long as Nora still lived up north they had kept a regular contact, at their respective homes in Gosforth and Jesmond. Later, when Nora was at York University and Janet managed to combine a catering course at some college in Hull with her role as a single mother, their contact became less regular, but they still kept it up. Now, Janet was in Bristol, where she could live with a cousin of hers called Linda, who was also a single mother and had offered to look after both children, her own girl Joanna and Janet's boy Bob. The happy arrangement was that while Linda was looking after the children and all the domestic chores, Janet would bring in the money. She didn't make a lot, but it was enough for their little household and even allowed for a few extras. The only drawback, Janet told Nora on the telephone, were her long hours. Working in catering, she often had to cover events in the evening, which meant she could only see her boy in the morning. But she was hoping for better times. Bob was twelve, and he was a lovely boy, devoted to his mother, and he often helped his "Auntie Linda", Janet's friend and flatmate.

Sometimes, Nora thought that she really had the calmest life of the three, with Debbie rushing about London's art world and Janet always being out and about at parties in Bristol, albeit in a servile capacity, but nevertheless in Bristol, the upcoming city of the young! All that while she herself was mostly at home, sitting over her books and her typewriter, soon over her new computer, delving into literary texts from all over Europe, but hardly ever going out these days. Yes, George often urged her to go out with him, but in the end, they rarely went, because their home was so comfortable, their baby so lovely and the TV programme often entertaining enough.

Most of what really mattered in a philosophical way happened in Nora's mind. In fact, she was so immersed in the dramatic stories about intrigues at Renaissance courts in Italy, about conflicts between men and women in small towns in Germany, or about jealous youths in the heat of Southern France, that she sometimes felt like waking from a dream when the news came on TV and threw her back with brutal force into the politics of the day, where she had to face the ugly images of people like Ronald Reagan or Margaret Thatcher, who, in her eyes, were about to destroy some of the best parts of Western culture.

Nora promised herself that she would bring up her own children with a better understanding of what really mattered in the world. She wanted them to learn to see behind all those lies of many politicians. She remembered how her father had taught her to recognize national pride as the seeds for nationalism and racism. She only wondered why not more people could see where things were leading when politicians went on and on about other leaders' faults, other nations' evils, merely to entice their people away from their own problems. And then there was corruption. Most African leaders and their entourage were soaked deeply in it. But where had they learnt it? Of course, from their old colonial masters, the English and French slave drivers. Nora had to pull herself away from such ruminations. She had to remind herself of what her father had taught her about the lies all those politicians were telling their people. They were just small lies, necessary lies in order to get re-elected, white lies.

ELEVEN

"Not before lunch."

"But you promised I could have an ice cream, didn't you?"

"In the first place, I never promised anything but only mentioned it as a possibility. In the second place, you know perfectly well that ice cream in the morning will only ruin your lunch."

"Is it still morning then?"

"Yes, it's only half-past eleven. We'll go for lunch in about an hour. So you've got another hour to play on the beach. Off you go! There's your sand bucket and your plastic rake still lying in the sand. Quick, before another child takes your things."

Although Andrew was only five, his mother talked to him in proper English. Sometimes she even used long and very complicated words, such as "idiosyncrasy", "perpendicular" or "disingenuous". Nora just didn't believe in baby-talk. Even when talking to little Lisa, who was going to be three this autumn, she didn't use what linguists call Motherese with that silly high-pitched sing-song intonation. Now she looked at Lisa, who was busy ordering and arranging pebbles according to some special secret plan between her pudgy legs spread wide apart in the warm sand. She observed her little daughter in her concentrated activity, wondering at the beauty of her child and taking note of the sand that stuck to her chubby knees and small shins.

While Andrew was a sturdy dark-haired boy with an extremely bright alertness, his baby-sister Lisa was a fair-haired little dreamer whose clear blue eyes struck everyone who took note of her fine face. An outsider wouldn't have taken them for siblings.

The sun was quite hot on this Saturday in August. Many mothers with little children were enjoying the summer, and Brighton was ideal for a day out on the beach. Nora felt truly happy.

She kept a watchful eye on her children, aware of her responsibility for these wonderful little human beings. She remembered how scared she had been during her pregnancy with Lisa. Andrew was a toddler, and she was expecting her second child when the threat of nuclear radiation hit them as a family. Some of her neighbours played it down, believing what some politicians told them about Chernobyl being too far away to affect their part of the world. But George knew better than the politicians. He explained how the wind could easily carry heavily radiated dust particles from so far in the east well over most of Western Europe. For several weeks, Nora didn't buy any fresh vegetables that were picked after the reactor catastrophe and no fresh milk but only long-life milk and bottled drinks. She could still feel the panic she'd felt in her heart when the full danger of that catastrophe hit her consciousness. She was pregnant, and her unborn baby might get radiated and be born terribly misshapen, a handicapped child. How relieved she'd been when, just after giving birth a few months later, she was told that Lisa was in perfectly good health. The baby was all there, in her arms, still unable to focus on her mother, sucking her thumb and making wrinkly faces at the world around her. What a relief it had been.

And now here they were: a complete family. A happy family.

They had lunch at a down-to-earth restaurant at beach level, just by the wall below the seafront parade. While Andrew was already well-trained in his eating technique and table manners, Lisa made quite a mess of her lunch, and Nora often had to give her a helping hand. But generally, the lunch went well, and they could return to their spot on the beach, where Andrew continued with the construction of his higgledy-piggledy sandcastle, while Lisa immediately fell asleep with her head in her mother's lap.

As it was getting a little cooler on the beach in the afternoon, Nora decided to head for home. She got her children safely back to the multi-storey car-park behind the Churchill Square shopping centre, buckled them up in her car, paid her fee at the machine and carefully drove out of the narrow car-park. Although the traffic was already building up, she got out of Brighton swiftly enough and reached home before five.

She was busy getting the children ready for bed while George was watching the six o'clock news on TV.

"Quick, my darling! Come and watch this," he suddenly shouted from the living-room.

It took her a moment before she could join him, so what he'd wanted her to watch had already disappeared from the screen. So she gave him a questioning look.

"It's a surprising development in Eastern Europe," he explained. "The Hungarians are letting the East German tourists out of the country, so they can escape to Western Europe. That's spectacular!"

"Why do you think that's so spectacular? Hungary has always been a half-hearted Communist country in the last few years. At least that's what my Dad told me. They seem to have abandoned some of the strict principles of the Communist system as it's being practised in the other countries behind the Iron Curtain."

"Right you are, Nora dear. But this is new. Now practically everybody from the GDR can escape to the West.

All they have to do is to travel to Hungary, which they're allowed to. This is practically a hole in the Berlin Wall."

"Do you really think that's possible? They're bound to stop the leak as soon as possible."

"I don't think that's likely. You see, there have been weekly demonstrations in many cities of the GDR lately. I think they started in Leipzig. The Church seems to be behind them. Every Monday evening, thousands of people peacefully walk through the streets. In Leipzig they've started to chant a slogan. I don't speak German, but on TV they said the slogan goes something like: 'We are the people!' What's it in German?"

"It's *Wir sind das Volk!* I think that's very clever of them. It's passive resistance, almost like Gandhi in India."

"Yes. The only danger is the uncertainty of the government's reaction. Nobody knows how long they're going to tolerate it. But then, the general mood has changed so much in favour of more freedom and democracy that it's probably going to be nearly impossible for the government to send out the army and shoot at their own people."

"Oh, these are very dangerous times."

"Yes. What's your dad's opinion on this?"

"I haven't spoken to him for a while. I'll meet him again soon. I'll ask him then. But right now, I've got to rush upstairs to make sure Andrew is going to sleep. He wants me to read another story to him. Thank God Lisa is fast asleep." And she left him with a smile. The love between them was still as fresh as on their first day together.

When Nora met her father a few days later, it was in London. Nora had been shopping in Chelsea High Street for most of the morning before they met at a nice restaurant in Sloane Square. After talking at length about the family, Andrew's progress and Lisa's health, while ordering their food in-between, they eventually arrived at the topic that she wanted to talk to him about, the developments in East Germany. She wanted to know what her father knew about the whole matter and what his opinion was.

"I fear the *Volkspolizei* will soon have to shoot at the crowds in the streets unless the government accepts a radical change," he said. "And I don't think they can accept a peaceful revolution. There's bound to be violence sooner or later."

"Are you going to Germany again soon?"

"Yes, quite soon, but not to the GDR, only to Frankfurt and Hamburg."

"Are you going to meet that fellow Wolfgang? You know, the man you told me about?"

"Of course not. Besides, he's still in East Germany." He hesitated. He took up his glass, took a long sip and shook his head slightly before he answered. "He's awful. He wants to ruin me. But I will find a way to get rid of him, I can assure you."

"Can't you tell me more about the whole business between you and Wolfgang?"

"Not now, maybe another time."

After this, their conversation turned to other things. They discussed Mrs Thatcher and Mr Reagan. This brought them to Mikhail Gorbachev, the Soviet leader.

"He's the GDR's only hope for a peaceful solution," the father judged.

"So, you think the Soviets will just stand by and watch while one of their colonies is being dismantled?" Nora wondered. "After what you told me a while ago, you know, after '56 in Hungary and '68 in Czechoslovakia?"

"This time they can't afford to interfere with tanks. Their system is nearly bankrupt. The arms race of the past decades has left them with very few options. They might try to threaten the West, but those threats would be empty words, and from what I have heard and read about Mr Gorbachev, his strategy is characterized by careful appeasement rather than confrontation. Ever since '86 he's been following his policies of *perestroika* and *glasnost*, which mean 'restructuring' and 'openness', and since then he has been working hard to restructure the Soviet Union and the Communist leadership of his country, and he's been offering the West a new relationship between the two super powers. You might remember his summit with Reagan in Washington. My hopes rest on Mr Gorbachev, I can tell you."

In the weeks that followed, Nora remembered her father's wise assessment of the political situation in Eastern Europe, because through September and October all the news programmes were full of comments and similar assessments dealing with the probability of a peaceful change in the GDR.

In the evening of the 7th of October, the news, both in the papers and on TV, were full of the Soviet leader's visit to East Berlin on the occasion of the 40th anniversary of the GDR. There were pictures of military parades, of flags all over East Berlin, of crowds cheering, of speeches being made and of critical voices against the Communist system. Journalists around the world had been speculating about Mr Gorbachev's comments on the most recent developments. And now the big surprise! He was reported as having said, "Those who are late will be punished by Life itself."

Three days later, Nora called her father. He answered the phone immediately. She asked him about his reaction to Mr Gorbachev's warning. His answer surprised her.

"You know, I do speak some Russian as well, don't you?"

"Yes, but do you mean you understood Mr Gorbachev as he made this declaration? He practically warned Mr Honecker to heed the people's voice and to change things in the GDR for the better."

"No, I didn't actually hear him, but I got a Russian paper that carried his exact wording. And I can tell you the world got him wrong. What everyone understood from the English translation – and from the respective German translation as well – is not accurate. You see, actually what he said was, 'If we are too late we will be punished by Life,' and 'Danger only awaits those who won't react to what Life dictates.' That's quite a different angle. His words weren't directed at Honecker and the GDR, but at his own country. He said 'we', didn't he, after all?"

"Are you sure?"

"Of course, I am. He could have said something like, 'If you're late you'll be punished by Life,' but he didn't. To me it's clear."

"Well, Dad, if you say so."

In the following weeks things suddenly took on new dynamics in the cities of the GDR, particularly in East Berlin. The people's protests in the streets reached a dimension where the government had to do something unless civil war was to break out. Lots of soldiers stood along the pavements of the streets that were full of protest marches. More and more soldiers joined the marchers, which was a thing that surprised everyone who saw it on TV in the West. Also, the news coverage in the West about such riotous activities in the East had been unheard of until now. Nora and George were glued to the TV screen every night. It was more exciting than the best who-done-it film on TV.

Then, on the 9th of November, the dam burst open. Nora and George couldn't believe their eyes and ears as they were watching the row of old men behind that long desk on the stage of the big press conference with the flag of the GDR on the back wall. Günter Schabowski, the man with the downturned lips and the sour face who had made most of the important announcements recently, was reading out the latest decisions of the *Politbüro* from a bunch of papers he was shuffling in his hands. He told the surprised journalists that private trips abroad could now be applied for "without proof of eligibility, reasons for travel, or family ties." Permission would be granted on short notice, he said. A journalist asked him when this new regulation was going to take effect. He hesitated and shuffled his papers, looking for some specific date in them, then turned to the waiting audience and announced, "As far as I know, immediately." That hit the journalists and the world at large like a bomb.

Nora and George looked at each other. They could hardly believe this. The English news reader explained the importance of this announcement to the TV audience. Of course, Nora realized much better what it meant than most people in England because she had all that background information about Germany from her father and from her own experience.

"What a pity we can't get German TV here," George said.

"Let's watch the news programmes on BBC, and there'll be commentaries and political discussions later."

They had a light supper and put the children to bed before they returned to the TV screen later in the evening. What they saw then was very moving. Ordinary people were crowding across the borders in Berlin, cheering and smiling, while some puzzled border guards were watching in disbelief and uncertainty. Some families crossed the borders to West Berlin in their little Trabant cars, others were marching, many were cheering, some had tears in their eyes. The news even showed West Berliners welcoming the people streaming in from the East.

On TV and in the papers over the following days, Nora and George saw pictures of people climbing the infamous Berlin Wall. And later the people began to hack at the Wall with pickaxes and other sharp tools. At long last, after 28 years, the hateful Wall was coming down. During these days, Nora often wondered how this would affect her father and his relationship with his old home country.

"Will you travel to Germany more often now?" she asked him when they met the next time. They were sitting in George's and Nora's large living-room at their house in Horsham, her parents being on a visit to see their grandchildren. The mother was spending a few days with them, while the father had business in London and was only down in Sussex for the week-end. It was Sunday afternoon, and they were all relaxing after lunch. Andrew was playing with his Lego set in the corner, Lisa was sitting on her grandmother's lap and enjoying the warmth and protection of her arms around her. Grandmother and granddaughter quietly cooed to each other, and the grandmother made funny faces. To Nora's annoyance, her mother was using baby-language whenever she spoke to little Lisa.

"I'll probably have to go there more often now," the father said. Nora detected a strange look that her parents exchanged. It was only the fraction of a second, but she realized there had to be something between them that concerned his trips to Germany.

"And will you visit East Germany more often, too? Will you visit your old home town?"

"I'll see how things turn out," he quietly answered.

"Come on, Didi," George burst in, "won't you have another cognac?" George always called her father by his shortened first name, never "Father" or "Dad", a very modern custom. But his mother-in-law was a different matter for him, so he called her "Mother", an appellation she particularly enjoyed since she'd never had a son of her own. Not that she regretted having only two daughters, but a son would have been nice, somehow more permanent, she felt.

The two men had a few more glasses of cognac, and eventually they fell asleep on the sofa and in the armchair.

Nora went to the kitchen to begin with the clearing away of the dirty dishes. While she was loading the dishwasher, her mother joined her in the kitchen.

"They've all fallen asleep, even little Lisa. Can I give you a hand, my dear?" she asked. Without waiting for an answer, she went to the sink and began to clear things from there, turning on the water tap in order to rinse things, helping her daughter.

For a moment, Nora paused in her work, a serving-dish in her hands, looking at her mother sideways. "Is there anything wrong about Dad travelling to Germany on business?" she carefully enquired. "You don't seem to approve."

Her mother didn't answer immediately but went on with her work at the sink. Nora wondered if she'd heard her, when the slow answer came.

"I don't mind as long as it's business."

"What do you mean?"

"Of course, he has to see other businessmen in Germany, but I'm sure he also has his private agenda. He usually stays much longer than his business requires."

"How would you know?"

"Well, his PR manager Bob Jenkins also thinks so. He told me so one evening when he was a bit tipsy at a party."

"Did he tell you what kept Dad longer in Germany, then?"

"Of course, he didn't have a clue either. He was just wondering, like myself."

Nora thought for a moment before she answered. "You know, he's been thinking back to his old days in Germany more often recently, don't you?"

"He never tells me. But I can see he's worried about something."

"It's probably because things have changed so much over there. Perhaps he wants to visit his old places, you know the places he knew as a child or as a young man, now that the borders are open, and you can travel all over Germany."

The two women were silent, continuing with their work in the kitchen, both of them lost in thought. When at last the kitchen was in perfect order again, the door of the dishwasher was closed, and the button was pressed, the mother remarked, "I only hope it's not a woman."

Nora was shocked. Her father would never deceive her mother. He had such high moral principles. He'd never start an affair with another woman.

"I'm sure it isn't," she said with firmness.

"Well, I'm not so sure," the mother slowly murmured.

"But you've got no proof, have you?"

"No, I haven't. But I have this strange gut-feeling. When you know your husband, you can feel when he begins to lose interest in you. He doesn't look at you the same way he used to, he doesn't always tell you everything, and things like that. I just feel there must be another woman."

Nora reassured her mother and comforted her with the observation that many older men were losing some of their former enthusiasm for their wives, and they needed their little secrets. Besides, what could it concern her even if he had a small affair with a woman in Germany who could never be a threat to her marriage, which of course was not the case with Dad?

Eventually, they dropped the subject. It was not mentioned again for many months. Meanwhile, Didi Woolf travelled to Germany more often. This was understood by his family and quietly accepted by everyone even though he gradually retired from his post with the American company.

Already in 1987, when he reached 65, he had taken what they called semi-retirement, and between 1987 and 1989 he still kept some of his duties, especially the company's important contacts with some of their Continental branches. They had said at the time that it was quite unusual for them to keep on an employee beyond his official retirement age, but because he was so popular with the Continental branches and his know-how was nearly indispensable for the company, he managed to convince them of the necessity of his continued service. He was generally considered as something like an *éminence grise* behind many of the more important decisions. However, by the beginning of 1990, he was finally an old age pensioner, a fully retired man with a golden retirement package in his bank account. Nobody, not even his wife, knew quite how much they'd given him, but Margaret, who knew more about these things and who spoke to Nora on the telephone from Boston, estimated a six-figure number.

Still he travelled to Germany from time to time. He said he wanted to remain up-to-date in German politics of the day, and he could keep on some of his former business contacts on a private basis. As he explained, he now had several good friends in Germany.

Later that year, as he was returning to England after his visit to Germany for the Reunification ceremony, Nora found another opportunity to speak to him privately, just between the two of them.

He was nervous. After telling his daughter everything about his activities in Frankfurt and Berlin, he fell silent.

Nora asked a daring question. "And what were your private activities over there? You know Mum thinks you're having an affair."

"Not really."

"What do you mean, not really?"

"It's a lot more complicated. I can't tell you everything."

"Well, just try. You know you can trust me. I won't tell anybody."

"You remember what I told you about that awful man who was following me around whenever I was in Germany?"

"Wolfgang, that was his name, yes?"

"Yes, Wolfgang Löffel. He made life difficult for me and an old acquaintance of mine."

"Just an acquaintance of yours? A woman?"

"Yes, she used to be my girlfriend when we were kids. Her name's Anna."

"Are you still in love with her?"

"It's not what you think. My feelings for her are not the issue. It's what Wolfgang has done to her and what he's told her about me. I can't tell you all the details. Please, don't tell Mum. Otherwise she will jump to the wrong conclusions."

"What would be the right conclusions then?"

The father didn't answer for quite some time. They both looked at each other. This was a crucial point in their relationship: Father and daughter asking themselves how much they could trust each other with sensitive information.

At last he found the right words. "Anna has never stopped loving me, but I have done some bad things which make it impossible for me to meet her again and face her with a clean conscience. Wolfgang has poisoned everything, he's destroyed everything that has ever been of value between her and me."

"And what are you trying to do now? What do you do when you're in Germany? Are you meeting people? Are you trying to clear your good name in her eyes, or what?"

"I don't think I'll be able to do that. And I think I should just let things be. It's no use. Perhaps I'm to blame as much as Wolfgang."

"So when are you going to Germany again? And where will you be going? Does she live in Berlin?"

"No, she still lives in our old home town, a small town called Gera. It's in Thuringia. I don't know if I can go back."

"Do you still have other old acquaintances in that town?"

"That's what I don't know. They're probably all dead by now. Certainly, my own family are all dead, my Mum died before the War, Dad died in 1955, and my older brother Thomas went missing during the War."

"Yes, I know," Nora said. "You told us ages ago. But what about other old friends? I mean, you're only 68. That's not so very old. You might still find some people you knew and who knew you in Gera. Have you been there recently?"

"No, I haven't been back for a very long time. And I probably won't. It hurts too much."

"So you haven't actually seen this Anna woman on any of your business trips?"

"The last time I saw her was in 1939."

"Then how do you know all those things about her?"

"First Wolfgang told me things, then he put me in touch with a cousin of Anna's in Leipzig, a younger cousin called Henrietta. I met her several times. She'd spent most of the War with Anna's family in Gera. So she knew her very well, and they kept in touch when Henrietta moved to Leipzig after the War. She told me many things I had missed through my absence in the West. There were good things, but also some terrible things."

The father looked into the middle distance. Nora detected some tears in his eyes and decided to let things be for the moment. What she had learnt from her father gave her a lot of food for thought. She needed time to reflect, to decide whether to do anything about Dad's story, whether to tell anyone, and if so, who could she tell?

***

In January, Mother had a heart attack. She was taken to the hospital, and after two weeks she was released. In March, Didi and Emily Woolf informed their daughters and their families that they were going to move south. The weather in Newcastle was too unhealthy for them, and they felt they were getting on in years. So they did what many retired people did if they could afford it: They moved to Eastbourne, the charming seaside town in East Sussex which, because of its attraction for retired people, was sometimes nicknamed "God's waiting-room." And indeed, the town had always had a very mild climate, with more sunshine than its neighbouring town of Brighton, due to the South Downs. This climate was ideal for elderly people. So the town boasted a great number of retirement flats, old people's homes and special care homes. On sunny days, one could always find large crowds of elderly people with walking-sticks or in wheelchairs sitting along the flower-beds on the seafront, near the Victorian pier, surrounded by screeching seagulls.

Due to Didi's substantial retirement package and because they got an excellent price for their big house in Gosforth, they could afford a very nice house in the more elegant part of Eastbourne called the Meads. It was only a five minutes' walk from the seafront and within walking distance from the local village shops, with life in the Meads still feeling like village-life. One didn't go down to the town centre of Eastbourne, which was below one's standards. If one needed things from big shops, such as fashionable clothes, one naturally went over to Brighton or even up to London. Shopping in Eastbourne was for the lower classes. In other words, the Meads area was full of what people up in Newcastle would have called "snobs from the South." However, the Woolfs soon found some friendly neighbours who were anything but snobs. Also, ever since his retirement, Didi had developed a taste for real ales, and the Pilot Inn, which was the local pub, offered some rather good brews. His regular visits to the pub got him in touch with even more friendly locals.

Of course, now they were much closer to Nora and her family. So, Nora often spent a pleasant afternoon with her parents, especially with her mother, on the seafront in Eastbourne or, when the weather was fine enough, up on the slopes of the South Downs. She was a little afraid, though, of the cliffs at Beachy Head. Whenever they walked up to the top of the cliffs she had bad nightmares in the following night, seeing her children falling down over the edge into the shingle below. This was because someone had told her that Beachy Head was the suicide-point number one in Britain, with an average of two suicides per month, because it was physically so easy just to jump down from the cliff. Her mother laughed at her. There was no need for fear if you were careful enough to stay away from the cliff edge. The children were warned accordingly, so on their usual walks over the Downs they always kept well away from the edge.

Mother's second heart attack came in July. This time, the ambulance was too late. By the time the paramedics bent down over her prostrated figure in the living-room, Emily Woolf had left this world behind.

TWELVE

The funeral was a very sad affair. There weren't a great many people, since the Woolfs had only moved to Eastbourne a relatively short while ago and hadn't had time to build up a large circle of friends. Some of their old friends came down from Newcastle, and Margaret managed to fly in from the States, albeit without her family.

Nora and George left their children with their neighbour. It was a fine day with a blue sky and only a few clouds travelling over the Downs. Nora hugged her sister in the car-park of the crematorium, which was situated at the town's eastern edge, just off the road to Pevensey. They didn't speak many words. They both felt that their mother had left them too early.

Later, Nora held her father's arm as they entered the Hydro Hotel for the wake. He hadn't shed any tears and hadn't spoken to any of the funeral guests. Nora acted as a sort of hostess for everyone, while George looked after the practicalities of the arrangements. Margaret couldn't dry her eyes, her tears kept pouring out even after they'd all left the crematorium.

Once seated, Nora sitting between her father and her husband, Margaret on their father's right, the general silence that always prevails at the beginning of a wake gradually melted as people started to talk in low voices, and eventually the room was full of chatter. Nora asked her father if anyone was expected to make a speech. Instead of answering her he stood up and touched his glass with his knife. The guests fell silent.

"Dear family and friends," he began, "I am not a great speaker, and I'm certainly not going to bore you with a long speech. However, I'd like to thank you for your sympathy and support in this dark hour for me. Thank you all for attending this last farewell for my dear Emily, I really appreciate it enormously."

Everyone expected this to be the end of his speech. But he didn't sit down, and after a long pause, which caused people to look at one another with puzzled faces, he raised his voice again.

"You know, I have seen many things in my life, and I have done many things, some good things and some not so good things. Sad as I am over dear Emily's passing, nevertheless there's a blessing in the fact that she could go before she had to learn about my bad things. Like this, she has left this world with a good image of her old husband."

He paused again. Nora could see that what he'd said was received with mixed reactions, some people obviously thought he was joking, others considered his words a misplaced understatement, while yet others were merely shaking their heads. There was general puzzlement in the air.

Would he say any more?

He stood for over a minute, hesitating, before he sat down. He uttered a puffy sigh and looked down at the white table-cloth.

"Are you all right, Dad?" Nora enquired in a kind voice.

"Just give me a moment," was his reply.

While everybody was busy with the food and the general conversation became more animated, Nora lost herself in deep thought. What her father had said struck her as part of a pattern which she had observed over the past few years. Sometimes there was no indication of such a pattern for months at a time, but occasionally – and more regularly in recent times, as it seemed to her – he said things that fitted the pattern. She couldn't exactly define what the pattern was, but it had something to do with her father's past, with his life before he'd met his wife, with Germany and with some of his former acquaintances there. He appeared to feel guilty about something that must have happened a long time ago. It might have been connected with that Wolfgang fellow, or perhaps with his old girlfriend Anna.

She remembered what he'd told her a few months ago and tried to put together all the different pieces in the puzzle of his life. For one thing, there was Wolfgang, who must have done some bad things that involved Dad and Anna. But Dad said that he'd done some bad things, too, something that he keeps referring to more often now. What else could he have meant in his speech now? Suddenly, Nora's mind fell back on her old interest in history and particularly in German history before and during the Second World War. How could her father have been involved? He'd said that almost everyone back then had done things that were not right. She could easily understand that. The Nazi system must have brainwashed most of the German people. So, he could just feel guilty about his own weakness when he believed what everyone else believed, namely that Hitler was a great leader and the German race was born to rule the world. But there had to be more. Why could Wolfgang bear him a grudge for which he was trying to make life difficult for him? Was it rather political? Or was it a private matter, involving Anna? Nora couldn't find a reasonable explanation, or only in parts. If she had more time at her hands, she could travel to Germany and meet some people who'd known her father in the past. Or would she have to go to Switzerland, rather than Germany? After all, he'd spent some time there after the War, and what bothered his conscience now might have something to do with what he experienced there. What a pity she didn't have the time to follow up these trails.

She was shaken out of her thoughts when her sister Margaret bent over her shoulders from behind. "Have you got time for a private chat later?" she breathed into her ear.

"Of course," Nora replied.

Then the man opposite her at the table asked her a question about how her father was coping with the bereavement, to which she answered with the usual formulas. The man was a former business colleague of her father's who had been quite a good friend up to his own retirement a few years back, when her father was still very active from his Newcastle base. His name was Ken Hughes and he still lived up north, she believed somewhere near Durham. She tried to be polite and responded to his friendly conversation with her best manners. But throughout the conversation, and indeed for the rest of the wake, her mind kept in touch with her former thoughts.

When people began to trickle away, while those who remained in the function-room of the hotel were increasingly having a good time – as it often happens at wakes – Nora joined her sister in front of the hotel. Margaret was smoking a cigarette. They smiled at each other.

"It's good to see you again," Margaret said.

"It's only a pity it has to be under such sad circumstances," Nora remarked.

"Let's walk a little," Margaret suggested. They walked towards the seafront. They reached the street that runs parallel to the coast, from where they could look down at King Edward's Parade and the rocky beach even further below. For a while they just looked at the horizon and the clouds in the deep blue sky above the metallic grey-blue sea.

"What was it you wanted to talk to me about?" Nora enquired.

"Well, I was wondering how you'd feel if I came back to England for a while."

"With your family?"

"I haven't worked that one out yet."

"Oh, what's going on? What about Doug and the children?"

Margaret hesitated before she answered. "We're having a big crisis. I feel I've just got to get away from Doug, for a while at least."

"Why is that? I understand he's such a caring husband, and only recently you told me how good he was with the kids."

"Yes, he's a wonderful father. And I accept the fact that he only means well the way he treats me. But I'm being smothered by his love. I simply can't breathe anymore."

"So, he loves you too much? Is that it?"

"Well, you could put it that way if you like."

"But don't you love him?"

"I don't know." Margaret's voice rose in desperation. "I'm telling you, I just don't know!"

"That's bad," Nora murmured.

"Of course, it's bad, as bad as it can get in a relationship. I mean, if he had an affair with another woman I think it would be easier. At least, then I would know what was wrong. But as things are now, I constantly feel guilty, guilty for wanting to be rid of him, and the only reason I can see is his overpowering presence over me, his over-protective love, the way he governs my whole life."

"How about your sex life?" Nora wanted to know. She knew she could ask her sister such an intimate question. They had always been quite open about this.

"The sex is great. We're having more than I can stomach. He can really satisfy me, but then again, it's almost too much, too good, too fulfilling. It's sometimes as if there was no life outside our bed. I tried to speak to him about it, but the only way he understood the problem was that he thought he wasn't good enough for me, and it had the opposite effect of what I was aiming for."

"That's a real problem."

"Yes, it is. I can hardly move without his approval or his supervision. I feel like a prisoner of my husband's love. This visit to England without him is a true blessing. I feel I can breathe again. Perhaps I shouldn't be smoking now. Now that I can breathe again."

The last remark made the atmosphere lighter because Margaret smiled in a self-apologetic way. The two sisters remained silent for a few minutes. Their minds evolved around what had just been discussed, while they were watching a sailing yacht making its way along the coast, heading for Beachy Head. When the yacht had disappeared from view, Nora resumed the topic.

"So, what are your plans?"

"Give me a few days. I need time to think. Let's keep in touch."

"Of course, we'll keep in touch. What else did you expect? Where are you staying?"

"In a charming little hotel on the seafront. It's an old fisherman's cottage called Sea Beach House Hotel. I found it quite by accident. You know, I came head over heels, I hadn't made any booking. So when I arrived, I just walked down to the seafront, looking for a suitable place, and that's when I found it, tucked away in that corner at the back of the green triangle near Fusciardi's, you know. Just like that. The owners are really charming people, my room overlooks the sea, and they serve you fantastic breakfasts."

"Just be careful you won't put on any weight," Nora smiled.

"Oh, no danger of that. But what I was going to say was how relaxing that place is. I think by staying there I might be able to get some order in my confused life."

"Okay then. But if you feel like it you can come and stay with us in Horsham. We've got plenty of space."

"Thanks, Sis. But I think I need to be alone. I'll let you know when I'm ready for further heart-to-heart talks with you. I know I have to find my own solution to my problem. You can give me advice, but you can't solve my problem."

After this, the two sisters returned to the Hydro Hotel, where they found their father in discussion with Ken Hughes. Nora asked him if she could do anything for him, otherwise she'd like to get back home to her children. In the middle distance she could see George who seemed to be ready to leave, too.

"No, my dear, I'll be all right. Off you go. We'll talk more a bit later. You'll have to come round some time to go through Emily's things. I can't face that on my own."

As George was manoeuvring their big Jaguar out of the car-park at the side of the Hydro Hotel, Nora looked back towards the hotel entrance, where she could see Margaret standing, smoking and looking out into space.

Back in her home in Horsham, Nora was busy with the children and had no time to think of either of the two issues which had burnt themselves into her mind at her mother's funeral. The question of her father's past had to be shifted to the background of her mind. There was no hurry with that. But her sister's problem appeared to her more pressing. As Margaret had correctly put it, Nora couldn't solve the problem for her, but she could at least offer to help her, to give her moral as well as practical support in this crisis. For example, she could be there for talks, and perhaps she might repeat her offer to have her at her home in Horsham for a while.

Margaret called her after three days. She said it would do her good to meet again soon. Nora postponed a few of her commitments and drove down to Eastbourne on the following day. It was half-past twelve when she found the pub where

Margaret was waiting for her. It was the Marine in Seaside, just more or less at the back of her hotel, quite a large pub with that red velvet atmosphere and a very long bar that sported a large selection of single malt whiskies, something that Nora had only become aware of through George's keen interest in Scotland and its distilled waters. She herself didn't like strong liquor, a good glass of red wine was what she preferred.

The sisters embraced for a long moment before they sat down. Margaret already had a gin and tonic in front of her, so Nora walked to the bar to get her drink. Now, before lunch, she went for a white wine, an Australian Chardonnay.

After some small talk they embarked upon the sensitive topic of Margaret's marriage.

"I've had a long discussion with Doug on the phone," she began, "and he seems to understand my problem, at least he says he does."

"I find that hard to believe, after what you told me," Nora said with a frown on her face. "How can he understand your problem, if he loves you too much to take note of your supposed imprisonment? As I understood the situation, it appears to me that he loves you in a selfish way, as a child loves a toy or as a man might love his car. Wasn't he treating you like an object rather than a living human being with your own feelings?"

"That's exactly what I've been explaining to him on the phone. You know, talking on the phone instead of face to face made it easier for me to insist on my view of things, to make him listen and try to see our relationship from my side."

"And you think you've been successful?"

"I'm not a hundred percent sure. And I told him."

"So, what now?"

"During our talks, and especially between our phone calls – which, by the way, cost me a fortune – I began to see my way ahead. So, I've come to a decision. I'm going to take a long break from my marriage. I can see that I need this in order to find myself again. I need to be on my own for a longer period, and only then will I be in a position to decide if we're going to stay together or break up."

"What does he say?"

"At first, he tried to talk me out of it, but eventually he came round. In the end, he even agreed that it might be a good idea. What seemed to be the hardest part for him was the sexual abstinence he could see ahead of him. I told him he could have affairs during my absence or see a prostitute if he needed it so badly. I told him I wouldn't mind. That was a lie, but it helped him agree to my plan. He must have sensed this. He said he didn't want another woman, because his sex life was completely focused on me. I jokingly suggested he could look at the photos he has of me, and he jumped at the idea."

"Isn't that a bit theatrical? I mean it's very operatic to be excited by a picture in the absence of the real woman and without any hope of getting the woman in the picture. Think of Tamino in the *Magic Flute*."

"Oh, it's not so stuffy," Margaret laughed. "It's a lot juicier. In fact, it's quite sexy."

Nora frowned. "Sexy?"

"Yes! You see, when we were first together, before we had children, we were both so full of our newly discovered sex life that we did all sorts of things I wouldn't tell anyone. One thing we did was taking pictures of each other. Nude shots, you know, in sexy poses. We have quite a stock of very special photos of each other. So, when I suggested photos, he naturally thought of those."

The two sisters were silent for a while, taking long sips from their drinks. Nora pondered what she'd just learnt. What a daring thing! Taking nude photos of each other! She couldn't imagine ever doing that with a man, not even with

George. She couldn't find it in herself to be so happy about her brother-in-law and his professed love for her sister. What sort of love was that? Only focused on sex and on looking at his wife in the nude? She kept her thoughts to herself.

"So how long are you going to be on your own? What are your plans?"

"I think for the time being I'm just going to stay here for a while. A month or two, maybe three? I'll see how I feel."

"Aren't you coming to stay with us in Horsham? We'd love to have you."

"Not now. I like it here, on my own. Maybe later."

The conversation turned to other things. The sisters discussed the new Prime Minister, who had only been in office since November. While Margaret admitted she'd lost touch with British politics and was more concerned with President Bush's speeches about the situation in the Gulf Region, Nora expressed her own mixed feelings about John Major's reaction to the American calls for support in that sensitive issue.

"Major seems a soft fellow, I don't know if he can be trusted. We'll see. At least I'm glad we've left the Thatcher era behind."

"People in the States admired her a great deal. She was as thick as thieves with Reagan, which gained her enormous sympathies."

"Well, I never liked her," Nora stated and put down her glass with an energetic gesture.

"Why?"

"Many reasons. Her personality, her egocentric ways, her arrogant language."

"But wasn't she very good for Britain? Wasn't she a very shrewd politician?"

"She may very well have achieved a few good things. Future history books will tell. But she'll also go down in history as the Prime Minister who led her people into the most ridiculous armed conflict."

"What do you mean?" Margaret wanted to know.

"Well, that stupid Falkland War, back in '82."

"I always understood that it had given a big boost to national pride in this country. Another country, and a dictatorship at that, had occupied one of Britain's territories, which gave Britain the right to take it back."

"How primitive must your critical historical understanding be? There are so many serious critical issues connected with the Falkland War. For one thing, the British stole the Malvinas, as they were originally called, from Spain in 1833, before they colonised the islands with British settlers, just like the Russians colonised the Baltic States and many central Asian territories with Russian settlers when they made them Soviet republics. The idea was to claim these areas as true Russian homeland, and the British have always been very good at that strategy, too. Colonial history is full of examples. Then there's the sense of proportion: all that money, all that military equipment and all that risk and even loss of human lives just to fulfil a weakened Prime Minister's strategy for re-election, which, as the whole world knows, was the only real reason for the War. Besides, you know what our father taught us about national pride. It's only the British themselves – and probably certain circles in the United States – who can't see things as they really are."

"You seem to have kept your interest in history, it appears," Margaret smiled.

"Indeed, I have. But my sense of history is different from many other people's interest. Most people think of history in terms of nationalistic narrow-mindedness, they'd glorify their so-called heroes from the past rather than look at the realities with a critical eye."

"Hey, Sis! Hold your horses. This isn't a university lecture. I was just surprised you didn't share most people's enthusiasm for Mrs Thatcher. I must say I can see your point, but let's change the subject. I don't really know all that much about politics or history."

The sisters decided to meet again on a regular basis. Margaret agreed to come to Horsham for the next Sunday lunch.

After their drinks at the Marine, they went across the street for lunch at the New Mum Taj Mahal Restaurant. Nora claimed she'd heard people say it was Eastbourne's best Indian restaurant. When they entered the restaurant, however, they were surprised to find it quite a low-class place. Old faded black-and-white photos on the walls, depicting the Taj Mahal, Delhi street scenes, elephants and political rallies of the National Congress Party; worn plastic-covered seats and plastic table-cloths: all in all, not a very inviting atmosphere. They were the only customers.

"We may as well sit down, now we're here," Nora suggested.

The middle-aged Indian waiter slouched across the room and stopped at their table without uttering a word. He looked as if he was sleep-walking. His eyelids were only half-open. He threw two plastic menus on the table and remained standing in silence. When the two women looked up at his face, trying to understand what they'd done wrong to deserve such treatment, he whispered: "Drinks?"

They ordered their drinks. The tall waiter shambled back to the rear of the restaurant and disappeared through a dirty door to the kitchen. Nora and Margaret looked at each other meaningfully. Presently, the waiter returned with a sticky yellow plastic basket containing two poppadoms. The sisters placed their orders.

After this unpromising beginning, their meal eventually turned out a great success. The place might have looked dirty and awful, but the food was a real revelation, indeed one of the best Indian curries Nora had ever tasted. Hers was a chicken dhansak, while Margaret had a lamb vindaloo, and they shared a portion of pillau rice and a sag bhaji.

After such a satisfying meal, they went for a pleasant stroll along the seafront. Their talks never returned to either Margaret's marriage or British politics. They spoke about books they'd read recently and about their children's activities. It was half-past three when they said good-bye, Nora jumped into her little car parked further along the seafront and drove off. Margaret remained seated on a bench facing the sea, looking into the distance and thinking.

***

It didn't come as a surprise when, about ten days later, Margaret told her sister on the telephone that she intended to stay in England for a longer period than originally planned.

"You see, I need to find myself in all this muddle," she explained.

"Would you like to come and stay here?" Nora asked.

"Actually, that's exactly what I was going to ask you, if it's not too much of an inconvenience. I'll pay you for my board and lodging."

"Nonsense. You are welcome. I was expecting this, and I've talked it over with George. It's quite okay. You can stay as long as you like, and we won't hear a word about payment."

"Are you sure?"

"Of course. We are sisters. When are you coming?"

"Well, I was thinking of tomorrow if that's all right for you."

"No problem at all. I'll be out all day tomorrow, but you can get the key to our house from Lucy next door. She'll be looking after Andrew and Lisa for me. Just come in and make yourself comfortable in our guest room. I should be back by about half-past five."

"Oh, what can I say!" Margaret sighed.

Nora had to repeat her invitation twice before her sister could bring herself to accept such natural trust and unlimited hospitality. But in the end, she was glad to accept.

When Nora arrived at her home the next day, Margaret was sitting in the downstairs lounge with Lisa on her lap and Andrew playing with his Lego set on the floor near his auntie's feet. Margaret was reading the captions of a picture-story for Lisa, who was obviously very happy listening to her auntie's voice and looking at the colourful pictures.

For a very brief moment, Nora's heart gave an extra beat of surprise, not without a hint of jealousy, before she collected herself within a fraction of a second, dismissing all traces of any bad feelings and welcoming the great relationship between her sister and her children. In her conscience, she scolded herself for her slip into a fond mother's exaggerated sense of protectiveness. She vowed to steer clear of any such negative feelings for as long as Margaret was going to stay with her family. After all, in the bright daylight of practical life, she was relieved to have her sister here. Margaret might turn out to be a great help.

The activities of the first evening indeed confirmed this vague hope. The sisters worked together as a team, preparing little Lisa's tea and the bigger meal for the rest of the family. When George came home, the whole evening seemed like a happy party for Nora. By seven, Lisa was asleep in her cot while the two sisters, George and Andrew finally sat down to their supper. George told them the latest news from his work, Andrew chatted away about his plans for the construction of a whole village on the moon, built entirely from Lego pieces. The two sisters also contributed to the conversation, but while the two males grew more and more enthusiastic about their topics, the sisters gradually fell silent, both of them realizing individually that they would have to come to a common agreement about Margaret's role within this family sooner or later.

After the evening meal, George got Andrew to bed while Nora and Margaret worked together in the kitchen, finally tidying everything. Margaret indeed turned out to be a great help for Nora.

In bed, later that night, Nora raised the subject of her sister's visit with George. They had this routine of discussing important issues in bed, before they finally relaxed and fell asleep. Sometimes they were so relaxed after everything had been said that they got aroused and made love before going to sleep. But not tonight. Nora felt she had to get some sort of perspective on the situation before she could relax. She explained her mixed feelings to a sleepy George, who was completely relaxed and couldn't see a problem if his sister-in-law wanted to stay in their house for a longer period.

"She's your sister, she's pleasant to be with, and she's a great help with the children, isn't she?" he asked.

"Yes, you're right, of course," Nora had to admit.

They continued discussing various aspects of Margaret's stay, and eventually Nora could relax, too, falling asleep in her husband's warm embrace.

The next three days were full of daily routines, before the sisters drove to their father's house in Eastbourne. They offered to help him with their mother's things, but he refused, maintaining that he had to come to terms with his own situation before any action could be taken into consideration. So, they just had a pleasant chat with him and invited him to a nice lunch of fish and chips with a pint of Bombardier at the Pilot Inn.

Driving home on the A27, Nora asked Margaret if she had any idea of how long she was going to stay. "It isn't that I would mind if you wanted to stay a lot longer. It's just that I could make my own plans if I knew," she explained.

"Of course, I understand," Margaret replied. "Would you have me for a longer period? Say, two or three months, perhaps?" She looked at her sister sideways. Nora was concentrating on the traffic along the Lewes bypass, which gave her an excuse for remaining silent before answering.

"I think it shouldn't be a problem," she said at last. "In fact, I've been thinking of a wild plan for myself in case you intended to stay for such a long period. So, yes! You're quite welcome."

"What's your plan, then?"

Nora negotiated the turn off the A27 and the roundabout that took them onto the A23 before she came up with her daring proposition.

"If you're willing to stay in our house and really look after things, I could go away for a few weeks for myself. You know, Lucy next door would be a great help, and as you've seen, George can look after himself, and he's willing to help with the children and with the evening chores."

"Oh, that's an altogether new ball-game," Margaret said with a heavy American accent. "Where do you want to go? Is everything okay between you and George?"

"Of course, everything is okay. In fact, I've hinted at such a possibility to George, and he was very supportive. I think he'd understand."

"Not every husband would, I can tell you that. But tell me: Where do you want to go? Have you got any definite plans?"

"Well, I've been hoping to do this for quite some time. I'd like to travel to Germany."

"What do you want to go there for? You were there during your university days."

"Yes, you're right. I was in Hamburg, and I visited Berlin. But this time I want to go to other places."

"Just to get to know other places? Or to brush up your German?"

"Partly yes, but I also want to find out a few things about the past, you know."

"Oh, Nora dear! Your old hobby-horse again? You want to dig up more stuff about Dad's past? Is that it? You can't let sleeping dogs lie?"

Nora let this sink in while she turned off the A23, idling down the slip-road to join the A272. Once on the new road, she let her VW Golf shoot off, accelerating faster than it was her custom, as if she wanted to rush to Germany faster than possible.

"You know perfectly well that I've always been interested in what had happened to Dad before he came to the States, especially during the War."

"Is your interest more professional or rather more personal?" Margaret raised her eyebrows and made a critically enquiring face.

"I don't really know myself. There's a lot of personal interest, too, of course. Did you know that Dad had a lover before the War? Her name was Anna. And he still has a problem with one of his old buddies, an awful fellow called Wolfgang."

"Isn't that his own business? Why do you want to dig up his past?"

"Because I'm convinced there's more than he's told us. There has to be some terrible secret. I want him to confront his own past and make his peace. But I also have to know for myself. I want to know our father for who he is and for what he was during that terrible time when everybody in Germany had to decide where they stood. Dad has told me a number of things that have definitely raised my curiosity."

"What things?"

"Well, what about his little speech at the funeral?"

Margaret didn't answer. They were silent for the remaining journey and reached Horsham in good time. As they were getting out of the car Nora stepped up to her sister and took her in her arms. "There's no hurry to decide. Also, I've got to talk things through with George and with Dad. I certainly need some more information from Dad before I can make my definite plans. Let's just think about the whole thing for a few days before we take it any further."

PART THREE

THIRTEEN

It was a cold Tuesday evening when Andrew White parked his Ford Escort in the narrow spot which was allocated to his flat in the dark back alley. Today it seemed particularly dark because the weather was bleak with low clouds and even a touch of sea-mist pushing in from the English Channel. He locked his car and realized that it could actually do with a wash, it was so dirty, but then what was the point with such an old car? It was a faded red and looked its age carrying an "M" registration, which belonged to the old system of registration marks and identified it immediately as a car from the last century. But he didn't mind, not belonging to the category of car-buffs like most of his friends. Any old banger would do for him as long as it took him from A to B.

He climbed the stairs to his flat. It was his first flat, and he was quite proud of being a property owner. Although, if you looked at it carefully, you had to admit that it was really the bank who owned most of it. He had just been lucky to get it on his minimal deposit. True, what had made it possible was not only the special deal offered by the bank to young people they called "first-time buyers", but also his parents' generous contribution. Both he and his sister Lisa had received fifty thousand pounds each on their twenty-first birthdays. Their parents had made it a condition that the gift was meant to help them buy their first homes. His twenty-first had been more than three years ago, while Lisa had only had hers last year. She was still at university up North, although at the moment she was down in Sussex because she could work better on her M.A. thesis in her parents' home. He, on the other hand, had left all academic efforts and ambitions behind him. True, he had his bachelor's degree in Social Studies, which had got him a part-time job in the local council offices, but what interested him much more these days was his piano. He knew he could never become a proper pianist, but his ambitions as an amateur were a constant challenge for him while he felt he could truly express himself through his musical activities. He never performed for an audience; his piano music was for his own enjoyment and personal fulfilment. On this Tuesday evening he was just coming home from his piano lesson. In his mind, he was still going through the Bach Fantasy which he'd been working on with his piano teacher.

The warmth of his flat surprised him. He found the switch and turned down the temperature on the thermostat. He took the sheet music from his briefcase and stacked it on his piano, which was a middle-aged Yamaha. Usually, when he came home from his lesson, he immediately sat down at his piano to try out his new achievements, to check if the things he'd been working out with his teacher still worked at home. But tonight, he had other plans.

He got himself a quick snack of bread and cheese with a glass of orange juice before settling down in front of the TV set. He wanted to watch the pictures of the Inauguration Ceremony for the first Black American President. He saw this as a historic date. Today, on the 20th of January 2009, the world was entering a new phase because its greatest super-power was about to change. Of this he was certain. This was going to be the end of America's backwardness and brutal inhumanity driven by its pioneer-mentality. At last the United States might find its way to democratic values propagated by figures like Abraham Lincoln. Some of the worst black spots in American un-culture might be overcome at last, such as the redneck madness with guns, the death penalty or the concentration camp of Guantánamo. Andrew felt that he was full of hope and expectation.

After his TV session, he felt tired. He walked to his small kitchen to make himself a sandwich. He loved a ham and tomato sandwich in the evening, often late at night. He had the illusion that it helped him fall asleep when he went to bed. As he was putting the remaining pack of ham back into the fridge, his eyes fell on his mobile phone that he had left next to the coffee machine earlier. It was still switched off from his piano lesson. He switched it on. Once it had made its connection with the provider, it beeped. There were two messages, one from his friend Dave and another from his sister Lisa. Dave's message suggested they meet for a late pint at the pub. He ignored it. It was too late now. He opened Lisa's message.

"Please call me asap. It's about Mum. Urgent! Love. L," it said.

Andrew sat down with his sandwich and wondered what Lisa could possibly have to tell him about their mother which was so urgent. He dearly loved his little sister, but he knew her well enough to understand that she tended to overreact at times. She was so emotional. Sometimes he listened to her emotional outbreaks in silence, knowing full well that what she was going on about was only half as dramatic in reality, and often he managed to calm her down once her energy was spent, and they could discuss the matter at hand much more realistically. So, he decided to wait until the next day before calling her.

When he woke up in the morning, he found three more messages on his mobile. They were all from Lisa, urging him to call her. She was considerate enough not to call him in the middle of the night, but she wanted to speak to him as soon as possible. It was now just seven o'clock, and it was still dark outside. Andrew loved getting up early in the morning. It gave him an opportunity to settle his thoughts, to look ahead at the new day and to sort a few things that needed sorting. For example, he usually answered his email messages and often did his on-line banking in the early hours of the morning. There was only one message from Amazon, the cheap on-line bookshop, informing him that the book he'd ordered had now been despatched. It was quite an expensive book about Germany in the Second World War, with lots of pictures and a host of facts. He was fully aware of the fact that he could find most of this information on the Internet, but he somehow felt that things were more accurate in properly researched books.

Andrew had inherited his mother's keen interest in history and particularly European history of the twentieth century. Lisa often teased him about it. Sometimes they had heated arguments about the usefulness of history, but he didn't mind. He was convinced that humanity could learn a great deal from a critical view on all history, particularly on more recent history. Besides, his mother had inspired him too much. History was in their blood, he felt. He knew his mother had found out lots of things about Grandfather's time in Germany, things she was keeping to herself. True, she'd told him a few facts, but there were still lots of open questions.

Just before eight he called Lisa. She answered on the first ring.

"So, what's up?" he demanded.

"Oh, my poor Andrew, it's so terrible," she answered, hardly able to suppress her sobs. "Mum had a stroke. She's in hospital. It's so unexpected, it's so early. She's only in her early fifties. Oh, poor Mum!"

"That's bad news, indeed," he said. "But what about her chances?"

"Oh, it's all so sad! I couldn't sleep all night. Why didn't you call me last night? What if I died and you never knew because you're not getting important messages! You have no consideration for your family, you have no feelings!"

"Oh, come on, Lisa. Calm down. Just tell me where she is, so I can visit the hospital and speak to the doctors."

Lisa sniffed for a moment before she managed to answer her brother in a level voice. "She's at the DGH, and I'm also going there this morning."

"Okay, I'll tell my office, and I'll be there by half nine."

"Oh, thank you. You're such a good brother. It's so kind of you to come, too."

"Of course. No problem. See you there."

He quickly organized his absence from his office and managed to be at the hospital by half-past nine, as promised. Lisa was already sitting there in the reception area. He kissed her on her cheek, which was still wet from crying, and sat down beside her.

"I've already asked to see the doctor," she informed him. "We can't visit Mum until later. She's in intensive care. Also, I've spoken to Dad on the phone. He's in New York, but he's flying home tonight."

Soon the doctor arrived. He introduced himself as Dr Banerjee. He was a friendly man of medium height with an extremely winning expression on his brown face. His sparkling eyes were nearly black. Andrew liked him immediately, feeling he could trust this doctor.

Dr Banerjee gave them a full report of their mother's case. She'd had a stroke, but she had a good chance to survive with only minor complications. One couldn't say much more at this stage. The doctor gave them a lecture on the exact medical condition. They understood that their mother might come out with a small handicap such as a partly paralysed left arm and possibly a weakened mind. Time would tell.

Later, Andrew and Lisa could visit their mother, but she was too weak and drugged to talk coherently. They held her hand for a while, then left. In front of the hospital, Andrew had to calm his sister down. She threw her arms in the air and concluded at last, "Such is life! In the middle of life, we are near death!" Andrew knew better than to respond to this, so he just took his leave. They agreed to visit again as often as possible. Lisa said she was planning to stay for another two weeks anyway before returning to her university.

Andrew spent the afternoon at work. At one point he got a bit bored. He had to fill in some lists. He stopped and sank into deep thoughts. What if his mother was dying? Dad would be shattered, but he'd be able to cope. He was more worried about Lisa. She was so close to Mum emotionally, while he himself was rather close to her intellectually.

Suddenly, the idea struck him that if she died a lot of valuable information would be lost, things she had researched about Granddad all those years ago. A pity Granddad was no longer in a condition in which he could talk about his own past in any coherent and comprehensive way. He was in a nursing home in Southfields Road. At eighty-six, he was suffering from a special form of dementia. Andrew had tried to talk to him on his last visit at the nursing home, but the answers he got from Granddad didn't make sense. Andrew always felt rather depressed after every visit, and he wondered how much the old man still realized.

He picked up his mobile and called Lisa.

"When's Dad due home?" he asked her.

"He'll be arriving at Heathrow early tomorrow morning. But Auntie Margaret's coming down from London. I'll pick her up from the station in twenty minutes and take her to the hospital."

"Okay, shall we all get together later?"

"Yes, let's meet at home, say after half six?"

They rang off, and Andrew fell back into his deep thoughts. He thought of Auntie Margaret. She was a very courageous woman who called a spade a spade. More than seventeen years ago, she'd left her family, her husband and her two children, back in the States, and moved in with her best friend Helen from Newcastle. At first, the two lovers lived in Newcastle before moving down to London. They'd now been in London for over five years and after some initial problems, the family – i.e. Mum and Dad – had accepted the situation. After all, this was the twenty-first century. Most people had a gay person in their families. In a way, he quite liked both of them, Margaret and Helen. Helen still had that funny Geordie accent, and they seemed to be very happy together.

Then his thoughts again took him to Granddad, who'd been in Germany during the last war. Now that his mother might be incapacitated to a certain degree it seemed even more important to talk to her about what she knew of Granddad's past. He decided to take up the subject with her again as soon as possible. Once she would have recovered from the worst of her stroke.

In the evening of the following day, the family assembled at their home in the Meads. It was an unusual situation. George, their father, was still suffering from a slight jet-lag, and the absence of his wife, Andrew's and Lisa's mother, created a strange emptiness in the living-room where they all sat down. There was no mother to serve them tea, so Lisa went to the kitchen and put the kettle on. Aunt Margaret hadn't arrived yet.

"I've been to see your mother," George began. "The doctors say she'll be left partly paralysed in the left half of her face, and she'll probably have difficulties moving her left arm. But he was quite confident that physiotherapy might improve things for her in due course."

"Did she speak when you were there?" Andrew wanted to know.

"Oh yes, she uttered a few words. Although they were quite slurred, her efforts at comprehensible speech made me confident that she might eventually be able to speak properly again. Let's be optimistic."

Despite his words, the father couldn't hide his worst fears from his own children. Lisa came through from the kitchen and put her arms round her father. There were tears running down his cheeks.

When they had their teacups in their hands, the beverage not only warmed their hands but gave them encouragement. They agreed to visit their mother at the hospital as often as possible and to exchange any information about new developments in her condition.

When the doorbell rang, they knew it had to be Aunt Margaret. As it so often happens, a stupidly funny idea flashing up in the middle of a serious situation, while appearing almost insolent, could reveal itself as extremely humorous and alleviating. This was the case in Andrew's mind when the ring of the bell reminded him of Algernon Moncrieff's statement that "only relatives or creditors ever ring in that Wagnerian manner", in Oscar Wilde's fantastic comedy, *The Importance of Being Earnest*. This unburdening thought brought a smile to his face, which made his sister frown at him.

"Hi, everyone," Aunt Margaret boomed as she was striding into the living-room, followed by her friend Helen behind her. Helen only uttered a quiet hello and left the field to her more powerful friend.

While all the different members of his family were chatting away, exchanging various ideas as to the way their mother ought to be looked after once she was out of hospital, Andrew followed a different train of thought. He decided to visit his grandfather in the nursing home, a thing he hadn't done for a long time. This time, he admitted to himself, it wouldn't just be a matter of doing his duty towards the old man. He felt a real urge within himself. Could it be what was just happening to his mother? Or was it the effect of his thoughts about certain aspects of his grandfather's history being lost unless he was going to do something about it? Whatever it was, he had to see his grandfather as soon as possible. During these ruminations, he felt as if he was drifting away from the other persons in the room. He was drifting away in a cloud, seeing his family as if they were the figures in a pantomime or, even more stunning for him, a shoal of fish in a tank. It was the first time in his life that he experienced anything like this. Up till now he had always felt connected with the people around him, even more inseparably so with the members of his family. Despite the small age difference, for example, with his sister Lisa, he had always felt this strong bond between them. A bond he'd never questioned. But now, although he knew they were just reacting to the situation with his mother, he somehow considered them all, even Lisa, to be running after destiny. They were all discussing things they couldn't influence in the slightest way. Was this all that we humans could do? Couldn't we try to make an impact? To learn from the past and apply those lessons learnt accordingly?

***

He was surprised at the relatively young nurse who received him at the nursing home. She could hardly be older than he was.

"Your grandfather is sitting in our sun-lounge," she informed him.

"Thank you. Is it this way?"

"Yes, just go through that door, and you'll see him."

Andrew did as the charming young nurse had instructed him. He pushed the door open, and indeed, there was his grandfather, about twenty feet away, sitting in an armchair by the large window. He crossed the room and stood by his chair. The old man didn't react to his approach.

"Hello, Granddad," Andrew addressed him cheerfully.

"I'm not buying anything from you. Go away."

Andrew waited for a moment before he tried again. "Granddad, it's me, Andrew, your grandson. I've come to see you."

"And you think you can hoodwink me, young man? I know what's going on."

"Of course, you do." Andrew sat down on a chair opposite. He gave the old man a pleasant smile. He hoped it was a natural smile.

"What's so funny, young man?"

"I'm just smiling because I like you."

"Ah, I see. I know what's going on."

Then the two men looked at each other in silence. Andrew decided to give him time, not to rush things. He knew from what Lisa had told him that it was quite possible for Granddad suddenly to see things clearly, just as suddenly as it was possible for him to slip away from a clear mind into the darkness of oblivion. He was wondering if he ought to keep up some sort of conversation, absurd as it might turn out, when the old man stared at him with a fixed expression.

"*He, he, du bist ein frecher Pimpf.* That's what you are."

Andrew's German was not very good. He'd studied it up to his O-Levels, but then lost most of it again. So he wasn't sure what a *Pimpf* was. It was probably something like a chap, a bloke, a fellow.

"It's all those things they tell you. *Mich können sie aber nicht hinters Licht führen. Mich nicht. Nein, mich nicht!* I know what's going on."

He tried again. "Granddad, can you remember your wife, Emily?"

"Who?"

"Emily! You loved her. She was your wife."

"I never married her. – *Anna war so schön. Sie war so schön.* – Why did you take her away?"

Andrew realized he'd never get anywhere. So, he just waited in silence to give his grandfather more time to remember who he was. He scrutinized the old man's face, then he looked out of the window at the nicely tended garden of the nursing home. He wondered how much of his physical environment his grandfather was able to take in.

Suddenly the old rasping voice began again, "The *Führer* didn't even give me a medal when he visited our camp. But I know what's going on."

"What do you mean?" Andrew enquired.

"Ah, I see, young man. You've come to get me. But I know what's going on. You don't know me, do you?" he chuckled. Then he laughed, louder and louder. "Ha ha! You think you know me, but you don't know me. *I cha scho Bärndütsch! Ja, jaaa, I bi kei Souschwab, nenei,*" he eagerly stated, nodding then shaking his head.

Andrew didn't understand what language his grandfather was falling into. Could it be Dutch or Russian? He knew that the old man had always been a very gifted linguist, but he wasn't sure how many languages he still spoke. Besides, it was highly uncertain whether any of his utterances really made sense at all. He was probably mixing together all sorts of different things in his life, even mixing them with his own dreams and fantasies. And in all this, despite some angry outbreaks, he appeared to be reasonably happy.

After another half hour of listening to the old man's ramblings, which were interspersed with bits from other languages – most of which he identified as German phrases and a few Latin proverbs – Andrew decided to leave. He stood up and bent down to kiss his grandfather on his forehead, which the old man allowed without protest.

"Good-bye, Granddad."

"Hey, don't leave your old Granddad like that," came the rasping voice.

Andrew turned round and saw that his grandfather was looking at him with great tenderness. Obviously, this was a brief moment of mental lucidity.

"Why didn't you bring your sister Lisa? And where's Emily? My dear girl, Emily?"

Andrew hesitated before he answered truthfully. There was no need to tell lies at this point, but he didn't remind his grandfather that Grandma had died years ago. "Lisa will come to see you soon, but Mother isn't very well. That's Nora. She had to go to hospital. But she's going to get better. Do you want me to give her a message from you?"

"Oh, I see," the grandfather said. "It's true. *Tempora mutantur et nos mutamur in illis*. Isn't it? If only Emily could be here. Tell her, it was all for the best. Tell her I didn't mean to do bad things."

"Yes, I will tell her."

After this, they talked about the weather, and Andrew told his grandfather about the first Black American President. Then old Didi was losing his grip on reality again.

Soon, Andrew left the nursing home. As he was passing through the front hall, he happened to see the young nurse again, the good-looking young nurse who had received him earlier. She smiled at him, and he smiled back. He wondered what her name could be and decided to ask her next time. He walked towards the station and turned right at the library. In Grove Road, he went into the newsagent's to get a paper. Of course, the headlines were full of the new American President. Andrew folded the paper away. As he was walking on he was thinking of all the things his grandfather had said or insinuated. If he put all the puzzle-pieces together it appeared that his grandfather was begging for some kind of understanding or even forgiveness.

He would really have to talk to his mother about this as soon as she was getting better. Hopefully, that would be soon enough.

When he reached his flat in the evening he first called his father, who told him that Mum was recovering slowly. He said she might have to remain in hospital for quite some time. After this call, Andrew had a snack and turned on his TV-set. He watched some more commentaries about the possible achievements the world could expect from Mr Obama. Some journalists believed he could really introduce a new era in American international politics, but more commentators were uncertain and warned of too high expectations. After all, there was too strong an opposition from the Republicans in the House of Representatives. Andrew found it hard to understand some aspects of American politics, particularly the prevailing frontier mentality, which was responsible for the power of the National Rifle Association, in spite of all those mass murders in public and shootings at schools. How primitive can you be to believe that the right to carry a loaded gun was a sign of freedom?

He was getting tired. As he was nearly dropping off to sleep in front of the screen he remembered the good-looking nurse. Lucky Granddad! To be looked after by such a charming young woman...

The next few days, he was very busy with various things. There were email messages to be answered, there were two of his friends who wanted to meet him for a chat, and there were the regular visits to his mother in the hospital.

Nora was gradually getting better. As Dr Banerjee had predicted, it appeared that she would remain partly paralysed in her left side and it was difficult for her to use her left hand. Otherwise, she seemed to be in excellent health. However, this stroke had an important effect on her mind. As she told Andrew after a week in hospital, she got the shock of her life.

"I suddenly realized how limited my life was," she explained.

"Oh, come on, Mum. You're going to live for much longer," he insisted.

"You're talking like your father. In his case it's inexcusable, but you are still young, so I can forgive you for your ignorance."

"Okay, I'm young. But can't you see that Dad must believe the same thing? He loves you. When a man loves a woman, he cannot imagine the end of her life, or vice versa. Or can you imagine the end of Dad's life?"

"I couldn't, up to now. Now I can. Does this sound harsh?" she asked, looking deep into her son's eyes.

He thought about it before he answered. "I guess it isn't, after what you've just gone through. But still, I don't believe it can help you to have such thoughts. Life is still so full of joy. I mean, you're only in your early fifties. There are still so many good things waiting for you in your life. It feels strange for a son to have to tell his own mother such basic truths, but I strongly believe in them."

"That's perfectly all right for you, my dear. But my perspective is a different one. I've seen things that can destroy even the strongest man's convictions. So, I'm also more realistic about my own life. You can't take this away from me."

The son frowned. "What things do you mean? What have you seen?"

The mother remained silent for a longer period before she took up the conversation again. And when she did, she spoke in a strange voice, a voice her son had never heard from her. It sounded as if she was speaking to him from some other sphere, but it was still his mother's voice.

"I have thought about these questions for a long time. Now, lying in bed here, with the prospect of going through my remaining days as a cripple – "

"Don't say that! You're not a cripple," Andrew protested. But she cut him short.

"Don't interrupt me. This is important, and I'm only telling you this once. I'm never going to repeat it. But the fact is, I've found out things that make you lose all confidence in humanity. Before this time in hospital I always thought I'd take those things into my grave with me. But now, I've come to the conclusion that someone in the family ought to know. Those things shouldn't be forgotten. They should never be allowed to be forgotten. But the problem is, they're so heavy. They nearly crushed me, and whoever is going to preserve them for the next generation might not be strong enough."

She broke off and directed her eyes to the window. He was just going to ask her a question when she continued in the same outlandish voice.

"Don't ask me to explain what I mean at this point. Listen, Andrew dear. I know you're a very strong man. You have enormous potential. Lisa is a good girl, but she's far too weak. She has such a soft nature, and you know how her emotions can get the better of her. So I'm convinced you are the person to be trusted when the time comes. You will know what to do."

"I still don't understand what you mean," he faltered. He felt a thick lump in his throat. "Why don't you want to explain?"

"Because the time is not ripe. But there will come a day when you can understand everything. One day, my heavy knowledge will pass on to you. It'll probably be after I'm gone, but it might be while I'm still alive, depending on my medical condition."

"You sound like Old Major in Orwell's *Animal Farm*," Andrew was joking, but he realized it was not the right time for lightness. "Sorry, but you scare me with such sombre predictions."

"I didn't mean them to be sombre. Knowledge is never sombre, though its contents may very well be."

"So, what do you want me to do?"

"Nothing. When the time comes you will know. Now, leave me, please. This has made me tired. I'd like to rest. Please."

With her right hand she grabbed both his hands and held them for a while. Then she dropped her hand, laid it down on her bed and closed her eyes. Her actions were a clear dismissal.

Andrew understood. He stood up from his chair by the bedside, kissed his mother's forehead, muttered a soft "good-bye, Mum," and quietly left the ward.

FOURTEEN

Life for Andrew continued very much within its normal groove. He did his job at the local council offices, he spent his free time either practising the piano or with friends playing tennis or football. Sometimes he went for a drink at the Dolphin or at the Dewdrop Inn opposite, about every two of three days or so he visited his mother at the hospital, and once a week he went to the nursing home to see his grandfather.

After what his mother had told him that afternoon, he often wondered what she could have meant, but he never asked her again. She never returned to the subject. As time went on, he put the matter to the back of his mind, although he couldn't forget it completely.

One day, about two weeks after his mother's stroke, he was sitting at his piano teacher's instrument. It was a fine Bechstein grand. Sam Westfield, his teacher, was talking about the piece they were in the process of getting to know. Andrew was immediately caught by the magic of the piece. It was Rachmaninov's *Prélude* in c sharp minor. Its general mood, especially in the opening bars, took hold of him in a very strange way. It reminded him of what his mother had told him about a hidden truth he was going to find out one day. Somehow, the heaviness of the first section of the *Prélude* drew him back into the emotions he'd felt at that time. The fast middle section, on the other hand, had an urgency that turned what he'd felt in the first section into some black being that was constantly escaping his consciousness, only to arrive, in the final section, in a land of superior knowledge. He wondered whether he should tell Sam. Even though they had quite a personal relationship – which was really a perfect thing between teacher and pupil in such an intimate subject as the piano – he wasn't sure if Sam would understand. After all, he didn't know Mum, and he hadn't been there when his mother spoke to him about those things.

Back at his flat, he practised the *Prélude* very diligently, trying to create the different moods in the piece according to his own sensibility. After a few days, he found he couldn't go back to his mundane every-day life after playing such a piece. He looked for a different piece that he could play as a buffer between the *Prélude* and the outside world. He tried the Bach Fantasy in c minor BWV 906 that he'd learnt only a few weeks back. It was only the Fantasy, without the Fugue, which had the right effect for him. But after a few more days he felt that Bach was altogether too logical, too mathematical and also somehow too deep to satisfy him. So he reverted to another piece within his repertoire that finally functioned for him as it should. And this was Schubert's *Impromptu* op.90 no.1. Its marching rhythm, together with its wistful main theme, gave him what he'd been looking for. Henceforth, he would practise the Rachmaninov *Prélude* to get it as near to perfection as possible – which was no child's play in the middle section – and always play the Schubert *Impromptu* before returning to normal life and the banality of his physical presence in his flat.

Today, he not only played the Rachmaninov, the Bach and the Schubert, but he leafed through his stack of sheet-music and pulled out various other pieces that took his fancy at this particular moment. Among others, he spent quite some time to work his way through Mozart's K 331, leaving out the all too often-heard last movement, but repeating several of the variations of the first movement. In the end, however, he got tired of the deceptively graceful A major of the Sonata and returned to the mood of the Rachmaninov. He was just reaching the climax of the third part with its gorgeous *fortissimo*, when his phone rang.

It was his friend Dave. He wanted him to come for a drink at the Bibendum, a pub-cum-bistro at the corner of Grange Road and South Street. Andrew had liked the pub a lot better before its recent refurbishment, when it had still been called the New Inn.

In the pub, Dave smiled, "Hi Andrew, old man, how are things?"

"Hiya, good to see you. I'm glad you drew me out of my place. I've been spending too much time on my own recently, you know, cut off from the world."

"Oh, have you? The good old piano, wasn't it?"

"Yes. That and other things."

"Aren't we growing into two old buffers? You with your music and I with my books?" Dave pulled a sour face.

"Well, I don't know. On the other hand, I think we are learning a great deal about the world, about humanity, only different things from what we can learn in a pub, for instance. Don't you think your extensive reading gives you insights you could never reach without your books? And I feel the same about my music."

Dave was indeed an extremely avid reader. Whenever he could, he had his nose in a book. Wherever he went, he always carried a book with him in case he might have some time to kill. Andrew envied his encyclopaedic knowledge of literature. He knew quite a bit about English and German literature, too, but Dave's expertise extended into many other literary fields. He was very well-read in all the Postcolonial literatures in English, and in French, German, Italian, Spanish and Russian literature. While he read most of those in their original languages, he also read Scandinavian, Chinese and Japanese texts in translation. No wonder Dave was working his way up the academic ladder and was hoping to get a chair in Comparative Literature one day. Andrew never stopped being impressed. The two friends respected each other's keen interests.

They got their drinks and sat down by the large window. Outside, the forecourt was full of smokers who were holding their pint glasses in one hand while gesticulating in the air with their other hand which also held their cigarettes.

"I can never understand how anyone can still be a smoker these days," Dave remarked. He had rather strict views on this, while he condoned the other most popular drug of today, alcohol.

The friends got into discussions about drugs, about the general decay of society and about their own positions between optimism and pessimism. Dave said he believed English society particularly was getting vulgarized more and more terribly year by year, much more so than other European societies. Andrew countered that he was obviously forgetting the *banlieues* of Paris. This got them talking about the general dangers of growing parallel societies in many European contexts. In the end, they arrived at the question of whether or not a society needed some sort of moral standards, some set of shared moral values, in order to keep its general coherence.

"What happens to individuals who violate such moral standards? And why do they commit such violations in the first place? That's what I'd like to understand!" Andrew said.

"Well, think of Raskolnikov! Every individual has the potential to commit a crime, for various reasons. The important thing, however, is for him to be guided back into the social system, to be reprimanded. That's Dostoyevsky's original title, you know. The Russian *Prestuplenie i Nakazanie*, generally translated as *Crime and Punishment*, really means 'Transgression and Reproof'. It is really that process of being reprimanded by the powers that govern human behaviour which is the important issue. Some individuals manage to survive such a process, albeit through phases of extreme difficulties, you know, through complete collapse and rebirth, while others are destroyed in the process, like Meursault in *L'Etranger* by Camus."

"It's funny how you're just trying to make me understand such important issues through some Russian mind. I mean Dostoyevsky. When you called me, I was just grappling with another great Russian mind, Rachmaninov." Andrew was quite excited about this coincidence. "The mood of his famous *Prélude*, you know the c sharp minor, especially in its third part, I now feel, has a lot in common with what you've just been explaining."

"Yes," Dave said and took another sip from his drink. He rubbed his chin and continued. "I used to think it was the Germans who carried with them a constant sense of guilt. I mean, just look at most of their classical literature. But more recently I've come to the conclusion that their hereditary guilt complex was nothing compared to the great Russian soul. Whereas with Tolstoy you never really know where you are, whether in the land of light or in the valley of darkness, it's a constant struggle for the spiritual survival of one's soul in Dostoyevsky, especially if a character allows himself to be separated from the essence of his society and from the healing power of love."

"I agree completely," Andrew nodded. "But why did you bring in Camus before? Surely, that's an altogether different case, isn't it?"

"You're right there. Meursault is different. He's the hero and the victim at the same time. The only insight he gains is the recognition of his own existence. He can be seen as the personification of Nihilism, in which case there's no parallel to Raskolnikov, but the similarity, at least for me, lies in both men's overstepping of absolute limits, their utter abandonment of the values of the society that nourishes them."

"But what about such cases in real life? What course of action remains for such individuals in our time?"

"Do you mean the Idi Amins, the Ghaddafis and the Saddam Husseins of this world?"

"Not even just those. They are lost to the world anyway. But take any minion within those dictators' machineries? Take the Stasi thug responsible for ordinary men's disasters, or the KGB agent helping to send innocent people to the Siberian Gulag. Those *aparatchiks* go to their offices like any ordinary employee but the results of their seemingly ordinary office jobs kill or destroy people. In their eyes, they're just doing their jobs. Remember Adolf Eichmann and all those defendants at Nuremberg who claimed they just obeyed their orders. How guilty can they ever be?"

"Of course, they're as guilty as their leaders. Remember Hannah Arendt's dictum, 'No-one has the right to obey.' But listen, Andrew. We'll have to go on with this conversation some other night. It's time for me to go home. I'm expecting a phone call from a colleague in the States who promised to let me know something I asked him the other day. He's due to call me within the next half hour. It's only late afternoon in Washington now."

Andrew was disappointed. He was enjoying such conversations with Dave, and his friend's insights often gave him a big boost. But he agreed to call it a day, and the two friends parted in the street in front of the pub.

Back in his flat, he sat down at his piano and played a light-footed *Arietta con Variazioni* by Haydn to unburden his spirit after the heavier pieces that he was normally working on. He added the second movement of Bach's Italian Concerto, to conclude his day. This relaxed him enough so that he could go to bed.

***

When, two days later, he ran into his Aunt Margaret in front of W. H. Smith's in Terminus Road he greeted her with real joy. She kissed him on his cheek and suggested they go for a cup of coffee together.

"I've just been to the hospital," Margaret explained when they were settled with their coffees at a wobbly table at the back of the café. "Nora is feeling a lot better. I'm glad. You know, we were all so worried."

"Of course, we were worried. She's given me such a shock as well. All of a sudden, I realize that my Mum is not going to live forever. But I guess that's a lesson every person has to learn sooner or later, isn't it?"

"Well, yes. Just think of your grandparents. My mother dead for ages and my father in a terrible state..."

"I don't think he is so terribly unhappy. Do you?"

"Not really. You may be right, it's more the people around him – that's us – that are unhappy. He may very well be okay within the cocoon of his dementia."

"On the other hand," Andrew mused, "there are obviously things that worry him a great deal. I mean things from his past. Mostly his experiences in the War. Don't you feel he seems to worry a lot about those?"

"Probably. But to tell you the truth, I am sick of all that talk about the War and all that. Nora has been going on and on about it for most of her life. I can't take any more."

Andrew mildly protested. "But I think it's important."

"Oh yes, I've nearly forgotten that you're just like her in that department. How come you also take such a keen interest in history, the War, Nazi Germany and so on? Does that really matter?"

"To me, it does."

"Just like your mother. Nora kept at it through most of our time as youngsters. But I understand she's no longer so keen. We all criticized her until she went on that trip to Germany, which seemed to have satisfied her at last. She certainly lost a great deal of her zeal after that trip."

"Have you ever talked to her about that trip?" Andrew asked.

"Well, yes, we did talk about it for a bit. But I don't think she told me everything. To tell you the truth, I wasn't all that interested."

Andrew wanted to tell his aunt how very much he would like to learn more about his mother's trip to Germany back in the 1990s. But he understood that his interest was not reciprocated, so he changed the subject. When, at the end of their time at the café, they said good-bye, Aunt Margaret quickly returned to the former subject. "Why don't you read her diary?" she suggested.

He was surprised. He'd never known his mother to be a diarist. But he decided to find out if such a diary really existed.

He was still lost in his thoughts when he walked into the National Westminster Bank. He wanted to ask something about his mortgage, but his mind was still engaged with his mother's diary. So he was turning the corner through the heavy wooden doors in an absent-minded state when he bumped into another person.

"Oh, I'm really sorry," he croaked. Looking up he saw the other person was a woman. They stood facing each other, dumbfounded for a moment.

"Can't you keep your eyes open?" the woman snapped, rubbing her nose.

"Sorry again. I don't know what else to say. Just that I'm sorry." He clearly felt it was all his fault. "Are you hurt?"

The woman took a moment to calm down. As it appeared, she felt a pain in her nose, which had hit Andrew's chin head-on, and she said she had a pain in her knee.

They stood aside to let other people pass by. They both felt a little awkward, not knowing what to say and still feeling reluctant to part without another word or some sign of reconciliation. While Andrew was searching the woman's face for signs of forgiveness, the woman was first looking down, avoiding his eyes. Eventually, she raised her face and met his. Then they just looked at each other. Neither of them managed to find the appropriate words. Andrew had never felt like this in his life. He didn't want to give up looking into this woman's dark green eyes. He forgot everything around them.

At last, he mumbled, "My name's Andrew."

"Hi Andrew. I'm Rebecca," she answered. She began to smile.

Suddenly, he panicked. He said something to the effect that he was busy and just walked away. He'd forgotten the bank and just walked across to the entrance to the Arndale Shopping Centre. He didn't look back.

Andrew spent the rest of the day in a state of nervous agitation. He was not himself. He went back to his office, but he didn't realize what he was doing. He functioned like a robot. After a fruitless hour of pretended work, he decided to go home.

Back in his flat he sat down to a glass of Chardonnay and tried to find out what was going on with himself. But his thoughts went round in circles, he felt drugged, and the wine added to his sense of intoxication. So he fell into a light sleepiness, a sort of trance. Like this, he spent what seemed to him something like ten hours but in reality, was only about half an hour.

Then it hit him like lightning.

"It's that woman," he breathed to himself. "What was her name? Rebecca. Yes, Rebecca. Her deep stare, her dark green eyes, her fascinating face, her breathing, her posture, her perfume."

The only adequate response to this shock was the piano. It had to be Beethoven. He sat down at his piano and played the *Grande Sonate Pathétique* from end to end. When he'd finished he first took some time to regain his normal breathing, then he felt utterly exhausted. So, even though it was only just after six o'clock, he went to his bedroom and collapsed on his bed.

He dreamed of Rebecca, of course. In his dream, she was staring at him in the same intensive way as in front of the bank, her face just a few inches away from his, and he wanted her to come closer, to put his arms around her, to kiss those lovely lips of hers, but whenever he had the impression that she was sinking into his arms and her lips were coming closer and closer, she vanished from sight, only to reappear in the same position as at the beginning of the dream. This scene repeated itself several times. Every time he wanted to draw her to him and to kiss her she vanished. In time, the dream became more blurred with every repetition, and he fell into a deep and dreamless sleep.

He woke up some time after two in the morning. After tossing and turning in his bed for another half hour, he got up and walked to the kitchen to pour himself a glass of cold milk. Normally, this helped him to go back to sleep. But back in bed he still couldn't relax enough, his mind kept racing around what had happened to him. That woman. Rebecca.

He thought about his experience with women. Most of the time he had been too busy with his studies and his piano to take note of women's charms. During his university years, he had been to several parties where he was attracted to one of the girls, he had even been drawn into some hot cuddling and kissing sessions with girls he liked very much. He had to admit to himself that he was really very fond of female beauty, and he still remembered how deeply he'd been impressed with the erotic quality of the *Toilet of Venus* by

Velazquez in the National Gallery. He used to go back again and again, standing in front of the alluring painting, following the wonderful curve of the woman's back with his eager teenager's eyes and admiring the perfection of her naked pink skin. Of course, he knew perfectly well what a naked girl looked like. After all, as a child he had often played naked with his sister Lisa during those hot summer afternoons. At the time, the fact that she looked different had just been a natural observation, without any particular attraction. The change had come when Lisa suddenly began to grow into some alien being, with her giggles and – more visibly – with those budding breasts. That was the time when they'd stopped their carefree games in the long summer afternoons. Lisa had begun to go out to play with other girls, while he had turned his interests to more academic subjects and to music. So, when the awareness of female beauty re-entered his consciousness during those hot university parties he experienced the whole matter as a pleasant but not very important aspect of his life as a young man. That was what men and women did, didn't they? Eventually, they'd get ready to produce children. But for Andrew that eventuality was still miles away. Although he was more than just aware of women and he loved looking at beautiful and sexy women, he still couldn't imagine himself wanting to be with a woman for more than a relaxed cuddling session, for an evening when he had nothing better to do perhaps. He liked the erotic quality of nude women in men's magazines or in French films, particularly with Isabelle Huppert or Eva Green, and at the other end of the scale he liked several women as friends or colleagues, just as fine persons. But up to now he'd never managed to build a bridge between these two quite contrasting images of women in his mind. Until now.

That Rebecca woman caused an earthquake within Andrew's entire being. He could neither categorize her among those erotic models and actresses, nor could he merely see her in the same sphere as his female friends, say like Zoe, the young woman who worked in the same office and with whom he often exchanged pleasant chats about everything under the sun. Zoe was a friend, yes, but what was this new woman, Rebecca?

He checked himself, telling himself that his feelings were ridiculous. He'd only bumped into Rebecca, they had looked into each other's eyes, and they had only spoken a few words. He knew next to nothing about her. Even if what was happening to him now could be called falling in love – a process which was utterly new and represented dangerous, unmapped territory – it was as futile as waiting to win the National Lottery.

He suddenly remembered the old Jewish joke of Samuel who went to the synagogue every day, praying to God for the jackpot in the lottery. Every day he would look up towards heaven and pray with the same words, "Please dear God, arrange it for me to win the lottery!" Back he went to the synagogue, day after day, until one day after many years, when he'd just completed his regular prayer, he suddenly heard a deep voice coming down from heaven: "Oh Samuel, please give me a chance. Buy a lottery ticket!"

Andrew had always considered that joke a bit silly, but now it suddenly struck him as a piece of old wisdom. It might apply to his predicament. He wanted to see Rebecca again. And the only chance he had was to do something about it, but what? He went through several courses of action in his mind.

He got up and had a shower. Over his early-morning coffee, he decided to explore his possibilities during the day. He was quite confident he would find her eventually.

In his morning break at the office, he happened to get his cup of tea at the same time as Zoe. He asked her if she had ever tried to find a person.

"How do you mean?" Zoe asked. "Do you mean someone whose name you don't know?"

"Yes, someone whose surname you don't know, so you can't consult the phone directory. Besides, many people no longer have a land-line. What would you suggest?"

They went through various options, most of which were too unrealistic, until Zoe concluded, "Your best bet is to place an advert in the *Herald*."

In the evening, Andrew went for a drink at the Dolphin in South Street where he ran into Dave, who was already on his third pint of London Pride. The two friends talked about their day and the latest news. Dave had some gossip about some scandal in the Labour Party, and Andrew told his friend what had happened to him the day before in front of the National Westminster Bank.

"So, what are you going to do about it?" Dave asked.

"I guess I'll have to put an advert in the paper to trace her down."

"Yeah, that's probably your only chance. Are you sure you didn't get her full name? I mean, if you were so taken with her, why didn't you ask her for her number?"

"I couldn't speak. I was so dumbstruck. Then, I would've found it vulgar to ask for her number. It's so crude. It's what people do in films, not in real life."

"That woman really got you, eh?" Dave chuckled.

Andrew just nodded. He decided to try the idea with the advert, and he changed the subject.

The next day, he went to the newspaper office to place his advert. He had concocted the following text under the bold title "Rebecca":

> *We bumped into each other in front of the NatWest in Terminus Road on Monday. I can't forget your beautiful green eyes. Where are you?*

If you'd like to see me again, just come to the Dolphin Inn in South Street on a Tuesday or Thursday between 7 and 9pm.

Andrew.

After the text had appeared in the *Herald,* he made sure to be at the Dolphin at the right time every Tuesday and Thursday. But it was all in vain. Rebecca didn't come. The first two weeks, Andrew still hoped for a miracle, but after that he gave up and told himself he would have to forget her.

Life went on in its usual grooves. Andrew was at his job, sometimes chatting to Zoe, he spent time with Dave, discussing politics and other things, and he played his piano. When his mother was getting better she was released from hospital. The next day, Andrew visited her at her home. After discussing various practical matters, her health, her therapy, her chances of a full recovery, as well as Andrew's latest news, they came to talk about some news items.

"Did you see the report about that old man who was charged with terrible crimes during the War? He's very old now, but they say he was involved with mass murder in a concentration camp."

"Yes," Andrew eagerly answered because it was an item that interested him as much as his mother. "He was an *Unterscharführer* of the SS at Auschwitz-Birkenau."

They discussed what had emerged about this case in the news. Then Andrew decided to ask his mother about her trip to Germany more than ten years ago.

"You know so much more about what happened in Germany during the War," he began. "So, I'm sure you could tell me a lot more. Aunt Margaret told me you'd been writing a diary."

Mother hesitated before she answered. "You see, I discovered so many things that nobody wants to know about these days. I just believed that one day, perhaps, someone might be interested, especially someone in our family who has enough understanding about history. Some of the things I found out are so terrible. You see, my boy, it's a proper dilemma. On one hand, I don't want to destroy our family's belief in the good things my father did, but on the other hand, I feel it as my duty to preserve the truth for the future, so that it can be recognized and assessed by the right minds when the time comes."

They remained silent for a while. Andrew poured himself another cup of tea from his mother's pot on the table. They were sitting in her lounge.

"You know, I'm just as interested in these things as you are. I envy you. You went to Germany to speak to the right people, but all I can do is guess."

"I know, my dear. And I think the time will come when I'll let you read my diary. But it's too early now. You're too young."

At the pub in the evening, Andrew told Dave about it. Dave showed the appropriate interest in his friend's news about his hobby-horse, Germany in the last war. But in reality, he only humoured him. What interested him rather more in this context than the raw historical facts were the philosophical implications.

"So, you keep blaming your granddad for his involvement in the atrocities of the Nazis in Germany?" he asked.

"Well, it's not even proved that he was involved. All I have are insinuations I gathered from my mum. But I want to know for sure, sooner or later."

"Why don't you let sleeping dogs lie, like everybody? Who cares about those events nowadays? Or do you believe that Kant's Categorical Imperative is still as valid for our moral behaviour as it was over two hundred years ago?"

"Of course," Andrew stated with conviction. "'Act only according to that maxim whereby you can, at the same time, want that it should become a universal law.'"

"Exact quotation, well done! But do you honestly believe it to be as valid as ever? Haven't things changed dramatically during the last century?"

"You may be right in many respects, but I believe in the moral philosophy of the Enlightenment. Otherwise I couldn't believe so passionately in Democracy and in the importance of Human Rights. These basic concepts can't be overturned so easily by some new technology, by the landing on the moon, by the Internet or by the possibility of pre-natal genetic diagnostics, to name just a few achievements."

"But some of the achievements you mention have obviously had some impact on some of our moral concepts, haven't they?"

Andrew emptied his drink before he answered. "Indeed, we have to agree on how to adapt the limits of our moral concepts because of the new scientific territory explored by some of these achievements. But that doesn't mean that our basic understanding of good and evil has to be changed. There are already enough challenges in the fact that other cultures are already drawing much narrower limits around even those basic concepts."

"What examples are you thinking of?"

"Take the Saudis and homosexuality, take the fundamentalist Catholics and birth control, or take the Americans and the death penalty, to name just a few examples."

Dave had nothing to add to this. So the two friends ordered another round of drinks and changed the subject.

"Tell me," Dave said confidentially, "any news in the girlfriend department?"

Andrew drew a long sigh. "She still hasn't come forward."

"She may have missed your advert. So just repeat the procedure. She may see it the second time."

"And then repeat it again and again? Spending all my money on adverts?"

"No. But give it just one more chance. Or let's agree on three adverts. If she doesn't respond the second time, I'm going to finance the third advert. And if there's still no answer the third time, we'll call it off. What do you say?"

"Okay, I'll agree to a second try. But I'm not going to have you pay for a third, you know, you have to see that."

The two men clinked their pint glasses on this agreement. Andrew was happy about Dave's optimism. In a way, he was hoping for better success the second time, too, but at the same time he was extremely doubtful if Rebecca would see the second advert if she didn't see the first. He even feared she might have seen the first advert but decided not to respond. Why should she get involved with a man she'd just seen once and hadn't even talked to except giving her name?

He placed the advert in the *Herald* a second time. It appeared on the last week in March.

As he was sitting over a gin and tonic in the Dolphin Inn around seven thirty on the next Thursday evening, not really thinking about anything in particular, but with the principal tune of Chopin's g-minor Ballad in his head, a soft voice behind his back asked, "Andrew?"

Utterly puzzled for a second, he turned around in amazement.

There she was. Rebecca was smiling at him.

FIFTEEN

The time came when Nora had recovered so well that her slight handicap was hardly noticeable, which was a development for which everyone in her family was grateful. Her sister Margaret still came down to Sussex at least once a month to help her, but recently her visits had become rarer and she seemed to prefer to stay in London with her partner Helen. Nora's husband George, although very busy at work in Gatwick, continued to be a great help and a wonderful moral support for her. Her daughter Lisa had completed her M.A. at university and got started on a job in the City, living on her own in an old flat near Hampstead Heath. Her son Andrew and his girlfriend Rebecca were her most regular visitors. They had been an item for nearly two years now. Their relationship had developed like a poorly constructed love-story in some cheap bestseller from the airport bookstall. Only the pink sunset had been missing. Even after nearly two years, they appeared to be very much in love. This made Andrew's mother very happy.

Andrew himself had hardly changed over the past two years, except for the fact that he devoted all his energy that wasn't directed at his music to his great love, Rebecca. She was his first and only love, the only woman he had invited into his life, body and soul. Her dark green eyes still fascinated him every day. They remained the most alluring part of her, even though he'd had the pleasure of getting to know other phenomenally beautiful parts of her. When they had first explored each other's bodies and made love for the first time – which hadn't been so very long after their meeting at the Dolphin Inn – it was as if a new world revealed itself to him. One of the effects of this new existence was that he no longer discussed women with his friend Dave. The two friends still met for occasional drinks and they still shared a great many observations about the world, about politics, about history and philosophy, but no longer about women. They could still make a casual comment about a woman they might see at the pub, but they had left their former juvenile male sexist comments behind them. Andrew didn't know why, but he felt his respect for women in general had been lifted to a higher level.

"I'm going to see Mum after work today," he announced one cool Wednesday morning in July. Rebecca had just stepped out of the shower and was beginning to dry her beautiful body with her large green bath-towel.

"Will you be home later in the evening?" she asked. "Or shall we have supper together?"

"I think Mum wants me to stay a bit longer. She seems to have something on her mind. At least that's what her short text message suggests. What about your plans for the evening?"

"I could stay out later, too, meet my Mum at the beach and take her for fish and chips on the Pier." She smiled at him, stepping out of her wrapping, throwing the bath-towel on the washing-basket.

"That's a very good idea," he said, looking at his beautiful Rebecca, who was standing stark naked in front of him, wriggling her large breasts in jest in front of his eyes. He swallowed hard, dumbstruck with admiration and desire. Her beauty was so perfect. Of course, she was fully aware of her effect on him. She loved to tease him sexually, especially in the morning. She knew how much he admired her full breasts with their pink puffy nipples, so whenever she wanted to arouse him, even just to celebrate life together, she knew how to present her physical beauty to him for maximum effect. Today, he didn't hesitate but immediately stepped up to her to fold her in his arms. She pulled off his light summer clothes, and they went back to bed to make love.

Afterwards, they got dressed and had a quick cup of coffee together, before leaving for work.

Throughout the day, Andrew found it hard to concentrate. His mind often returned to the love-making of the morning. In his mind, he could still smell her skin and feel the soft touch of her flesh. Even after two years, he still found Rebecca the most beautiful woman in the world, and their sex life hadn't lost any of its initial fascination. If anything, it had become even better every time. He kept wondering how it was possible for a man like himself to be so happy, not only with a woman as a person, a companion, but also with a woman as a sexual partner, an object of such wild sexual desire with all those physical pleasures. He was convinced that it represented one of the great powers which lay behind all artistic creativity. How else could Velazquez paint such pictures, how else could Schubert or Chopin create such music, and how else could Keats or Wordsworth write such poetry?

Rebecca also proved to be a very pleasant and reliable partner in every-day life. She was very capable in practical matters, she was efficient and caring. Ever since they had moved in together she had been looking after their common flat. She did the cleaning, the washing and most other household chores. Andrew was very happy about this. He often offered to do more, to do what he considered his share, and she sometimes let him empty the dishwasher or allowed him to clean his own shoes, but she wanted to be the true mistress of their set-up. She had her standards in everything. So even if she let him do the occasional household job he had to do it to her standards. She was extremely opinionated when it came to standards of cleanliness and often reproached him for not having cleaned his hands enough, for having forgotten to clean his teeth after a meal or leaving a spot of water on the floor in the bathroom. And if he left a single stubble of hair in his face after shaving she would refuse to kiss him. He didn't mind these things, he rather considered himself fortunate to be with such a beautiful, sexy and competent woman. If there was one drawback about her that he became aware of over the first few months that they lived together, it was perhaps her limited intellectual capacities. For example, her mind was not capable of abstraction. So she could never tell him what she'd just read in the paper, she couldn't summarize a story, she couldn't even tell a story so that it made sense, she mixed up marginal matters with the central issue of a story, a report or a news item. For example, only recently she'd gone to the cinema with one of her friends to see the new film about King George VI called *The King's Speech*, which Andrew hadn't seen yet. When she came home he asked her about it.

"What was it about?"

"It was a charming film, you know, we nearly cried when we saw the girls, Elizabeth and Margaret, that's the Queen when she was young, and they were so cute. Their mother was very strict with them."

"Yes, but what was the main plot about?"

"The Queen, that's the queen we know as the Queen Mother, she was Helena Bonham Carter. I never really liked her, except in that old 1980s film about the girl playing the piano in Florence, you know when she had such a lot of thick hair. Wasn't that impressive? Do you remember?"

"Yes, that was in *A Room with a View*, based on the E. M. Forster novel. But what about *The King's Speech*? Was it more about the politics of the day, the Second World War, how the Royal Family coped, and the support they gave their people? Or what was the story?"

"Colin Firth, he was the King, you remember he used to be Mr Darcy. Well, he got together with some Australian and they became friends, but before he had to become king, he never wanted to become king, but it turned out he was a good king, his brother should have been king, and his wife, Helena Bonham Carter that is, she gave him a lot of support. Oh, it was a fine movie. They really got the atmosphere of those days during the War."

Andrew gave up. He decided to see the film for himself. But it took him a lot of intellectual tolerance to cope with his darling Rebecca's weakness in this matter. He admitted to himself that he had originally expected her to have higher intellectual abilities. He swallowed his slight disappointment and told himself that she was a charming woman anyway.

Another aspect of her intellectual limitation was something that often cropped up when they were sitting comfortably either at home or in some pub or restaurant, having a relaxed chat about things in general. As it can happen quite normally between any two people in such an every-day situation, he sometimes didn't get what she had just said because there was some noise around or it was spoken too softly, whatever. When he asked her what she'd just said she almost invariably repeated the only bit that he'd understood instead of the part he hadn't. At first, he thought he hadn't asked her clearly enough, but eventually he found that she couldn't grasp such a task, she just repeated what she considered the most important word of her utterance.

"Fiona said she'd seen him on the Pier." She stressed the word "Pier".

"Who – *whom* – did she see?"

"On the Pier!"

Or: "Fiona asked if we could meet at the pub next Wednesday," stressing "Wednesday".

"Sorry, I didn't get where. *Where* does she want to meet you?"

"Wednesday."

"Yes, but where?"

"Fiona, I said. On Wednesday."

Situations like this were so frequent that the idea hit him that she might have a problem with her hearing. But he found out that it couldn't be the problem, her hearing often proved to be excellent. So it had to be her intellect.

Over the months, Andrew learned to live with this. It was a small price to pay for being with such a lovely woman, after all. And weren't all love-relationships a challenge? And, to top it all, the sex they had was so satisfying. He truly believed he'd won the jackpot when it came to finding his ideal partner for life. The sex, yes, the sex was so overwhelmingly fantastic.

By the time he walked up to his mother's front door, after work, he had sufficiently recovered from his morning's sexual earthquake to focus on what his mother might have to discuss with him.

"I wanted to talk to you, but now I find it difficult to begin," his mother admitted. "You see, it's not easy. I have been in two minds about it for quite some time. Should I involve you, yes or no? And if so, when was the right time?"

"Don't say anything unless you really mean it," Andrew warned. "Don't say things you might regret afterwards."

"Oh, it's not that, my dear. I won't regret anything. It's only that I don't know when you will be ready for it. How will it affect you if I involve you too early?"

"Please, Mum, don't speak in riddles. I'm a big boy, and you know you can trust me with everything, even if you're going to tell me you've had a career as a chain-saw murderer." He thought this exaggeration could lighten the mood, but he was wrong. It was the wrong thing to say, he realized at once.

"I'm sorry, I was just – "

"I know. I'm sorry if I can't joke about these things. They're too serious."

Mother and son went on beating about the bush for a while. Eventually, after a short moment of silence, she took a deep breath and said, "It's that awful man, Wolfgang, again."

"Now you'll have to explain," Andrew begged.

Then it was time for the truth. For the first time in her life, Nora White, née Woolf, who had always been such a strong woman, became a humble narrator of events beyond her control. She began to tell her son Andrew a story that was bound to affect his life as much as it had affected hers for so many years.

"You may remember, we used to talk about people who must have known my father, your granddad that is, in his young days. And in that context, you might have heard of a man called Wolfgang. What you probably don't know is that Wolfgang tried to blackmail your granddad through the 1980s. But you know that I went to Germany in 1996."

"Yes, I know. And I probably guessed more than you may think. You know that I'm also interested in the past. Just like you. And I'm equally intrigued by what happened in the last war, especially in Germany. Also, Granddad sometimes says very strange things when he's so puzzled in his mind. He keeps on about having done bad things, but I can't make head or tail of it."

"There you are. This is the point. Are you ready to take my old diary and read it when it suits you?"

Andrew looked at his mother. With her question she gave him such a wonderful proof of her confidence in him. Was he worthy of such unconditional trust?

He realized that she might expect him to show some surprise, but he didn't want to be too enthusiastic either.

"Your diary?" he only asked.

"Indeed. There's only one problem," his mother said. "I can't find it. I know it must be somewhere, either in the attic or in the garage. I'm sure it isn't anywhere among our books or our documents. So I'll have to look for it. Only, at the time I simply haven't got the energy."

"Oh, you'll find it. I'm confident. Or do you want me to help you?"

"No, I prefer to find it myself."

"Perhaps Dad might know where it is," Andrew suggested.

Nora hesitated before she answered. "Your father doesn't even know this diary exists. He knows about my trip to Germany, of course. But I never told him everything. I only told him the more pleasant stories about my time over there. He knows I went to trace my father's past, and he asked me a few general questions, but he has no idea of the depth of my enquiry. I also did tell him that my father had changed his name twice after the war, but he wasn't really interested in the details. George said he married Nora Woolf and made her into Mrs White, and that was enough for him. He could never understand or even support my interest in my father's past."

"So, it's a thing between you and me?"

"Absolutely. That's why I want you to read my diary when the time is right. Oh yes, Margaret knows about the diary, too."

"Has she read it?"

"Of course not. She hasn't even seen it. I only told her in a moment of weakness shortly after my return from Germany. We both got a bit tipsy one evening when we were on our own. George was away on business and Helen was with her parents in Northumberland. So we spent a sisterly evening together, first at the Pilot and later back here. I can't tell you how much we had, but the bottles of Pinot Grigio lost their contents pretty quickly. It was just one of those evenings. We both felt so relaxed and free, and very close as sisters. We've never felt like that again. Anyway, that's when I confided in her. I told her about the diary. She's never asked me about it, and it has never been mentioned between us again. So, there you are. Margaret knows but doesn't seem to be so interested in it."

"And what about that Wolfgang man?"

"Well, that... That's another problem. He called here a few days ago, he was at the door. I was alone, and he gave me quite a fright. You know, he's an octogenarian but looks a lot younger, quite threatening. The vulgar type of an ugly German, if you know what I mean."

"What did he want?"

"Guess what. Money."

"I can see. But what do you expect me to do?"

"Well, I was hoping you might have an idea of what to do, how to react to the fellow's demands."

Andrew was silent for a few minutes, while his mother went to the kitchen to make a cup of tea. When the kettle was boiling she asked him if he wanted a cup, too, and he said yes, please. Then they sat down together in the living-room again.

After they'd had their first sips Andrew came to a decision.

"Here's my suggestion, Mum. You do your best to find that diary. How can I decide what to do if I don't know the full story? Whatever that man knows, it can't be all that bad. If he contacts you again, just put him off. Invent some story about ill health or so, just put him off. Let him think there might be some money if only he'll be patient enough. Meanwhile I will think of an appropriate strategy."

Nora sighed and nodded.

Back at home, Andrew gave the matter a great deal of thought. He told Rebecca that his mother wanted him to help her. He gave her a rough outline of the problem, playing it down as much as possible. He didn't want her to worry too much but being so much in love with her, he couldn't exclude her from something that occupied his mind so much.

"Do you want me to help in any way?" she asked.

"Not unless you desperately want to get involved with things of the distant past, I mean my grandfather's time during the War."

"I know how important those things are for you, my darling. I don't need to get involved. Only if you want me to. I trust you will do the right things. But if ever you or your mother should need my help, just let me know."

"Oh yes, there's something you could do. You could help Mum with her visitors next week. Some old friends of hers from her young days in Newcastle are coming down south to visit. They're quite decent women, in fact very nice people, and I'm sure Mum would love you to take them round, show them a few things, you know."

"I'd love to do that," Rebecca smiled. "You know I like your mother very much, and I'm glad to give her a hand with things."

"Well, I don't think she needs a lot of help, but she could do with some support with the tourist thing."

"Okay, I'll arrange things with her."

"You are such a darling."

Andrew decided to involve Dave. The next day, he called him, and the two friends met at Dave's apartment at the bottom end of Grange Road. After some small-talk and a few comments about the current political situation, they came to what Andrew had on his mind.

"So, what's that problem for which you need my help?" Dave asked.

"Don't laugh, but it's got to do with the past, with the time of the last war, and my grandfather's role in it." Then Andrew told him what he knew about his grandfather, his mother's investigations and finally about that Wolfgang fellow and the blackmail. Then he asked Dave for advice.

"I think it's clear," Dave answered. "Just ignore the idiot. Whatever he knows – *if* he even knows anything that's shameful or whatever – it can't be that bad. Besides, who cares? Nobody gives a hoot about petty little crimes committed some sixty years ago. Why dig up the past? So, your granddad may have stolen a gun from some Nazi bloke, or whatever. Let it be. Let sleeping dogs lie."

This advice appeared very sensible to Andrew. Even if that fellow published what he knew – say, in a TV talk-show or in some tabloid paper – it would never have a big effect. Granddad was an old invalid. So, what would be the worst thing that could happen? Neither Mum nor Dad were important people, people of interest to the general public. Nobody would blame an ordinary person, a law-abiding decent citizen, for anything that one of their ancestors had done during war-times in the last century.

Andrew's decision was taken. He told his mother. She was uncertain. "And you'd really take the risk. You'd let the man publish what he knows?" she wondered.

"Indeed, I would. Let him do what he likes. Let him do what he wants with his scanty knowledge of no importance. Let him put it in his pipe and smoke it!" Andrew smiled.

"Well, if you think so," his mother answered, hesitatingly.

They changed the subject. The mother was full of excitement over the impending visit of her friends. This was going to be much more than a casual visit, it was the first – and perhaps the only – reunion of Nora's school friends. While she had been staying in touch with Debbie in London and Janet in Bristol, she had not seen any of the others since her school days. Debbie, who was still the great communicator and who kept in touch with many other people from her Newcastle days, had now organized this reunion.

She had been planning this for over two years, but it had taken so long to get everyone to agree on a common date.

"There will be Janet, of course, but there will also be Christine, Sophie and Amy," she'd informed Nora in her latest email message. Whereas Janet had kept in touch with Nora and had been to see her in Eastbourne on several occasions, neither of the other three women had ever been to England's south coast, so Debbie invited them all for an extended weekend in Eastbourne, hoping that Nora would be their local guide.

"Are you going to natter about the good old days in Newcastle when you get together?" Andrew asked.

"Those good old days weren't all that good. We had our disagreements, our rivalries and a few big conflicts. But we never really broke up as a loose group of girls in a male-dominated and narrow-minded society. The biggest conflict we had was about Janet, when she got pregnant at fifteen."

"Was that when Bob was born?" Andrew had met Bob when they visited Janet in Bristol the first time. Bob was twelve years his senior. Andrew had never really liked Bob because he considered him vulgar. Bob was a hands-on type who only considered manual labour real work, he called all university graduates pussy-footers, and he used four-letter-words in almost every sentence; that is if he ever produced a full sentence.

"Oh, don't judge him," Nora said. "He had such a hard time when he was young."

"Why?"

"Well, Janet and her child were social outcasts. You know, in those days it was considered a great shame when a girl got pregnant as a teenager and without being married. It was always the girl's fault, never the boy who got her pregnant, and she was made to feel it. I remember in Newcastle, people pointed their fingers at her and warned their daughters not to have anything to do with such a bad girl."

Andrew changed the subject and promised his mother he would help her when it came to hosting her friends. He suggested he might show them round, showing them Beachy Head, Pevensey Castle and other sights in the area.

When her old friends arrived, Nora put them up at the Hydro Hotel. It was arranged that Andrew would join them for the evening meal on their first day.

He parked his old car in the hotel car-park and walked through the lobby to the dining area. He was just stepping through the open doors of the elegant partition between the hotel lobby and the dining area when he was stopped by a middle-aged man in a dark suit and a silver-grey necktie.

"I'm sorry, sir," the man said and stopped Andrew with his right arm.

"I'm just going to join some friends – " Andrew began.

"You can't come in like this, sir."

"What's wrong about me?"

"We are an elegant hotel, sir. I'm afraid you have to wear a jacket and a tie."

"But it's summer, and it's warm, as you must feel yourself."

"Again, I'm sorry, sir, but these are the rules."

So Andrew could only wave to the table where his mother was sitting with her friends before he walked out of the hotel. He found the situation too ludicrous to make any more comments. But he couldn't help mumbling "ridiculous" as he left the hotel through the front doors.

Back in his flat, Rebecca asked him if he didn't want to let his mother know. So he sent her a short text message and explained the reason for his absence.

The next day, he went to his mother's house and walked to the hotel with her. In the lobby, at last, he was personally introduced to everyone. As he already knew Debbie and even Janet, he was particularly interested in the other three women. They all greeted him with enthusiasm, and Christine even kissed him on his cheek. He'd never been kissed by a middle-aged woman he'd never met before. And as the conversation among all of them took off, he soon realized that Christine was the most charming woman of the group, obviously a woman of the world, in her early fifties, with well-groomed clothes and a stylish hair-do. When she spoke, she betrayed a higher level of education than the others. She liked to round off all her statements with comment like, "Don't we all know?" or: "I know you all agree."

Observing the group of middle-aged women, Andrew tried to imagine them as teenagers when they were all schoolmates in Newcastle. It was difficult to imagine them as young girls. This made quite an impression on him.

The weather being nice, with only a few white clouds in an otherwise deep-blue sky, they went off for a walk along the seafront. Andrew went along with them as far as the Pier, then he excused himself and went to work.

In the evening, sitting comfortably in his living-room with Rebecca, he told her of his impression.

"I was trying to see those women as young girls, as a group of naive schoolgirls, but I found it extremely difficult."

"Why should they have been naive? They may very well have been quite sophisticated. But I can see your point. Life goes on and on, and it has its impact on us. We won't be the same at their age, too, and it's a good thing."

"Of course, you're right, my darling. But it just made me realize how the ageing process works on us. My granddad used to like his Latin proverbs, and one of them was '*Tempora mutantur et nos mutamur in illis*,' which means 'Times change and we change in, or with, them.' So, if our bodies change so much within only twenty or thirty years, what about our minds? Are we still the same persons at fifty or sixty that we were at twenty?"

"You worry too much. Is it about your granddad? About his past, as you told me several times? I can understand that we will always be confronted with such questions whenever we see our grandparents, or even when we look at ourselves in the mirror. It's a fact, we're all growing old."

"Yes, but for me it's much more."

Rebecca just looked at him with a tender expression. She loved him so much. While she could understand his interest in topics like this she nevertheless tried to cheer him up when he fell into one of his gloomy moods. He was such a positive person, but sometimes he lost himself in such deep questions. It was clearly connected with his keen interest in history, particularly with the history in which his grandfather played some dubious role.

The next day, Andrew took the day off and devoted his time to his mother and her friends. He went with them on all those local excursions that they had talked about before the arrival of the friends. When they stood on the lawn in the middle of the ruins of Pevensey Castle, having paid their admission fee to the woman from English Heritage, Andrew gave them a lively and very informative lecture on the Norman Conquest, showing them where the coastline had been in 1066, and giving them a very lively, almost theatrical account of the hardships the Anglo-Saxon soldiers had suffered on their quick-march from Stamford Bridge in Yorkshire all the way down to the south coast. His audience was attentive, and they could all see how the Anglo-Saxons under King Harold of Wessex didn't stand a chance against the waiting army of the Normans under Duke William.

So they were well-prepared for the next stop on their exploration tour, the battle-field itself. Andrew made sure they could visualize the battle, the battle-cries, the bloody fights, the dying men, the King's death, William's oath and his founding of Battle Abbey.

When he delivered the group back to their base camp at the Hydro Hotel they were a little tired but very happy. They thanked him for his interesting and entertaining tour. And of course, Nora was extremely proud of her clever son.

SIXTEEN

It was a pleasant summer evening. Andrew and Rebecca were sitting on the shingle beach, leaning against one of the wooden groynes, enjoying the light breeze and talking about their situation in life, something they had begun on a regular basis a few months ago.

Up to now, their talks about their relationship had usually consisted of what amounted to a celebration of their mutual love. More recently, they had sometimes brushed against the subject of a family. But they had never really spoken about it openly. Now it seemed the right time.

"Have you ever thought about the future?" Rebecca asked. "I know you're so involved with the past, but there's also a future for us, isn't there?"

"Of course. Sometimes I try to imagine our lives in about twenty years or so. But it's all a big blur."

"Have you thought about a family?"

Andrew hesitated before he carefully answered. "Yes, I have. But I don't know if it's right, these days, you know."

"Are you worried so much about the future?"

"Not really very seriously, but I just don't know. Look, now with Fukushima I don't know if it's safe to have a family in the near future."

"I see. But isn't Fukushima a long way from here?"

"Indeed, it is. But it could happen here, in this country, in France, elsewhere in Europe. Yes, particularly in France. You've heard about the French unwavering belief in nuclear power, and they have some of the oldest and most dangerous power stations."

Rebecca sighed. "I am confident the European politicians will have sense enough to phase out all the nuclear power stations, now, after what happened in Japan. It's being discussed in most countries."

"History even today remains true to itself in many ways," Andrew mused. "There's always some big danger looming just over the horizon, and there's always hope. It's this constant balance between danger and hope that we humans have to cope with. But can you see any great hope at this point in time? Anywhere in the world?"

"Yes. Isn't there a great deal of hope in what's going on in North Africa at the moment? You know, what they call the Arab Spring. Only this year, so much has already happened down there that can give us a great deal of hope for the future. Most of the dictators are disappearing, and more democratic systems are emerging, in Tunisia, in Libya, in Egypt. I know things are not perfect yet, but there are clearly visible movements that allow us to hope for better times."

"I'm glad you can be so positive." Andrew smiled at his beloved Rebecca. "So, you'd like to start a family?"

"Well, not right now. Let's wait and see, but I think we should try for it soon."

They let it stand at that. The sun was throwing longer shadows over the beach and they felt hungry. So they stood up and strolled off the beach, holding hands, still very much in love.

Over the following days, Andrew often returned to their talk about a family in his mind. Again and again, he asked himself if he wanted to become a father or not in the near future. For a while, his quest moved in circles, always returning to the same position of indecisiveness. His conclusion was always to put it off. He was confident that he – or he and Rebecca together – would eventually arrive at a positive decision. But not yet.

One day in October they drove up to London to attend a concert. He would later remember the date; it was

Wednesday, the 26th of October. The traffic was horrendous, but they still made it in time to the Barbican Centre, where they parked their little red car in the car-park. Andrew had booked the parking on the Internet in advance. They walked the short distance through those doors to the lobby of the concert hall. When they entered the hall itself, looking for their seats, the gong sounded to announce the immediate beginning of the concert. They found their seats, settled down, sealed their pleasure about the treat to come with a quick kiss and relaxed.

The Leipzig Gewandhaus Orchestra was ready, all the instruments tuned. Their chief conductor, Riccardo Chailly, entered, bowed, turned round to face his orchestra, and the music began. While the maestro's long wavy hair danced in the air and the musicians were getting into the strange mood of the modern piece, which was first on the programme, Andrew's mind refused to be taken in straightaway. The music was a new composition of a man called Steffen Schleiermacher, something that Andrew had never heard. Although it was quite good, he just couldn't really get into the music. And before he could adapt to the new sounds, the piece was over, and the audience applauded politely.

The next item on the programme was Beethoven's first symphony. It was a great performance; the conductor and the musicians did justice to their reputation among the best of the world. It was during this symphony that Andrew's mind travelled through galaxies and what he saw as a thick fog in his mind began to lift gradually. When the piece reached its end and the audience applauded frenetically, he knew he had reached an important decision, but he wasn't quite clear as to what it amounted to.

In the interval, they drifted to their drinks that they had pre-ordered before the concert. He had a glass of prosecco, while Rebecca sipped her gin-and-tonic.

"You are very quiet," she remarked, looking him in the eyes.

"Am I?"

"Yes, normally you have something to say about the music we just heard, the pieces, the interpretation, the musicians, the conductor... What about the new piece, the contemporary one? Did you like it? I quite enjoyed it. It was very unusual. But then, what can one expect from a contemporary composition?"

"For me it wasn't a question of like or dislike. Both works, the Schleiermacher piece and the Beethoven symphony, had an unusual effect on me. I can't tell you what it was exactly, whether it was the Germanic quality of the music, of both compositions, of both composers and of the orchestra itself, or the style of the performance. Two German composers, one who lived two hundred years ago and another one who is alive now, one from Bonn and the other from Halle. I just don't know, but they have had a very strong effect on me. It's even possible that the mood comes from my own subconscious quests, but it can be the music."

"Well, you'll have another chance after the interval. We're in for another treat, Beethoven's Seventh," Rebecca smiled.

And it was just as she had predicted. The second half of the concert with that truly great symphony helped Andrew to get through to the end of the fog, and when the concert was over he saw light.

Again, he was silent. They walked back to the car-park and drove out into the late evening traffic of London. Rebecca must have felt that he needed the silence to come to terms about how to communicate to her what he felt. They drove out of the big city in silence. It was only when they reached the M23 and the movement of their car had become more regular that Andrew spoke at last.

"You must have wondered, my darling," he began, "but I needed to sort things out first. But now I'm one hundred per cent sure I have come to an important decision."

She glanced at his face in the semi-darkness of the interior of the car. But she did not say anything. She let him continue at his own pace.

"My first priority will be to find that diary of my mother's. I want to read it, and I want to find answers to all those questions about the past before I'm ready to engage in the future. In other words, only when I've found out about Granddad's role in the War can I take on the responsibility of parenthood. I promise you we'll try for a child once I have my answers."

She was silent for several minutes. The M23 had become the A23 before she answered in a level voice.

"I have been expecting this, and I respect your decision. I know how much all that means to you, and I love you. So, I will go along with it as long as it won't be for years and years. For both of us and our happiness I can only hope it will not take too long."

"Thank you, my darling."

They didn't speak anymore during the rest of the trip. They were both deep in their thoughts. When they were back at their home they prepared for bed in silence. It was a happy silence. In bed, they were happy to cling to each other, to feel the smooth texture of the skin of their naked bodies. Even though this gave them both a moderate erotic feeling they didn't do anything to intensify it. They were both very happy as they were. It was a celebration of togetherness. In this happy and relaxed mood, they gradually fell asleep, the lovely music still in their ears.

The following morning, Andrew decided to make a special effort to find his mother's diary. He wondered what new aspects he would find in there. Could it be that Granddad was all wrong about his fantasies? How long did he actually stay in Germany, how long did he spend in Switzerland? Was he really in Germany up to the end of the War? What role did he play when called up? Men of his age must have been called up in 1943 by the latest? Did he do his national service in the *Wehrmacht*? Did he fight against Poland, France, Russia, the Allies? What was his political allegiance? Was he perhaps even in agreement with Nazi doctrine? Or was he in the underground, fighting the Nazis?

Would the diary reveal anything in that direction? Did Mum actually manage to find out anything about the background of that Wolfgang? And what about the woman called Anna, for whom Granddad seemed particularly concerned? Was she his great love before the War? How long did the relationship last?

Questions over questions kept boiling up within him as he was planning to take a week off from work in order to search his mother's attic and garage.

He started with the attic. Strange feelings crept up on him as he got started. He thought it was like going through his mother's things after she'd died, but he knew she was still alive, and she had given him full permission to go through all her old things. She was too tired of such searches herself.

In the late afternoon of the first day that he spent in his mother's attic he got tired of all this rummaging through his parents' things. When his father got home the two men sat down on some wooden boxes in the attic. The father had brought some bottles of beer.

"So, you're hoping to find some of Nora's old stuff, she told me."

They clinked their bottles, and each took a swallow of beer.

"Yes, it's her diary. She wrote down everything she found when she went to Germany, back in the nineties."

"Oh yes. She only told me a few days ago. I never knew she'd actually written a diary."

"You don't mind, then?"

"No. Why should I mind? She has obviously given you permission for this search. She trusts you to read it in the right spirit."

"But wouldn't you rather read it yourself first? There may be very personal passages. There usually are, in a diary."

"Heaven forbid!" George exclaimed and slapped his left hand on his left thigh, leaning back on his box. "I have had just about enough of your mother's crazy interest in all those old stories from the War. You just go ahead, and don't mind me. You obviously have the same passion for that sort of stuff."

In a way, Andrew was glad that his father didn't interfere, but gave him *carte blanche* with his search. Even though he loved and respected his father, he still felt that what he was about to launch into was something between himself and his mother. Granddad would have been involved if he was still in a better mental condition. But as things stood, it was now a matter between mother and son only. They were the ones who cared about history.

"Let me ask you one thing, though," George asked his son. "What are you going to do once you've found out things you didn't know before? Not that I believe you're going to find out any spectacular things, but what if you find out terrible things about your old grandfather? Would that change anything? Would that make the world a better place?"

"I don't know."

The father had just finished his beer and prepared to get up and climb down the ladder. He smiled at Andrew. "I'll leave you to it."

"I think I've had enough for today," Andrew replied. "I'll call it a day."

After his father, Andrew also climbed down the ladder, washed his hands and left. He went back to his flat, where Rebecca was ready with a light supper. She had some good news.

"Dave phoned. He wants to celebrate with you. He's been appointed as a full professor. He's all over the moon, and he'll call you again later or you call him."

Andrew met Dave two nights later at the pub. Rebecca didn't want to join them. "It's a thing between you two. Old buddies celebrating. Only don't drink too much," she had warned.

The two friends discussed every aspect of Dave's new position, his opportunities in research, his new routine, his new salary. Dave promised to remain Andrew's best friend. Then, after their third round, their talk drifted to other topics, the weather, current politics, the general state of the world and such things.

"I think it's a pity that Europe didn't grasp the opportunity it had after German reunification," Dave mused.

"Well, at least the former Soviet Republics of Eastern Europe freed themselves and became democracies. That's something, isn't it?"

"Yes, but what about leaving the Cold War behind? The way things are going these days Russia and Western Europe are in opposition as much as before the fall of the Iron Curtain. That guy Putin keeps heating things up whenever he can."

"I can understand him," Andrew suggested. "Imagine how the Russians have always been in fear of the West. They never trusted any Western leader. What could have improved the situation, built up some form of trust, would have been for the West to work together with Russia right from the early nineties. I know that Gorbachev shouldn't have been ousted by Yeltsin. Gorbachev knew how important for world peace a good understanding between East and West was, whereas Yeltsin, and in his wake Putin, opted for confrontation, reviving old Russian nationalism, directed against the West. But even with Putin, we could have come to a better understanding. I think the worst mistake was for NATO to incorporate all those buffer states, from the Baltic States down to Bulgaria. Like this, the West poses a direct threat to the Russians. So if in the future, Putin is going to do some silly things to demonstrate his power, NATO will bear the main burden of guilt. But let's hope Putin won't have to go to extremes, even though one may never know with him."

"But what could he do?"

"Well, just bear in mind that Stalin made sure most of the Soviet Republics had enough Russians living and working in them. He implemented a huge relocation programme in the 1930s. Like this, there is still a considerable proportion of Russians in all those new countries. What could happen if Putin should call upon them to rebel against their new governments? Is Western Europe going to help those countries if new civil wars break out, perhaps in Latvia, or in Ukraine?"

"You're really painting a black picture. Putin must be interested in peaceful relations just like everybody else."

"I only hope you'll be proved right," Andrew said and emptied his glass.

Discussions like these often took place between Andrew and Rebecca. With time, he realized that she wasn't going to be of any great help, she just wasn't involved enough. So he had to be satisfied with her general support without her enthusiasm. During the weeks that he spent looking for his mother's diary he tried to get more information out of the other members of his family. He was looking for any bit of information concerning Granddad that might be helpful in his quest. Mother had already told him what she was prepared to share with him without her diary, while Lisa refused to discuss the topic and even warned him not to get crazy. "You'll end up in the loony bin if you're not careful," she threatened.

One evening at the pub Andrew was surprised to find David in an extremely happy mood. Whereas usually his friend was a more serious person, always full of thoughts about literature and its contribution towards a better world but without the belief in its success, he now appeared to be a lot more relaxed. What could be the reason behind such a change of mood?

"I say, you really seem to be in a fantastic state. What's up, old chap?"

"Well, guess," David answered with a mysterious smile. "Can't you guess? What can make a guy really happy?"

"A woman?"

"Bull's eye, old chap!"

"Come on, tell me all about it," Andrew urged his friend.

"Well, what do they say in such situations? I don't know how to describe it; my feelings are beyond words."

Andrew laughed. "You can say such a thing, you of all people? You, who are a man of the word, of the power of language?"

"It's not so easy when it comes to your own feelings, you know."

"If you were a poet you'd know what to say, wouldn't you?"

"Not all poets wrote about the theme of love."

"Those are poor quibbles. Just tell me in plain words."

Then David told him about the woman he had met at that conference in Canterbury a while ago. They had kept in touch, and as things stood, they had fallen for each other and were now a serious item.

"Why did you never tell me?" Andrew asked, a little disappointed at his friend's secretiveness over the past few weeks.

"Things were not clear to me for quite some time. But now I know where we stand. But what's the problem? I have told you now."

"What's her name?"

"Marie-Claire. She's French."

"Great. I must say I'm very happy for you. When am I going to meet her?"

David promised a meeting in the near future. Then he continued telling Andrew about his feelings for her, about her fine character, about her gorgeous looks and about all her other attractions. In the end, Andrew had to put an end to their talk, otherwise David would have gone on and on with his eulogy. After a serious promise to introduce Marie-Claire to his best friend as soon as possible, David agreed to call it a day. The two men downed their last drinks and went home.

Over the following weeks, Andrew and Rebecca had the pleasure to make the acquaintance of Marie-Claire and to experience David in his new role as a fond lover. This new setting as a quartet, as Andrew remarked to David, gradually changed their friendship. Their old camaraderie as two buddies had disappeared, and they were now two couples, well, as he'd said, a "quartet".

Marie-Claire proved to be a very charming woman, although Andrew was a bit disappointed at first. He didn't really consider her beautiful. Her face was a bit too broad, with slightly drooping eyelids and puffy cheeks, and she wore a pair of quite thick spectacles. Her figure was a little too full for Andrew's taste, and her legs a bit too short. However, he managed to check himself and to see her as his friend's partner, in which role she didn't have to be sexually attractive for himself, and her otherwise very charming nature had to be enough for him. As, during their second or third meeting, he reached this more mature view, he felt a bit ashamed of himself. He ascribed his former error of judgement to the silly old male camaraderie he'd enjoyed with David and admitted to himself how some of their comments had been of a sexist nature. He realized that as a man you no longer needed a sexist view of the world when you'd found true love with a woman. And, after all, he was very happy for his friend. It was so obvious that David loved Marie-Claire and found her the most lovable and beautiful woman in the world. This had to be enough for Andrew. And it was.

***

He coughed. The dust coming down from the top of the old wardrobe and spreading over his head was nearly choking him. He got an old dining chair and stepped onto its faded green fabric seat. He tested its stability before he planted his full weight on the chair and stood up, stretching to reach the whole area on top of the wardrobe. With the torch in his left hand, he searched the otherwise dark space and, to his surprise, he detected a cardboard box at the back, right in the corner. He had to put the torch aside to reach the box with both hands, before he pulled it out of its corner. When he got hold of the box at last, he carried it down, carefully stepping down from the old dining chair.

He cleared a space on the dusty floor of the attic, which he cleaned with a broom. Then he placed the grey box, which was heavier than he'd expected, between his feet on the floor and bent down to open its lid.

Andrew gasped.

The box, which he'd never realized had been hidden on the top of the wardrobe for so long without being detected, appeared to be full of old black-and-white photographs. But as he was carefully digging deeper with his hands along the rough sides of the uneven piles of photographs he felt the edges of what appeared to be old school-books, not the thick textbooks but the slim books you were given for your own school-work, exercise-books, books for mathematical constructions or for your own essays.

He pulled out one of the books. He found it full of hand-written texts. His heart began to race as he recognized his mother's handwriting. This must be her diaries!

Andrew took the box. He went home, took a shower to get rid of all the dust and dirt from his parents' attic, made himself a nice cup of tea and settled down at his desk with the old box in front of him.

With the air of a religious ceremony, he opened the box again and took out all the old photographs, placing them on his desk. Then he took out the pile of school-books.

When he'd cleaned their covers with a slightly wet cloth he detected the faint pencil-marks on them. Clearly legible, the captions said, "Quest 1", "Quest 2" and so on. All in all, there were seven school-books, and as he flipped through them he saw that they were all full of written text in his mother's fine and regular hand-writing.

This was it.

Andrew picked up his mobile phone from the living-room and called his mother.

"Hiya, Mum. Listen. At last! I've found your old diary."

"Oh, my dear boy, are you sure you're prepared for what's written down there?" Nora responded.

"I think I am. But now is the time to stop me if you don't want me to find out all those things you'd kept hidden from me, from us, from your family."

"Our family couldn't have coped with it. You know that. For one thing, they just don't want to know about the past. Then there is the uncertainty of how they would react to the truth about my old father. They're not interested in history and could never understand some of the things. Whereas you have always shown such a keen interest in history and in your grandfather's life during those dark years, I feel – no, I'm fully confident – that you can deal with those things in the right spirit."

"You may be right. I can only tell once I've read your diary in full." He paused before he continued. "But tell me. Is it okay for me to read it now? Do I have your permission, your authorization?"

"Yes, you do. Now let me get on with my things. Remember, I don't want to hear any comments about the diary from you before you've finished reading it right to the end. Is this understood?"

"Yes, Mum. I promise."

With that, Andrew rang off and sat down at his desk again. He knew he had at least three hours before Rebecca would come back from her Sunday visit to her friend Karen. So he decided to start right now. He hesitated for a few moments, wondering whether he should take notes as he was working his way through the text of the diary, but eventually he decided against it. He would just read the whole thing as if it was a novel he was reading for his own pleasure.

Before delving into the diary, however, he let himself drift off in his thoughts. He knew he would find out more about events and people of the past. He wondered why he couldn't find out anything about that woman called Anna, the woman who had been Granddad's first love, or about that horrible old man called Wolfgang, who had tried to blackmail Granddad. He had tried to find their names on Peoplefinder and on Facebook, but no success. His mother wouldn't tell him if any of those people were still alive.

Andrew suddenly realized that it would be a good idea if he brushed up his rusty German. Flicking through the pages of the diary he'd found several German words and expressions in the otherwise English text. Well, he would see. But he decided to do something about his German anyway. To be honest, he admitted to himself that he found it a very interesting language, and to him it sounded very nice. Somehow, the complicated word-order of the spoken language gave the English listener the impression of a higher degree of intelligence, to some people perhaps the aura of arrogance, but to him it sounded beautiful and intriguing.

He remembered that Marie-Claire thought it a barbarian language. She believed that there wasn't any language more beautiful than French, but that was a normal view shared by many people. In the end, Andrew thought, there was beauty in every language. Some sounded a bit nervous and stressful, like Arabic, while others sounded so languid and well-rounded, like Russian, and yet others sounded utterly mysterious, like Japanese. He regretted his lack of linguistic expertise and envied David's vast competence in so many languages.

Only a few days ago, David had told him in confidence that he was now learning Turkish, explaining to him the wonderfully sweet aspect of that language. Andrew remembered how he admired his friend's ease with which he explained some Turkish grammar to him, the vowel harmony of the language, the agglutinative nature of its syntax and the fine simplicity of its vocabulary, enriched as it had become over the centuries by its contacts with Arabic through religion and with Farsi, the Persian language, through mysticism, while Turkish had for a long time influenced those other near-Eastern languages through government and military matters, due to the Ottoman Empire. To Andrew, yet another proof of how past history will always influence the future.

Andrew was shaken out of his thoughts by the town hall clock striking the hour of three in the afternoon.

PART FOUR

THE DIARY

Preamble, inserted much later

When I decided to explore my father's past I had no idea of the scope my enquiry would eventually take, neither did I expect to meet with such a lot of people with such great hearts. I had assumed I would just spend a fortnight in Germany and Switzerland before returning to England with a full account of everything that had happened with my father during the Second World War. Little did I know that my search would lead me to many more places and take more than six months. Most of all, I started out with a naive conception of the challenges and temptations my father had been faced with, and I had to realize that my conceptions had been those of the post-war generation.

SEVENTEEN

This is perhaps not a diary in the strictest sense of the word. The word "Diary" is derived from Latin and means "a daily report" or "a daily notebook". In my case, I will probably be unable to keep to a daily routine. I have neither the inclination nor the time to add my regular entries on a daily basis. Also, I could never muster the necessary discipline.

I used to write a diary that could more aptly be called such when I was a young teenage girl in Gosforth. I diligently wrote down my daily reports, but when I re-read them after about nine months I realized the futility of my enterprise. My daily entries consisted mainly of a list of persons I had met during the day, of the food I'd eaten and sometimes of descriptions of the clothes certain friends had worn on that day. There were only very few real entries of substance, and they concerned things I'd discussed with Margaret or with my parents, mostly with Dad. However, after all, my diary appeared completely worthless to me. So I destroyed it.

Now, in my middle-age, I have therefore decided to write down only or mainly my experiences which appear to be of a certain importance. I have a presentiment about my search for my father's past. While I am confident that I won't really find out any spectacular things, I nevertheless expect a few unpleasant surprises, simply because my father's reticence and stubborn silence about certain parts of his life have made me curious, and because some of the things he told me don't match with what I have learnt about life in Germany during the Second World War. This is the reason behind my diary: to understand things more clearly and, should there emerge certain unpleasant things, to protect my father while at the same time to preserve my findings for future generations in my family. As it appears, my son Andrew has already shown a keen interest in history and in his grandfather's role during those difficult times.

My entries will be mostly undated because they normally comprise my experiences over several days, if not several weeks. I begin with March 1996.

***

To begin with, I decided to start my search with a visit to the German Embassy in London. Unfortunately, however, the staff there was extremely arrogant and didn't want to have anything to do with my quest. One of their office minions, however, happened to leave the building at the same time as myself. He saw my disappointment and asked me if he could help. I told him I was looking for information about my German ancestors during the War, but obviously the Embassy was either unable or unwilling to be of any assistance.

"What is it you're looking for?" he asked.

I told him I was looking for a starting point in my enquiry into my father's past. I had assumed there was some sort of office with all the relevant records, probably in Berlin. But since I hadn't found anything of relevance on the Internet, I thought the Embassy might have an address of such an office.

"Was your father Jewish?" the young man asked.

I told him no, but he may have had something to do with the Jews. I believed he had helped them in some way or other. He'd obviously been in a concentration camp for a short while.

"Then your best bet is to start from the Simon Wiesenthal Centre in Paris. Its headquarters are in Los Angeles, but Paris isn't so far, and the Paris guys are just as efficient. If

it's rather the documents of the Jewish Holocaust you're after, then visit the Jewish Documentation Centre in Vienna. I'd start in Paris if I were you."

I gave the young man my email address and he promised to send me the relevant addresses and contacts. I thanked him, and before I could ask him why he was helping me he had disappeared down the stairs to the tube station.

When I had the contacts, I phoned the Paris centre and asked if it would make sense to call there in person. They said yes, they might be in a position to help me. They added they might be interested in my case, too.

I hadn't expected to travel to Paris originally, but when it became necessary, I didn't hesitate. It dawned on me that my search might take me to many more unexpected locations. So I negotiated with George about a longer absence from home. At first, he wasn't really happy about my zeal and particularly about the prospect of having to fend for himself for a longer period, but after several serious discussions about what really matters to me in life he consented. In a way, it was a learning process for both of us. I had not been aware of how important my quest really was to me until these negotiations with George, whilst he had never been conscious of how much my personal happiness actually mattered to him. In the end, we came to the conclusion that I was free to roam the entire Continent in search of the truth that I was looking for. He agreed to look after himself for whatever length of time I needed. I had his promise that I wouldn't have to be under stress if my search took longer than expected. Also, I wouldn't have to worry about money. We had enough to finance my enterprise for up to six months if necessary.

So I packed my suitcase and travelled to Paris by train. The people at the Centre were very keen to help me. They took down everything I could tell them about my father and told me to come back two days later. I killed the time walking around

Paris, enjoying the spring atmosphere in that lovely city. I spent hours just sitting in street cafés sipping a strong café au lait *and watching people.*

The result of the Centre's research was disappointing. They found no trace of a Didi Woolf or a Dieter Wolff. According to their records there had been no survivor of any of the German concentration camps by that name. I told them that he had probably changed his name, to which they replied that they couldn't know all the new names that people had given themselves. When we discussed this aspect of my father's case they became suspicious.

"Why did your father change his name? Why should he have felt the need to change his name at all? Are you sure he was in a concentration camp?"

This suspicion made me angry. My father had obviously suffered, and now these wisecracks were questioning the facts that I had gathered from him. They even seemed to insinuate that he'd done something to be ashamed of, something that forced him to change his name in order to escape the law. I decided to find out more about his name change before I could face such suspicious bureaucrats again.

The only person who obviously knew my father's original name before the war was probably that awful man Wolfgang. I was afraid of facing that man, but it became the only reasonable next step. So I went through my notes to find his name and address. The only bits of information that I had told me that he was called Wolfgang Löffel (the German word for "spoon", quite a strange name, I found), and that he lived in Gera, a small town in Thuringia, which was in East Germany. Well, it was no longer a separate country, with the great reunification that had taken place only just over five years ago. I only had the name of the town, no exact address, but I knew he had been born in 1921, one year before Dad. So he was seventy-five now. I thought about my chances of finding out more from him without giving him a lot of money. I also thought about other things I might try to find out once I was in Gera. Of course, one other person that I was extremely curious about was Dad's childhood sweetheart Anna. She might still be alive, and she might still live in Gera. People in East Germany normally either fled the country, risking their lives, especially between 1961 and 1989, or they stayed put, not having the means to move to other places. So there was a slight chance she might still be in Gera. She probably had another name as a married woman, but Wolfgang Löffel had to know her name.

My decision was taken. I had to travel to Gera. The idea dawned on me that I would have to do quite a bit more travelling. But where to go first? I knew I could also travel to Switzerland, where Dad had spent several years as a refugee after the war. I had read that Switzerland had very accurate records in their council offices and archives.

Because of my impending travelling plans and because of my wish to be independent in my search, I took a train back to England, where I only spent two nights at home. Of course, George was overjoyed, but he had to let me go again. The reason for my quick visit home was my need of a car. Two days later, I drove back to the Continent in my VW Golf. I only stopped for petrol and for coffee in France and reached the city of Bern, the small capital of Switzerland, late in the evening.

***

My time spent in Bern was very interesting. I had studied German and visited several places in Germany, where I had acquired a certain skill in detecting various German dialects. I was proud enough to boast that I could understand most people in Hamburg, Frankfurt and Munich, and with some alcohol inside me I could even imitate several phrases with a Berlin accent. However, what I encountered here in Switzerland was really completely and utterly unexpected. When I asked someone for directions in the hotel lobby on the first morning, I got a friendly answer that I thought couldn't be German. I repeated my question, but the good woman who tried to explain things to me made her answer even longer this time, probably giving extra bits of explanation and embellishing her statements with flowery terms. All I could gather were sounds that didn't make sense to me at all. They were something between Dutch and Czech, the rhythm and the intonation had no similarity to any German dialect that I had ever heard. I couldn't even detect the word endings and the beginnings of new words, and I had absolutely no idea of the topic being treated. In this case it was probably the required directions through the streets of Bern. I was suddenly reminded of that time back in Newcastle, where we couldn't understand the Geordies at first. I begged the woman to speak High German, the standardized variant of the language that I had studied at university. She switched over, so I could understand at last. However, even speaking proper German for her had a very strong accent, with very funny vowels and very guttural consonants. While I was leaving the good woman, on my way to the council offices, I promised myself to study the special features of Swiss German when I had the time.

My search in the council offices led me to other offices and archives in that charming medieval city. The result was that there had actually been a certain German refugee called Dieter Wolff living in Bern between 1946 and 1952. His address had been in a northern quarter called Lorraine (like the French region so terribly fought over in the Great War), in a boarding house (called Pension in this country). His occupation was given as "Büroangestellter" *which translates as "office clerk", not a very accurate piece of information.*

So Dad had actually lived here for six years, before he moved to the States. Now I could have left Bern, because there probably wasn't much more that I could find out about him. But I felt I wanted to try to find a person who had known him in Bern. Such a person might give me some useful details. Besides, I felt a keen pleasure in walking round a foreign town, aware of the fact that my father had walked through these very same streets half a century before.

I bought a good town map and walked north, across Lorraine Bridge. I identified the big railway bridge on the left. As I watched, there happened to be one of those high-tech high-speed ICE trains from Germany moving slowly into the station. To my right, I detected a prominent building with the letters "Kursaal" *across its top, wondering what it could be. Far below the grey bridge the blue-green waters of the Aare River flowed at alarmingly high speed. The weather was quite pleasant, still a bit cool, but mostly sunny with only a few white clouds racing across the sky. As I was crossing the bridge, I was suddenly overcome by an exciting sense of adventure. Here I was, at last tracing my father's footsteps in a foreign place. I felt no stress, because I knew I didn't have any obligation to anyone else, only my own motivation. It was I who wanted to find out the truth about the past, and if I failed I would only disappoint my own eagerness.*

It was easy to find the house. I checked the bell-buttons with their name-tags. Obviously, the pension had been converted into flats. There were eight flats in all, and there were mainly names that sounded Swiss, such as Meyer, Leuenberger or Wunderlin (to name just the ones I can remember), and one Italian name, Merazzi. One name sounded outlandish, it was Kleibenzettl. What sort of name could that be? I was wondering what to do when the heavy wooden door with its curtained window covered by its wrought-iron grid suddenly opened. An elderly woman stared at me, asking what I was looking for. She seemed friendly enough, with curly grey hair and a round face that corresponded to her generally roundish appearance. She wore a thin green raincoat and carried an old and rather worn dark brown handbag. She was obviously on her way out, probably for some light shopping or to see a friend, I guessed. Her blue eyes observed me with intelligence. I told her I was looking for the flat where my father had lived between 1956 and 1952.

"What was his name?" she wanted to know.

I hesitated at first but then I told her the name he had taken before he arrived in Bern, Dieter Wolff.

The woman frowned, trying to remember. Then she said yes. She told me she had been born in 1938, so she was still a girl at the time Herr Wolff lived in what was now the top-floor flat.

"Yes, now I remember. You see, I was away for a long time. I lived in Austria during my married life. That was – let me see – that must have been between 1963 and '92. When my husband died I moved back here, and fortunately my parents' old flat became available last year, so I moved back to where I'd originally grown up. Both my parents died in the 1980s, and my husband in '91, Heribert Kleibenzettl that was, he was quite a bit older than me."

I tried to stop the good woman in her flow, but checked myself, aware of her need to talk about the things of her past. After all, her need to talk about her past was as legitimate as my interest in my father's past. So, I let her talk.

"People here have difficulties with my name. They laugh at it, it's so ridiculous. You see, my dear husband came from a Jewish family in Vienna. When the Nazis took over, they forced many Jewish families to adopt ridiculous names.

Whereas before Nazi occupation my husband's family was called Rubinstein, a beautiful old Jewish name, they were given the name of Kleibenzettl. That wasn't even the worst name, two of my friends' families fared a lot worse. They were given the names of Kanalgeruch and Achselschweiss. So Heribert's family made their peace with their new name."

I asked her why she didn't have her name changed after returning to Switzerland. The authorities were bound to allow her to adopt her maiden name. But she answered she wanted to keep her Austrian Jewish name in memory of her husband, whom she had loved very much.

By this time, we were both beginning to feel a bit awkward, standing on the doorstep in front of the grey apartment-block. Frau Kleibenzettl must have felt the same as I, she asked if I would like to come again in the afternoon. Then we could have a cup of coffee in her flat and she could tell me a lot more.

I walked back to my hotel and used the time to take notes and to update my diary. I also sent an email message to George, informing him of my progress and asking about the family. After a light lunch at the hotel I took a short nap before I changed into less elegant clothes and walked across Lorraine Bridge again. I felt that Frau Kleibenzettl might be less embarrassed if I didn't look too upper-class.

When she let me step into her flat, which was on the first floor, I noticed that she had changed into more elegant clothes. This made me smile at myself. I would have to be more careful about my clothes. Obviously, dress codes in Switzerland were not the same as in England. I couldn't exactly remember what they had been in Germany at the time of my stay there. I had been a student and as such moved mainly in circles where people wore denim jeans and simple tops or jumpers. Now, here in Switzerland, people in the streets appeared to be a lot better dressed than in England, not really in expensive or very elegant outfits, but just more stylish, more in harmony with their personalities, and generally cleaner. If I wanted Continental people to trust me and give me sensitive information, I would have to adapt to the correct dress codes. I made a mental note of this.

We sat down in her living-room, which was furnished in very good taste. The coffee I was served tasted delicious and there was also a plate of biscuits. I was glad I'd only had a light lunch, because they tasted very nice, too.

While we were warming up with small-talk I observed Frau Kleibenzettl. She looked younger than her age. Whereas in front of the house I had taken her for an elderly woman, now in her own surroundings and nicely groomed she seemed just in her best years. She really had a very charming face, her smile took me in, and her warm voice had a fascinating timbre. I only threw in a few remarks and mostly let her do the talking.

She told me she remembered Herrn Wolff for his learned talks. As a small schoolgirl she was deeply impressed by his Latin phrases and proverbs, many of which she didn't understand at first, but when she took up the courage to ask him he explained them all in detail.

"He should have been a teacher. He could explain things so well. I came to adore him. To me as a little girl he stood for all the great things in the world. He knew everything about languages, about geography and science, and he could explain the world."

I asked her what she meant. "The world?" She said that when the midday news came on the radio she had to be quiet at the dinner table while her parents were listening attentively. It was almost a religious ritual. The station was called Radio Beromünster. To her, it always seemed the same news items, always about the Swiss Bundesrat, *about the German* Bundeskanzler, *about Mr Churchill from England*

and about the American President. There were always meetings between politicians, sometimes problems with people in Africa, sometimes quite worrying news from Russia. Because she wasn't allowed to ask any questions during the news she sometimes asked after the news, but the only answers she got from her parents were things like "It's not for small girls" or "You'll understand when you're older".

"One afternoon, I asked Herrn Wolff. He was so natural and friendly about it, and he really took time to explain things to me. So from then on, I would ask him such things from time to time. His best and most detailed explanation was the one in June 1953. I can clearly remember what he told me about the events in East Berlin, when the people protested against the Soviets in the streets and the whole thing was crushed by Russian tanks within such a short time."

I was so happy about all that information about Dad. I didn't want to appear unfriendly, but I gently tried to get more facts out of the good woman. However, because my father's residence in her house was so long ago and because she had been a small girl at the time – only eight when he moved in and fourteen when he left – there wasn't much more that she could remember. Of course, there were no bits of information that might help me in any concrete way in my quest, but it was genuinely heart-warming to listen to Frau Kleibenzettl telling me about her memories of my father.

I asked her if she remembered her parents mentioning anything about their German neighbour. She hesitated before she answered.

"You see, there was a deep rift between my parents and myself when it came to Herrn Wolff. Germans were not popular here at the time. Everybody hated them. They were abused and sworn at wherever they were known as Germans. Many people didn't make a distinction between refugees and other Germans, they considered all of them responsible for

the War. The most often heard name for them was 'Sauschwab', *which translates as 'pig of a Swabian'. The Swiss still call the Germans Swabian, even people from Berlin, although the Swabians are only people of the southwest corner of Germany. It's a common phenomenon, like the French calling the Germans* 'allemands' *for the same reason."*

Her socio-linguistic explanations made me compliment her on her knowledge of languages. I also admired her proficiency in English. She explained that she had been a student of languages, first at the University of Bern and later in Vienna. "Besides," she added, "everyone with any higher level of education has at least three or four languages in this country." Then she went into a lengthy account of the funny accent the Austrians had when they spoke French, and I let her talk for a while before I steered her back to the subject of my father.

She explained that her parents considered Herrn Wolff a Nazi. It was no use arguing with them. So she kept her admiration of their neighbour secret. She liked him very much and she trusted him when he explained the world to her.

"He had such sad eyes. And he warned me against any nationalist or racist arguments, again and again. At first, I didn't understand what he meant, being too young to understand such big words, but later it became clearer to me. Those constant reminders of the dangers of nationalism and racism became his hallmark. To tell you the truth, I got a bit fed up with that constant litany of his. But I still respected him for it. In a way, his warnings have remained a beacon throughout my adult life."

When I asked her if she knew about any friends of my father's at the time of his residence in Bern, she shook her head. Then she remembered a middle-aged man who sometimes called and a young woman that he sometimes brought back to his flat. She said some of the neighbours considered that immoral. At that time there was a law against unmarried couples spending the night together. Frau Kleibenzettl called it "das Konkubinatsverbot", *but she didn't let on about her own view of such matters. Neither could she remember the names of either the woman or the male visitor.*

The remaining parts of our conversation didn't give me any more insights. Frau Kleibenzettl elaborated a great deal about differences between life in Austria and life in Switzerland. I couldn't quite make out which of the two lifestyles she preferred, but I just liked to listen to her. Eventually, she ran out of steam, and the time came for me to take my leave. I thanked her profusely. When she led me to the door of her flat, we shook hands. Then, quite suddenly, she pulled me to her bosom and kissed me on both cheeks. Her warm embrace showed me that our long chat about the past must have awakened some strong emotions in her, too.

I gave her my mobile number and my email address. She said she didn't know about email, but one of her neighbours, Herr Wunderlin, who was very much into these newfangled technologies, had actually promised her to show her how she could send messages from a computer. She had already decided to get herself one of these machines, but she would need a lot of coaching. So, she accepted my address but said she might never text me. I told her I'd be happy if she could let me know when she remembered any more facts about my father.

Back at my hotel, I took stock of what I'd found out. I knew now that Dad had told us the truth about coming to live in Switzerland in 1946 and leaving it for the States in 1952. Also, there was the evidence from Frau Kleibenzettl about Dad's character and personality. Already at that time he was against nationalism and racism. He had a decent occupation and he was just trying to get away from all the horrors he had experienced in Germany. Then there was his love of the Latin language and his keen interest in all areas of knowledge and learning. That was Dad. That was my father as I have always known him. With this confirmation, I could now leave this country and head for Germany.

I could leave now. But what about the man and the young woman that Dad had been friends with? There was no way of finding out any more about them. Who could they have been?

The next morning, I checked out of my hotel. I was on my way to the station when my mobile phone rang. I was surprised to hear Frau Kleibenzettl's voice.

"I am so sorry to disturb you," she said in an apologetic tone, "but I just remembered the young woman's name. You know, the young woman your father was friends with. She was called Marianne Grossniklaus."

I thanked Frau Kleibenzettl and asked her if she knew anything else about that Marianne. Where did she live? Where did she come from? What did she look like? And then what about the middle-aged man? But the good woman couldn't give me any more information. So we said good-bye and rang off.

What was I to do? I walked to the post office and looked up the telephone directory for Bern. There were some two dozen entries under "Grossniklaus". I stood there for a while, wondering what to do.

I took courage and dialled the number of the first Grossniklaus. There was no answer. The same thing under the second number, although there was an answer-phone under that number, but I didn't know what to say. I swore that the third number would be my last try. It clicked, and a woman's voice answered. She sounded very friendly. I gave my name and told the woman about my search in as few words as possible. She said it was impossible to find such a person if I only had her name. We chatted on for a few more minutes, and as we were about to terminate our conversation she said I could try the village of Beatenberg in the Bernese Oberland, because that was where almost all Grossniklaus families originally came from. That was all I could do. And even that seemed a very remote possibility.

I sat down in one of the cafés and considered my next steps. It didn't take me long to come to a conclusion. There was no hope in a trip to that mountain village. How could I ever find out about a Marianne in their tribe who had lived in Bern in the 1950s? Impossible. So my obvious next step had to be Frankfurt, because Dad had stayed there for a short while just after the war, probably only a few months between 1945 and 1946. He had worked for an American company as a translator before he decided to emigrate to Switzerland. I said to myself that I could still come back to Switzerland at a later stage in my search if I still considered it to be of importance to find out about Marianne Grossniklaus or that mysterious middle-aged man.

I had to accept the fact that I wouldn't be able to find out everything down to the smallest detail about Dad's early life. After all, he also deserved his share of privacy. What I had to find out was his role in Germany during the war. How did he get into the concentration camp? What was his exact stance in the face of the general hysterics? Did he openly oppose the system? He, the man who hated all nationalist ideas, who always uttered his most venomous criticism whenever the world news reported about totalitarian systems... I remembered his hard words directed against the Soviet Union and about the German Democratic Republic and, of course, against various African dictators. Then there had been the Nazi's love of military aggression. Dad had always hated soldiers' uniforms and military equipment. He had most certainly been in the worst moral conflict in his life. The fact that he never really told his family was proof of that. He had to live with a very bad trauma throughout the rest of his life.

I thought of Dad's tattoo. It was a pity he'd had it removed. Although it had still left an ugly mark on his skin, it was no longer legible. Otherwise I could just write to that Centre in Vienna or the one in the States and trace my father's fate in the concentration camp on the basis of his number.

I had high hopes about my visit to Frankfurt.

EIGHTEEN

I found a relatively decent hotel in the Gallus area. The district owed its name to one of the old watchtowers of the city that had remained unscathed in the terrible bombings by the Allies in the 1940s, the so-called Galluswarte. *The word Gallus itself was misleading. When I first read it on my city map I thought it referred to the medieval Irish monk, Saint Gallus, who had founded the Swiss monastery of St Gallen which had later become a substantial city in the east of the country, near Lake Constance. But later, when I asked one of the historians that I consulted at the university I learnt that "Gallus" was a distortion of the German word* Galgen *which means "gallows". So the* Galluswarte *marked the site where the city's executions had taken place. I wondered if that was the place where the young poet Goethe had witnessed the execution of a young woman who had murdered her own baby, a traumatic experience which later led to the character of Margarethe in his* Faust, *the great play about the legendary Doctor Faustus, probably based on Marlowe's play.*

During my period in Frankfurt I came to like this district. I liked to walk along Mainzer Landstrasse as far as Griesheim or to the public baths at Rebstock Park. The street was lined with mostly second-hand car dealers, office buildings and petrol stations. The Ausländerbehörde, *the alien citizens' registration office, was also to be found in Mainzer Landstrasse. I read that the district had once contained a Nazi concentration camp on the site of an old factory, the* Alderwerke. *The site had later been used to host the Frankfurt Auschwitz Trials between 1963 and 1965.*

My first port of call was the chamber of commerce. It took me quite some time and effort to find a person who could help me. I wanted to know which American company my father had been working for just after the war.

"There were no American companies in this city right after the war," the man explained. "The only American employer during the summer of 1945 was the U. S. Army. It's more than likely that your father got a job with them if he could speak English. You see, they desperately needed German translators and interpreters to get things going in their administration, and there was a shortage of such linguists."

I asked him if there had been any other employers that were hiring educated men later in 1945. The man replied that the only other potential employer for my father would have been Hoechst, the old Farbwerke, *a company that was just beginning to establish its new direction and identity after the war, throwing off its former Nazi connection and later developing into a large manufacturer of chemical and pharmaceutical products as well as fertilizer. The result was that I called at the HR department of Hoechst, which was situated in a western suburb of the same name, only spelt differently, Höchst.*

It took me a great deal of patience and persuasion before I could speak to the man who had access to the list of former employees. They had kept that list on paper in a drawer and only digitalized it last year, "for the sake of the records," as the man remarked.

It turned out that they'd had a certain Dieter Wolff in their employ, but only on a temporary basis. Immediately after the war they had been looking for men who were proficient enough in English to deal with some of their correspondence with international business partners. "You know, practically overnight English had replaced French and become the most important language in international business," the man added. "So we needed those translators immediately." He went on to explain that they hadn't been allowed by the Americans to employ people on a permanent basis before they'd been vetted in view of their Nazi connections. From their records it appeared that Dieter Wolff had come to Hoechst from the American Forces, where he'd been employed first, from September 1945 to January 1946. But he only stayed a few months before he left. The man said the records didn't show where he'd gone from there. But I knew.

Interesting as the information from Hoechst was, it didn't really reveal any new aspects of my father's history.

I stayed on in Frankfurt for a few more days, hoping to find out where Dad had lived. He must have lived in that city, which must have been a ruin at the time. Where could he have stayed between his escape from the Russian Zone until his hasty departure for Switzerland?

His second escape – if indeed it was another escape – from Frankfurt to Switzerland puzzled me. Wasn't he safe in Frankfurt? And from what I remembered, based on the information I'd gathered in Bern, the Swiss were quite strict. Why would they have accepted him as a war refugee, not being a Jew and coming from Frankfurt? I thought about that puzzle a long time, and my thoughts often returned to it. It was my constant companion for several weeks in the course of my research expedition in Germany. I never found a full explanation that appeared satisfactory. I just had to live with this open question.

As I was wandering through Frankfurt, in search of clues about my father's stay in this big city half a century before, I sometimes sat down in one of their cafés. One afternoon I was sitting at a table in a café in what they call the Fressgass, *which translates as "Food Alley", "Gobbling Alley" or something like that. The street is really called Grosse Bockenheimer Strasse, and it is an upmarket shopping street with restaurants and fine food shops between Opernplatz and Börsenstrasse, but everyone calls it* Fressgass. *It was a place where you could meet everybody. It helped my mood to sit there and do nothing but stare ahead of me, sometimes watching people in their shopping activities, sometimes observing couples and wondering how they might be getting on with each other.*

"Verzeihen Sie bitte, ist dieser Stuhl noch frei?" *It was the voice of a friendly face popping up from my left.*

I allowed the young man to take the other chair from my table. He thanked me, carried it to a table behind my back and sat down with some people there. I only turned round once, just to see what kind of person he was. That was when our eyes locked for a split second. I faced in my direction again and tried not to think of the young man behind my back. I made every effort to concentrate on an elderly couple at another table just a short distance away. I forced my mind to get involved with what they were talking about and what their situation could possibly be. The man wore a blue suit with a light blue shirt and a flowery tie while the woman's dress looked a little shabby in comparison. Were they a married couple? Hardly. Their discussion was quiet and quite relaxed, but there seemed to be some sort of disappointment. At least the man's face betrayed that.

It was no use. I had to listen to what the people at the table behind me were saying. Although – or because – I couldn't see them I found it much more exciting to listen to them, rather than guessing at the problem between the two elderly people at the other table.

It was extremely annoying that I couldn't understand most of their lively conversation. But to my surprise, I found that I was satisfied when I just heard the voice of the man who had asked for the chair. His voice had that exciting timbre that you can sometimes get from good actors. I had to think of

Alan Rickman. I admitted to myself that such a voice could be very sexy.

When the group behind began to break up, saying their good-byes, I had still not come to the point where I would normally question my own behaviour in order to know why I'd been doing that. In other words, I was still uncertain why I had been eavesdropping and was therefore caught unawares when the young man addressed me as he was replacing the chair on my left.

He asked me if I was on my own. I didn't take offence at the question, which I would have considered a bit forward in other circumstances. On the contrary, I was overjoyed when the man sat down on the chair he'd just brought back and introduced himself. His name was Christian.

***

More than one week has elapsed since my last entry. The fact is that I simply didn't feel like writing down anymore of my observations. I didn't have the energy, and for over a week I haven't been in the mood.

The reason was Christian.

Now I don't want to go into any details of what happened between this charming and wonderful man and me. I cannot know who will read this diary; that is, if anybody will ever read it. Not that I have to be ashamed of anything. Nothing really happened. Nothing that George could find objectionable.

Nothing? Well, almost nothing.

And yet, what happened in my mind, with my feelings and my secret desires, what made those days in Frankfurt so special and so unforgettable... all that, plus the secret knowledge of what could have happened and the confidence that I had been strong enough not to let it happen... all that has given me a new lease of life. I now know that I'm not an old woman yet.

I am satisfied. I am strong.

All that is history. I will never see him again. But I'll be carrying his memory in my heart to the end of my days.

I could easily tear out this page, but I won't. Whoever might read these lines at some indefinite point in the future will allow me to be a real human being, a real woman.

***

I drove from Frankfurt to Gera. In his job for Hoechst – and probably for the American Forces before – my father had given the Thuringian town of Gera as his place of birth. Indeed, I'd heard him mention that place before. That was obviously where I might stand the best chance of finding out more about his life as a young man. Christian, who knew a lot about German bureaucracy, had advised me to go to the town archives in Gera and the Thuringian archives in Erfurt, where records were kept as far as they still existed after the War.

The last time I had travelled through the German Democratic Republic had been nearly twenty years ago, as a student of German, on my way between Hamburg and Berlin, via Hannover. At that time, I hadn't been allowed to leave the motorway, the so-called Interzonen-Autobahn, *the transit road between West Germany and West Berlin. What I had seen in the course of my passage had been extremely depressing, a country that got stuck in the 1930s and had never arrived in the second half of the twentieth century. Nobody found out, but on one of my transit trips I had left the Autobahn somewhere near Magdeburg, just to have a look. I was very lucky. I wasn't stopped by the* Volkspolizei. *What I can best remember was the smell of burnt brown coal and two-stroke exhaust fumes.*

Now, with the corrupt system gone and East Germany being part of the Federal Republic, the whole place presented itself as a strange mixture. On one hand, there were still lots of things that reminded one of the GDR, such as the cobblestones in streets, dirty grey houses or the still considerable number of Trabant cars. On the other hand, there was so much that was new. The Autobahn itself – formerly a bumpy array of concrete slabs with wide gaps in-between – was now a great deal more elegant and smooth than in the West, six lanes all the way through and relatively little traffic. Everywhere around the old decrepit towns there emerged new building sites, especially for new industrial estates. I didn't wonder where the sudden money had come from. Christian had told me how the Federal Government – formerly from Bonn, more recently from Berlin – was pumping billions and billions of deutschmarks into building projects in the East. If this is going on, who knows? East Germany might one day have an industry and an infrastructure which would be a lot more modern than what the West would be able to maintain, given the enormous financial burden of building up the East. True, Helmut Kohl had promised that the reunification wouldn't cost the people a single deutschmark. But who believed him? I certainly couldn't.

On my way, I left the motorway at Weimar and at Jena. I did my tourist thing, particularly in Weimar, where I visited Goethe's house and admired the places that Goethe and Schiller had haunted together. I thoroughly enjoyed my dip into Classical German literature, and I found it a pity I didn't have the time to attend a performance at the German National Theatre. I was sad to leave Weimar behind to continue my journey and my mission.

I could have visited Erfurt first, but I thought I wanted to start at Dad's roots. So I went to Gera first. When I arrived, I checked into a modest hotel, which was called Hotel am Galgenberg. It was within walking distance of the town centre, and it was cheap but clean.

Thinking of my strategy, I started from the main problem that I was facing. It was my father's name. He himself had told me he'd changed his name at the end of the war, but he'd never told me his original name. So where was I to start my search? I couldn't just walk into the town archives and tell them I was looking for a man whose name I didn't know, could I? I decided to go for a walk around town, just to clear my mind. Also, I had a feeling that I might be lucky and detect some clue or other that could give me an idea. It was a lovely day, and I found it very refreshing to walk down the street to the big intersection, then left towards the town centre.

As I was getting into the densely built-up part of the town centre I noticed the old tram tracks in the cobbled streets and wondered how long this town would take to upgrade these. In one stretch, the town still looked exactly as it must have looked through those forty-one years of Communist dictatorship.

The people gave a very happy impression. Everyone seemed to be busy but cheerful. However, some older people still wore that standard sour expression I used to find on the faces of the people in all Socialist states, the expression which meant something between resignation and hopelessness. Interestingly enough, I found that the older people who still had that expression were also wearing shabbier clothes than the younger generation with their cheerful and confident faces.

I bought a town map of Gera and began to study it over a cup of coffee in a pleasant little café which was most certainly a business that had only sprung up after the Wiedervereinigung. *It was very stylish and must have meant a big investment for its owner, given the fact that almost everybody in this town must have started with almost no assets right after the fall of the Iron Curtain. Except perhaps those that had been members of the Party before and therefore privileged or those that had come over from the West to take advantage of the lack of business experience among those in the East. I had read quite a lot about the growing unease between the* Wessies *and the* Ossies, *the people from old Western Germany and those from the former GDR. Sharp businessmen from Hamburg or Frankfurt had come over to the East to take over some of those rotten businesses that found it hard to cope with the new Capitalist order. Some were honest and really managed to save old* VEBs (Volkseigene Betriebe) *and give them a new lease for the future, but others – and those were probably in the majority, it was to be feared – were real sharks. They took out what assets they could and then let the companies go bankrupt or gave them a completely new structure, a process which was really illegal but in many cases, went unnoticed by the authorities and was generally referred to by the new German verb* "abwickeln", *which translates as "wind down" or "phase out". It was a euphemism for a criminal procedure that left thousands of people in the East unemployed.*

I thought about my search. What were my next steps? Yes, I had to find out my father's original name. In the hotel I had consulted the telephone directory for Gera, but there were no entries under "Wolff", which was no surprise. What strategy could I follow to find out the name?

What facts or nearly established facts did I have?

My father's family had lived in this town before the War. My grandfather had owned a delicatessen shop in the town centre. The family had lived in a house somewhere on a hill. My grandmother died in the 1930s, my grandfather probably after the War. My father had had one brother who was two years older. I remembered Dad referring to him as Thomas, but he hardly told me anything else about him, except that he was conscripted into the German Navy at the beginning of the War. Dad obviously didn't know if his father and brother had survived the War or not.

It was clear to me that I couldn't walk into the town archives on the basis of such scarce information. I had to find out more by other means.

Perhaps I should talk to people, elderly people who might still remember my grandfather's delicatessen shop. That seemed my best bet.

I stowed my map in my handbag and strolled through the streets in the town centre. In the market square, which was simply named Markt, *I sat down on a bench. There was an elderly woman who was feeding some pigeons. I watched her for a while, studying her face. At first, I had the impression that she was very old, with all those wrinkles down her cheeks and her sunken eyes, but the longer I watched her throwing her breadcrumbs and cooing to the birds the younger she appeared to me. It was one of those rare moments in life where one realizes how subjective and fleeting certain impressions of other humans can be.*

The woman noticed me. She smiled. She had an extremely charming smile despite a hint of earnestness behind her façade. I liked her immediately.

"Do you often come here to feed the birds?" I asked.

"Whenever I feel like it," she smiled. "It relaxes me."

"But only in fine weather?"

"Well, mostly. But in winter this square has its particular attraction, so I sometimes come in spite of the cold."

We were silent for a few minutes. She continued feeding the pigeons until her paper bag was empty. Then she sat down beside me.

"Sie sind nicht von hier," *she remarked. "Where are you from? You have a strange accent."*

I told her I was English, leaving out my American roots. This surprised her, and she said my German was very good. Then she asked me if I was here as a tourist. I explained to her that I was looking for the history of my father's family who had lived here before the War.

"What was their name?" she asked.

"I'm afraid I don't know," I replied. "My father changed his name at the end of the War."

"Were your people Jewish?"

"No. At least, not that I know of. My grandfather had a delicatessen shop in the town centre."

"Oh, I remember. I often walked past that shop. It was in the Sorge. That was the main shopping street, just over there, behind those houses. Still is."

"Do you remember the name?" I suddenly became excited.

"I'm afraid I can't think of it at the moment. You see, we were too poor to go shopping there. That delicatessen shop was for the rich. When the Nazis took over it was mostly them that went there. I remember the elegant people or their servants coming out of that shop, with their noses up in the air."

"And you really can't remember the name?"

"I am so sorry," the woman shook her head. "It's too long ago."

What a disappointment! But at least I now knew where about the shop had been. I asked the good woman if she could show me the exact house where it had been. She said yes. So, we stood up and walked over to the street called Sorge, where many new chain stores that were familiar from other German cities had recently established themselves. The woman, who introduced herself as Trudy Kleinschmidt, stopped in front of one of the buildings which now housed a new pharmacy.

"This must be it," she pointed at the front.

I looked at the building. It was one of those that had obviously been rebuilt after the war and refurbished again now after reunification. It was clear that the people who owned it now would certainly be unable to tell me anything about the owners before the war.

Trudy Kleinschmidt and I stood there and went on chatting for a while, until she said she had to leave. I gave her my mobile number and told her the name of my hotel, "just in case you suddenly remember the name of the shop," I added.

We parted, and I walked back to Markt, where I sat down on the same bench again. There were only few people about. I studied the large building across. It looked as if it had seen better times. A most impressive building with a wide front facing the Markt. What could it have been? Today it was apparently uninhabited and observing it carefully, I detected some cracks in the walls and some rotten beams under the eaves. But its size meant it had at one time been a building of considerable importance. A government building? A modest town palace? A guildhall? A foreign embassy? I was reminded of yet another of my father's Latin catch-phrases, sic transit gloria mundi, *"such is the decline of former glory". Somehow, I felt I wanted to find out more about this building.*

I bought a newspaper and walked back to my hotel, where I caught up with my writing. My diary was behind schedule. The rest of the day I spent reading the paper and staring at the map of Gera, hoping to draw some information from it and wondering where my grandfather's house had been.

I spent three days wandering around the town without any significant results. Then, quite out of the blue, I got a phone call from Trudy.

"Can we meet?" she wanted to know.

"Of course. Have you found out the name?" I asked back.

"Yes, I have. But I have found out more information that might interest you."

That afternoon, we met at the same café where I had started out on my first day in Gera.

Our talk was mostly about the town of Gera in general. I couldn't get away from the impression that Trudy was afraid of something. She seemed to shy away from the sort of information she had made me believe she had found out for me on the telephone. While we were discussing the progress of modernity in the Eastern Länder, *the awful behaviour of some arrogant* Wessies *and the good things that the reunified Germany ought to have taken over from the GDR – such as certain patterns in the education system or a commitment to full employment among the people – I observed her face and her body-language. She was really a very good-looking woman despite her advanced age. Whereas at first I had judged her to be in her seventies, I now estimated her age to be in the mid-sixties. Her slight nervousness showed in the movement of her hands and her blinking eyes. As I was to find out later in the course of our acquaintance, whenever she was nervous her hands moved in the air very quickly, especially her left hand, which she flapped in front of her as if she could emphasize a certain point like that, and she accompanied this hand-flapping with repeated winks which gave the impression of a person who was dazzled by bright light or beginning to cry any moment. But with her these idiosyncrasies were signs of extreme nervousness. Though I had not been able to interpret those signs yet at the time of our meeting at the café, I still caught her nervousness. And I wondered what she could be so nervous about.*

Eventually our general topics had run out of steam and we sat in silence for a few minutes. We both ordered more coffee. Then I decided to take the initiative.

"On the telephone you mentioned something that is of great interest to me," I ventured. "You said you'd found out the name of my grandfather's delicatessen shop in the Sorge. If you don't mind, would you be ready to let me know now?"

She looked at me. "Yes, it was called Weidmann's, and it was a very elegant shop, as I think I told you." She hesitated. "But you see, there's a lot more to tell. Only, I don't quite know where to start."

"What is it, then?" I asked.

"It's all so long ago. But it suddenly came back to me when I spoke to my cousin. She was... well, she could remember it all. How could I ever have forgotten that name? Of course, it was Weidmann's."

I felt there had to be a lot more behind this information. Why else should Trudy and possibly her cousin be so emotional about the name of that old shop?

"Did you know the family who owned the shop?"

"No, I didn't. But my cousin did, and only too well."

"So, can you tell me more about your cousin and what she knows?"

"I think you should talk to her. I don't know how much I can tell you. Some of the things are too private, so she'd better tell you personally."

"But what do you feel entitled to tell me? Or can I talk to your cousin soon? What's her name anyway?"

"Well, these are a lot of questions all at once," Trudy frowned at me.

"Oh, I'm sorry. I didn't want to be impolite. But you see, I'm really interested in the family, the Weidmann family, as you said. They could be my ancestors. So I think I have a moral right to know the truth."

Trudy reflected for a few moments. Then she shrugged her shoulders and uttered a deep sigh.

"I guess you are right," she finally said. "If you are the granddaughter of the owner of Weidmann's Delicatessen, then you have the right to know the truth, as you say. But I'm warning you."

"Why?"

"You see, I like you. I liked you from the first moment we met on that bench in Market Square. And some of the things my cousin could tell you, well, they might not be so pleasant, and I wouldn't want you to worry too much about the past. It's all so long ago."

I looked her straight in her eyes and solemnly declared that I wanted to know the truth, whatever the outcome, even if it was hard to stomach. She replied she wanted her cousin to be free to decide for herself.

"Let her be the judge of how much of the truth she is ready to tell me," I suggested.

"I will call her, and I'll ask her," Trudy promised.

"What's your cousin's name?" I repeated my earlier question.

"She's Anna."

NINETEEN

Anna Kleinschmidt was indisposed for about ten days after my meeting with her cousin Trudy in that café, where I had first learnt the name of my ancestors, Weidmann. Trudy assured me that Anna would eventually talk to me. She was in a retirement home in Gera-Lusan, but she was suffering from a bad pneumonia and couldn't be visited until she was better again.

I spent these days with further enquiries. My approach was a personal approach at first. I just addressed older people in the streets and asked them if they had known Weidmann's Delicatessen or even the owner's family. The responses I got were very few. Hardly anyone could remember the Weidmanns, although some people remembered the shop.

One elderly woman could tell me a little more.

"Old Herr Weidmann was a very strange character, and so were his two sons," she stated. "He was known as a liberal freethinker in the thirties, but when his sons left for the War he suddenly adapted to the new order and became as thick as thieves with the Nazi big-shots in town."

"And his sons?" I wanted to know.

"Well, I don't really know. I was too small at the time, a mere child. But I remember what I learnt from my parents, who went along with the system but always kept their heads low. They didn't like the Weidmanns. They said the boys always thought they were better than everybody else. One of them was sent to the Nazi elite school near Dresden where they made a real arsehole out of him. The other boy just disappeared in the War. Old Herr Weidmann died in the early fifties. He was a broken man after the war."

I was very excited about this information. Obviously, my unknown uncle, my father's brother Thomas, had become a staunch Nazi after he was sent to a special school where he was brainwashed.

"Do you think I could talk to your parents?" I asked very politely.

"I don't think so. My father is dead, and my mother is very weak. I'm sorry. But tell me, why are you so interested in the Weidmanns?"

"As it appears, old Herr Weidmann could have been my grandfather, but I'm still not quite sure. That's why I want to find out."

"Ah, I understand. If you can give me your name and telephone number I might call you when I've spoken to my mother and she's agreed to talk to you. But don't count on it."

So I now had two elderly informers whose relatives could tell me more. I had become dependent on the good-will of Trudy Kleinschmidt and of this woman, whose name was Renate Erdinger.

But it was more than just a start.

I got a few more bits of information from elderly people, but I suspected most of the so-called information to be based on rumours. A conspicuous delicatessen shop in the town centre with an owner who changed his political attitude during those troubled times must have stood out. But then, of course, such a long time makes people forget or mix up things. Moreover, some of my would-be informers were reluctant to talk about those times, probably because they had either suffered too much or because they had been sympathizers of the Nazis and now wanted to erase that part of their biography. After the War, things must have been similar to the situation now, in certain respects. I am convinced that many of the good citizens that I see in the streets of Gera today must have been agents of the Stasi, *the secret police of the Communist dictatorship. A good number of them might even have blood on their hands. And it must have been similar, or even worse, in the late forties and through the fifties. As my readings in history have taught me, many men even in high positions in the early years of the Federal Republic must have been Nazis with blood on their hands. I remember that one of them, Hans Filbinger, even became prime minister in one of the* Länder. *And then, later, there was Kurt Waldheim from Austria who made it all the way up to the position of Secretary General of the United Nations. Fortunately, both of them were uncovered and had to resign. As far as I know, the Filbinger chap is still alive. I wonder if they will give him a state funeral when he dies.*

For days, I had time to reflect and assess my own picture of my father. Of course, as a young girl I had admired him as a hero. But after my adolescence, I had begun to see him in a more critical light, even though I still felt very close to him. Whilst I admired his pacifist views, I became increasingly curious about his role during the War. The fact that he'd changed his name and his consistent reluctance to talk about those days made me more and more suspicious. It's strange how you can love your father unconditionally and at the same time question some of the things he wants you to believe. For one thing, I found it odd that he had those scars on his arm, scars that he claimed stemmed from tattoos that he'd had removed some time after the War, which meant that he must have spent a certain time in a concentration camp, but he absolutely refused to tell me more about it.

***

Neither Trudy Kleinschmidt nor Renate Erdinger has called. It's time for some sort of reckoning or position-finding. I don't know how long I'll have the patience to wait for my kind informers to contact me. It's possible I might have to return to England with the scarce information that I have accumulated up to now.

So, what information do I have?

First, my grandfather's name was Weidmann. His shop was in the Sorge.

Then, he had two sons. Thomas, my uncle, who was obviously a Nazi, disappeared during the War. He's probably dead. The second son, Dieter, – if that is his real name – is my father.

Furthermore, my father must have known the Kleinschmidts.

What will my next steps have to be? What questions will I have to ask those old women if and when they're ready to talk to me? What stumbling blocks are there when I interview them? I'll have to be polite and careful and ask my questions with empathy. Those old women might have suffered during both periods of dictatorship, the Nazi times as well as the GDR times.

***

Several days have passed. It's only now that I find the time and the energy – or should I say courage? – to return to my diary and write down what I have found out in the course of my research. It is not easy to stomach. But let me begin at the beginning.

One morning, Trudy Kleinschmidt called to say her older cousin Anna was now ready to talk to me. As she pointed out, Anna only agreed after Trudy had told her I was a daughter of one of the Weidmann boys.

We took a tram to Gera-Lusan. It was a quarter or suburb that must have grown up during GDR times. Most of the huge apartment blocks were constructed out of those standard-sized grey slabs, so-called Plattenbauten, *which you can find in all former Socialist states of Eastern Europe, but most widely spread and conspicuous in the former GDR.*

The retirement home was located in such a building, but it had had a thorough refurbishment, probably right after Reunification.

A male nurse showed us to Anna Kleinschmidt's room.

As we entered, I was surprised to meet the bright smile of an extremely good-looking woman who hardly looked older than in her mid-sixties, but who had to be in her mid-seventies. Her bright eyes beamed and exuded an emotional warmth that I immediately liked. Her hair was well-groomed and tinted a pleasant bluish grey. Her lipstick was elegant but not overdone, a hue between red and dark pink, emphasized by the woman's winning smile. The wrinkles produced by her friendly smile didn't make her look older because her skin was of such smooth and soft quality to make many a younger woman envious.

We shook hands and sat down in two elegant armchairs, while Trudy busied herself with the tea-making paraphernalia in the background. I imagined we would begin with the usual small-talk, but Anna went straight into the heart of the matter.

"Yes, I can see, my dear young woman," she said, looking at my face with what seemed like fascination, and I was touched to detect a tear running down one of her cheeks. "I can see it in your features, you must be Manfred's daughter."

I was so puzzled, I couldn't respond immediately.

"But my father's name is Dieter," I managed to croak eventually, in full knowledge that I had to be wrong and she had to be right.

Anna slowly nodded her head. "I can understand why he had to change his name after the war. But to me, he is still my beloved Manfred, Manfred Weidmann, the great love of my life. How could I ever forget his features? And you are his spitting image. What did you say your name was?"

"Nora. Nora White."

"And your father?"

"Dieter Woolf. He said it was Wolff in Germany, but actually he must have changed his name before, as you say, because he betrayed that one day when he had a slip of his tongue and mentioned his escape from the East. Originally, he maintained that he'd changed from Wolff to Woolf when he went to America, but when he told me of his dangerous escape from the Russian Zone right at the end of the War, he accidentally mentioned that he had to change his name during his escape. At the time it didn't strike me as important – I was only a young teenager – but more recently, as I was trying to put together all the pieces of the puzzle that was my father's biography, it suddenly dawned on me as an inconsistency."

"I see."

"So, you are quite sure his name was Manfred Weidmann, and we are actually speaking of the same man?"

Anna thought for a moment. Then she began to describe her young lover of the nineteen-thirties, giving me his exact date of birth – which indeed was my father's – and she added some of his typical idiosyncrasies, such as the twitching of his left shoulder when he was nervous.

"And he was always so fond of quotations from Latin," she added.

I had to swallow hard. There was no doubt. We were really speaking of one and the same man. And Anna had been his girlfriend before the War.

"Tell me. How is dear Manfred today? Is he well?"

"I'm afraid he isn't very well. Physically he is okay for his age, but he seems to worry so much. His mind seems to go funny, if you know what I mean."

"Please, tell me more about him and about your family."

So I told this charming woman the whole story. I told her of Dad's time in Frankfurt, then in Switzerland, in Chicago, and finally in England. I told her of my mother Emily and of my sister Margaret. I gave her a history of my father's professional career, as far as I knew about it, and I concluded with a report about my own family, my husband George and my children Andrew and Lisa. I could see that my listener was very pleased with what I told her.

We were silent, all three of us, digesting what we had just found out, when a young nurse entered and put an end to the intimate atmosphere.

"You'll have to leave now. Frau Kleinschmidt needs a rest. You can come back tomorrow."

We left the retirement home in silence and took the tram back to the town centre. When we parted in Weimarer Strasse Trudy sighed, "I hope it hasn't been a disappointment for you."

***

The next day, I went back to visit Anna at the retirement home in Gera-Lusan. And after that I spent at least three hours with her every day for two weeks. During this time, we became very close. I can even say, we became very good friends, and I learnt to love her very much. On the first three days, Trudy came with me, but then it became too much for her, so I went alone. This made it possible for us to grow so intimate.

What I learnt about my father and about Anna during these two weeks was so dense and at first so unbelievable, that I simply didn't have the energy to write down my new findings in my diary every day when I was back at my hotel. So, now, after two weeks, at last I have at long last found the energy and the courage to write down what I know today.

The greatest shock for me was that it was not my Uncle Thomas who became a staunch Nazi; it was my own father, Manfred Weidmann.

***

If I start chronologically, I have to begin with my grandfather's family, the Weidmanns. They lived in Ypernstrasse on the Galgenberg. The street was re-named after the war and is now called Niemöllerstrasse, named after Martin Niemöller, the famous anti-Nazi theologian and Lutheran pastor who died about ten years ago. My grandparents' house is still there, and it's only a five minutes' walk from my hotel.

My grandfather was Thomas Weidmann, the successful delicatessen retailer of Gera between the wars and during the Second World War. His wife Elfriede, my grandmother, was a very frail woman who died early after giving him two sons, Thomas and Manfred. Thomas senior had been a member of the NSDAP for a short period before 1933, but he left before Hitler came to power. Anna remembers him calling the Nazis a dirty Lumpenpack. *He was set against the growing dictatorship, first because he simply thought the Nazis' ideas stupid and dangerous, later because he lost many Jewish friends who disappeared overnight. He wanted his sons to have a good education, which he strongly believed to be the best safeguard against Nazi propaganda.*

Manfred was an excellent student. He went to the same school as Anna, and they became good friends. Anna carefully told me of their growing love. Of course, she didn't give me any details, but from certain parts of her report I gathered that they must have been very much in love. They used to discuss the political situation and they agreed on many things. One night that Anna can never forget was the night in

November 1938, when Jewish homes and businesses were raided. She told me how she and Manfred had witnessed the burning of the local synagogue.

"And the worst of it all for us personally was the fact that we happened to seal our love forever on that same night," she said with tears in her eyes.

Manfred and Anna must have planned a future together. But then, very suddenly, he was accepted by a special school near Dresden, something every young fellow in those days would have been proud of. It promised him a brilliant career for the future, it was commonly assumed.

More or less at the same time as Manfred's career at Pirna, the Second World War began.

At first, they often wrote letters to each other, but gradually these letters became less frequent and then stopped altogether. Anna was heartbroken. During the war, it was generally accepted that the young men had to be away from home for long periods, but Manfred's absence seemed much longer than usual.

There was a terrible thing that happened to Anna only about three weeks after Manfred had left for Pirna. Something so terrible that she couldn't find the words to tell him in a letter, she had to wait until his return to tell him personally. She felt so ashamed. Even now, after all those years, she found it hard to tell me.

"Please, don't judge me as a bad woman, dear Nora," she begged. "What happened after Manfred left destroyed my whole life, and I knew that he would stop loving me when I told him. That's why I didn't want to tell him in a letter, but in person."

"Are you sure you want to tell me now?" I asked, holding her hand.

"Yes. You have a right to know the truth."

She stood up from her armchair and walked over to her bureau, where she searched among her papers in a drawer and eventually found a piece of paper, which she carried back to her armchair. She drew a long sigh before she spoke again, obviously collecting the courage needed to tell me what she had to tell.

"Has your father ever mentioned a man called Wolfgang Löffel?"

"Yes," I answered but decided to keep back what I'd heard about that character from my father.

"Wolfgang was one year above us at school, and he was an awful bully. I soon realized – in fact I knew from childhood – that he fancied me. I never told Manfred, but I found Wolfgang spying on me several times. I was only about ten when I found him spying on me in the changing rooms at the local swimming baths, and later he often ambushed me on my way back from school. He became a real pain for me. When Manfred and I eventually fell in love and it became general knowledge in town, Wolfgang retreated, and I was ever so relieved. It was a true liberation. I assumed that he'd understood that Manfred was the boy of my heart and he stood no chance. That was how things stood through '38 and most of '39."

I cannot write down the continuation of what Anna told me in her own words. Her report was too broken, often interrupted by emotional cries. I have to give the facts in my own words.

Three weeks after Manfred had left for his new school at Pirna, suddenly Wolfgang accosted Anna in the street. He told her he had news from Manfred. He claimed he'd had a letter from him with a photograph enclosed, a photograph which showed Manfred in his new uniform, his arm round the shoulders of a fine girl. Anna couldn't believe that, but Wolfgang insisted. He said he could show her the photo, he had it in his attic. She hesitated, fearing some sort of trap, but eventually her curiosity was too great and her anxiety about such news from Manfred too irresistible. She followed the awful fellow to his house, where he led the way up the dark stairs to his attic. In his room, he closed the door behind her and immediately caught her in his strong arms. She struggled for her life, but he was a lot stronger. He brutally ripped her clothes off her body, flung her on his bed, threw himself on top of her and raped her in the most horrible way, injuring her in body and soul. It was perhaps a blessing that she lost consciousness.

After this crime, Anna took a long time to regain her consciousness. When she shakily returned to her senses, she found herself lying naked on Wolfgang's bed, covered with her own clothes. The perpetrator was sitting in the swivel chair at his desk at the other end of the room, smoking a cigarette and smirking.

"You liked what you got?" he asked.

She was too stunned to answer and just began to cry. She felt herself shake with her whole body. She could no longer withhold her tears.

"Oh, you cry-baby! Don't be such a fool. You've had it coming for a long time, that's for sure," he chuckled.

She managed to groan something like "you dirty pig", but he only grinned.

"I'm sure your milksop Manfred couldn't give it to you like this," he boasted.

She preferred to remain silent. Eventually he allowed her to get dressed, which she did in great haste. She was eager to get out as quickly as possible.

As she stumbled down the stairs he called after her, "Don't think you can tell anyone. No-one would believe you. Besides, nothing really happened, you wanted to seduce me, but you were no good!"

When Anna had finished telling me this part of her life, she had to stop for the day. She needed to rest and could only go on the next day.

In the days following her rape, it was clear to her that she couldn't tell anybody. No-one would believe her, as Wolfgang had said. So she kept her pain and her humiliation to herself. She found her only consolation in the letters that still arrived from Pirna. She wrote back without telling Manfred because she was so deeply and utterly ashamed, and she was afraid of losing his love if she told him.

Meanwhile, the War was claiming sacrifices from everyone, and Anna, although not interested in politics, began to doubt what she heard on the radio. If the things that the Führer *was saying in his speeches were true and correct, then why did he have to yell and shout as he did? Her parents never discussed these things with her, but she found out that her father sometimes listened to the BBC from London. He did that at very low volume so that the neighbours wouldn't hear, and when he realized that Anna had found out, he gave her very serious injunctions not to tell anybody, not even her best friends, not even Manfred in her letters. He warned her that sometimes teachers were instructed by the Party to ask their pupils what radio programmes their parents were listening to. One day, Anna's class teacher, Herr Niederberger, whistled a tune while the class was busy with some written exercises. All the boys and girls were bent over their exercise-books and writing with their pens, from time to time dipping these in their inkwells. Anna at once recognized the tune of the BBC News. She just continued writing, keeping her head down. Gerhard Heckel, who was not the brightest boy, looked up and nodded to the tune, only for a few seconds.*

"A lovely tune, isn't it?" Herr Niederberger asked, fixing his stare on Gerhard.

"Ja, Herr Lehrer," the boy promptly answered.

"Do you know it?"

"Yes, of course."

After class, Gerhard was taken to the staffroom for official interrogation. He didn't return to class for three days. And when he did, he was very quiet. He kept his mouth shut and just looked around with a shy expression.

Later, it was whispered that his parents had been arrested. To Anna, it was clear that the teacher's whistling was a trap he was instructed to set his pupils. Like that, the authorities often found out when people were listening to enemy radio stations, something that was officially declared a serious crime, a form of treason, a premeditated Landesverrat. *People went to prison for several years for such a crime. Anna admired her parents' civil courage.*

Another consequence of the ongoing state of war was the gradual disappearance of young men. Suddenly, everybody seemed to be in uniform, only to disappear to some battle or other. In her school, Anna found new posters on the walls. They called upon people with special talents to come forward and offer their talents to the great cause. They all said something to the effect that Germany had to be made great again. At home, she asked her father why Germany had to be made great again. He hesitated before he answered.

"Before we can discuss such things in times like these, dear girl, I have to be absolutely certain that nothing ever goes beyond these four walls. Is this clear?"

Anna promised she would never discuss such things with anyone else. While she was giving her promise, she knew that she would most definitely discuss them with Manfred once he was back, but she was confident that things would have changed for the better by that time. Besides, Manfred would marry her, she was sure. So, her promise to her father today was a small lie, what some people call a white lie.

Herr Kleinschmidt told his daughter how wrong it was to think one's country was better or greater than any other country, or that it could ever be greater, or that it somehow had to regain some imaginary former greatness. The only true greatness for a nation lay in the happiness and political freedom of its people. Anna completely agreed to this.

"So, you don't think that what our fatherland is attempting in these times makes any sense?"

"That's an extremely dangerous question, my dear. And my answer would be even more dangerous if it could reach the ears of the Gestapo. We would both go to prison for it."

Clandestine discussions like that happened from time to time between Anna and her father. With her father's opinions on her mind, she managed to construct her double-life. She was a good student, a good Jungmädel *in the BDM, and she never criticized any official statements. But inside she was convinced it was all wrong, and it would be over in a few months. Hopefully.*

In mid-October, she missed her period. She kept it to herself, but when, towards the end of November, her mother found her being violently sick on a Sunday morning, she could no longer ignore the truth.

Anna found herself pregnant.

TWENTY

Trudy called one morning and wanted to know how I was getting on with her cousin Anna. Had I found out any interesting things about my ancestors? I told her yes, but things had been so complicated during the War that we needed more time to sort them out properly.

When I went to see Anna again after her terrible revelation the previous afternoon, I had a strange feeling in my stomach. I wondered if it wasn't prying into her most private affairs if I continued to question her about the past. I asked her straight out when we were sitting over our tea again.

"Not in the least," she exclaimed. "I'm so relieved that I can tell someone at last, and who else but my dear Manfred's daughter should be entitled to be the recipient of such difficult and personal news?"

"I thank you for your confidence in me," I said and regretted it immediately. It sounded so cheesy after I had first asked her about her past. But I decided to let it stand.

Her pregnancy was without any medical complications. However, there were considerable social complications. She was expelled from her school, and her parents had to fight hard to convince the authorities to let her keep the baby once it was born. The argument which did the trick involved Manfred. They told the authorities that the child's father was preparing to fight for the fatherland. The Kleinschmidts thought they might not get away with such a lie, but when the identity of the alleged father was established, and it became clear that he was a student at Pirna, suddenly all questioning ceased, and the family were told to look well after the child of a German officer.

Anna wrote to Manfred and told him of her pregnancy. Of course, everyone was convinced that he was the father of the expected child. Anna was sure, and so were her parents. Only in her worst dreams did she admit to herself that the child might just as well be Wolfgang's.

The Kleinschmidts took Anna to see Thomas Weidmann in Ypernstrasse and told him about Manfred and Anna. Herr Weidmann congratulated Anna on her pregnancy but refused to have anything to do with the affair. He told them it was up to his son Manfred to acknowledge the child once it was born, but they couldn't expect to get any money out of him. He would speak to Anna again when the baby was born and when she showed him a letter from Manfred in which he officially acknowledged his parenthood.

He added a quiet remark: "The silly boy! Destroying his career like that!"

The Kleinschmidts pretended they hadn't heard the remark and took their leave. As Anna was a bit disappointed, her father explained to her that he was not surprised at all. It was what he had expected from that snob, Thomas Weidmann.

So Anna gave birth to a healthy boy. She named him Manfred. One of their neighbours who called in to congratulate the young mother asked if she didn't want to give the boy a middle name to honour one of the country's great leaders.

"You know how it is," she explained, "these days it can only help a young lad in his career if he has an Adolf, a Hermann or a Joseph in his name."

"We shall think about it. You may be right," they lied.

And what about Wolfgang?

Ever since the horrible crime, Anna had never seen him again. It was possible he was just taken to some battlefield, as many young men of the town were, but she didn't trust the simplicity of this interpretation. As she was walking along the pavement around town, pushing her pram with healthy little Manfred gurgling in it, she constantly looked behind her, afraid that her rapist might jump out of nowhere and rape her again.

And Manfred?

He got the message of her pregnancy, after which he wrote back several times, but with decreasing frequency until, about two months before her confinement, his letters stopped altogether. He never acknowledged to be the father of her child.

Apart from his apparent withdrawal from their relationship, there was another problem which worried her a great deal. It was the reference made by the authorities. They referred to Manfred Weidmann as a future officer. Also, in his letters he no longer mentioned anything about politics. That might be because of the general fear of the Nazi régime among the people who could see more clearly what was going on in the country, but Anna had a bad feeling about his withdrawal. She feared they might make a Nazi sympathizer out of him at that school. After all, everybody referred to it as an elitist school where only the most gifted students were accepted. She knew that Manfred was brilliant in every subject at school, but the suspicion began to creep into her brain that qualities like "gifted" or "brilliant" these days might only refer to complete subjection to Nazi ideology. There were rumours about Pirna to the effect that proper Nazi hardliners were bred there. If they thought a young man was pliable and gullible enough and showed academic talent at the same time, he was the right material for their brainwash. From Manfred's earliest letters, Anna had gathered that the school was led like a military camp. There was a lot of drill and indoctrination. But gradually he stopped telling her about such things as time went on.

Herr Kleinschmidt had some good connections, although he was set against the Nazi system. "You can learn a lot more about your political opponents if you pretend to be one of them," he used to say. Anna and her mother warned him to be careful. They had heard of too many people who disappeared. But he was a very clever man. He would go to the Stammtisch of the Nazis in Untermhaus and listen to what they had to discuss. Like that, Anna got some information about Manfred's progress and his activities over the war years.

The other source of her information, strange as it may seem, was Wolfgang. It was late in '43 when, all of a sudden, Wolfgang accosted her in the street. She panicked and was about to run away. She was glad she didn't have little Manfred with her. But Wolfgang stopped her with a firm grip on her right arm.

"Listen, stupid bitch, I have some news for you. It's about your weakling of a lover-boy," he laughed.

This stopped her. "All right, I'll listen to what you've got to tell me, but I won't go anywhere with you."

"Hey, hold your horses. I'm not going to hurt you. You don't interest me. I've got better women I can get if I want. Real knock-out women, classy women any man would be proud of."

Anna decided to listen to him. But she was careful not to provoke him. Her eagerness to learn anything about Manfred even made her follow Wolfgang to a café in the Sorge, where they sat down at a table in the corner and ordered tea. They had the table between them, and the café had people in it, so she felt safe enough. She wondered what this awful man had to tell her. He was in a uniform of the Wehrmacht.

He registered her scrutiny of his uniform. "As you can see, I'm only a sergeant, which is a type of non-commissioned officer."

"I wouldn't recognize the difference between any ranks anyway," she said with a dismissive gesture.

"Well, you should, with your lover-boy such a big shot these days."

"What about him, then?"

"Didn't you know he's an Untersturmführer *in the* Waffen-SS*?"*

"That's impossible!" she cried. "You're only saying that to annoy me."

"Not at all," he smirked and chuckled. He must have known how to shock her best.

"How can you know such a thing anyway?" she asked.

"Well, I have my connections. Although I didn't make it into the officers' ranks while your lover-boy made it into the super class, I have my secret connections. Believe me, what I'm saying is true. Your Manfred is one of the Nazi hardliners. The SS wouldn't have made him an officer otherwise."

"But why are you telling me? You wouldn't do this unless there's something for you in it."

"Isn't that obvious? For years I had to listen to your intellectual babble. You and your loverboy with all your liberal freethinker attitudes, ridiculing the good cause for our fatherland. You always thought you were better human beings and looked down on chaps like me, but now look who is on the winning side? It's us, the proper ruling party of our great nation, and we'll build our empire, we'll make Germany great again. Das tausendjährige Reich! *And as you can see, your boy has turned his back on your floozy intellectual ideas. He's joined the winning side. Let that be a lesson to you, you silly woman."*

"So you've had your satisfaction, or as they say, your innere Reichsparteitag, *haven't you?"*

Wolfgang only smiled his dirty smile.

Anna left the café and ran home. Back in her father's study, she told her parents what she'd heard from Wolfgang. They couldn't believe her at first, but then the father said he'd seen stranger things and many young men could be led astray by the promises made by the Nazis. It was the brainwashing process of Pirna which might have changed Manfred so sadly. After all, the fact that he had given up writing to her could be an indication of his volte-face, *couldn't it?*

"Can't you find out about this, with your connections at the Stammtisch?*" Anna begged her father.*

"I'll do my best, my dear girl. But we've got to be very careful. One doesn't just ask questions about SS officers, just like that. I'll have to see what can be done to find out. But listen, you'd better get used to the idea that your Manfred might have become a staunch Nazi. It will be easier to forget him."

"I'll never forget him."

"Well then, put him behind you, as they say."

***

I received a phone call from Renate Erdinger. She said her mother was having a good spell, and I was welcome to come and talk to her. So I decided to give Anna a break and see Renate's mother before returning to Anna's report. So I told her I would be back after a few days to which she replied, "I know you must have other sources for your search."

"And do you mind?" I asked.

"Not really," Anna replied. "It's only possible you might hear some really bad things about my dear Manfred, because many people hated the SS, especially after the War. So they invented all sorts of crimes for them. But I just refuse to believe that your father could have been involved in really awful crimes. He was too good for this world."

I decided to let this stand and promised to be back after a few days.

Renate received me in her flat near the town centre. It was an old house which hadn't been refurbished yet. The plaster was peeling off the walls and there were cracks all over the façade. The staircase creaked as I was climbing up to the third floor, and the banister didn't really look very trustworthy. There were smells of cooked cabbage and spicy sausages oozing out of other flats, but when I entered Renate's flat, I was surprised to find a fine smell of lavender and an extremely tidy place. There was no dust, everything was nicely polished and smelt good. If fact, the entire flat had a very elegant atmosphere. Quite a contrast to the dilapidated outside of the building and the decrepit staircase.

"We like to keep up our dignity," Renate explained when she ushered me in, as if she had read my thoughts.

I handed her a small parcel, which contained some sweet confectionery from a nice shop in the Sorge. "It's really very kind of you to remember me," I added.

"Oh, that's quite all right," she answered. "My mother has been very eager to see you these two weeks, ever since I'd told her about your search."

We exchanged a few more niceties and made some brief comments on the weather, before she led me into her grand parlour with the polished parquet floor and her elegant and stylish Biedermeier furniture.

Her old mother was sitting in a comfortable armchair which was a stark contrast to the rest of the furniture because it was obviously a modern Stressless easy chair. Quite an aesthetic shock within the context of the lovely Biedermeier parlour. She looked like a tough woman with her short black and grey hair.

"So, you are the daughter of one of the Weidmann boys," she croaked, as she was offering me her shaky hand.

"Yes, my father was Manfred Weidmann, you know, the son of the family with the delicatessen shop in the Sorge."

"I know who Manfred was. My husband went to school with Thomas, the older Weidmann boy."

"Oh, I see. Did you know the family personally?" I asked.

"Not very well, not personally, but we knew of them. My husband Gerhard didn't get on very well with Thomas. He considered him the most arrogant prick. But he admired Manfred. I'm afraid my dear Gerhard passed away a long time ago, otherwise he could tell you everything himself."

"I am sorry. If it is too difficult for you to talk about those times, I perfectly understand. It must have been a very hard time."

"Not hard at the time," Frau Erdinger said. "It became hard after the War."

"Yes, I see. But how did you cope with the difficulties during the War? I mean the depravity, the food and fuel rationing, the political indoctrination."

"There was no political indoctrination, as you call it. We had a thoroughly good time. Gerhard was assistant to the Stadtrat, *a protégé of Walter Kiessling, he had joined the NSDAP very early and managed to rise to important posts. He was awarded several medals of honour, two of them even from the* Führer *personally. In such a position, we never suffered from any rationing or other disadvantages."*

I hesitated before I asked my next question. "So, you were proper Nazis?" For a split second after uttering the question I regretted it, fearing to offend Frau Erdinger, but then quickly remembered that I had resolved not to condemn any former Nazis – or former SED members – in the course of my search. For, who knows how I would have reacted had I lived at that time? Let those who are without blame throw the first stone.

"Of course, we were. And I'm glad we were, whatever people said about us after the War."

Now this was a new situation for me. While, after the War, all the big Nazis tried to hide and pretended to be ashamed of their crimes, here was a woman who openly admitted that she and her husband had been Nazis and were even proud of it. I wondered which was more honest: Frau Erdinger's open confession or all those liars. After the fall of the GDR a few years ago, we had a similar problem. There were those who couldn't escape their criminal past in the SED and those who became what people referred to as Wendehälse, *the German word for wrynecks, birds that could turn their necks around and face the other side of reality. Many who had been Nazi criminals under Hitler managed to erase their pasts and move into high positions after the war. They became top politicians, bank managers or industrial tycoons. And today, as we are sitting here, several of the top politicians in Germany are former SED members or Stasi sleuths.*

After digesting my slight shock, I continued with my next question. "Did you hear about Manfred after he'd left Gera for Pirna?"

"Of course, we did. Once he was an Untersturmführer *in the* Waffen-SS, *he visited the town several times, usually in the entourage of a* Sturmbannfüher, *a* Standartenführer *or some other high SS-officer. One evening there was a big reception in the* Rathaus *when an important delegation of the SS happened to be in town. I think it was in '43 or thereabout. There was some function or other going on, I don't remember what it was, but I remember the reception. It was very grand indeed. Gerhard and I were invited. I wore my long red evening dress that one of his friends in the SS had brought back from Rome. It was ever so elegant, and I felt like a princess."*

"That must have been a big occasion. But what about Manfred Weidmann?"

"Oh yes, Untersturmführer Weidmann was presented to us, and of course, we recognized him immediately. He was so wonderful, resplendent in his impressive black uniform. He had a short chat with us before he moved on to other people who were obviously more important for him. But I won't forget what a dashing young officer Manfred was."

"So, you are absolutely sure he was in the SS?" I wanted to know for sure.

"Absolutely."

"Then how is it possible that he could get himself arrested and deported to a concentration camp later?"

"Who told you such rubbish?" she asked, surprised.

"It was what he always told us. Ah yes, and he had a tattoo on his left arm, which he had removed after the War, of course. All we ever saw was the scar."

"Where was the scar, between his wrist and his elbow?"

"Yes."

"And that was the only scar on his left arm?"

"Why do you ask? He was in the camp only once, and I don't think they tattooed their inmates more than once."

"Well, did he have another scar or not?" Frau Erdinger was quite persistent.

I had to think for a moment. Then I remembered. "Oh yes. He did have another scar, but that was on the inside of his upper arm. He told us it was from an accident in the swimming baths when he was a young man. He'd slipped on the metal ladder and scratched the inside of his arm as he was trying to grasp one of the railings. So that's got nothing to do with a tattoo or with his time in the concentration camp, I can assure you."

Frau Erdinger sighed. "I am sorry, young woman, but I have to destroy an illusion of yours. The scar on the inside of his left upper arm is proof of his membership of the Waffen-SS. All their officers had their blood type tattooed there. The idea was to ensure quick first aid in case they were injured. They all had it. You can believe me."

I was stunned. When I'd first heard that outrageous accusation in Anna's report of Wolfgang Löffel's verbal attack, I still believed it was probably wrong. But now it was confirmed by this old woman who had known my father personally. And she had seen him in his black SS uniform.

I needed time to reflect on this. So, I steered the conversation away from the SS, the Nazis and the War. When, shortly afterwards, I thanked Frau Erdinger and took my leave, she urged me to come back soon, because she had a lot more to tell me. I promised to call again and climbed down those creaking stairs with a heavy heart. I needed the fresh air outside.

***

Anna had some information that she had got from her father back then. As he'd said he had good connections and could find out things that were not openly accessible.

"And did your father really find out more about my father's career?" I asked on my next visit to the retirement-home in Gera-Lusan.

"Yes," she replied. "It's no use pretending. We knew by then that he'd become an SS officer."

"Indeed," I said, "sad as it is, I have to get used to the fact that I'm the daughter on a proper Nazi." I paused. "But please, do tell me what your father found out. Did Manfred just disappear within the construction and protection of Hitler's empire and the machineries of the War? Or is there any definite information about his career at that time?"

Anna told me how her father had found out that for a certain time Manfred had to work for a man called Bernhard Krüger, whose job it was to forge foreign banknotes, especially pound sterling. He was working in a secret printing factory at the Concentration Camp of Sachsenhausen with a workforce of 142 inmates. Manfred, who by then had reached the rank of Hauptsturmführer, *something equivalent to a captain, was also responsible to channel the newly printed banknotes to the right squadrons of the* Luftwaffe *that were to drop them over British towns at night. The idea was to weaken the British economy by flooding the country with money, which would eventually lead to an inflation that the British economy would no longer be able to cope with. Not all the money was dropped by the* Luftwaffe, *some of it was also channelled to Swiss bank accounts. The idea was to flood the world market with sterling.*

Of course, this job gave him the unique chance to get enormous sums stashed away for himself, albeit in counterfeit money. Nobody knows if he succumbed to the temptation or, if he did, whether he could use any of that money after the War. I asked Anna.

"But wouldn't Krüger have found out? Wasn't he his boss?"

"From what my father found out, Sturmbannführer Krüger was indeed one rank above Hauptsturmführer Weidmann, but it appears the two were as thick as thieves, in the real sense of the phrase. Manfred probably covered Krüger's thefts and Krüger covered Manfred's. Nobody can tell for sure after such a long time."

"And was their counterfeit operation successful? Did they manage to weaken the British economy?" I asked.

"It seems that Operation Bernhard, as it was called, didn't have a heavy impact on the British economy, although they produced some six million pounds in high-quality

counterfeit currency. You tell me how much that would be today."

"From what I know, about six billion pounds. Was that where my father worked for the rest of the War?"

"No, not at all. He was only part of Operation Bernhard for a relatively short period. When, in 1944, the operation was transferred to a different concentration camp in Austria and switched from sterling to American dollars, Manfred was promoted to Sturmbannführer *and assigned to the security service of the Nazi legal system. He had to work with a man called Hans Filbinger, a Nazi judge."*

"What did he do there?"

"I don't know. You'll have to extend your research to Filbinger and his role during the last years of the War in order to find out anymore. All I know is that Manfred disappeared towards the end of the War. Nobody knows what happened to him in the end. It was general knowledge that SS officers who were caught by the Russians were shot on the spot. So, we all assumed that Manfred didn't survive. It would have been extremely difficult for him to escape."

After I had all that information from Anna, we spent a long time chatting about my father, what sort of person he was after the War, what kind of a father he was to me, and also about his declining health these days.

Anna and I parted as good friends. I returned to the hotel to write my diary and to do some research about Filbinger. I remembered the name Hans. Dad had mentioned it several times after his trips to Germany. It must be the same Hans.

TWENTY-ONE

I only saw Renate Erdinger and her mother once more. Even though the old woman had been very friendly and very helpful on my previous visit, I wasn't completely comfortable with her. Renate sensed this.

"I could see how my mother's report shocked you," she admitted when she fetched me from my hotel a few days later.

"It wasn't only her report," I replied.

"Yes, I know," she said. "It was also her pride in being a Nazi, wasn't it?"

I confessed that it was. Renate nodded and told me how she had been trying to change her mother's mind for the past thirty years. She said she used to be ashamed of her parents' stubborn adherence to the Nazis when she was at school. The schoolchildren throughout the first twenty years after the War had to learn to cope with their country's past. They had many lessons dealing with recent history in an extremely critical light. Vergangenheitsbewältigung *was the watchword for many years.*

"We learnt to be watchful of populist politicians, we learnt to abhor any form of racism, we learnt to be heedful about national pride and feelings of superiority. Words like Heimat *or* Volk *were tainted and became practically banned from our vocabulary. We were even discouraged from flying the German flag."*

"And did you all go along with this reassessment of your nation's recent history?" I asked.

"When we learnt how many crimes were committed in the name of xenophobia, nationalism and racial purity, we had to go along. None of us ever wanted such a system back in power. We saw all the films about the concentration camps,

about mass executions and about the rounding up of thousands of Jews, Gypsies, Homosexuals and other Undesirables, and we had guided tours through some of the defunct concentration camps, where we were shown the torturing tools, the gas chambers and the ovens where they used to burn people. We saw photos showing mounds of naked bodies, emaciated prisoners, heaps of clothes, shoes, jewellery, things they had stolen from the poor people they sent to the gas chambers. We saw pictures of some of the so-called medical experiments they used to perform on prisoners, and, last but not least, we saw lists of numbers, huge numbers of deported people." Renate became very heated.

I told her I could understand. While I knew about all those atrocious crimes too, having read about them, I was nevertheless impressed when Renate placed them in front of my eyes again.

"So, you had a serious conflict between what you had to learn at school and what your parents believed?" I asked.

While we were discussing like this, we were walking up the hill, turning right into Niemöllerstrasse. There, at last, stood my grandfather's house. Of course, there were other people in it by now, but still it touched me. We walked on in the direction of the town cemetery.

She took up my question after a long pause. "It was more than just a conflict. It was absolute hell. I couldn't take any friends to my house. The first few who did come were wise enough never to come back. My mother would go at them with Nazi slogans. She would tell them how everything we were learning at school these days was full of lies. She told them what a wonderful leader Adolf Hitler had been and what a crime of the Allies to kill such a great man. I stopped taking friends to my home. But those who had seen my mother told stories about her, and soon the whole school knew that my parents were Nazis."

I was impressed. And I had to think of the type of history teaching I'd had myself in the States and later my children in England. What a contrast! In America, it was full of the victories of the good ones over the bad ones, the good ones always being us, the bad ones being first the English, then the Native Americans – or Red Indians, as they were called at that time – later the Southern States and in the end, the Japanese and the Nazis. We were always on the good side. If any war crimes were committed, it was always by the others. From what I learnt from my children, it was even worse in England. They had to learn the names of the English kings and queens, the greatness of the British Empire and the Commonwealth and, of course, they were inundated with heroic stories about how the English and the Allies saved the world from Hitler and the Nazis. The teaching of modern history at my children's schools consisted mainly of hero worship. And flags as symbols of nationalism? Well, public buildings in America are full of the Stars and Stripes, and the English love to fly their Union Jack on every possible occasion.

Quite recently, in the course of my research into Fascism in preparation for my present search for my father's past, I came across some interesting documents showing how many people in Britain, particularly the aristocracy, hailed Hitler and welcomed the fact that the Nazis – in fact all the Fascists in Europe – set up a stern rule and put the Jews in their place. Such facts are never taught in schools. And which English schoolchild ever learns about the British concentration camps in South Africa, the massacre of Amritsar, the Indian Holocaust – often euphemistically referred to as the Bengal Famine of the 1940s – or the financing of the Hitler dictatorship by the British? Of course, all the war crimes committed by the British appear a lot slighter than those of the Germans in the twentieth century, but my discoveries still made me wonder why they were all swept under the carpet and therefore completely ignored by the history lessons in British schools.

I felt I had to tell Renate something I'd heard when I was in Hamburg as a student. Julia, one of my fellow-students, told me what had happened to her as a girl on a school-trip to England. "When I was at secondary school," Julia had explained, "we went on a school trip to London. It was in 1970. One afternoon, we were all allowed to go for walks in Hyde Park and relax from the sight-seeing programme. My friend Ursula and I were leisurely strolling through the park, chatting, when an elderly woman heard us, ran up to us and banged her handbag in our faces. She yelled at us, calling us monsters and dirty murderers. We were so shocked and just stared at her with open mouths. She cried that we had killed her father and her husband in the war. We realized there was nothing we could say to contradict her, because, in a way, she was right. Well, it hadn't been us personally, but our country. That was an awful experience, I can tell you." When I told Renate now, I expected her to be as shocked as I was when I heard the story.

But she answered, "Yes, I've heard of similar experiences among the West Germans on holiday. Here in the GDR, we couldn't travel to England or other western countries. But for West Germans, it seemed to be quite common to be verbally attacked in shops in Holland or Belgium, or they were not served in restaurants when they spoke German."

I had to admit that such experiences were alien to people like myself. We have always been the good ones. So, it is quite a different matter in my generation whether you grew up as an English or a German child in the first decades after the War. In Britain – and in the States, for that matter – you grew up in full consciousness of the noble past of your country and with a perfect understanding that your fathers and grandfathers had all been great heroes. After all, there were, and still are, numerous ceremonies and memorials to remind you of that wonderfully comforting fact. Even to this day, every British town celebrates Remembrance Day in November. In Germany, on the other hand, you grew up with the full knowledge that your fathers and grandfathers had been either murderers or cowards. Murderers if they were Nazis – like my father – or cowards if they couldn't prevent the Nazis from committing all those crimes. For us, it was very comfortable to sit on our moral high horse.

While I was following my own train of thoughts and occasionally exchanging a few words with Renate, we were walking along the hill-slope, through quarters that were obviously built after the War, until we reached the cemetery.

I found the grave of my grandparents. It was overgrown with lichen and looked untended. I decided to buy some flowers and come back another day. There was no grave of my Uncle Thomas. I asked Renate if she or her mother knew anything about my father's brother. But they obviously didn't know anything. It was generally understood that he'd died in the war. He had joined the Navy, so it's possible he went down with one of their warships.

"Would you like to see my mother again?" she asked.

"Only if you think she can tell me anything I don't know yet. You know, since I talked to her the last time I have accepted the fact that my father wasn't just a Nazi but an active member of the Schutz-Staffel. *Do you think she might have any more shocking news for me?"*

"I don't know. But I think she would like to see you again."

"I'll see her once more, then."

So, I went to see Frau Erdinger in her clean apartment a second time. She received me with a friendly smile.

After the usual small-talk we came to talk about the old times again. I asked her how she got all that information about my family. She said her husband used to have good connections, as she had pointed out before, but this time, she added that he had been good friends with a man called Löffel. Wolfgang Löffel, a man of many talents, as she said.

When I heard that name I was all ears.

Apparently, that Wolfgang fellow had spread a lot of bad news about the entire Weidmann family. Nobody really knew what role he played in the War, but Frau Erdinger was told he was involved in some pretty important work for the Gestapo. Her husband found out that Löffel was one of the Gestapo's thugs for the dirty jobs. He wasn't the intellectual type who would cross-examine important dissidents before they were sent to prison or executed, he was more the hands-on fellow, he had to go to people's homes and teach them lessons with his truncheon or his gun. It was rumoured that he blackmailed lots of people, even some Nazis themselves. But because Gerhard Erdinger and Wolfgang Löffel had always been such good buddies, they could protect each other.

"And did you learn anything about my father's further career?" I asked.

"Not much. His name was only mentioned once more after the War. It was a few months after the Russians had taken over Thuringia from the Americans. One day, Gerhard told me he had found out how Manfred had escaped to the American Zone. After the end of the war, my husband considered it his duty to fight all forms of Wehrkraftzersetzung, so he bribed lots of farmers near the Zonengrenze, *the area near the border to the West that had to be crossed by cowards who tried to escape. Of course, most of them were caught by the Russians, but some obviously made it. Gerhard told me he knew about Manfred's escape and he knew his new name."*

We were silent for a few moments before I asked my next question.

"And do you happen to know what Herr Löffel did with his dangerous information?"

"Well, I don't know exactly. But my Gerhard told him he should use his knowledge to make money. You know, we were all so extremely destitute after the Zusammenbruch *of the Reich."*

"You mean blackmail the people who made it to the West?"

"I don't know. I only know that Wolfgang was never a poor man. While we all had to struggle to make both ends meet in the newly established German Democratic Republic, he always had enough money. He was one of the first friends of Gerhard's to own a motorcar. Have you got any idea how difficult it was to get a car in those days?"

"Well, how did he manage that? What do you think?"

"I believe he did a complete turn-around. From being a Nazi, he switched over to being a Communist. His broad experience in dirty work for the Gestapo must have given him an entry ticket to the Stasi in the new system. Gerhard considered him a traitor. But they remained good friends. You see, we tried to keep a low profile, and I believe Gerhard could be quite useful for Wolfgang on several occasions."

I decided to change the subject.

"Do you know anything about Manfred's girlfriend at the beginning of the War?"

"You mean the Kleinschmidt whore?"

I gulped. "Yes, if that's what you called her."

"I don't know what became of her. She and her family should have been dealt with by the Gestapo. They were traitors, British spies. At least that was what Wolfgang told us. He told us how she would jump into bed with any man who paid her. Now that you mention her, I think I remember there

was some talk about an illegitimate brat, and Gerhard said it was Wolfgang's. It seems the Kleinschmidts were trying to blackmail the Weidmanns, believing the baby to be Manfred's. But of course, it was Wolfgang's."

"How can you be so sure about that?" I asked.

"It was obvious. It was Wolfgang who fancied her after Manfred had left. And he told my husband how she had seduced him, the slut."

I really had to swallow hard and keep my impulses back.

"Do you know what happened to the baby, the little boy?"

"No. And I don't care. Never thought much about that lot."

I thanked old Frau Erdinger for what she had told me and wanted to leave, but she kept me back, wanting to know what I could tell her about my father.

"I've given you all the information, now it's your turn to tell me how your father got on after his escape. Wolfgang told us he'd escaped to Switzerland. That was the last I knew."

"I don't know anything about his life until we lived in Chicago, in America," I lied. "From there, we moved to England, where we still live now."

"Was your father involved in anymore political work?"

"Not that I know of. He worked for an American company. His interest lay more in spreadsheets and trade agreements, in profits and losses."

"Ah, a true Capitalist, then."

"If you like. Yes."

I threw her a few more raw bones, but I avoided to tell her too much about Dad. I wanted to protect his reputation in the eyes of that awful old Nazi. It was really pointless, but I followed my instinct.

Soon, I managed to get away. Renate walked down the stairs with me and bade me good-bye at the front door. I walked away, along the grey street, with a heavy heart.

***

I am back at the hotel. It's raining. This gives me an opportunity to stay in my room and catch up with my diary. I haven't written down the latest findings yet. This has been partly because of my emotions. Some of the things that Frau Erdinger told me shocked me, whereas my heart felt very joyful when I talked to Anna Kleinschmidt. I find it strange, but it is a fact that I can't ignore: I have grown to love the old woman. I feel as if Anna was my own mother. Or is this bad? My own mother died only six years ago. I'm not very good at psychology, but I wonder if it's possible that I might have adopted Anna as my surrogate mother, as it were.

When I saw her yesterday, she told me more about her son Manfred. He grew up in Anna's family with her parents and a young cousin, Henrietta, who came to live with them as an orphan in '42, when her own family was killed. They had lived in an apartment block in which the SS found a Jewish family hidden away in the attic. The SS killed everyone in the apartment block. They just broke down the doors, entered every apartment and shot everybody dead. Henrietta managed to hide in the bottom of an old wardrobe under a heap of old linen. She escaped from the building at night and walked to the Kleinschmidt apartment, which was about two miles away. Anna's family took her in. It was quite difficult to explain the little girl's presence to the authorities. They declared her as a refugee. Had they registered her as who she really was, she would probably have been shot.

Henrietta was very good with little Manfred. When she came she was ten, while Manfred had just turned two.

Through the remaining war years, the girl was a great help. While Anna went to work – she had found a job, sewing insignia and rank badges on tunics in a uniform factory – Henrietta would look after the boy.

"What became of her?" I asked Anna.

"She lived with us until 1952. Then she fell in love with a returned soldier. They got married and moved to Leipzig. But we kept in touch. She still lives in Leipzig, a widow."

"And what became of Manfred?"

"He was a happy child and a lucky boy. He started his apprenticeship as an electrician in 1956 and completed it successfully. Then, in 1960, when he was working for VEB Elektroinstallationen, he fell in love with a girl from Berlin. He often travelled to Berlin for the weekend, and I thought he would move in with her. She was a lovely girl. Her name was Angelika. He often brought her to see me."

"Well, did they get together?"

Anna hesitated before she answered. "They had great plans together. They only argued about where they were going to settle down. Manfred liked it here. Gera was his town. But Angelika was a girl of the big city. She wanted to remain there. So, things went on like this for months, she visited him here and he visited her there. Until the 13th of August 1961."

"Oh, the building of the Berlin Wall. What happened then?"

"Angelika was visiting her aunt in West Berlin when the wall was built. She was staying in the West for a few days. Nobody believed they would make the border so watertight as they did. When she was trying to get back two days later, she was shocked to see the wall and the border guards in reality, not only in the paper or on TV. She was too frightened to cross back into East Berlin, hoping she might get an opportunity later but really only putting it off. The machine

guns of the Grenzpolizei *frightened her so much. She wrote a letter to Manfred, explaining it all."*

"And what did he do?"

"He went very quiet. He stopped telling me everything. He became more outspoken against our political system. Eventually, the Stasi got wind of his critical attitude. One day two Stasi thugs fetched me in handcuffs and took me to their interrogation rooms. They wanted to know what I knew about my son's seditious activities. After two days they let me go, but I was intimidated enough to be careful from then on. When Manfred heard of the questioning I had undergone, he went berserk. He said he was going underground, he might even leave the country."

"Did he become a rebel?"

"You can say that, in a way. I don't know what he was doing or where he was hiding for several months, until late in 1962, when the Stasi arrested me. They kept me in a dark room for about three or four days, feeding me on dirty water and mouldy bread. There was no bunk or chair. I had to sit or lie on the floor, which was cold and wet. Then they led me into a brightly lit room where a strong lamp was aimed straight at my face. I went blind for a while. I was tied to a chair, my hands tied at my back. My clothes were dirty from the dirty room in which they had kept me in the dark. When the Stasi interrogator left the room, the two guards stepped up to me and started to tear the front of my clothes. They said their boss had given them permission to do with me what they liked. They boasted to each other what they were going to do to me, how they were going to rape me and what injuries they would like to inflict on me. But then the Stasi man entered again, and they stepped back to the wall. He told them off, but it was only play-acting, I could tell. The men's actions and threats were meant to intimidate me. As if I still needed intimidating!"

"How awful!" I had to breathe.

"Yes, it was an ordeal. The Stasi interrogated me about Manfred, what I knew about his activities, in what way I was involved in his crimes against our great republic and so on. I couldn't tell them anything. They kept me for about three weeks, torturing me from time to time, then being extremely friendly and mock-conspiratorial, but always trying to get information out of me. Then, suddenly, I was let out. They must have given up. However, I had to sign a document stating that I was bound to absolute secrecy. I was forbidden to talk to anyone about what I had experienced during my time at the Stasi headquarters. If I violated that secrecy, I would be convicted as a Staatsfeind, *an enemy of the state, and sent to prison in Bautzen."*

"What happened to Manfred?"

"He tried to cross the border, probably hoping to make it to his Angelika, but they caught him between barbed-wire fences somewhere near Creuzburg, just north of Eisenach. They shot him in his legs and arrested him. He was convicted for attempted Republikflucht, *which was a very serious crime, and sent to Bautzen for a long sentence. In the first years, he could sometimes write a letter. All our mail was checked by the Stasi, of course."*

"How long did he spend at Bautzen?"

"He stopped writing to me in the late seventies. I didn't know how he was getting on for many years. It was only after the collapse of the system, in 1989, that one of my neighbours, who had been an IM *– that was the abbreviation given to those nearly 200,000 spies of the Stasi – and who regretted it afterwards, wanted to clear his bad conscience by telling me what he knew about my boy."*

"What was it? Did he get out?"

"Yes. He was released after 25 years, which was in 1987. Because the Stasi considered him a dangerous element, they deported him out of the country."

"So, he is in the West now?"

"I don't know. I never heard from him again. Henrietta said she could find out, but I haven't had the courage yet."

We were silent for a while. Then I took her in my arms. I held her tight, and I could feel her heartbeat. Slowly, she began to weep. She wept in silence for several minutes, and I felt very close to her. In a way, it was good, just holding the dear woman tight with my arms around her shaking body.

When we let go and sat back, she swept the tears from her eyes with her handkerchief and was going to apologize, but I told her there was no need. I said I felt honoured and privileged to have her confidence. She gave me another hug.

Now, back at my hotel, I feel I have to do something for Anna, the woman who could almost be my mother. But how realistic is that? One thing that must be my next step is to find out more about Manfred, find out his whereabouts, not only for Anna but also for my own peace of mind. After all, he is probably my half-brother. I would love that.

So, what can I do next? I think I will travel to Leipzig and find Henrietta. I'm sure Anna will give me her address. As far as I remember, she indicated that her cousin might know more.

Thus, to Leipzig.

TWENTY-TWO

I dropped my bags in my room at the Ibis Hotel in Leipzig. I was impressed by this city. Everything was in a process of change and transition. Especially along the ring road lots of houses were being either pulled down or being refurbished. Across from my newly built hotel there was a hand-painted poster saying, "Leipzig retten – alte Bausubstanz erhalten!" *So the people of the city were obviously divided between those who wanted to preserve the historic buildings, dilapidated as they may be, and those who were all for rebuilding.*

After a quick snack at the reception area of the hotel, I grabbed a free town map from the reception desk and looked for Yuri-Gagarin-Strasse. It was not very far; I decided to walk.

When I rang the bell, there was no answer. So I went back to my hotel. I realized I should have called first.

I spent the time reading through my report, trying to phone Henrietta Scholz from time to time.

At last, about five o'clock in the afternoon, she answered the telephone. I introduced myself and explained how I came to contact her. Henrietta was very polite. When I mentioned Anna, she cried with joy.

"Oh, how is dear Anna? I hope she's all right."

"She is very well, thank you," I replied.

It took a lot of explaining. At last, Henrietta declared herself glad to be of assistance in my search. We arranged to meet the next morning at her flat.

When I arrived there, she immediately opened the door and greeted me with a beaming smile. If I noted earlier on how beautiful Anna was, I now had to admit that her younger cousin was just as fine a woman. In a way, she looked very much alike, only a little younger and with dark hair. She must be in her early sixties, but there wasn't a single grey hair on her head, and it was her natural colour. A very striking woman indeed!

"So, you are the daughter of dear Anna's first love?" she asked when we were sitting over our cups of tea in her nicely presented living-room.

"Yes, I am. And I understand you can tell me more about my father's fate in the War and afterwards."

"Well, I only met him once after the War. But tell me, what is it you're trying to find out?"

I told her I had reason to believe that my father had been a member of the SS and had possibly committed some awful crimes, which was hard to accept for me as his daughter. But if she could confirm that there was no alternative, I would just have to live with it. If, on the other hand, she could tell me that my information was wrong, I would be more than happy.

Henrietta sighed. "I'm sorry, young woman. May I call you Nora? What you've heard is true. Manfred – your father, that is – was an active member of the Waffen-SS. *Those were the hard-boiled Nazis with the black uniforms and the emblem with the dead skull on their peaked caps."*

"I see."

"Anna and I are as sad as you are, you can believe me. Poor Anna has suffered a great deal. She loved him so much. And you probably know she bore him a child and called him Manfred, too."

"Did you tell my father when you met him so much later after the War?"

"No, I couldn't. Besides, all he was concerned about was his new identity. He even tried to lie to me. He insisted he'd always been called Dieter Wolff. I think he'd lost his mind, if

you ask me. Nothing of what he was trying to make me believe made any sense. So sad!"

I had to digest this before I could ask my next question.

"What do you know of his son, Manfred the younger? Anna told me his story up to 1987 when he was released from Bautzen and deported out of the country."

"I don't know everything, Nora. But quite by accident I met him again after the reunification. I didn't tell Anna that I'd actually met him. It would have been too much for her. But I told her I'd heard from him."

"And how did that happen?" I wanted to know.

"As I was saying, it was such a coincidence. I believe it was in '92. I was shopping in town when, all of a sudden, I bumped into him in front of a shop. It only took me a split second to recognize him, and he also recognized me at once. We just stood there for what seemed like an eternity, looking at each other and trying to believe what we were seeing. I said 'Manfred' and he said 'Henrietta'. And when we had recovered from our shock we went to have a cup of coffee together."

"Had he changed much?"

"Of course, he was quite a bit older than the last time I had seen him, but he was his old self." She looked at me. "Actually, if I'm honest, I have to admit you look a bit like him."

Then she told me what she had learnt from Manfred. He had spent a few years travelling after his release from the GDR before settling in a small town somewhere in Norway. He had now been contemplating to move back to Germany and wanted to test himself with the idea of returning to one of the Eastern Länder *to live there. But as he explained, he found it too depressing. There were too many bad memories for him. He'd been to Gera and other places he used to know well, and he'd even driven to Bautzen, but he couldn't find it in himself to forgive those who had made his life so miserable. He told her he was just going to see a few more places in Germany before his emigration to Canada. He had a friend who was about to buy an electric company in Vancouver and who was eager to take him on as an electrician and possibly as a partner later on.*

I asked her if young Manfred knew about me and my sister. After all, he might be our half-brother. She said yes, she had told him.

"How did he react?"

"He was overjoyed and wanted to know where he could find you. But I couldn't tell him. I knew that your father wanted to keep the two versions of his life apart. I don't know if I was right. Perhaps I should have told him."

After this, we drifted off to other subjects. At the end of my two-hour visit, she invited me to have dinner with her and her husband on the following evening. I was happy to accept.

When I found myself at her door again the next day, better dressed and with a bunch of flowers in my hand, I wondered what Henrietta's husband would be like. We hadn't talked about him, which I now realized was a social blunder. We had discussed such a lot about my family, my father, my life in England and about trivial things, and it had never entered my head to ask her about her life, her family, her husband. I decided to catch up and do better now.

Friedrich Scholz was a very large man with a broad and winning smile. His voice was loud, and his friendly statements didn't allow any contradiction. He was a head taller than his wife, who looked up to him with fondness. Even though it took me a while to get accustomed to his overbearing but extremely heart-warming manner, I was very glad to note that this was a very happy couple.

"Call me Fritz," he boomed, as he was shaking my hand with a firm grip.

"I'm pleased to meet you, I'm Nora," I replied and found my own voice sounded like the peeping of a small mouse in comparison to his.

After the couple had stood there, facing me together and displaying their happiness, he took my arm and led me to the living-room.

We had a very pleasant chat over a glass of white wine, which wasn't so pleasant. They were very proud of the wine and explained that it came from the vineyard in the northernmost location in Europe, yes, even in the world, they said. It was called Saale-Unstrut and tasted like stale dishwater, but I was polite enough not to let them know. They were both so happy to have me as their guest.

"You know," Fritz said, "my darling Henry – I just call her Henry, she likes that – she's told me about you. You must know she has the fondest memories of your brother Manfred. They more or less grew up together. But there it is, the poor chap had to do time at Bautzen, what a shame, but he's been out for quite some time now. Yes, life can be very unfair, but there it is."

He rambled on while Henrietta slipped out to the kitchen to get the meal ready. I tried to listen to everything he was saying, but it turned out quite a challenge. He jumped from subject to subject – from the difference between the Wessies and the Ossies to the rise of unemployment, from the warm weather to the exchange rate with the US dollar – and he punctuated his speech with an occasional "there it is."

During the meal, we touched mostly general topics. My hosts wanted to know about my travel experience. They asked me what countries I had visited and what I had learnt about humanity in each country. They were particularly interested in Spain because they were saving up for a trip to that country. I could only give them very limited information. I had visited Spain about half a dozen times, but my destinations *had usually been the culturally fascinating cities. I could tell them about Zaragoza, Salamanca, Toledo, Sevilla and other old cities full of cultural treasures, but such things didn't interest them. What they were after were the beaches and the nightclubs of Mallorca and Ibiza, possibly also Torremolinos. "We want to meet the real people of Spain," Fritz explained. I tried to tell them that the places they mentioned would allow them to experience other German and English tourists, but mostly of the less pleasant sort. However, Fritz was so convinced that those would be the right places to visit, it was no use arguing. I realized that I would appear arrogant if I insisted on conveying my views to them.*

So, I concentrated on the lovely food we were enjoying together and gently steered the conversation to less controversial topics. One such topic was the superiority of the Capitalist system over the Communist experience in the GDR. Another common topic was German Vergangenheitsbewältigung. *Henrietta drew my attention to a new book published by Niklas Frank. He was the son of one of the worst Nazi leaders, Hans Frank, the so-called slaughterer of Poland, who was hanged in Nuremberg in 1946. Niklas, a good journalist, is very active today. He has published a number of books and articles on the poorly managed process of De-Nazification after the War. Henrietta considers him a modern hero. He has shown us how many old Nazis got away with very few scratches to their social prestige, and many of them just slipped into posts of responsibility in the 1950s.*

"I tell you," Fritz confirmed his wife's report, "even now as we speak there are still many old Nazis who manage to live comfortably and who are respected by the communities in which they live. Most of them were never found out and only few of them had to appear in front of a Spruchkammer *after the War. But there it is."*

I didn't know how to feel about such comments. If I was honest, I had to admit that my own father was one of them, an old Nazi who got off unscathed. My best strategy was to steer the conversation to more general perspectives. In the end, we agreed that the ideas of the Nazis could probably never be completely eradicated in Europe.

As I was walking back to my hotel, I thought about everything that had been said during the evening.

***

I am an open-minded person, and I believe I am a critical observer of what's going on in the world today. I am neither a clever philosopher nor a sharp politician. But I can clearly identify some of the dangers in today's world. I'm not merely thinking of environmental problems now, but of social conflicts. With the new catchphrase of Globalisation, we are certainly deceiving ourselves. From what I have seen of this process so far is that it makes the rich even richer and the poor even poorer. Multinational businesses are internationalizing their profits, while the financial and social burdens are being debited to the national governments. The nations face increasing problems because they haven't got enough money to fulfil their tasks, while the big international companies don't pay taxes which would be needed for those national duties.

What are the dangers for our future? I am afraid the system is increasingly drying out the middle classes in most Western countries. Only very few are getting very rich, while more and more middle-class families are falling into poverty. If we lose our middle classes, we'll lose the most important pillars of our societies, the sections of society that defend law and order, the people who pay taxes and who are interested in social peace.

Will such a development favour the rise of new Nazi systems? Is there a danger of a growing unease about the existing democratic systems, an unease which will allow new populists to rise and to lead the weak-minded and disappointed masses into new versions of Hitler's dictatorship? Once a critical mass of the losing part of the people find out that they have been cheated all along, they will be an easy prey for a populist politician who will promise them to solve all their problems. The strategy for such a rat-catcher will simply be to create enough fear and anxiety in order to announce to the gullible people that he will have the solution and save them all from the existing – democratically elected – politicians if only they will elect him. Once that happens we will be back to square one, meaning a situation like the one in 1933. Is it possible that we may already have reached a stage that can be compared to the situation like 1914, before the First World War, when rampant nationalism led people to believe that the cause of their problems lay in another country and the only solution was to go to war against their neighbours in Europe? I will be watchful over the emerging developments in the next few years.

***

I travelled back to Gera, hoping to pick up a few more traces of my father's family. For example, I was hoping that Anna might have more information. Also, I wondered whether I would be able to find the whereabouts of that awful fellow Wolfgang Löffel. If I could find him, I would silence him once and for all. I would make it clear to him that blackmail was a serious crime, and I would have the law on him if he ever tried to contact my father again.

At the Hotel am Galgenberg, a message was waiting for me. It was from Anna. "Dear Nora, I would so much like to see you once more before you return to England."

It was clear to me that Anna was the only source of information that was left to me. I didn't trust Renate Erdinger or her mother to be of any further help, and really there wasn't anyone else I could ask about members of my family or about the Löffel fellow.

Just to make sure to exploit every possible angle, I paid a visit to the Thuringian archives in Erfurt. They had a list of all the War casualties. It was far from complete in its section on the civilian population, but it gave a complete account of all the members of the Wehrmacht *that had either died or gone missing during the War. When I saw this list, I had to remember the numerous war memorials that we can find in every British town or village, and it made me wonder. What can be the significance of such lists or memorials? Are they meant to invest the dead with a particular sense? And if that was their purpose, the question remains if they really succeed in their purpose.*

The list of the missing soldiers contained my Uncle Thomas's name. He had gone missing on board the Prinz Eugen, *which was a* Schwerer Kreuzer, *off the coast of Norway on 23rd February 1942. The vessel had been hit by a torpedo fired by the British submarine* Trident. *So the British had killed my uncle.*

The list didn't mention my father's name. I spent another hour scanning the list, but I couldn't find any names that rang a bell in my mind. This wasn't surprising, since I didn't know any of my father's friends' names. I didn't even know any names apart from Anna Kleinschmidt and Wolfgang Löffel. Not very much, I had to admit to myself.

When I saw Anna again, it was at a pleasant restaurant in the town centre. I had decided to treat her to a nice meal out.

"Are you satisfied with your findings?" she asked.

"It's very difficult to know for myself. What would 'satisfied' mean in this context, I wonder? It would probably mean that I've found out that my father was a victim of the Nazis, but instead I've found out that he was a really bad accomplice, a horrible criminal himself. I will need a lot of thinking to come to a conclusion as to how to cope with such knowledge."

"Don't be too hard on him, please."

"How can you say such a thing? You who have been treated most abominably by him?"

"He was the love of my life, and he is the father of my child. How could I condemn him?"

"But you always knew about his Nazi career from early on. And yet you never hated him?"

"I was brought up a Christian, and as such I learnt to forgive. Yes, I was bitterly disappointed when he stopped writing back from Pirna, and I was almost equally disappointed when I heard about his career in the Waffen-SS. *But as a Christian, I couldn't find it in me to hate him. Do you know that even the worst Nazis were accompanied by a priest when they were taken to the gallows in Nuremberg? People like Keitel, von Ribbentrop, Frank or Streicher. I can't remember all their names. But they were all informed about Heavenly Grace by the priests who escorted them to the gallows."*

"And you believe they deserved that?" I wondered at Anna's understanding of Christian forgiveness. This was something I just couldn't believe in.

"It is not for me to judge that."

I was going to ask her if she believed that there shouldn't be any judges, any courts of justice. But I checked myself. The woman's generous conviction impressed me so much that I decided to keep my thoughts to myself. Instead, I came to the conclusion that I should really admire her and be grateful to her. Admire her for her strong character and be grateful for her love, the love she felt so strongly for my father, despite all the adversities.

It was then that I realized I had myself learnt to love her. It was true. I felt a very powerful love for this wonderful woman.

I stood up, walked round the table and gave her a long hug. She responded very gently.

Back at my place, I looked at her beautiful face, onto her clear eyes, and I understood her tears.

After a long silence, we took up our knives and forks and resumed our meal. As I was taking a forkful of potatoes to my mouth, I realized that our minds had been so completely absorbed by the topic we'd been discussing that we hadn't even tasted our food. That is, we had started to ladle small amounts of food into our mouths before, but we had not actually tasted any of it. It had been a mere mechanical action, and only now, after the recent emotional climax in our intercourse did we begin to taste our food. It tasted like something I never tasted before.

Eventually, I managed to open our conversation again by asking her about Wolfgang Löffel. I asked her if he was still alive and if he still lived in Gera.

"He lives in Gera all right. He is still a constant threat for me, to tell you the truth, although I haven't seen him for over three years. But I know he's there." Anna's whole body shook with disgust.

"I'm sorry. Perhaps I shouldn't have brought him up. But I think I have to know more about him before my mission

is complete. He has made life for everybody – I mean for you and for my father – so difficult that I have to be sure he can no longer torture either of you."

"I don't want to talk about him, please. You can find him and form your own opinion of him. But please, do leave me out of this."

"All right. I'm sorry. Again, I am deeply sorry. I only thought you might know where I could find him."

"I'm afraid I can't. Why don't you go to Einwohnermeldeamt*, the residents' registry office?"*

"Oh, that's a very good idea. I haven't been aware of the existence of such an office. But of course, that's where I'll go to find him. Thank you for giving me this idea."

After this, we drifted off to some more pleasant topics. Anna wanted to know more about my music taste. I explained to her that I have a very broad taste, but I don't really know much, neither about classical music nor about modern music, jazz or pop. I told her about my boy's keen interest in classical music. I told her how proud I am of Andrew's piano-playing. This pleased her very much. She told me how fond of classical music she was, particularly of Bach and Beethoven. I let her teach me many interesting facts about her music.

When we parted, we embraced again. I gave her my best wishes and thanked her for her openness and her confidence in me.

Walking back to my hotel, I thought of how different my life would have been if Anna had been my mother. But I immediately dismissed the fantasy and returned to the world of facts and of reality.

***

Anna's advice was perfect. The people at Einwohnermeldeamt *were very helpful and found Wolfgang*

Löffel's address for me. He lives in a small house in Zwötzen, a southern suburb of Gera.

The house looked in a very poor state. It still had the worn grey plaster façade of the GDR times, and the front wall was streaked with bad cracks. The tiny front garden was unkempt, really neglected in every way. In one of the corners of the garden there stood a faded sunshade in bad repair. Behind the window to the left of the front door, I could detect a yellowed curtain which wasn't hanging straight. The outside lamp above the front door was cracked and the bulb was missing.

I rang the bell. No answer. I rang a second time. Still no answer. I waited.

As I was preparing to walk away, I saw a face peeping over the wall on one side of the garden. I stopped in my movement. The face disappeared and a few seconds later popped up again. It belonged to a middle-aged man with a peaked cap on his head, greying stubble on his cheeks and glasses with round lenses pulled low on his broad nose, the type that used to be called John-Lennon-glasses when I was a teenager in England.

"Keine Sau da," *he grumbled.*

"Verzeihung," *I replied. "What were you saying?"*

He seemed to understand that my German, though quite good and very fluent, wasn't up to every vulgar saying. He smiled and repeated in proper language that there was nobody in.

"Is Herr Löffel away? Will he be back soon?" I enquired. I thought if he as a neighbour knows when the man is out, he might also know when he could be back.

"Der Scheisskerl macht ja, was er will!" *was his comment. "The son of a bitch does what he likes anyway!"*

"You don't seem to like your neighbour very much," I said.

"Of course not. Everybody knows what a crook he is. Are you a friend of his? Or are you family? For if you are, you may as well pay me back the five hundred deutschmarks he owes me."

I saw the importance of keeping my distance. "No, I'm neither. I just want to find him, but I'm not a friend of his. On the contrary."

"Then you're on our side. Come over, let's have a chat about that crook."

I hesitated, but then decided to walk over to the neighbour's garden, which was a lot better kept. We introduced each other. His name was Karl Brettschneider.

After our introductions, he bent down to where he had his garden tools and produced a bottle with two small glasses.

"Have a sip of Korn," he said and poured me a glass.

We both downed our Korn in one gulp, as they do in Germany, and sat down on one of his clean garden benches. The alcohol loosened our tongues, and we had quite a long and pleasant chat about his unfriendly neighbour Wolfgang Löffel. I learnt that the fellow was obviously considered quite a criminal, no-one trusted him, he was unmarried and lived alone. But he was hardly ever at home. He seemed to be involved in strange projects all the time, always promising his neighbours to pay them back once his projects were successful. But they never were. At the same time, he kept bragging about his hidden wealth. He said he had a lot of money stashed away, but he couldn't get at it. Nobody believed him, his life-style was so poor. He always wore the same old baggy trousers, the same old army-shirt and the same old dark grey jacket with holes in its elbows. He told everyone he was very educated and spoke several languages, but again nobody believed him. Sometimes he was away for three or four weeks at a time, and he always came back in high spirits, boasting of more riches that were coming his way.

Obviously, Wolfgang Löffel was disliked all around, he owed money to everyone, and he had cheated everyone. This general image suited what I had already found out about him from various sources, my Dad, Anna, Henrietta and others.

Herr Brettschneider – I didn't follow his advice to call him Kalle – wanted me to stay for lunch, promising his wife would be happy to have me, but I politely declined. The man was getting a bit too familiar with me. Also, I didn't like the way he looked at me with his blood-shot eyes. Again and again, his eyes travelled down my front, inspecting my figure, or so it seemed to me. I was uncomfortable. So, I kept my distance, thanked him for the Korn and especially for his useful information, and took my leave.

As I was driving back into Gera, I realised I should have taken the tram because I felt the alcohol of the Korn hammering in my brain, and I wasn't sure if I'd pass a police check with a breathalyser in my present condition. Al least the strong schnapps had loosened Karl Brettschneider's tongue, and he could give me a good impression of his unpleasant neighbour.

Back in my hotel-room I lay down on the bed and took stock. I concluded I didn't really need to see the Löffel fellow. Nothing new could be gained from an interview with him.

***

Two days later. I am on my way back to England. I'm looking forward to being with George again. I don't know what to do with my diary.

PART FIVE

TWENTY-THREE

Andrew felt exhausted after reading his mother's diary. It was not only a physical exhaustion, but also a mental and emotional one. What a story!

He had asked Rebecca to leave him alone while he was reading his mother's diary; he needed to concentrate on what he was reading, and the presence of another person would have bothered him too much.

Now, as he was slowly recovering, he gradually began to realize that what he had read wasn't just a story, it was reality. It's possible that Mum may have got a few details wrong, but not very probable. The main facts of her report must be true.

Now the big question: What to do with the knowledge of this truth? Throughout his life since his puberty he had always assumed his grandfather to be a victim. Now the old man had been found out as a perpetrator, a Nazi criminal.

Andrew tried to come to a decision about an adequate reaction to this shock. But he was too dumbfounded to keep his senses together and decide what he should do.

He left the apartment and went to the Dolphin. Once there, his most important question was how to get drunk. What was the right drink now? He asked for a white wine, and when Sandy behind the bar asked him what white wine, he just croaked, "Any old plonk will do, I just need the booze."

Sandy tut-tutted but gave him a glass of Chardonnay because she remembered that he often had that. He refused the glass and asked for the bottle, which Sandy first hesitated over but eventually served him.

When David entered the pub about an hour later, he saw that his friend was already in a state of considerable inebriation – he often thought of this beautiful expression for a state which was anything but pleasant.

"Come on, old chap," he said, trying to pull him away from the bar. "I think you've had just about enough."

Andrew made a feeble attempt to protest, but David managed to get him out of the pub, supported him along the pavement to his doorstep, helped him find his key in his pocket and then helped him to his flat. He got him out of his clothes and put him to bed. Then he wrote a note for Rebecca, which he left so she would see it when she came home. In it, he begged her to be gentle with Andrew. He wrote: "He's had such a terrible experience reading his mother's diary." David had expected something like this. He didn't know why.

When Rebecca came home, she saw the note and decided to sleep on the settee in their living-room. The next morning, she met Andrew in the bathroom. She could tell he had a bad headache. He didn't say very much. Later, after some medicine and two cups of coffee, he slowly got back to his old self.

"You must've had a very interesting evening," she teased.

"Oh, my dear! I'm sorry, but I needed to get drunk. It was my first reaction. Now I have to cope with what I've learnt about my family's past."

"Why do you have to cope? Can't you let sleeping dogs lie? What does our family's history matter? What has it got to do with us?"

"I know, it's hard to understand for you. But your family are all good people. You haven't got a Nazi criminal among your ancestors."

"A Nazi criminal? Your Granddad? Are you sure?"

"Absolutely."

"But even then... I mean, there may have been murderers, rapists and arsonists among my own ancestors, only not just recently. Back in the eighteenth century or so, what do we know?"

Andrew reflected for a few moments. "The crimes of the Nazis are too recent. It's too early to forget them. Besides, many of their inhuman ideas are still around. Look at all those populist right-wing politicians that you can find in many European countries. Their ideas are extremely dangerous. It's only to be hoped that they'll never get to power. So we have to know these dangers in order to prevent such developments."

"Isn't that a bit far-fetched?"

He decided to leave the subject. Rebecca wasn't interested enough, and her political sensitivity didn't amount to very much. He took another sip of coffee and only remarked, "I'll have to discuss it with Dave first."

But she wasn't prepared to let him off. "Can't we just forget the whole thing? Look, we are so happy. We live in great times. Our nation isn't at war, we are gradually moving towards something like world peace. We are all growing happier and richer every day. If we play our cards right, we might be able to buy our first house soon."

He did not respond to this. Any adequate answer would be either too complicated or too detrimental to their relationship.

"I think I'll ask Dave to spend a men's weekend with me, just the two of us. If you like, you can arrange something with Marie-Claire or with any of your other friends."

"If that's what you want. Where will you go?"

"We shall see."

***

It was two weeks later when the two friends managed to get away for the weekend. They took David's car, a relatively new Ford Mondeo, and drove to Weymouth. David knew a nice hotel there. It offered a pleasant view of the bay. When they were checking in, the receptionist, who was Irish and seemed to be the owner, explained to them that the bay in front of his hotel was going to host several water-sport events in the upcoming Olympic Games.

After settling in, they walked along the seafront and began to talk. During the trip they had discussed all sorts of things but avoided the all-important topic, saving it for now.

"So, what about the worst part of your findings? Or should I say your mother's findings?" David introduced the sensitive topic.

At first, Andrew had difficulties finding the right words, but then decided to dispense with all embellishments. His best friend deserved to get the unmitigated facts.

"My own grandfather was a Nazi criminal," he began. And during the following forty-five minutes, he managed to tell his friend the whole story of Manfred Weidmann, SS-Hauptsturmführer Weidmann, the man's escape to Frankfurt under the name of Dieter Wolff, his move to Switzerland and eventually his emigration to the States under the name of Didi Woolf. He also mentioned his grandfather's love affair with Anna Kleinschmidt before the War.

"There's even a half-uncle living somewhere in Canada, I understand," he added, before he concluded his report.

"Tell me," David asked, "which aspect of the whole story hurts you most? Which part really gets under your skin?"

"I think it's the injustice, most of all. The injustice. How did he manage to get away like that? How could he have the cheek to lead the life that he's been leading from 1945 to this day? How could he escape without being caught? Why did he never have to appear in front of an inquiry, a so-called *Spruchkammer*?"

"Well, my dear fellow, that's another story."

"What do you mean?"

"What I mean is that those *Spruchkammer* procedures were anything but just. Yes, we all know they represented at least something like a public effort in the whole process of *Vergangenheitsbewältigung* in post-war Germany. But only too often in reality, they were mere fig-leaves."

"Why?"

"Because most of those inquiry boards called *Spruchkammern* had a fair share of old Nazis among their members. You know, after the really big shots were condemned at the Nuremberg Trials, there was a general feeling that that was enough. The new democratic Germany needed educated men, teachers, university professors, lawyers, judges, policemen and politicians. Almost every man they could recruit had some brown spots in his biography. So, the watchword for those *Spruchkammern* was leniency, clemency with the men they had to assess in view of their Nazi pasts."

"You mean they didn't get their deserved punishment?"

"Most of them got off with a mild reprimand, and some bad guys were even transformed into heroes and heaved into important positions."

"Yes, Mum mentioned people like Hans Filbinger and Kurt Waldheim."

"Right you are. But there were thousands of Nazi followers who had only obeyed orders but caused misery to unwanted individuals by just doing their office jobs. They wrote lists of Jewish families, they copied and filed Gestapo documents needed to persecute and imprisoned dissidents, they helped the Nazis in power in many possible ways."

"We don't know what we would have done in their situation." Andrew threw in.

"Exactly. So why punish everyone? If the *Spruchkammern* had been set up with members of the Allied

Forces and if they had been as strict as possible, Germany would have been even more depopulated than it already was through the numerous casualties. You can't build up a new country without people."

"I'm just disappointed. So, the whole process of *Vergangenheitsbewältigung* was just a sham? A big show to pretend that the German people weren't so bad after all?"

"Not at all. The process was the best thing that could be done in that situation. It was impossible to deny the past, and it was equally impossible to throw a whole nation into prison. But what was possible was some large-scale action to prevent such horrible crimes from ever being repeated. The German people had to be re-educated."

"I see."

The two friends stopped at a street-café and sat down for some nice refreshment. Andrew looked out to the sailing yachts in the bay.

"But Granddad was more than a small follower. He was in the SS. He must have blood on his hands."

"Do you remember? One evening at the pub a few years ago we were discussing Dostoyevsky's *Crime and Punishment* in view of what can be done with a heavy guilt?"

"Yes, and you drew a comparison with *L'Etranger* by Camus. I can clearly remember."

"Now, if we want to explore the moral sides as well as the social sides of a heavy guilt, we have to do a lot more thinking."

"Indeed. But listen, Dave. Only half an hour ago we agreed that we can't know how we would have reacted if we had been young men during Hitler's dictatorship. Young men without the type of democratic education that we have today! Wouldn't we have joined what was presented to us as a great cause?"

"Yes, possibly."

"So how can we sit on our high horse and judge those men and women on the basis of today's enlightened insights?"

"We aren't judging them, and you shouldn't judge your grandfather either."

"What are we doing then, I'd like to know?"

"We cannot judge them because we are individuals."

"What do you mean?" Andrew raised his voice.

"Remember Dostoyevsky," David replied. "His view isn't that of an individual either. His great novel asks what society as a whole can do to cope with such aberrations as Raskolnikov's. So, if we take the view of our post-war society in Europe as a whole, including not only Germany but all the European nations, even the ones who won the War, we can and we should try to assess the whole phenomenon from a moral, a legal and a social position on the basis of democracy and Human Rights."

"Those are big words, my friend."

"Indeed, they are. But they aren't any less appropriate for that, are they?"

The two friends spent the day walking around Weymouth. The weather was fine, so their extended walk offered them many new views of this seaside town. Andrew loved the fishing boats they found moored to the quay, while David was more interested in the expensive yachts. They also admired the modern car ferry for the Channel Islands, promising each other that they would visit Jersey and Guernsey with their girlfriends one of these days.

Their conversations were mostly about the topics of the day, but from time to time they returned to Nora's diary and Granddad's role in the War.

"Actually, we don't know any details of what he did during the War. So, he may have been just one of the followers," Andrew suggested.

“If he was an officer of the *Waffen-SS* you can bet he committed his share of horrible crimes, I am sorry to say.”

“The question is: Do we have to find out?”

“Didn’t you say your grandfather is already far advanced in his dementia? He probably couldn’t even remember everything himself, let alone share those awful memories with you.”

“You’re right.” Andrew heaved a long sigh. “And what about that son of his in Canada? My Uncle Manfred, or rather half-uncle? Do you think I should urge my mother to find him and visit him in Vancouver? Or should I go?”

“That’s for your mother to decide or to negotiate with you. If it was me, I would certainly be curious about a new uncle popping up on the horizon.”

They left it at that.

The next morning, they had a long breakfast. Between mouthfuls of bacon and eggs they uttered occasional comments on what they had discussed the day before. Especially David felt the urge to place everything he had said then in the right light. He was afraid that Andrew might get things the wrong way. It was important for him to make sure his friend didn’t get the impression that he had to do what he told him. Andrew was completely free to act in any way he considered right. There was no hard and fast rule about how to speak to his grandfather or what to say to his mother.

“Then there’s that fellow, Wolfgang Löffel,” Andrew said at the end of their long breakfast session. “What am I to do with him?”

“I don’t think there’s anything you can do,” David replied.

“He must be in his late eighties. I only hope he’ll kick the bucket soon.”

***